"Benny's not there anymore."

Travis joined Susannah at the window. "He has to be," he said.

"I have to find him, Travis."

He heard the fear in her voice. "Don't panic, sweetheart. We'll both go."

Larene chimed in. "That child shouldn't be wandering down by the water on his own this time of night. Who's there to hear him if he falls in?"

The question galvanized Susannah. She reached the dock in thirty seconds flat.

On the dock, his giggle a high-pitched thread of sound on the still air, was Crazy Abe. The hulk of him cast a shadow over Benny, who was already dangling half off the edge as Abe held him mere inches from the dark, bottomless water of the fjord.

ABOUT THE AUTHOR

Catherine Spencer left teaching in 1981 to pursue two other professions she loves, restoring and selling antiques and writing romances. She soon decided to keep the antiques for her own pleasure and devote her full professional attention to her writing. She says that writing a book is like having a baby. New plots are tiny at conception. Their parent creates a carefully enriched environment in which they grow until they're ready to leave home. Then they fall under the influence of strangers and often, it seems, change their names. Of course, the only solution to that is to start another one. Catherine lives with her husband in British Columbia, Canada, and *Fires of Summer* is her first American Romance.

Books by Catherine Spencer

HARLEQUIN PRESENTS
910–A LASTING KIND OF LOVE

Fires of Summer
Catherine Spencer

TORONTO • NEW YORK • LONDON
AMSTERDAM • PARIS • SYDNEY • HAMBURG
STOCKHOLM • ATHENS • TOKYO • MILAN

For Floyd,
my husband and my best friend

Published May 1989

First printing March 1989

ISBN 0-373-16296-0

Chapter One

The path leading down to the road was empty, and below the deck last year's dead weeds—facetiously called "lawn" in the ad—swayed indolently above the bright green of their new growth, quite undisturbed by the passage of human feet.

She called her son, Benny, without success. The mountain behind the house flung back distorted echoes of her voice, gradually fading into nothing. The silence was a bit unnerving for someone born and raised in the city: it sort of underscored the isolation of the town and the vastness of the land to which it clung, which brought her back full circle to the question of where Benny had got to this time.

Common sense told her he couldn't have gone far, but a thread of worry unraveled inside her just the same. She was never quite easy when he wasn't where he was supposed to be, and she'd thought he was out back in the toolshed "exploring," to coin his favorite word of late.

The trouble was, there were a hundred new things for him to discover, and he wanted to experience them all. It made keeping track of him difficult, and although she tried hard not to hover over him, she'd been a single parent too long to be casual about his absence. Responsibility, as much as buried memories, made her cautious.

Down the hill and around the corner, Cameron's Landing dozed placidly in the sun. That thought reassured her, reminding her of one of the reasons she'd created such mammoth upheaval in their lives by exchanging the conveniences and familiarity of Seattle for the more primitive comforts of rural existence. The country was safe. It wasn't overrun with traffic, hell-bent on speed at the cost of safety, and it wasn't riddled with crime. Thugs and lunatics didn't populate places like Cameron's Landing—clinging as it did to the isolated coast of the southernmost tip of the Alaskan Panhandle—not when all manner of big city temptations lay ripe for the plucking a scant few hundred miles to the south.

As for Benny, well, he was a cautious little person. He wouldn't just wander off, and he wouldn't tread carelessly in alien territory. Exploring might be big on his list of pleasures right now, but he was a transplanted city child, still more at ease in a suburban playground than the vast hinterland that encroached on the perimeters of this small town—breathtaking country, beautiful beyond imagination, but decidedly untamed and echoing with that majestic silence. He couldn't be far away. He was just too engrossed to hear her.

She cupped her hands around her mouth and imitated the call that he'd invented his first day at playschool. "Cooo-eee-ooo-eee-ooo-eee!"

To her left and out of sight someone snickered softly, a high, childish smothering of laughter. Planting her fists on her hips, Susannah turned toward the sound. There was nothing to be seen, but she hadn't really expected there would be. "Very funny, Ben," she said. "Now get your buns up here and lend me a hand."

Nothing. Not a sound, not a movement. Until suddenly something smacked the back of her neck and fell inside the collar of her shirt, buzzing furiously.

Her shriek split the air and filtered down the hill to the town. Caring nothing for modesty or local custom, she tore the shirt over her head and shook it vigorously. The king-sized ant did a little soft-shoe number along the collar before sailing off the deck and taking a nosedive into the weeds below. "Good riddance," she muttered, the skin on her neck still vibrating with distaste. If there was one thing she couldn't abide, it was insects—winged or otherwise. They were a part of country living that she'd neglected to take into consideration, until now.

There was another snicker from just around the corner. Benny was enjoying his mother's mild hysterics, it seemed—that, or the sight of her prancing around in broad daylight with nothing on but a pair of jeans and a bra. "You get up here this minute, young man," she ordered, and swung back into the living room.

Here she was, miles from her parents and everything else familiar, bent on proving that she was able to take charge of her own life, and within a week of her arrival, ants an inch long were parading over the Delft plates she'd hung on her kitchen wall and reducing her to the screaming meemies.

"Someone up there's got it in for me," she muttered, inspecting her shirt for any other trespassers before shrugging into it again. It ate at her, but the fact remained that she was going to have to ask someone for help in getting rid of the ants, or they'd chase her out of the first house she and Benny had been able to afford since Mel's death. And that was absolutely out of the question. There was much more at stake here than cheap accommodation.

"Mom? You crying or something?"

She lifted her head, then felt her jaw drop with astonishment. Benny stood halfway down the stairs, his hair rumpled and his face all creased down one side from lying on the quilt he'd slept with since he was eighteen months old. "You're in the house!" she said.

"So are you," he replied with the uncomplicated logic of a seven-year-old. "Were you crying?"

"No, of course not."

"Well, I was," he informed her with more than a little belligerence. "I hate it here. There's nothing to do and no one to play with."

He looked so pitiful, so lost and absolutely adorable, that her heart ached. Was he really miserable, or was it just a passing thing, brought on by loneliness in a new place? God knew the last thing she wanted, ever, was to cause him unhappiness. Everything she did was because of, or for him.

She'd agonized over this move, juggling the pros and cons. The hardest thing about being an adult, she'd decided in a burst of late-blooming wisdom, was realizing that most of the time there weren't any straightforward right or wrong answers, and almost never any simple solutions.

For all sorts of good and right reasons, they'd moved, climbed on a plane, left behind her bad experiences and painful memories. Now all the wrong reasons had to be dealt with, like long-distance relationships, severed friendships and the lack of daily contact with the people who'd been the mainstay of their lives for years.

"Mom!" Benny tugged at her sleeve. "I said I want to go home." What he really meant was: Mom, make everything right again, because he wasn't old enough to understand she really couldn't work miracles. Moms communed with Santa Claus, after all, and made fiscal arrangements with the elusive tooth fairy, so why not this, too?

"But what about exploring?" she asked, hoping to distract him.

"Exploring's boring by yourself. I miss everybody."

Her heart sank. This was what she'd been afraid of. Maybe if they'd moved before spring break, or after, he wouldn't have felt like so much of an outsider, but it had seemed better to make the switch between semesters so that they could find their bearings together in the new town. Now, all she could see were the drawbacks of such a choice. Benny was feeling left out and had yet to meet any kids his own age to replace the friends he'd left behind. Whatever else the locals had been doing to keep themselves entertained during the long, dark winter eight years ago, it wasn't something that resulted in children.

"Let's go home, Mom."

"Oh, Benny..." She reached down and hugged his warm little body till he squirmed. "This is our home, at least for now, and things'll be better when school starts. You'll make new friends, you'll see. And remember, it's only for a year. We can stick it out that long, can't we?''

''A year takes forever,'' he objected.

''Not really, honey.''

''Well then, why are you looking sad, too?''

Susannah quickly arranged her face along more cheerful lines. She tended to forget how observant Benny had become. ''I'm not sad. I'm just a little bit upset because we've got ants in the house, and you know I don't like insects.''

Right on cue, another ant lumbered across the room and headed straight for them. The squeal she couldn't quite repress had Benny tittering. ''A lot of help you are,'' she accused, trying to keep her own face straight. ''One of these things flew inside my shirt just now, and I heard you giggling in the bushes, you little weasel.''

Benny gave her a look that suggested she was suffering from premature senility. ''Not me, Mom. I told you, I was upstairs.''

Susannah looked at him reproachfully. Over the last year, he'd started to tell lies. Just little ones, to be sure, but lies just the same, and they always had to do with where he'd been and who he'd been with. In a way, she couldn't really blame him, what with his mother and his grandmother hovering over him all the time. City living imposed restrictions that were necessary for his safety, but children, like plants, needed space and freedom to grow. The problem was she wasn't one of those casual mothers who could sit back and trust a benign God to keep her child safe. Experience, as much as temperament, made her watchful. Not overly protective, as her good friend Megan Frost had once suggested, just vigilant and responsible.

''You were outside, Benny. I heard you,'' she insisted.

He looked at her out of soulful brown eyes. ''Not me, Mom. Cross my heart.''

She had to believe him. Fibbing was one thing, but he'd never gone so far as to tell a bare-faced lie before, and the truth of what he was saying was clear enough to see. He *had* been upstairs in bed. "Good grief," she said, covering her mouth with her hand to stifle a nervous giggle. The idea that someone other than Benny had been spying on her was a bit unsettling, but she could see that it might have been awkward for that person to come forward and make an introduction to a squealing, half-naked stranger. "Don't tell me I stripped for the neighbors?"

Benny looked embarrassed. "You mean you got undressed *outside*? Just because of some dumb ants? Gee, Mom, how'm I supposed to make friends here, if you go around doing things like that?"

She laughed. "If I promise never to do it again, will you come down to town with me? I want to phone Grandma and Grandpa, and you can spend your allowance a day early. Then we'll have to find someone to get rid of these ants, because if we leave them here much longer, they'll probably start to have babies."

"Hey, neat!" Benny's face lit up a bit.

"Not neat, Benjamin," Susannah said, planting a kiss on his head and relieved beyond measure to see that something could make a dent in his homesickness. "Just gross."

She hated to admit it, even to herself, but Benny wasn't the only one having a few doubts about their new situation. She wasn't nearly as confident as she sounded, either. However, since she'd boasted to her parents that she and her son were going to find life in a small town rewarding and fulfilling, she put on an act worthy of an Oscar when she talked to her mother a short while later.

Lois Johnson's voice was eloquent with relief when she heard her daughter at the other end of the line. "Susannah, you've arrived!"

"Three days ago, Mother," Susannah replied dryly.

"And you only just got the phone in, which is why you haven't called us sooner."

The gnome of a storekeeper wheezed gleefully when he heard that. There was only one phone in the entire town.

"I don't exactly have a phone," Susannah said into the microphone and glared at the loudspeaker hanging on the

wall. "I'm calling from the store. On a radio telephone."
And anyone within hailing distance can hear every word we both say, Mother.

"I suppose they're a bit slow up there," Lois said sympathetically. "How long do you really think you'll be able to stick it out?"

"A year, Mother. I haven't changed my mind."

"What a pity. Your father and I were hoping you'd had time to come to your senses. Is it snowing?"

Oh, grief! Susannah rolled her eyes.

When she'd heard her daughter's plans, Lois had predicted Susannah would find that Alaska was just a segment of the Arctic Circle that had slipped a bit during a blizzard, and that Cameron's Landing would be populated with little else than wolves and other fur-bearing creatures.

"It's the beginning of May, Mother, and this is the southern end of the Panhandle. There are forget-me-nots and lupins blooming in the gardens." *And king-size ants flying all over the kitchen.*

"That's all very well, but what's the house like?"

"Charming."

"And Benny? How's our little grandson surviving?"

"He's in heaven, Mother—just loves it."

"Let me say hello to him."

Not a chance. This would be one time he'd feel compelled to tell the truth. "I don't see him right now, Mother. He's spending his allowance."

Her mother's squawk crackled through the loudspeaker. "He'll get lost in the wilds, Susannah."

"You looking for your boy, girlie?" the gnome bellowed helpfully from somewhere at the other end of the store. "He's right here with a fishhook stuck in his finger. I'm just performing a bit of frontier surgery, as you might say, to get it out."

The loudspeaker carried Lois's wail to the four corners of the store and out into the street beyond. "You see, Susannah? You see the sort of thing you've exposed yourself to? You should never have left Seattle. If the rent on that dreadful apartment was too high, you could have moved back in with us. We've got plenty of room and everything you could possibly want.''

Susannah contained a sigh. It was pointless to go over it all again. She'd had to sever her dependence on her parents, and an apartment six blocks away just wasn't the answer.

She loved her folks, but she'd leaned on them long enough. New widows, their lives shattered by grief and violence, were allowed to be weak. For a time. But five years was stretching things a bit, something she'd realized with a sense of shock when she looked at Benny one day and saw a boy instead of a baby.

"You know why I moved up here, Mother, so please let's not get into it again."

Static crackled, obliterating Lois's reply, which was probably a good thing. "I'd better go," Susannah said. "We don't have a good connection. I'll call again soon. Say hello to Dad, okay?"

It was just as well her mother was too far away to visit, she decided, hanging up. This was a classic case of ignorance being bliss. What her mother didn't know, wouldn't hurt her.

IT WAS LIKE COMING HOME, Travis thought, a smile curving his mouth the minute he set foot in the door of the only hotel and bar in Cameron's Landing.

"Travis O'Connor, as I live and breathe!" Larene Kelly screamed in welcome. "Don't tell me the season's upon us already. Saints alive, I'm not yet done paying my Christmas bills, and here the forest fire fighters are back in our midst. Lock up your daughters, folks!"

All hundred and eighty pounds of Larene's five foot frame shook with laughter as she hauled out beer and a glass. "Sink your nose into that, my lad, then let's be hearing what's brought you up here so soon, and no spinning yarns. Is the Firecat with you, or did you come up by sea and if you did, who brought you and how come no one knew to expect you?"

Travis hooked one leg around a stool and propped a booted foot on the brass rail that paralleled the base of the bar. "In order, sugar plum—no, yes, I came alone, and I missed you so badly, I couldn't bear to take the time to call ahead."

"You're a liar," Larene sighed, "but a gifted one, I must admit. Is it too much to hope, Travis O'Connor, that you've decided the hotel's good enough accommodation for you this summer, or are you planning to be staying with herself again?"

"Now, Larene!" He shook a reproving finger and tried not to smile. "Don't take it so personally. I have a standing arrangement with Judith—when I'm not flying around putting out fires, I help her fix up the house, and in return she gives me bed and board."

"I was afraid that's what I'd be hearing," Larene returned darkly. "Tell me, is her bed so beguiling, you couldn't wait for the beginning of the fire season to sample it again?"

Discarding the glass, Travis cradled the bottle of beer and shook his head dolefully. "You're a wicked old woman, Larene Kelly. You know full well I have a single bed in my room at Judith's."

"I know full well that woman'd creep into a hearse with you, if she thought she'd fit. And don't be turning your face inwards like that, Travis O'Connor."

"Larene, I don't intend to say another word on the subject," said Travis firmly. Small-town gossip had a habit of running amok faster than a forest fire. It was too early in the season to get drawn into the ongoing hostilities between Judith and The Crones as she so unflatteringly labeled the trio of women that included Larene. "I may be a retired navy pilot and technically no longer an officer, but I pride myself on still being something of a gentleman."

"Then find yourself a lady," Larene shot back tartly.

He smiled at her. "I did, the day I met you."

"Spare me your dimples, my lad, and don't be thinking you'll change my mind with your flattery." Larene tossed her head until her curls flew around her face like a faded red whirlwind. "That woman," she pronounced, "is a madam if ever I clapped eyes on one."

"You're just jealous because she's tall." It was a well-known fact that Larene would have given her right arm to stand six inches higher—not to mention fifty pounds thinner—to be built, in fact, along the willowy lines of the much maligned Judith.

"Bite your tongue, you young devil, and save your wits for what you really know! At this rate, you'll be needing them. It's a dry mild winter and an early spring we've had. For all that I hate to be seeing herself smirking from one side of her face to the other because you're back, I have the feeling we'll all sleep safer in our beds knowing you're here to protect the old town, should the need arise."

She halted her cheerful tirade long enough to cast an inquisitive glance at the door behind him, then resettled her features in anticipation, her nose practically twitching with excitement. "Finish your beer and hush your noise," she whispered. "There's another, more deserving soul needing my attention."

Intrigued, Travis turned and found himself gazing on the face of a stranger and drowning in a pair of eyes as darkly beautiful as newly opened pansies—near-black, velvet eyes, wide and huge and doing their damnedest to hide behind lashes tipped with gold.

Blinded by the sun, the woman scanned the room unseeingly then turned to speak to someone outside on the road, revealing as she did so a profile as delicately fashioned as a cameo. "Larene," Travis whispered, the words sliding out of his mouth in hushed admiration, "who's the vision? Does she come from around these parts, or am I hallucinating?"

"Down, Rover," Larene ordered with lightly sugared malice. "She's not your type. Looks nothing at all like herself who offers bed and board."

"Who is she?"

Larene's expression softened alarmingly. "She's a sweet and lovely young widow, come to live up here with her boy," she crooned, bestowing on the newcomer the smile she normally reserved for Sundays, confession and or- phaned kittens. "She's taken a lease on the Company house at the top of the hill, and she's planning to operate the mobile library when she's not busy with her school book."

Why would a face like that want to isolate itself so thor- oughly from city lights? Travis wondered. Cameron's Landing was accessible only by water and air. The first was inconvenient with the ferry running just twice weekly; the second expensive. "A widow with a child," he asked, eyeing the stranger with some skepticism, "and she's still in school?"

Larene clucked impatiently. "Of course not! But she's writing a very important book for those who are, is all."

"Really." Travis contained his amusement at the awed delivery of this morsel of information. Larene might have been quoting the Fathers of Confederation. "How old's the boy?"

"Going on eight. He'll be joining Sonja's class after spring break."

"Hmm. Where'd they come from?"

"Seattle."

Larene's voice came distantly to Travis, impinging only slightly on a mind already working at one of the things it was trained to do best: record with the speed and accu- racy of a camera the most minute details of all that the eye observed. Young pilots who lacked the ability to develop such a faculty seldom lived long enough to become vet- eran flyers.

The woman, backlighted by the sun slanting in the door, was slight, weighing about a hundred pounds. Small- boned, narrow-waisted, with wonderful red-gold hair and a mouth that might have reminded him of a rosebud if it hadn't been so tightly pursed in displeasure that it robbed her of beauty and left her frozen-faced instead. Regard- less, she belonged in an elegant, city setting, not a bar in Alaska and looking for all the world as if she'd like noth- ing better than to start a brawl. "Cameron's Landing's a far cry from Seattle," he said. "I wonder why she chose this neck of the woods?"

"Because she's after some peace and quiet, you great lump. Why do you think?"

Travis grinned. That was something he'd believe if she was still around in a month's time, after she found out there wasn't a beauty salon in town, nor a gourmet deli down the street; and that garbage disposal was something each resident took care of on his own, and the only movie theater in town was the VCR in the Kelly's back room. Leaning forward confidentially, he whispered, "How old would you say she is, Larene?"

Larene snorted disparagingly. "As if I'd know, and this the first I've really seen of her up close. But the way you're after gawking, no doubt you'll be able to draw me pictures in another five minutes. Sure, and your mother'd be ashamed if she could see the way you're staring."

Travis made big, innocent eyes at her. "You mean you've yet to meet the lady? From the way you've got the details of her life memorized, I figured she might be related. How'd you come by all your info, sugar plum?"

Larene looked at him witheringly. "And why wouldn't I know about her? It's common enough knowledge to anyone with ears to hear. There are precious few secrets about these parts, my lad, as well you know."

A discouraging observation, Travis thought, if the rumors about his own life were a case in point. He and Judith were friends, not lovers, whatever the local gossip decreed. By the same token, maybe the newcomer wasn't widowed, but had a husband waiting somewhere in the wings. Not that it mattered to Travis, one way or the other. He wasn't looking for involvement with some porcelain princess who'd pout and complain when he had to stand her up. And standing up women went with the territory in his job.

He cast the redhead one last, regretful glance. She was definitely the wrong type in the wrong place at the wrong time, pansy eyes notwithstanding.

Chapter Two

Leaving Benny outside with a handful of shoestring licorice for company and diversion, Susannah stepped inside the bar, thoroughly ticked off. The interior was dark after the glaring light of afternoon. At first it seemed to her, hesitating on the threshold, that the place was empty, which shouldn't really have surprised her.

"Try Bob Kelly in the bar, girlie," the gnome in the store had cackled, shoving the visor of his baseball cap more firmly over one ear after she'd finished her phone call and asked, reasonably enough she'd thought, if there was an exterminator in town. She'd half believed he'd been leading her on and only the prospect of those giant ants, making themselves at home in her house, had persuaded her to leave her child outside a hotel and enter its tavern. Chalk up one more demerit if this was the way things were done in small towns.

To add to those mixed feelings, she heard a low, amused chuckle coming from the far end of the bar that stretched the width of the room. Blinking, she focused on the couple huddled together in conference there, sending sly glances her way.

They're laughing at me, she decided with faultless logic, and felt herself grow a more annoyed shade of pink. Why couldn't the exterminator be found in the yellow pages, instead of hanging around the local watering hole for lounge lizards? The woman behind the bar looked approachable enough, but the man on the stool across from her was something else again. In fact, on closer inspection, *lizard* wasn't exactly the term Susannah would use to describe him. He brought to mind the story of Little Red Riding Hood, and there was no doubt about who was the wolf. Talk about a lean and hungry look!

"Excuse me," she began in her most frigid tone, moving toward the couple but directing her request to the woman. "My name is Susannah Boyd and I'm new in town, and I was told at the store that I could get help here."

"Saints alive, if we weren't just this minute wondering how you and the boy were liking the house and all, dearie," the woman beamed. "Were we not, Travis O'Connor?"

Travis O'Connor, draped over the polished mahogany of the bar, seemed taken aback by the remark. "We were?" he echoed, and Susannah wondered uncharitably if the wolf had brain damage.

"We were," the woman replied firmly. "I'm Larene Kelly, dearie, and this is Travis, and surely between us we can be looking after you. Wouldn't you say, Travis?"

"That depends," the wolf hedged, "on the sort of help she needs."

Susannah's hackles rose another inch. Hardly the chivalrous type, she decided, fully prepared to dislike the man intensely. She was not unfamiliar with body language, and there was no missing the message conveyed by his semi-supine posture, great long legs entwined negligently around the stool to anchor his lower half in place, the rest of him sprawled forward and supported on his elbows, and the whole effect one of supreme boredom. If she could have laid hands on a firecracker, she knew exactly under whose stool she'd choose to set it off. "I have flying ants," she announced baldly.

"Well, that lets me out," he replied, lazily amused. "I'm not the man you're looking for."

Do tell, Susannah was tempted to snap back, and debated telling him that if she had been *looking for a man* as he so quaintly chose to phrase it, she would have been searching for someone like Mel. Someone good and honorable, with a darkly handsome face and powerfully compact body. This lean and lanky blonde hardly fit the bill.

She'd learned the hard way that there weren't nearly enough quality men to go around, and spent the last five years reconciling herself to the fact that she'd had more than her fair share when she'd found Mel. The guys she'd come across since she'd been widowed seemed to fit into one of two categories: those who had sex on the brain and were certain they could cure all that ailed her with a romp in bed; and those of more material persuasion who were equally certain that, having lost one meal ticket, she must be desperate to find another. Neither type had the slightest interest in taking on a ready-made family, or showed the least patience with her maternal concerns. She had no use for either specimen, and this one looked as though he combined both in one package. Oh joy!

"It's my Bob you're needing, dearie," Larene decided, clearly of the opinion that every right-minded woman needed a man in order to be complete.

Susannah smothered a sigh. "Really?"

"Yes, indeed. He'll know what's to be done. Is it them big black flying beasts that's bothering you?"

Among other things, Susannah thought as she nodded agreement.

"They don't attack, you know," Travis remarked between sips of beer. "In fact, they probably don't like you any better than you like them."

Susannah ignored him, concentrating instead on the far more sympathetic Larene. "What can Mr. Kelly do?"

"Oh, not Mr. Kelly, dearie. There aren't many misters around Cameron's Landing. You call him Bob, like everyone else."

Susannah's irritation dissipated a little in the face of such friendliness. It was some consolation to find at least one person in town who didn't find her predicament hilarious. "You're very kind," she murmured cautiously. "Do you think I could talk to him?"

"Surely you could if only he were here, but he's away to the city for a few days and won't be back before Friday."

Three more days of flying insects infiltrating every corner of the house? Susannah's flesh crawled. "Is there no one else?"

"Once the sun goes down," Travis O'Connor supplied, "you won't be bothered by them anymore."

She felt a surge of hope. "That'll be the end of them?"

"Uh-uh. There'll be another swarm of them tomorrow, and another the day after that." He looked sideways at her, cradling his beer in long, elegant fingers. "That's something you can always count on with ants. Where there's one, there'll be a hundred others."

Susannah renewed her resolve to dislike this man, even though he did have nice-looking hands. "You're such a comfort," she said sweetly.

He shrugged. "Hey, don't get after me. I'm just telling it like it is."

"Well that is not how it will be with me," she declared coldly. "I'll get rid of them. I'll buy Raid and spray them to death."

"Save your money," he advised with a laugh that, at a different time and under different circumstances, might have been rather appealing. "Raid'll knock off the ones you can see, but it won't touch those still in the nest. You might as well face it—either you live with them for a few days, or you move into one of Larene's upstairs rooms till Bob gets back."

Let herself be chased out of her house, after only three days? Not on her life! She had run as far as she intended running. One way or another, she'd stay put and deal with the problem. "Believe me," she announced, flinging him a departing glare before turning to the door, "there will be no more ants by tomorrow, if I have to crawl inside the nest myself and stamp out every last one."

Larene couldn't hide her disappointment at Susannah's leaving. "Will you not be staying for something?" she called. "There's coffee at the back, or I could be making you tea."

"Another time," Susannah said. "My son is waiting for me outside. But thank you, and I'll be in touch when your husband gets home. It was nice—" she paused a moment, reluctantly including Travis in her farewell "—meeting you both."

He nodded amiably and turned toward her for the first time since her eyes had adjusted to the dim light inside the bar. "Ma'am," he said, releasing a smile of unexpected charm. "I'm sure we'll meet again."

"Perhaps," she replied, striving to look as composed as she managed to sound. Stealing one more surreptitious glance just to make sure her eyes hadn't deceived her, she escaped through the door to the safety of the street outside.

It had been a long, long time since her heart had stalled like this. Even after she'd drawn in a lungful of air to clear her head, she kept seeing that smile and hearing that voice, and had to remind herself that she'd decided not to like the man who owned them, not one little bit.

"Dearie!" Larene shrieked behind her, just as Susannah and Benny prepared to start back up the hill. "Don't be rushing off like this. There's people wanting to welcome you, and things you need to be knowing…about the town and the house and the job and all."

"I thought perhaps in a day or two—"

"The bus has to run on Thursday, dearie."

"Thursday? But that's tomorrow! We're not finished unpacking yet."

"But the men in the camp've been without the library for over a month now," Larene protested, then added darkly, "and there's no telling what they're doing for recreation without it. Like wild creatures they are, living away by themselves in the middle of nowhere."

"I didn't know. I was—"

"There's a lot you don't know, dearie, and I'm just the person to be filling you in. You come along with the boy now, and we'll go in the back way. There's a fresh batch of cookies cooling in the kitchen," Larene said, reaching forward and mussing Benny's hair affectionately. "It was as if something told me there'd be a boy the size of this needing a bite extra to see him through 'til supper.''

"What sort of cookies?" Benny wanted to know, looking, Susannah thought, as though he might take a bite out of Larene if she messed around with his hair again.

"Sure they're peanut butter with chocolate chips, darling," Larene assured him, zeroing in on Benny's favorite so unerringly that Susannah suspected her of having mothered a dozen others just like him. "Come away now and give them a taste while your mama and I enjoy a pot of coffee in peace."

Peace, Susannah shortly discovered, was Larene's euphemism for a salvo of information, delivered with scarcely a pause, on the life and times of the inhabitants of Cameron's Landing. In short order she learned that the Turners, from the store, had remained childless all these years, despite their most earnest efforts to be otherwise. "Probably his fault," Larene confided, "what with them morning swims he takes every day, and the temperature enough to freeze a man into an early grave." She learned that Jan and Joe, her neighbors from the dock, almost starved in the winter, but made a killing in the summer chartering out their fleet of Boston Whalers to the tourists who wanted to go fishing. And their four sons—"good boys, every last one, and handsome as sin, dearie. Makes me glad I don't have daughters!"—made good money as fishing guides.

Refilling their cups and settling in for the duration, Larene hitched her bosom into place and leaned closer to confide that there were some scandalous goings-on around town that a nice girl like Susannah might find hard to believe.

"Amazing," Susannah murmured, resolving to be discreet in all her dealings. It struck her that hangnails would be public domain within an hour of sprouting. "It seems such a sleepy little town."

"Not at all. It's a regular little Peyton Place," Larene boasted. "The things I could tell you, dearie, if I weren't a person to keep my own counsel. It comes of working in the bar, you know. People in their cups…'' She wagged her head sagely and let silence speak volumes.

The thought of how the gossip circuits would buzz if it ever leaked out that Travis O'Connor had almost reduced the newly arrived widow to palpitations had Susannah choking into her cup.

''Finish your coffee,'' Larene urged. ''I promised I'd take you down to the store to meet Marg and Henry if I got to know you before they did.''

The couple who hadn't been blessed with children, Susannah remembered, and thought that if they were as garrulous as Larene, she couldn't face them today. ''I'm not sure we have the time,'' she said, coming up with the first lame-brain excuse she could think of.

''Sure and what else do you have to do, what with your house not being fit to live in for the next while.'' Larene scoffed, adding cheerfully, ''No doubt you'll be thinking I'm a nosy old woman, and it's a fact that I am, but there's no malice in me. It's just filling in for your mama I am, seeing that you're a stranger here with no family.''

Loading Benny up with a handful of cookies, she led the way out of the hotel and across the road to the store, barely stopping to draw breath. ''We're a very caring community, you understand. We share each other's lives, good or bad, and it's thrilled to pieces we are to have you here. Cameron's Landing's short of children and young folk.''

Susannah hadn't taken time to look around when she'd made her call earlier. The general store was a fascination to a woman city born and raised. A great rambling structure, with beams a foot thick and a wealth of alcoves and corners, it sat perched at the top of the ramp leading down to the docks. Not only did it appear to be the spot where everyone congregated from midmorning to late afternoon to listen in to the long-distance calls coming over the radio-telephone, it carried everything, from flour to floor tiles and garden tools to garbanzo beans. It reminded Susannah of something out of one of those museum villages. The only thing missing was the blacksmith's shop next door.

"You can't find something, m'dear," Marg Turner, a pleasant dumpling of a woman offered, after Larene made the introductions, "you just ask. We're not fancy, but we try to keep a bit of everything."

"Your bread smells wonderful," Susannah told her.

"Oh, that!" Marg shrugged off the compliment. "Henry bakes it up himself every Tuesday and Friday. You come down around noon, I'll have a loaf ready, or if you're busy, we'll send it up."

"I was telling her," Larene said, "that it's a close-knit community we are here."

"Close-knit?" a voice from the next aisle scoffed. "Lordy, lordy, Larene Kelly, a body can't sneeze around these parts without the whole town saying bless you!"

"I do declare, Henry Turner, you get more miserable with each day that passes," Larene informed him cheerfully. "Come out from behind them sacks of meal and try to be pleasant for a change. There's someone come to meet you."

"I met her already, Larene Kelly, afore you did for that matter. Reckon that sours your milk, eh?" Henry Turner shambled around the corner, baseball cap firmly in place, looked Susannah over and nodded a confirmation. "Yessir, it's the little widder from the company house that don't like ants. I seen her half an hour past, when she came looking for an exterminator man." He let fly with a cackle that had Larene pursing her lips with outrage. "She don't know much about country living, does she?"

"Henry Turner's a bit lacking in social graces, dearie," Larene declared, acting as if he weren't there. "But, though it grieves me to admit it, he has the lightest hand with pastry of anyone I ever fell across, including my own grandmother who turned out cakes fit for the angels. Come Christmas time, there's not a soul in town that gets overlooked when himself bakes his gingerbread men."

Henry shifted from one foot to the other as if his shoes pinched, an acutely uncomfortable expression on his face.

"If they smell as good as your bread," Susannah said, "I can't wait to taste them."

Henry's expression softened into a smile and he patted her shoulder briefly before making off behind the counter. "Why, girlie, it's a real pleasure to hear you say that. When you have a minute, you come to the back room and I'll show you where the mail's kept, so you'll know where to look if we're too busy in front to get it for you."

"Henry's a good man," Larene announced in a thundering whisper. "He just doesn't like people to be knowing it. But if there's ever anything he can be doing for you, all you have to do is ask. He'll be on the job before your mouth's had the chance to close again."

The tips of Henry's ears turned bright red. "Not in your case, Larene Kelly. Yours don't close long enough for a body to wink."

Close-knit community, hmm? Susannah stifled a laugh as Larene slapped at him with her mail. "Who should I talk to about the library?" she asked, hoping to prevent a riot by changing the subject.

"Me," Larene said.

"Rosalind who runs the school," Henry said.

"She won't be back till school starts," Larene persisted, "and the bus goes out on Thursday."

"That reminds me," Susannah interrupted. "I'll have to find a baby-sitter. Is there anyone you'd recommend?"

"No," Henry replied.

Simultaneously Larene beamed. "I was just getting to that, dearie. Of course there is. He can stay with me. There's a tree swing back of the hotel just made for a lad of his years, and I'll have another batch of cookies ready and waiting for him, as well as a bowl of soup and a sandwich."

"If you're sure, that would be wonderful, but I don't want to put you to any trouble," Susannah began.

"It ain't no trouble, that's the whole trouble," Henry predicted gloomily. "Larene Kelly's never happier than when she's in charge of somebody. Give her a chick to mother and she damn near sprouts feathers."

Marg settled things. "Here's the key to the bus, Susannah. Go take a look around and pay no attention to Henry.

He and Larene'll spend the rest of the afternoon bickering. They enjoy it so much that if you hang around waiting for them to agree, you're liable to grow roots.''

"I guess I should get organized, if I'm to start work so soon.''

"Go with an easy mind, dearie,'' Larene urged. "And come Thursday morning, just drop the lad off at the back door. He'll be fine with me, and just to make it a bit easier for you, we'll wait for you up at the house so you don't have to come all the way back down to the hotel to pick him up your first day on the job.''

THE NEXT MORNING, it seemed to Susannah that half the town turned out to see her off. Jan Hamilton brought her a map and a schedule. "It's best to go up to Camp Angus first, then make the other stops this afternoon, on your way back to town.''

It was the first Susannah had heard about other stops, but a glance at the schedule showed that there were several families, living in the middle of nowhere, who also liked to receive regular reading material. And she soon learned that delivering books was only part of her job.

An ancient little lady with bright, malicious, black eyes appeared at the door of the old yellow school bus that served as a mobile library. Her hair was drawn back so tightly from her face, she looked almost bald. "I'm Mrs. Dawson,'' she declared, hoisting herself up into the bus with remarkable agility, "but you're just about old enough to call me Vi. Marie Allen's baby's due anytime, and this here's the knitting I done for her. Drop it off for me, like a good lass, and tell that husband of hers to get his family down to town as soon as she's up and about. I aim to inspect that baby before he gets to talkin'. If there's one thing I can't abide, it's a lippy child.''

She doddled off and was promptly replaced by Marg Turner and Larene, with Benny trailing self-consciously at the rear. He'd been less than thrilled at having a babysitter, especially one so disposed to hug him. "I'm not a baby, Mom,'' he'd complained.

Unhappily, while that was true, he'd been behaving a bit like one: clinging to her as if he feared she was going to disappear, and easily upset over small things. Susannah knew he was lonely all by himself, and it was souring all the good things for him. What he really needed was a friend, someone to share with him the thrill of exploring his new environment, and for lack of an alternative he'd begun turning to his mother to fill the void in his life. It was a temptation that, for both their sakes, she had to resist.

"You're not old enough to be left on your own, Benny. You know that," she'd said firmly.

"I could come with you," he wheedled.

"I'll be busy working and the bus is small enough as it is. Not only would you be in the way, you'd also be bored stiff. Make up your mind to enjoy the day with Larene, and when I get home we'll toast marshmallows on the hibachi."

Now, seeing his unhappy little face, she was assaulted with doubt. Maybe she *should* let him come with her. Maybe she expected too much of him. Maybe they should have stayed in Seattle. Maybe . . . maybe this whole move had been a big mistake.

"We brought along a lunch pail for you, dearie," Larene confided, outscreaming the gulls that had also gathered for the event, "just so you don't find yourself peckish. It's a long day you'll be having, and I wouldn't like to think you'd be setting foot in any of them cookhouses, or eating with any of them savages. The less you have to do with them, the better. They're not used to quality company."

Her tone suggested that Evil personified lurked in the camps, which didn't make Susannah feel any better. She was nervous enough as it was, without having to worry about fending off a pack of unwashed, semicivilized men.

"Hush your noise, Larene Kelly," Henry Turner panted, arriving in the school yard with a bundle of something under one arm.

"Go mind your store and your own business," Larene snorted genially. "If you had daughters to begin with, would you be wanting them spending time up at them camps?''

"For the love of God, woman, the boys are looking for books, not favors. They'll not bother Susannah at all.''

Larene resettled her bosom and bestowed a pitying glare on him. "It's half-baked you are, without a doubt, Henry Turner," she pronounced grimly, "but let us all pray that for once, you know what you're talking about.''

"Seems to me your job's to look after the boy," Henry retorted. "Why don't you fix your mind on that, Larene Kelly, and leave Susannah to take care of herself? Strikes me she's more than capable—long as she don't have to worry you aren't holding up your end of things.''

Larene reached out an arm and hugged Benny to her ample girth. "He's in safe hands, dearie, never you fear," she assured Susannah. "It's such great plans I have for this one, he'll likely never be wanting to come home again.''

That made Susannah feel better, but Benny's face, squished lovingly to Larene's midriff, turned puce with mortification.

Joe Hamilton's arrival created another diversion. He appeared on a bike that looked as if it belonged in a museum, towing behind a sort of trailer made out of packing crates. "Morning, Susannah," he said, poking his head inside the bus. "I'll stack Solly Smith's washable Latex paint behind the driver's seat, and Arnie Swensen's bottles at the back. They won't be in the way there.''

"Solly's wife's making him paint the bedroom again," Henry explained, his head joining Joe's in the doorway. "And Arnie needs the empties for his hooch. Now, girlie, this here's all the mail. Elaine Sharp'll take all the old magazines, and whatever you do, don't bend the brown envelope for the Coopers. It's got picture snapshots in it that Annie's been waiting on for the last six months.''

Installed, by then, behind the steering wheel, Susannah decided it was time to leave before she lost her nerve completely. They were all watching her expectantly, except for Benny who was conspicuous by his shifty eyes and still-pink face. He'd never been given to public displays of affection, especially not from people he didn't know well.

"Do you have the map?" Jan asked, just before Susannah swung the lever that closed the bus door.

"Map?" Henry scoffed. "She don't need no map, woman. There's only one road in and one road out. She don't come home by five this afternoon, we know to go looking in the ravine for her."

"Ravine?" Susannah's anxiety level rose a fraction higher. It occurred to her that maybe the reason her rent was so low was that no one else could be persuaded to take on the job of visiting librarian, and that what she'd really done was not swing a good deal for herself so much as fall prey to a bribe.

"Just remember," Larene interjected, loath to let Henry have the last word, "if you have engine trouble—or any other kind, for that matter—stay with the bus and keep the door locked, dearie, until someone from town comes looking for you. At least then your virtue'll be safe."

It was just what Susannah needed to make her day complete. She'd have asked Henry to ride shotgun with her, but he and Joe had already left to go about their business. She'd have to rely on her own wits and Henry's assertion that Larene was all mouth and no sense.

Benny deigned to glance her way at that moment, and she wanted to hug him goodbye, or at least blow him a kiss, but he pointed his "I'm not allowed to talk to strangers" face straight at her, making it plain he would never forgive her if she made a spectacle of him in front of everyone.

She swung the bus door closed. Larene's parting advice was drowned out by a chorus of farewells. Acknowledging them and ignoring her son, Susannah engaged first gear and pulled away from the parking lot.

It took her almost two hours to cover the twenty-five miles to the logging camp. The road, narrow at best and at times little more than a dirt track, hugged the bare rock of the cliff to her right as though it was as terrified as she of slipping over the sheer precipice on her left. She really hadn't expected a four-lane freeway, but what she got was so primitive, the pioneers would have shunned it. About the only thing missing was hostile Indians.

The bus rattled and clanked, grinding along in second gear. Susannah clutched the steering wheel in a death grip and repeated "The quality of mercy" speech from *The Merchant of Venice*, because she couldn't remember any appropriate prayers. Every once in a while, the road would flatten out and she'd notice trails cut into the hillside. From the map, she knew they led to the cabins she had to visit on her way back. The prospect filled her with dread. She hoped each place had room enough in front for her to turn the bus around. She'd walk home before she'd try backing down to the main road.

Except for a swarthy little Frenchman, who identified himself as the cook and moved more like a ballet dancer, the camp was deserted when she arrived just before noon. "For you, madame," he announced, handing her a mug almost as thick as his accent, the minute she set foot on the ground. The aroma of fresh-ground coffee revived her slightly. "That street," he informed her cheerfully, "she makes you pale. Drink, and you will feel better, then we will open for business. The boys, they are impatient."

I'll just bet they are, Susannah thought, Larene's predictions suddenly seeming not quite as far-fetched as they had in the school parking lot. She decided she'd better establish a few rules at the outset, just to be on the safe side. "Now see here, Mr.—" she began.

"Call me Chef, madame. Everyone does. And what is it we call you?"

The coffee was delectable. It sort of undermined her determination to remain aloof. "Mrs. Susannah Boyd," she replied, feeling distinctly foolish but deciding it was up to her to set the tone of their relationship.

Chef beamed. "The others will call you Miz Susie," he declared, "but for me, you will be Madame Suzanne. Please take your coffee with you into your *autobus*. I hear the boys coming, but I will make them wait in line for their business and visit you one at a time."

Larene's warnings really came home to roost at that. Susannah would have beaten a fast retreat if she hadn't suddenly found the bus surrounded by loggers.

As it turned out, her imagination had once again gotten stuck in overdrive, and she didn't have a problem in the world. Chef took charge and orchestrated everything beautifully.

"Wipe clean the boots," he insisted, weaving nimbly among the crowd of men lined up outside the bus door. "We will not have the mess in here for the madame. You, Archie, you may go first."

The next two hours were a revelation. Susannah shed a number of misconceptions and learned, among other things, that loggers pursued a variety of interests, from studying Japanese to knitting Cowichan Indian sweaters. Science fiction was big on their list of recreational reading, and one young hopeful cleaned her out of everything she carried about making a fortune on the stock market. She also discovered that men in the logging industry had mothers who'd taught them manners just like everyone else; that some called her Miz Susie, as Chef had predicted, and some called her ma'am; and that Larene was full of hot air.

She made all the requisite stops on the way home, without incident. Marie Allen was charming and cheerful, despite being so far advanced in pregnancy that she looked as if she might deliver momentarily. Jed and Annie Cooper were thrilled to get their mail, which did indeed contain pictures of their four grandchildren. They fed her strong tea while she admired the album that contained every snapshot ever taken of their family. Arnie Swensen smelled like a brewery, but gave Susannah a bottle of berry wine that he swore was better than anything "them folks in Californ-eye-a" could come up with. Solly Smith sent back the washable Latex and said he'd wear a dress before he'd let his wife paint the bedroom pink. Elaine Sharp didn't have time to talk because one of her dogs had a badly cut paw and needed attention.

The drive back to town was no picnic. For all that Benny was in good hands, Susannah wanted to see for herself that he'd survived the day without her. It was the first time they'd been so far apart, and she felt disconnected from the mainspring of her life. She knew, too, that until she actually arrived back at her starting point, all in one piece and under her own steam, she couldn't claim to have survived the day, or to have accomplished what she'd set out to do.

She was tired, and the muscles in her shoulders and the back of her neck felt as if they'd been stitched into place with red-hot darning needles, but when she turned the last hairpin bend into Cameron's Landing, it was worth every last stabbing pain and qualm. The town looked like Shangri-la and the house, when she reached it, a palace—until she walked in and found no sign of Larene, just Benny hanging precariously from a ladder in the living room, and above him a pair of legs that on further examination proved to belong to Travis O'Connor.

Chapter Three

She was so paralyzed with horror that all she could manage was a whimper, but it was enough to alert Benny and Travis to her presence.

"Hi, Mom," Benny sang out, his face wreathed in more cheerfulness than it had worn in over a week. "See what I'm doing?" And just to emphasize his situation, he hung on by one hand and waved to make sure he had her undivided attention.

"Oh, Lord!" She sprang forward, grasped him around the waist and hauled him down to safety, certain he was about to break a leg at the very least. "Benny, what in the world do you think you're doing, and why isn't Larene here looking after you?"

Benny's chest puffed out with pride. "Me and Travis're fixing it so the ants can't get out. I helped him with the drill. I climbed up eight steps, Mom. I was higher than you."

She thought her heart was going to fail. "Are you out of your tiny mind?" she barked at Travis O'Connor as his upper regions descended into view.

"Good afternoon to you, too, Susannah," he replied, and swung down the ladder with careless agility, stopping halfway to toss her a reassuring grin. "Don't worry, Ben's been in good hands."

"Impossible," she snapped, "if by that you mean he's been in your care while I was gone. Why isn't Larene here?"

"She developed a migraine. It happens only about once every six months but when it does, it lays her out flat. Since I had nothing else to do, I offered to step in as baby-sitter. I was sure you wouldn't mind. And we had fun, didn't we, Ben?"

Benny glowed. "Yeah. We did the neatest things, Mom. I made a holder for my pencils and stuff. Travis let me drill holes in a piece of wood, so all my crayons can stand up. And we built a shelf on the wall for my treasures. He's real smart at things like that, Mom."

"Well, I had some pretty good help," Travis chipped in, beaming down on them both.

"I know." Benny, who had never been afflicted with false modesty, nodded agreement. "He prob'ly couldn't have done it if I hadn't hammered the nails in and held on while he sawed the wood. When he saw I was a good helper, he let me climb up the ladder with him and hold the drill."

Susannah felt her blood pressure rise another notch. "Saw?" she spluttered. "Hammer and nails? Climbing ladders and holding tools? Good grief, man!"

Travis opened his mouth to speak, but Benny beat him to it. "You shouldn't yell at Travis," he protested. "We had fun."

"We wanted to give you a surprise when you got home," Travis added, indicating the beam overhead which she gathered was where the ant nest was located.

"Consider me surprised," she told him coldly. "Not pleasantly, perhaps, but definitely surprised. I thought Bob Kelly was supposed to take care of the ant problem when he gets back."

"You're welcome," Travis rebuked her mildly. "And I'm sure Larene will feel much better knowing how pleased you are at not having to put up with them a moment longer than was absolutely necessary. I imagine concern for your welfare had something to do with her migraine attack in the first place, but don't feel you should go rushing down to thank her, either.''

Susannah had the grace to blush a little at that. "I don't mean to sound ungrateful," she muttered, "but I don't think you should have allowed my son to help you, especially not on that ladder. In case you haven't noticed, he's just a little boy, not a man. He's not nearly big enough to be handling tools like that.''

The grin that was so beguiling she could learn to hate it, grew again. "Relax, Mother," Travis soothed her. "All he did was pass things up to me." He leaned his weight against the rungs and held out both hands for her inspection. "I have only one pair, see?"

She saw. They were beautiful hands, lean and capable, with the long elegant fingers and short-clipped nails of a pianist. Neither an exterminator's hands, nor a logger's. What *did* he do for a living?

She caught her straying attention and yanked it back into place. "Well, okay," she conceded. "As long as you didn't let him do anything really dangerous. I don't want him getting hurt.''

"Truce then?" He stood casually, dangling one leg, completely at ease.

Susannah, looking up the length of his legs to his neat, narrow hips, decided that it was her poor head for heights that made her feel dizzy. "Truce," she agreed, averting her eyes. "Now come down from that thing before you kill yourself.''

He complied with more speed than sense, jumping down the last three feet to land lightly beside her. He wasn't heavily muscled like Mel, built more along the lines of a track star than a football player. Lean was a good description, but lanky was safer. It made him seem less attractive. "Thank you," she said.

"Anytime," he murmured, his summer-blue eyes studying her disconcertingly. "At least now you can sleep in peace without worrying that the ants are chewing the floor out from under you.''

A little snort of mirth escaped Benny's lips. "She screams," he confided, "when one gets on her. Pretty dumb, huh, Travis?"

Reaching up to remove the kerchief she'd worn around her hair, Susannah couldn't help laughing at Benny's delighted revelation. Disloyal little toad, she thought. It wasn't a son's prerogative to expose his mother's frailties so acutely to a man already possessed of more than enough ammunition to blow away her composure.

"Not so dumb," Travis remarked, wishing he could run his fingers through the subdued red-gold of her hair. Allowed to hang loose, it fell half an inch short of her shoulders; not curly, not straight, just curved. And so rich and smooth, it might have been spun from pure silk.

"You're staring," she accused, catching his fixed expression and retaliating with a cold tone, as though she'd caught him committing original sin.

I'm also letting my lascivious imagination run riot, he felt like replying. The truth was, he was bowled over. She couldn't possibly know how that spontaneous burst of laughter had transformed her, or she'd surely laugh more often. The frozen-faced doll he'd met yesterday had just come alive and turned into a woman. Her laugh brought animation to her features, sparked them with vivacity and touched them with humor and grace. She was lovely, and he was tempted enough to cast aside caution.

He realized that Cameron's Landing didn't allow for much privacy and an affair gone sour would soon become public domain. The last thing he needed was to have the entire community on his back because they thought he'd dealt unkindly with the widow. But where was the harm in enjoying each other's company, provided that they established the rules at the outset? A summer encounter, perhaps. Mutual pleasure between consenting adults. Nothing heavy, no serious entanglements and no broken hearts at season's end.

He held out his hand in a friendly overture. "Can we start all over again? I'd sort of like to make a better impression this time." He angled a smile at her. "Travis O'Connor at your service, ma'am."

The corners of her mouth softened. "Susannah Boyd," she said, taking his hand, "and I believe you've already met my son, Benny."

"That's a baby name," the boy objected. "I'm Benjamin Melville Boyd, but you can call me Ben."

The smile she brought to bear on her son told Travis more clearly than words that her whole life revolved around this child. For some weird reason, it made him feel empty inside, as though he were missing something, which was bloody ridiculous considering he had his life arranged exactly as he wanted it.

"Well, Benjamin Melville Boyd," Susannah said, stroking back the hair from his face, "we should let this kind man go. I'm sure he's got better things to do than hang around here, and I'd better start thinking about dinner. Knowing you, you must be starving."

"Travis doesn't want to go, do you, Travis? He could stay for dinner, too, Mom."

Gold-flecked lashes swept down to cover those expressive eyes of hers, but not before Travis had time to register the objections mirrored there. "Another time, maybe," he suggested, ignoring the shaft of disappointment her rejection produced.

Ben's face fell. "But—"

"I hadn't planned on company tonight, Benny," Susannah interrupted. "I think we'd find ourselves a bit short of food."

Ben tried to worm his way past the obstacles his mother kept throwing up and managed instead to ignite her wrath again. "We aren't very hungry, are we Travis? We had a big lunch, Mom—potato chips and wieners and Hershey bars and root beer and all sorts of good stuff."

"Hardly what I'd call a balanced meal," she said shortly. "You were supposed to have a bowl of soup and a sandwich."

"Heck, Mom!" The child didn't see where he was headed with his revelations, but Travis did and closed his eyes in silent farewell to his short-lived efforts at a truce. "We went down on the dock, and had a picnic instead. Right Travis?"

"Dock?" Her voice was rapier sharp.

"Yeah." Ben grinned heedlessly. "We sat on crab traps and Travis showed me how to tie bait, and I met all sorts of neat guys. It was fun, Mom."

"Go wash your hands," she said.

"But—"

"Now, Benny." Her tone allowed for no compromise. He scuttled upstairs, flinging an apologetic glance over his shoulder at Travis.

Too late, kiddo, Travis thought, bracing himself. She was glaring at him, and her eyes weren't black as he'd first thought, but the dark and turbulent purple-gray of thunderheads crouched up against the mountains. He offered her a weak smile. "I was just getting to that part," he said.

"Were you?" she replied silkily. "Well, don't let me stop you. I'm all ears."

"It was a long day for him." He gestured up the stairs. "He seemed kind of low . . . lonely, you know? I thought he might like to meet a few other people, like the Hamilton boys. Well, they're men, I guess, but they've not really outgrown being kids yet either—not like Larene and the Turners—and that makes a difference to somebody Ben's age."

"So you took him to play at a nice safe place like a dock, where he could have fallen in the water and drowned. How very thoughtful and kind."

That really ticked him off. "Hey, listen, lady—"

"No, you listen. That child means everything to me. He's the reason I get up in the morning and one of the chief reasons I moved to this town to begin with. If all I wanted to do was to worry myself sick over his safety, I could have stayed in Seattle. Bad enough that he's finding it hard to settle down here and that I had to leave him with strangers practically as soon as we arrive, without you barging in uninvited and encouraging him to do things that any fool could recognize as risky."

Even his mother wouldn't pin his ears back this far, Travis decided, hitching up his jeans to ride more comfortably on his hips and turning for the door. "Ma'am," he said in a weary voice, "this may come as a shock to your delicate sensibilities, but I'm a very responsible adult. I've never been to jail, never been arrested even, and I don't get my kicks from endangering people, regardless of their age. I'm sorry if I didn't perform according to your high standards and I promise that you won't have to suffer because of me again. Frankly, I don't need the aggravation any more than you do. Life's too short. Good day."

And then he walked out before she had the chance for the last word.

"Mom," Benny mourned from halfway down the stairs, "you went and yelled at Travis again and now he won't come back anymore."

"Good."

"But I like him, Mom. He's neat."

Susannah made an exasperated face after Travis O'Connor's departing shadow. She had the feeling she'd been too hard on him, especially considering that he'd managed to accomplish something she'd been trying unsuccessfully to achieve almost from the day they arrived: namely, to make Benny feel more at home here.

"Oh, by the way," Travis said, reappearing in the doorway before she had her features properly in place again, "these are for you. They were outside the back door and I forgot about them till now. They're a bit past their best but I think they might recover if you put them in water." He held out a wilted bunch of forget-me-nots, their heads drooping sadly.

What a sneaky move, she thought, taking the pathetic little bouquet. Only a jerk would wait until she'd torn strips off him before offering her flowers. How was she supposed to remain self-righteous if he was going to do things like this? "Poor things," she murmured, trying to save face by reminding herself that the flowers were a casual, meaningless offering from a man she barely knew. "You shouldn't have left them out in the sun, but thank you for the thought. You've been very kind—to both of us."

"Before you say something you might regret," he cautioned her, "you should know they're not from me."

His smile washed over her, warm and unapologetic, which made her own disappointment all the more illogical. "I hardly need a bribe to be civil," she said, half-irritated at the knowledge that when he put his mind to it, he could be thoroughly charming.

He heaved a comical sigh of relief. "I knew you weren't as heartless as you wanted me to believe."

Well, heaven knew there'd been times enough in the past few years that she wished she were. When she'd finally accepted that Mel was gone, she'd very firmly turned all her affections on Benny, and put romance into storage. She'd derived all the emotional nourishment she needed from motherhood. Some might call it sublimation, she'd called it survival. Still, she felt her mouth lifting in a smile at his words.

Travis watched her, enjoying the sight of her all golden with sunlight. "You know something? You should smile more often. You make me wish the flowers were from me, after all."

"I'd almost forgotten they weren't," she said, startled, and looked up at her son who was sliding up and down the bottom three feet of the stair bannister. "Did you find them someplace, Benny?"

He spread his arms wide and balanced himself astride the rail. "Nah. See Travis? I can do it without hands."

"Are you sure?" A thought struck her and she looked at him more closely. "Benny, you didn't steal them out of someone's garden, did you?"

He shook his head in further denial, too absorbed to take note of her concern.

"Benny, I'm talking to you."

He looked frustrated. "I already told you, I didn't."

"I think he's telling the truth," Travis interjected, bringing a restraining hand to her shoulder. "They were on the doorstep when we arrived here this afternoon, and in any case why would he lie? It's not as if it's a crime to give flowers."

It was, if he'd filched them from someone else's garden, Susannah thought. She didn't want him picking up any more bad habits—telling fibs was enough. "Well, if it wasn't him and it wasn't you, then who was it?" she demanded.

"It could have been anyone."

"Gee, thanks! Why doesn't that make me feel better, I wonder?"

"Search me. I've always been led to believe women like to receive flowers."

"Not when they're half-dead and anonymous, we don't. That's creepy."

He aimed a level look at her. "Susannah, this is Cameron's Landing, not Sodom or Gomorrah. It was just someone's way of saying welcome."

Well then, she wished people around here weren't so covert with their good intentions. The idea of someone sneaking up to the house without announcing himself unnerved her. Where she grew up, that sort of behavior was reason enough to call in the law, for Pete's sake. "Then why didn't whoever it was knock at the door or leave a note or something?"

"Because although this is a very close-knit community, you're a stranger here, and people will respect your privacy until you invite them to do otherwise. But that doesn't mean they won't welcome you. Before the week's out, you'll probably find a dozen eggs on your doorstep, or a jar of preserves, or a pie hot from someone's oven, and very possibly all three."

"And what if you're wrong?"

"I'm not wrong." He shook his head emphatically. "I know every single person in this town, and there's not one that would harm you or Ben, nor anyone who'd stand by and let someone else harm you. For crying out loud, woman, whatever made you this paranoid?"

"That," she said, in a cool remote voice that exactly matched the face she'd worn yesterday, "is really none of your business."

"What if I decide to make it my business?"

"I thought you said people around here respect each other's privacy."

His hand trapped her wrist, his eyes relentless on her face. "They're also very friendly."

"I'm trying to unpack, make a home for Benny and get used to a new job," she objected feebly, noticing that his eyes were as blue as the forget-me-nots on the table beside her. "I'm too busy for socializing right now."

"How long do you think it will take you to settle in?" Travis asked, and lifting her hand, turned it over to inspect the palm.

"Weeks," she gasped. She felt exposed, as if her whole life, past, present and future, were spread out for him to read.

"Much too long," he murmured, and whispered his lips over her inner wrist as though to seal the lightly uttered words into a promise. "You have until next Thursday."

Her flesh burned where he touched it. Burned and froze. "Why... next Thursday?"

"That's when I'll be knocking on your door again, to see how you're doing. Maybe by then you'll have forgiven me enough—" He paused for a moment, then shrugged. "What the hell, the worst you can do is refuse. Maybe you'll invite me to stay for dinner next time, seeing as you'll be expecting me. I'd make it sooner, but I'm going fishing and won't be back before then."

He was the most tempting diversion she'd run up against in years, Susannah thought, feeling her cheeks turn peony pink with awareness. She was terribly conscious of Benny standing quietly on the sidelines, his wide brown stare taking in the unlikely sight of his mother blushing and holding hands with a strange man.

Shaken, she pulled back her hand and tried to dismiss the emotions that had come from nowhere. When she found she couldn't do that, she tried to belittle them. They were nothing but biological urges, set free by Travis's audacity. He wasn't the first man who'd tried to tempt her, for heaven's sake, so why react like Eve confronting the serpent?

It would help if he were homely instead of so attractive, but there was more to it than that. Some elemental force was at work that paid no heed to wisdom or convenience. It set him apart from the other men she'd known. She wished it were not so. She didn't need the complication of him, not here, not now.

Oh brother! Travis thought. It was a dynamite setup: sexy mom, cute kid, no dad . . . and ants. The perfect opportunity for him to show off his rescue tactics.

"Well . . . ?" He stretched out the question, hoping to disguise the nervousness in his voice that was as uncharacteristic as it was surprising. But the room was humming with undercurrents of tension suddenly, and Ben was watching him, wide-eyed, as if he believed that only fathers should mess around with mothers' hands. "Don't keep me hanging this way, Susannah. Am I invited to dinner or not?"

Chapter Four

Susannah sucked in a deep breath and spoke before she lost her courage—or found her senses, depending on how you looked at it. "If you like," she said off-handedly.

His grin blossomed. "Wow! I'm swept away by your enthusiasm. Thanks. About seven okay?"

She shrugged. "Fine. Have a good trip."

In the act of turning to leave, he stopped, and she knew he was examining her face with eyes that had stolen for themselves the richest blue the ocean had to offer. "I'm sure I will," he said gently, "now."

Then, to her intense relief, he disappeared before she could ask him just what he meant by that.

DURING THE NEXT SIX DAYS she had so many other things occupying her mind that if anyone had asked her what she thought of Travis O'Connor, she could almost have looked them full in the eye and asked, "Travis Who?"

Almost but not quite. He had a habit of cropping up when she least expected him, if not in conversation, then in her thoughts.

Just as he'd predicted, people came quietly when she was busy doing other things and left offerings on her front porch: two fresh-baked loaves with a cordial little note from "Marg and Henry (the store)"; a lemon meringue pie and a potted hyacinth with a card from Judith Petersen, who invited her to drop in for coffee, "the big house, four up from the school'' when she was more settled; and a pail of mussels from ''Jan and Joe Hamilton, your neighbors down on the dock.'' Susannah filed away the forget-me-nots as yet another unobtrusive gesture of welcome and persuaded herself to discount the rather unorthodox method of delivery.

The first day of school arrived and Susannah escorted Benny personally to his teacher, braving the curious stares of the other children who seemed to find her presence highly amusing. She spent the rest of the morning wondering how he was fitting in and was there waiting to meet him at noon. Her worst fears were confirmed when he came slinking out alone after the rest of his class had erupted into the school yard in a noisy, exuberant pack.

His reaction at seeing her was something less than flattering. ''Why did you come?'' he muttered out of the corner of his mouth, looking all shifty-eyed.

''I wanted to,'' she said. ''You've never walked home by yourself before, and I missed you.''

''Well, wait behind a tree,'' he begged, as if she were some sort of pariah whom he was ashamed to be seen with.

''Why?''

''Because the other kids think you're weird,'' he said, ''especially when you try to hold my hand. I'd rather be by myself.''

She suffered a little pang at that, but decided she'd do as he asked. It was safe enough, she supposed, since the school was practically within sight of the house, and she had no wish to do anything further that might jeopardize his being accepted by his peers.

He arrived home five minutes after school was out that afternoon, moody and quiet.

''Tell me about your day,'' she said, when they sat down to dinner. ''Do you like your teacher?''

He shrugged. ''She's okay.''

''Did she introduce you to the class, the way she said she would?''

He nodded glumly and shoved his food around his plate.

''Well? What did they do?''

"They looked at me."

Even to her ears, her laugh sounded forced. "I guess they would. What did you do, love?"

"I looked back."

"Were they friendly? Did they talk to you after school?"

"One guy did."

Only one? "That's nice. What did he say?"

"That I talk funny."

"What?"

"Then he said I was a simp and should play with the girls."

The little toad! "Why did he say that?"

"Because I need my mother to bring me to school."

"But that was just this morning. He'll change his mind when he sees you coming and going by yourself."

Again, that apathetic little shrug. "I don't care."

With mixed feelings, she waved him off the next morning and thought that if he felt one-tenth as lonely as he looked, her heart would break.

Later in the day there came a knock at the door that would have roused the dead had they been inclined to resurrect. Susannah opened up to find herself dwarfed by the man who stood outside. Easily six foot four, with hands like hams and ponderous jowls, the stranger identified himself the minute he opened his mouth.

"Morning, dearie. My Larene tells me you had them big black flying beasts bothering you," he boomed. "Just thought I'd stop by and spread a bit of poison along the beam in case they show up again."

"I haven't seen any. Travis O'Connor came up and took care of them."

Bob Kelly let forth with a great bellow of laughter that reverberated through the rafters. If there still had been an ant colony, Susannah thought, he'd surely have shaken it loose.

"Strikes me," he chortled, digging her in the ribs, "our Travis might have got a bit distracted, if you follow me.

Hear he spent quite a bit of time with the boy the other day.''

Susannah cringed at the ripples that would be created if word ever got out that Travis O'Connor had been seen kissing the wrist of the newly arrived widow, and decided he could trail his lips up someone else's arm in future—she didn't need the notoriety.

Later that afternoon, she went down to sort inventory in the library bus which was parked in a corner of the school yard, timing her visit so that she'd still be there when classes ended for the day. She planned to appear occupied with her job and not embarrass Benny needlessly, she decided, but if anyone started anything with him, she'd make her presence felt in no uncertain terms.

Shortly after she arrived, a young woman came out of the building and introduced herself as Rosalind Basehart, the principal.

"I'm so glad to meet you," Susannah said. "I'm afraid Benny's not settling down very well. He seems very lonely and unhappy."

"It's not easy for him, arriving partway through the year, especially with the school being so small," Rosalind agreed, "but I'm sure, given time, that he'll fit in."

"What can I do to make it easier for him?"

"Be there for him . . . and try not to let him see that you're concerned. He'll pick up on your anxiety, you know."

"He's my only child and we're very close. It's hard not to worry."

Rosalind looked at her out of compassionate eyes. "Of course it is. It's only natural under the circumstances. Benny told us this afternoon about his father."

Mel's death wasn't something they discussed much anymore, and it came as a surprise to Susannah that Benny would have talked so freely to people he didn't know. "He did?"

"Yes, and it's my guess that he'll find himself less of a stranger, now that the other children know something about his background." Rosalind smiled. "He told us about you, too."

Oh, grief! Susannah thought in mild trepidation. She'd heard about Show and Tell, and knew that when Benny waxed loquacious nothing was too private to reveal. No doubt the whole class was now aware that she talked in her sleep, was afraid of heights, allergic to walnuts, and threw up if she drank liqueurs. "Really. How interesting."

Rosalind's smile widened. "Don't look so nervous. I hear you're a writer."

"Not exactly." Susannah relaxed. "Nothing very creative about me, I'm afraid. I'm working on a language textbook for senior grades in high school."

"Well, I hope you'll be doing something similar for the elementary grades when you're finished that. It's about time we had something new and exciting for the really captive years." She studied Susannah for a minute. "This is just a suggestion, Susannah, but it might make Benny feel more accepted if he brings lunch to school instead of going home at noon. Nearly all the children come in by bus and lunch hour's when they do most of their socializing. I think he'd find friends and settle in faster if he were here then, too."

Rosalind was obviously a sensible woman, and her point was worth taking. Susannah had harbored a few doubts about the quality of small-town education, but it was clear Benny was in good hands. Maybe things weren't as bad as they'd seemed half an hour ago.

"By the way," Rosalind said, preparing to leave, "I wanted to mention that if you'd like Benny to stay here until you get back to town on the days you take the bus to the camps, he's very welcome. I'm here until six most days, and if I'm not, someone else will be."

Susannah hesitated. When she'd brought up the subject of having Larene baby-sit for the days when she had to work, Benny had nearly had a fit.

"I'd appreciate that," Susannah assured Rosalind. "He's never been left alone before."

"That's settled, then. Let's keep in touch, but I'm sure we won't have any problems. By this time next week, he'll have forgotten he ever was a stranger."

Half an hour later, Susannah was left wondering. School ended and the yard was suddenly full of children. From her vantage point in the bus, she saw Benny detach himself from a small group and head for the road home.

"Hey, Ben," a tow-headed boy yelled, pointing to where Susannah lurked behind a stack of paperbacks. "Your Mom's here. Don't ya want to walk home with her no more?"

"Shut up, Peter Fleming," a doll-faced little girl ordered. "Ben's new and we're supposed to be nice and help him."

"Wazoo!" retorted Peter Fleming who looked, Susannah thought, rather the way Al Capone might have appeared at the tender age of seven: tough and lawless. She tensed, prepared to defend Benny and the girl, if need be. Benny had explained wazoo to her as something between a baby and an idiot.

But the girl had matters well in control and was quite unmoved by the insult. "You're *such* a dope, Peter Fleming. No wonder your cat hates you," she said and ran to catch up with Benny. "I live next to the Petersens. You can walk with me, Ben, if you like."

The last Susannah saw of Ben, he was speeding up the hill as if the hounds of hell were in pursuit.

IT STARTED TO RAIN late Wednesday afternoon, a gray and dismal drizzle that shrouded her ocean view in veils of mist and dampened everything but Susannah's spirits. Benny was marginally less withdrawn about his day, though he wasn't exactly brimming over with enthusiasm. After dinner she set a flank steak to marinate in ginger and wine then settled down to give herself a manicure, preferring not to look too closely at her motive for doing so and telling herself that the menu for tomorrow night's dinner was in no way influenced by the fact that she was expecting Travis O'Connor to be there to share it with them.

"What's that?" Benny demanded, rummaging through the refrigerator in search of a snack and finding the steak.

"Tomorrow's dinner. Get a move on, Benny, it's past your bedtime."

"Yuck. It looks like something fell in the bowl and drowned. Do we have to eat it?"

"Yes."

"How come? We never did before. Are we having company or something?"

"Sort of."

"Who?"

"No one—well, sort of no one. Mr. O'Connor." Good grief, she was blushing again. That, or there was something wrong with her hormones, because thirty-two was a mite young to be having hot flashes.

Benny was looking at her as if she'd just admitted she might be expecting pups. "You mean you got a date with Travis?"

"Certainly not."

"Good," he said with more animation than he'd shown since the last time Travis had graced them with his presence, "because he won't eat that stuff."

"Go brush your teeth, Benny."

That night a full-fledged storm blew in from the Pacific, bringing squalls and cool temperatures with it. Lying awake and listening to the wind soughing through the fir trees outside the windows, Susannah wondered if she could, just once in her life, bake a decent pie. She had tender young stalks of rhubarb in her freezer, and Benny liked rhubarb. That Travis would probably be ready for something rib sticking if the rain kept up was purely coincidental.

IT JUST WASN'T LIKE HIM to be chafing this way. Normally he'd be happy to hole up in a deserted anchorage and let the weather blow itself out. Days like this became rare with the advance of summer, and although he enjoyed the company of his buddies, there were times when Travis liked to be solitary.

So why, he wondered irritably, was he unable to settle down with the latest bestseller? Instead he was leaping up every five minutes to check on the weather outside. He couldn't do anything to change it, and from the way it looked out there, it was likely to get worse before it got better.

It had been a good trip, until tonight. If the fine conditions had held, he'd have been back in Cameron's Landing by early afternoon, with a fifty-pound halibut, a salmon and his limit of crab. To be reasonable, whether he arrived back tonight or tomorrow made little difference to most of his plans. Larene would still be delirious about the halibut and would invite the whole town to supper, Judith would still freeze the salmon for later, and the crab would probably still be alive and fresh enough to eat. It was his one other plan that would go awry, and he was as sore about that as a kid who'd missed a birthday party.

He was going to be a day late getting back to town, a day late for his dinner date with Susannah, and that fried him. It disconcerted him, how much he'd thought of her during the last week. He wasn't used to that. Of course there'd been other women, but never to the point that they crossed over into the other compartments of his life. He preferred it that way: a place for everything and everything in its place.

His work shaped his life-style and it simply didn't lend itself to a serious relationship. A woman needed a man who was going to be around, not one always coming or going and too often gone for days at a stretch. He knew firsthand how tough that could be on the one left behind to carry the load. He'd seen what it did to his mother.

The way he remembered it—back when he was about ten, his sister Patsy still in diapers, and the other four somewhere in between—if the furnace broke down in the middle of winter or the car wouldn't start in the rain, his mother always had to call in an outsider for help. When he or his brother needed stitching up after a fall, it was his mom who drove to the doctor's office with the injured hero in the front next to her, and the other five crammed into the back seat, silent with awe at the sight of a bit of blood.

Even the fun times were something his father had too often missed: the school concerts, the birthday parties—and the memorable time all six O'Connor children were members of a former baby-sitter's wedding. Easily the worst day of his life, Travis recalled, smiling at the memory, until he and Rick had started shoving each other and wound up in an ornamental lily pond, soaked to the skin. The blue satin bow ties had never been the same again, and while the O'Connor girls had been mortified, the boys had had a ball.

Not necessarily a bad life for a child, he concluded, but a wife deserved something better. To him, marriage meant sharing his life, with a woman and with their children. Yet flying had been his first love for so long that he had a hard time envisioning another passion taking its place. And that thought made it difficult to explain why Susannah's beautiful pansy eyes invaded his dreams at night.

Frustrated, he flung his book across the cabin, turned down the wick on the oil lamp and crawled into his down sleeping bag. He didn't recall falling asleep, but when he awoke around five on Friday morning, the wind had dropped to less than a breeze, the seas were calm again and the sky the pale milky blue of early summer. He could leave now, and it would still take him the better part of the day to make it back to Cameron's Landing, but he found himself reluctant to make a move, unwilling to shatter the mood left by the picture that had formed in his mind during sleep. He wanted time to examine it, to try to analyze it.

It hadn't been a dream in the real sense of the word, just a series of images that even the dawn couldn't fade. He had seen Susannah, up behind her rented house, naked in the deep, cool grass of summer, the shadows flirting over her skin in the filtered sunlight. She rose and walked toward where he waited.

The image evoked an unfamiliar mixture of feelings in him. Desire he understood and could cope with; tenderness and this strange urge to protect were something else entirely. He was way out of his depth on this one.

IT WASN'T FAIR, the way contentment could hinge on such inconsequentialities, Susannah decided. In a word, Thursday had been lousy. First, the weather was so foul that she could scarcely distinguish the mouth of the harbor, much less see the arrival of any boats.

Then Benny, who'd seemed as if he might be settling in, had come down to breakfast clutching his quilt as if it were a life preserver and announced he didn't plan to go to school anymore.

She'd been stunned. "Why ever not?"

"Because." He hugged the quilt close, rubbing his cheek with it.

Oh grief, Susannah thought. He'd be sucking his thumb next. What had she done to him, uprooting him this way? "But you've always liked school," she said helplessly.

"Not this one. I don't have any friends."

"You do so. I saw you talking to them the other day."

"They live too far away. After school they go on the bus and there's no one left."

"I'm sure some of the others live in town, Benny."

"Yeah," he agreed mournfully, "but they're babies or big guys who don't want me hanging around. The rest are girls, and they're wazoos, Mom."

Susannah felt trapped. "I can't do much about that, Benny."

"You could let me go down to the dock and watch the guys fishing," he suggested with such shining innocence that she knew it was what he'd had in mind all along.

"Out of the question," she had said firmly. "I thought we'd settled that last week. What if you fell in the water? You could drown."

"I can swim," he'd burst out resentfully, "and they like me down there. You never want me to have any fun. You don't even listen. You just always say no. All the time, Mom."

Did she? Was that why he'd resorted to telling lies, to avoid deliberately disobeying her? She looked at him, saw the angry tears sparkling in his eyes and the trembling mouth, and knew he was torn between being a baby and a boy. She wished she could keep him a baby just a little longer but knew she'd be doing neither of them any favors with that sort of attitude. "You said it would be different here," he had accused her. "You said to Grandma that it would be good for me because I was growing up, but you didn't really mean it."

"Tell you what," she had offered. "No more complaints from you about school and I promise I'll think about it. Maybe we can work something out."

After he'd left for school, she'd paid a visit to the dock where the Hamiltons lived above the boat shed. "Benny wants to come down here and watch people fishing," she told Tony, the eldest Hamilton son, "but I'm not sure it's a very good place for a boy of seven."

"Hey, no problem," Tony assured her. "Kids hang around all the time, and if you're nervous or anything, we have a whole bunch of vests in the boat shed. We can let you have one if you like."

Jan Hamilton, who'd come out when she saw Susannah, put in her two bits' worth. "It's a good place for kids down here. We have some pretty strict rules about them always wearing life preservers and not fooling around, and there's always at least one of us out here when the weather's good."

She rummaged around inside the shed and came out with a junior floater vest. "This should fit him. We'll print his name on it and hang it with the rest just inside the door where he can find it."

Unwilling to appear unreasonable and unable to come up with a better solution, Susannah swallowed her misgivings and agreed to give the idea a try. "But you have to promise me," she warned an ecstatic Benny, "that you'll play by the rules."

That afternoon she tackled the pie, forming little petals of pastry around the steam vents and brushing the top with beaten eggs so that it would bake nice and golden. Unfortunately she forgot it was in the oven, and by the time she remembered, it had passed through all shades of golden to an unrelieved brown that looked far from appetizing. As things turned out, it didn't matter worth a damn. Travis O'Connor never showed up, and she served baked beans for dinner.

"Beans, beans, the musical fruit," Benny caroled, delighted not to have to swallow meat that had to be washed overnight before it was fit to eat, and still high on the fact that he had won the battle to become "one of the guys." "The more you eat, the more you toot."

"Shut up," Susannah snapped, in no mood to appreciate his childish exuberance. In fact she decided she'd be very glad when he outgrew the need to giggle immoderately over simple body functions. Boys could be so vulgar at times.

Of course, once her whole week had been spoiled and it didn't matter if it snowed for a month, Friday dawned mild and sunny, promising great things for the weekend. But what really annoyed her was the way she reacted to the knocking at her door just before lunch. Deciding, irrationally, that it must be Travis and that, somehow, she'd find it in her heart to forgive him for being a few hours late, she flung wide the door only to discover Bob Kelly outside.

"How's them big pests?" he wanted to know, disgustingly cheerful. "Seen any more of them?"

"Not one," she admitted glumly, a picture of Travis springing immediately to her mind's eye.

"Ah." Bob grinned. "Reckon you've seen the last of them, then."

She reckoned he was right, unfortunately. "Um... Bob...?"

"Something on your mind, dearie?"

Travis O'Connor, Susannah thought, but she'd die before she came right out and said so. "Not really. It's just that...well, what's-his-name who plugged up the nest—"

"What nest?" Bob inquired, scratching his bald spot and looking, she thought, unnecessarily stunned.

"The ant nest…last week, when you were out of town, remember?"

Comprehension dawned. "Ah, you mean Travis. Nice guy, our Travis. Everyone's glad to see him back in town."

"He's back?" The louse! It was the last time she'd invite him to dinner.

"Well, of course he is, dearie. He plugged up your nest, didn't he?"

Susannah took a deep breath and prayed for patience. Talk about a dog chasing its own tail! The conversation was going around in circles. "But that was before."

"Before what?" Bob's stunned look returned, intensified.

She let fly with a gust of exasperation. Being discreet was getting her precisely nowhere. "Before he went fishing last week. He was supposed to be back yesterday."

A light went on in Bob Kelly's head. She could tell by the way his eyes gleamed. "Why, that rascal! Stood you up, did he?"

Susannah went clammy at the thought of Larene sinking her teeth into that little tidbit. "Well, not exactly…"

"Must have been held up by the weather," Bob offered, comfortingly. "Happens all the time with the spring storms. He'll show up sooner or later, never fear."

Ridiculous the way her heart soared at that little morsel. "Oh," she said in the most offhand, uninterested voice she could drum up. "I wasn't really worried."

"Just as well," Bob said, promptly spoiling everything. "Them fire-fighting pilots have a habit of not turning up when they're expected. If you and Travis are going to be keeping company, you'll have to get used to him being a bit late now and then."

Fire-fighting pilot? Forest fires? Her heart stopped spinning and came to a shuddering halt somewhere around her navel. She'd rather have heard he was married with nine children, or a convict on the run.

Well, she thought, this was one little romance that was about to be nipped severely in the bud. She'd had her share of nail-biting anxiety with Mel when it came to hazardous occupations. He'd be alive today if he'd been content to lead a quiet life, and she'd long ago resolved that if she ever became involved with a man again, he'd have to be an accountant or computer analyst; anything, as long as it was safe.

All things considered, she should be glad Travis hadn't shown up. So how come she still felt so bleak with disappointment?

That afternoon, Benny came home from school in high spirits, collected his allowance, submitted to forty or more reminders to wear his life vest at all times and took off for the dock. She waved him off cheerfully then went sneaking down after him, determined to keep her distance but stay close enough to fish him out of the water, or any other kind of trouble, should it be necessary.

Unfortunately she overlooked the fact that small boys get distracted rather easily, and rounded the corner so fast she almost stepped on him where he was bent over examining a caterpillar.

"Hi, Mom," he said. "Where're you going?"

"I—uh . . . for a walk." She offered him her most guileless smile to no avail.

His face darkened stormily. "You can't come to the dock," he announced flatly. "If you do, I'll go home."

"Why?" she asked. "I won't *do* anything. I'll just . . . sort of stand there."

"Geez!" Benny flung an agonized gaze toward heaven. "It's not for girls down there. You're supposed to be at home."

She had raised a tiny little male chauvinist piglet, Susannah decided, horrified. How had it happened? "For your information, I once caught a jarful of tadpoles," she told him sourly, and forbore to mention they'd all died overnight and been flushed down the toilet the next morning.

"That's dumb," Benny said. "Go home, Mom. You're spoiling things."

"Don't be rude, Benny."

"Well, but," he objected, "you're breaking your promise, and you're not supposed to do that."

He was right. She kissed him again and slunk back the way she'd come, determined to spend the time working on lesson eight of the textbook. But becoming engrossed in the sophisticated use of the comma was a lost cause when her attention kept hopping from Benny to Travis and back to Benny again. Finally she decided she'd be better off taking advantage of the weather and devoting her energies to rescuing the honeysuckle which was in danger of being choked to death by crabgrass and dandelions at the foot of her deck. She might not need Travis, and her son might not need her, but the honeysuckle could surely use some help.

It was a good decision. She felt better as soon as she was out in the sun. This far north the air had a clarity to it seldom found in Seattle, etching the landmass lying west of the fjord dark and blue on the horizon. The sky was clear, the breeze a sigh and there was nothing to disturb the peace. The distant purr of a power boat approaching the harbor accentuated the utter silence, rather than detracting from it.

Susannah's discontent melted. This was what country living was all about, she decided: inhaling the scents of early summer, playing farmer and pretending she knew what she was doing.

An hour later she surveyed her efforts with some dismay. She had blisters on both thumbs, the dirt had somehow crawled through her new gardening gloves to lodge under her fingernails and she doubted her knees would ever be the same again.

And what had she to show for it all? A miserable little patch of earth and a scrawny-looking honeysuckle vine that had some sort of blight afflicting most of it. Add to all that a ruined manicure and a sunburned nose, and she had two more reasons to be glad that Travis O'Connor had chosen not to show.

But what the heck! If the honeysuckle died, she could get another. She had the rest of the summer to work on the garden, the whole weekend in front of her to spend with Benny and there was still time for a snooze before he came home for dinner. Luxuries! Travis could go take a jump off the end of the dock, and as of this moment she would stop worrying about things she couldn't change.

Later, when she relived the horror of what followed, she tried to remember if she'd felt his presence, and discovered that what chilled her the most was that she'd remained completely and utterly oblivious to the approaching danger.

She was lying with her eyes closed, soaking up the late-afternoon warmth, somewhere between awake and asleep in that hazy half-world that placed reality at a distance and reduced a person's perceptions until everything ran in slow motion. Lethargy dulled her senses, left her limbs heavy. Only the prolonged shade, cast by his leaning over her, roused her.

She opened her eyes very slowly and with the certain knowledge that she was no longer alone. Before she had a chance to move either head or body, she heard his voice, and the sound of it, high and thready, reassembled the uneasiness that had nibbled at her over the past few days, and crystallized it into cold and immediate menace. Pitched exactly to the smothered laughter she'd heard over a week ago when she'd first discovered the ants, it drifted over her now, secretive and somehow deranged.

"The little boy liked the flowers. Did you?" it asked, close by her ear.

Against reason and every other instinct of self-preservation, she turned her head to look at him, and horror rose in her throat to choke her. He loomed over her, a solitary giant, his spine a black arc silhouetted against the sky, his scant hair a halo of thistledown. The face was that of a child, curiously unlined or touched by age, with vacant beautiful eyes the color of Devon violets. The broad arc of a scar, faded to silver, curved over his nearly hair-less skull and disappeared in the tuft of one eyebrow.

All the peace vanished, the sense of well-being so swiftly eclipsed that she felt as though she'd been trapped in this nightmare all her life. She was never so conscious of the silence as she was in the seconds after his words. Not a bird, not an insect, disturbed the late afternoon calm. Just this pathetic wreck of a man, hovering over her, his hands working nervously, his lips drooling and loose. Even her scream emerged thin and strangled. All it did was startle him into a frantic whimpering, and bring his hands close to her face, to stop the noise.

Panic-stricken, she hit out at him, and he retaliated by letting loose a bellow of noise and springing away from her. "No!" he wailed. "Don't, don't! You aren't nice." His face contorted with emotion. "I'm going! I'm going to get the little boy. He's not like you. He's nice."

And he was gone down the hill and into the under-brush, loping away like some great injured animal, his head hunched down between his shoulders.

Only then did the paralysis leave her, swept aside in a rush of dread. "No...no...!" she croaked, her whole body beginning to shake. "Oh, please, God, no...not again...not my baby, please..."

She struggled to her feet, the old memories as close and oppressive as if they had happened just yesterday. She didn't see that she was no longer alone, didn't hear her name called on the soft spring air. Beset by devils that she'd hoped had been left behind five years ago, she cannoned into Travis, blinded by fear.

Chapter Five

She didn't hear him. *Couldn't* hear him. Couldn't see him, either, come to that. Holding her at arm's length, Travis searched her face then pulled her close again.

Her eyes were sightless, their color hidden behind a sheen of fear that turned them silver, and the way she trembled in his arms reminded him of the time he'd seen a hummingbird snagged in a net. He watched her swallow once, twice, as though trying to dislodge a terror that was leaving a bad taste in his mouth, too. "I'm here," he whispered. "Whatever it is, Susannah, I'm here, and it will be okay."

But gentleness, he quickly realized, was powerless to lessen the panic engulfing her. "I can't help you," he insisted, the urgency of his tone at last penetrating the quiet wall of hysteria that separated her from him, "until you tell me what's happened."

Her eyes flooded, and she sank against him, her strength temporarily spent. "Benny..." she whispered, his name emerging as a plea, fractured with anguish.

Travis frowned, puzzled. He'd seen Ben on the dock, when he'd nosed the boat to its mooring. "Ben's okay, love. I saw him not fifteen minutes ago."

"No!" Adamant, she stepped away from him and raised her hands, palms out. She was hearing him now, but she wasn't believing. Her gesture closed out any attempt at logic or reason. "I saw *him*. He was here. He touched me, threatened—'' A spasm crossed her face. "He's gone after Benny. That...*psycho* is after him. Fifteen minutes—''

For a moment, fear choked her words. It took only seconds for disaster to strike. She knew; she'd lived through it, twice, first when Benny was taken, and again when Mel was killed. But not a third time, please God. She caught hold of the panic and shaped it into action, wrestling to free herself from Travis's hold. "I have to find him—''

The raw fear he detected in her eyes, coupled with the absolute determination in her voice, shook him. "Susannah," he protested, restraining her with difficulty even though he outweighed her by at least seventy pounds, "there are no psychos in Cameron's Landing, and Ben is just fine, I promise you.''

Fragile to begin with, her control snapped then. "Don't say that," she cried, spinning away from him. "I saw him, I tell you.''

"Who? Who did you see?''

"Him!"

"That doesn't tell me a whole lot." Damn it, her fear was contagious. Even though logic dictated that whatever had upset her posed no immediate threat either to Ben or to her, Travis found his body tensing with apprehension. "Describe him. What's his name, what does he look like, what exactly did he do?''

"Big," she breathed, urgency vibrating through her. "Very big. And weird. Drooling, and babbling like an ape." Her eyes widened, and Travis knew the terror was gaining ground, making it harder for him to reach her.

Forcibly holding her back, he intervened, his voice soothingly low. "Take a deep breath," he insisted, "and calm down.''

She tried to do as he asked. "He was bald, with a scar, and his voice...'' Her own failed briefly at the memory, and a frisson of distaste rippled over her. "It was strange—high, sing-song, like a little child's.''

"Ah!" At the mention of the scar and the voice, he knew at once. Relief swept over him. Poor old harmless Abe; if only he knew what an impression he'd made!

"Oh, sweetheart," he said, "he won't hurt Benny. He wouldn't hurt a fly. Ask anyone in town, they'll all tell you the same thing. He's called Crazy Abe, but the truth is, he's as sweet a person as you'll ever come across and no more dangerous than you or I."

She opened her mouth, the words ready to trip over themselves in their anxiety to be born, and left it gaping as the import of what he'd said sank home. She leaned away to get a better view of him, as though she hoped her eyes would tell her that her ears had deceived her. She felt as brittle as glass under his hands. "You think this is all a big joke?" she snapped. "By your own admission, my child is at the mercy of a madman, and the best you can do is stand there and tell me not to worry because you know his name?"

Her voice shook with outrage, and when he tried to stroke her again, to explain, she wrenched away, her features tight with shock. "Well, I'll tell you something. He's not the only madman around here. You're a lunatic, too. Let me go and get the hell out of my way!"

"Why? What do you think you're going to do?"

"Rescue my son!"

Gad, talk about a lioness protecting her cub! Spitting mad and with all claws bared, she'd uttered the words, Travis thought, caught midway between amusement and alarm; as if nothing but her frail weight and mighty determination stood between Ben and damnation. "Susannah," he began again, all echoes of laughter dying from his voice, "Ben's hardly in need of rescue. Abe might not be exactly normal—whatever that means—but he's no madman. He had an accident when he was just a kid, and he's ... simple-minded, I guess you'd say, but he's neither dangerous nor violent."

The stormy purple-gray of her eyes darkened ominously. "Don't you *dare* try to minimize the situation,

Travis O'Connor. This is my child's safety we're talking about—not that it probably matters a damn to you!''

"That's uncalled for, Susannah, as you'd realize if you'd calm down enough to hear me out. You've had a bit of a fright, I'll grant you that, but nothing more. Abe's harmless and probably more terrified than you are, if truth's known."

He sounded so sure of himself, she was half inclined to believe him. Lord knew she wanted to believe him. She'd come too far and worked too hard to find herself back at the starting post, learning all over again to stare fear in the face until it backed off. But the incident with the stranger had unnerved her and unlocked a door she never again wanted to open.

It might have been that other time, with Benny little more than a baby, sweet-smelling from his evening bath, his fat little cheeks flushed pink all the way up to where the dark smudge of his eyelashes drooped heavily. Benny, his quilt clutched in one chubby fist, his teddy bear in the other, asleep in his government-approved crib, in his snug little nursery, where he should have been safe enough—and wasn't.

"But," she said, her voice quavering as she blinked away the images and fastened her gaze imploringly on Travis, "you said yourself, the man's mad. You called him crazy...Crazy Abe...?"

Travis wanted to hug her for the courage she fought to regain. He could see how difficult it was for her, how hard she struggled not to let panic swamp reason. "Yes, but not in the sense you think. It's a cruel name and I don't know where it came from. I almost didn't tell you about it, but you'd have heard it from someone else in town sooner or later. No one means it unkindly, it's just the way they talk."

He took a chance and let go of her arms, capturing her fingers loosely in his, and when she didn't pull away, he went on, "Abe's different, that's all. He spends hours talking to the birds and the trees. He'll sit and watch the sun set and wait for the first star to appear, as entranced

as if God had created them just for him. He'll cry when the
first frost turns the buttercups black, and clap his hands
with glee at the first snowflake. He believes in four leaf
clovers and Santa Claus. He's as timid as a deer and as full
of wonder as a child.''

His voice washed over her, dark and gentle, lulling her
into too-easy acceptance, displacing her fear, making her
ashamed she'd screeched at him earlier, shrinking the
proportions of her panic into lesser significance. It didn't
seem right, any more than it was right for her to have been
devoting so much thought to a man who'd stood her up for
dinner the night before. ''Why should I believe you?'' she
demanded, making a last stab at righteous indignation.

''Well,'' Travis said, amusement suddenly shimmering
again in his eyes, ''is the fact that Ben's just come charg-
ing around the corner at the bottom of the hill, full of
beans and not a hair out of place, reason enough?''

She flung him a look of pure suspicion laced with hope,
before hazarding a glance over her shoulder. The sight of
Benny, haloed in sunshine and as cheerful as Travis had
proclaimed him to be, sent relief shooting through her in
such waves she felt almost giddy.

''I'll accept your apology,'' Travis murmured, still
holding her hands soothingly, ''any time you feel ready to
extend it.''

Drat the man for being right! ''Don't hold your breath,''
she muttered.

''You wound me, Susannah,'' he chided her soulfully.
''What have I done to make you view me so unkindly?''

She ought to have been warned by the current of laughter undermining his words. If she hadn't been so light-
headed about Benny's safe return, she'd have proceeded
more warily. As it was, relief rendered her incautious.
''You're unreliable,'' she accused him. ''A person can't
depend on you to do what you say you'll do. That being
the case, why should a person believe anything you might
have to say?''

He cocked his head to one side and regarded her from under outrageously lowered lashes. "Why do I get the feeling we've just changed the subject?"

She dismissed the question with a flick of her hand. "I don't know what you mean."

"You're upset with me," he observed, stating the absurdly obvious, "because I'm a bit late for dinner, right?"

Benny was almost within earshot. She had no wish to continue this conversation, but she couldn't bear to keep her mouth shut on this subject, either. "Certainly not," she retorted, aiming for a lofty tone and missing. "And you're more than a little late. You didn't show up at all. Today is not yesterday!"

A dimple appeared beside Travis's mouth. "No, it isn't," he agreed, "but since we're trading earth-shaking truths, here's another you might like to consider—better late than never."

Halfway up the path leading to the porch, Benny stopped and waved something white and floppy at Susannah, his seven-year-old radar picking up the fact that all was not harmonious on the home front. "Hi, Mom. I brought dinner."

A peace offering if ever I saw one, Travis thought, smothering a grin.

Susannah snorted and turned her attention to Benny, knowing Travis was waiting for her to make a mess of handling the situation. Well, she wouldn't give him the satisfaction, she decided, and promptly said, "It's about time you got home, young man. You and I have to have a little talk."

Benny climbed the last few yards warily, his feet dragging. "Why? What've I done?"

Oh brother! Travis rolled his eyes, feeling for the kid. He was ankle-deep in trouble not of his own making, his new-found freedom likely to enjoy a short lease on life from the looks of things. Travis had hoped he'd made his point about Abe, but he had a feeling Susannah aimed to have the last word on that subject.

Supremely conscious of Travis's critical gaze fixed on her mouth as it spilled out evasions, Susannah replied pointedly, "We'll discuss it after Mr. O'Connor's gone home."

"But you said he was going to stay for dinner. You seemed happy about it, Mom."

The sun rolled down behind the mountain as though it couldn't compete with the fire in her cheeks. The air gusted out of her lungs in a sigh of pure exasperation. "That was yesterday, Benny."

"Why can't he stay today?"

"We don't have enough food."

"Yes, we do," her child informed her.

"No, we don't, Benny, and it's rude to talk this way in front of a guest."

"I don't mind," Travis put in, his grin bringing out his dimples.

"Well, gee," Benny grumbled, recognizing an ally when he saw one, "you spent enough time cooking—all that gross stuff that's in the fridge, and that pie thing that got left in the oven too long. It was enough yesterday, why isn't it now?"

"Yes," Travis agreed, undeterred by her glare. "Why isn't it, Susannah?"

"Because—"

"I know!" Benny's face lit up with feigned innocence. "Travis can have my share, and I'll eat this." He pressed his offering into her hand. It slithered over her palm, cold, wet and very dead. "It's a fish. I caught it," he informed her pridefully, running a loving finger over its limp back. "See, Ma? Now we've got enough to eat. No probs!"

The situation was fast getting away from her. Listen to him: "Ma"! "No probs"! Altogether too cool for a kid his age. It was time she took a firm stand.

Susannah looked down at the fish. It stared glassily back. Revolted, she turned her attention back to her son. He grinned at her guilelessly, and the words she'd been about to visit on him died unspoken. He looked too apple-cheeked and expectant for words. Beleaguered, she risked a glance at Travis. He was quite unable to control the smile twitching over his mouth.

Sometimes, she thought, it would be nice to have a child who wasn't quite so bright and observant. As for Travis and his cute little dimples, she'd like to wipe them off his face with the fish except that it deserved a better fate. "We eat in fifteen minutes," she announced, averting her gaze and addressing the distant mountain peaks. "Go wash your hands and get out of that smelly T-shirt."

"What about my fish, Mom?" Benny sounded crushed with disappointment. "Aren't you proud of me for catching it?"

He made her ashamed of being so crabby when truly she hadn't a reason in the world to be so out of sorts. He was home safe, after all. Whatever else she might think about Travis, he had been right on that score. "Yes, love," she said. "It's the most beautiful fish I've ever... held."

Benny let out a howl of delight and scampered off.

Travis showed no urge to follow him and seemed not to find the silence in the least awkward. Under the pretense of checking her watch, Susannah managed to sneak another glance at him. He seemed as disinclined to speak as he was to move. Instead he fixed her with an expectant stare, as though he hoped that, given enough time, she'd see the error of her ways. She clamped her lips shut and lowered her eyes. Settling in for the duration, he folded his arms across his chest, and in doing so, pulled his knit shirt taut across his stomach.

It was a very flat stomach, she couldn't help noticing, lodged neatly above a very trim waist that was hooked onto hips that were every bit as narrow and sexy from this angle as they had been when she'd looked up a ladder at them. Susannah swung her eyes back to the dead fish she still clutched in her hand, and wished Travis had a paunch, or was short. Maybe then she'd have found herself less disposed to dwell on how elegantly he wore his clothes. And maybe then she wouldn't have found her gaze loitering immodestly on the way his khaki pants hugged the lean curve of his thigh. And if she hadn't done that, her face wouldn't have turned the shade of an overripe tomato.

"You've got to stop that, you know," Travis remarked conversationally.

She was so horrified, she almost dropped the fish, which slithered around in her hand as though it had been resurrected. Grief, he'd seen her...*examining* him!

"Stop what?" she sputtered, feeling helplessly trapped.

"Making such a fuss about little things," he replied blithely, and Susannah hiccuped with nervous laughter.

"Ben's likely to pick up on it, if you don't," Travis went on, "and the next thing you know, *he'll* be looking for trouble around every corner, too."

"I'm sure I don't know what you're talking about," she huffed, torn between relief that his thoughts were not in the same groove as hers and dismay that he wasn't about to let the subject of Crazy Abe drop.

Travis crossed his ankles and tipped his head to one side. "Well, I don't profess to be an expert on children but I do know Abe, and I can't help thinking you'd do well to keep quiet about today's incident, at least until you can judge it a little less emotionally. Because, whether you like it or not, Abe's a part of this community and you're going to have to accept that."

The pause that followed struck Susannah as decidedly pregnant. She found it difficult to meet Travis's gaze, and when he resumed speaking, his voice had an edge to it that had been missing before. "I wouldn't like to think, Susannah, that you'd hold a person's disabilities against him."

Incensed, she prepared to defend herself, but Travis didn't give her the chance. His eyes looked cold as he surveyed her. "Nor would I like to think," he continued undaunted, "that you'd want to influence a nice, outgoing kid like Ben into viewing anything a bit out of the ordinary with the sort of suspicion you showed today. I think you'd be doing him a grave disservice if you did."

He had his nerve, preaching at her like this. "Talk about judging someone unfairly!" she exclaimed. "Where do you get off lecturing me about my attitudes, or anything else come to that? You don't know the first thing about me."

He grinned disarmingly. "I'm willing to keep an open mind, if you are," he offered.

"Well, now that you've had your say," she snapped, unappeased, "perhaps you'll let me have mine. I have every right to be concerned about my child's safety and well-being."

Travis sighed. Hadn't she heard a word he'd said? "No one's denying that. It's the witch hunt part that bothers me, especially when it's based on ignorance."

She drew in an injured breath. "I agree I *might* have overreacted a little bit," she conceded, "but that doesn't mean I'm neurotic and narrow-minded. The plain fact is that man scared me witless. You should be glad I'm not filing a complaint against him."

Travis straightened to his full height, and she had the satisfaction of knowing she'd finally put a dent in his good humor. But the pleasure was short-lived. If his charm was irritatingly endearing, she found the cool displeasure that replaced it nothing short of intimidating. "No, *you* should be glad," he announced flatly, "because under no circumstances, Susannah, will I allow you to make a fool of yourself by denouncing poor old Abe, unless you can come up with some concrete evidence to support your accusations."

Poor Abe, nothing! The man brought out all Travis's protective instincts. Why couldn't he just accept that she felt the same way about Benny? "I have evidence, sort of..."

"Oh?" He fixed her in a gimlet-eyed stare.

"Yes," she said. "He came creeping up here when I was sleeping, sneaking around—"

He pounced on that. "How do you know he was sneaking around, if you were asleep?"

"Because...because he scared me. I woke up and he was there, with his weird face—"

"Aha! You'd file a complaint because you find him ugly, is that it?"

Damn him anyway, putting words in her mouth and making her look and sound like a nincompoop. "He said..."

What had Abe said, exactly? That he didn't like her, that he was going to find Benny who was nicer. Recalling his words now, they lost most of their menace and left her feeling uncharitable and rather foolish.

"You see?" The chill melted from Travis's voice and eyes, and somewhat shocked, Susannah realized that it mattered terribly to her that he not think poorly of her.

"I was scared. That's not so strange, is it?"

"Of course not, but it is kind of strange to expect that Ben's going to wind up in danger or trouble every time he runs up against something a bit out of the ordinary. Life's full of potential pitfalls and it's too bad, but that's just the way things are, and most kids manage to survive, despite them."

He reached out and cupped her jaw with one hand. "You act as if it's your fault that the world can't be made perfect for him, as if it's your job to anticipate trouble and protect him from it," he said, "but that's not the route to survival, Susannah. Ben's got to live with the flaws like everyone else. You owe it to him to let him learn how."

With horrible accuracy, Travis had put his finger on the real problem. Perhaps because he was too young to remember, or perhaps because children had no real concept of their own mortality, Benny had let go of the past. And she thought she'd done the same—until today when time had suddenly taken a backward leap and left her face to face with that old, consuming terror again.

Now she wondered if a thinking, feeling person ever really forgot that sort of trauma, or ever accepted the helplessness of knowing that not all the love or prayers or vigilance in the world could fully protect anyone. Ultimately each life hung by a thread that dangled from Destiny's finger, to be broken at whim. It was not an encouraging insight.

"You make it sound so easy," she said. "I wish it really were." For reasons she couldn't explain even to herself, she wasn't angry with Travis anymore.

"Not easy, perhaps, but possible. All it takes is a little trust in other people, beginning with your son. Ben's a good kid. He's got good instincts."

She sighed. "He's a child. What does he really know?"

"He knew enough to look out for himself this afternoon, even though you were so certain he was in some kind of trouble that he couldn't cope with."

"Maybe he was just lucky."

"Or smart."

"If something happened to him, I'd never be able to live with myself."

"You're a mother, Susannah, not God. You do the best you can. You love him and that means giving him the freedom to grow."

She looked up at Travis and found herself trapped in his gaze. His eyes were as calm and clear as tidal pools reflecting the deep and endless blue of summer. "How come you're so smart?" she wondered. "Do you have children of your own?"

It was a relief to Travis to be able to laugh. When she looked at him like that, her eyes brimming over with softness and uncertainty, he was surprised to find himself wanting to do for her exactly what he'd counseled her not to do for Ben: to take her to him and protect her from everything that was hurtful or disagreeable or threatening. "No, I don't have children of my own," he told her, and startled himself even further by adding, "And in case you're interested, I've never been married, either."

There was something so candid and fearless in his vivid eyes, so compelling in the curve of his mouth, she wished he'd stop talking and just kiss her. At length. The only trouble was, that sort of thing wasn't on the blueprint she'd mapped out for her life.

Travis might have almost read her mind. "You know, Susannah, life doesn't always have to involve choices or confrontations," he observed. "You're more than just a mother. You're a person—a woman in your own right. You're entitled to a life of your own, too.''

He shifted, letting his hands move down her sides until they rested lightly on her hips, inching her closer to him. "In this instance," he went on, his words rumbling softly over her, "I'm here, albeit a day late, and hungry. Ben is home safe and no doubt also hungry. What say we stop wasting precious time and enjoy the evening?''

And then he kissed her, just as she'd wished he would.

He thought he knew what to expect. He meant just to alert her to his future intent with an acceptable gesture that involved the blending of his lips with hers. He should have known better. Nothing about Susannah, or his reaction to her, was ordinary. Why had he thought this time would be different?

His mouth merged with hers, and at the feel of her lips, soft and receptive to his, the evening was suddenly shot through with rainbows. The miracle of it lured him past caution. A second stretched and became a minute that promised a lifetime.

She might have stayed there indefinitely, letting her mouth linger under his in dreaming wonder, had it not been for Benny's noisy descent from upstairs.

"What happened to my fish?" he demanded, barreling out of the house to the porch and, impervious to the hushed intimacy of the moment, he groveled on the floor under his mother's unsteady feet. "You're standing on it, Ma. Geez!"

Susannah felt terribly tangled in limbs that weren't her own. Not just Benny's though they were certainly creating confusion enough, but Travis's, too. It was hardly fitting for her son to find her wrapped in this stranger's arms, even though it felt absolutely right for her to be there. "I must have dropped it," she muttered lamely and stepped back, hoping Ben hadn't noticed what she and Travis had been doing.

Chapter Six

Benny promptly disabused her of any such notion. He surveyed the pair of them with heartfelt disgust. "You sure did," he agreed, taking time from dusting off his fish to cast her a scathing look. "You were more interested in getting all kissy-faced than in looking after my dinner."

So much for a life of her own! "I knew you'd want me to cook it," she said, "but I didn't realize I had to baby-sit it, too."

"You dropped it," Benny accused. "It's a good thing it's dead already."

Travis hooted with laughter. "Let's go run it under cold water," he offered, shepherding Benny in the direction of the kitchen, "then I'll show you how to fillet it, if you like."

"There won't be anything left of it if you do that," Susannah objected, following behind as Benny, appeased, raced ahead.

"There's something you should understand," Travis replied, draping an arm over her shoulder. "A guy's first catch either has to be eaten, or stuffed and mounted over the fireplace. I reckon you'd rather it was eaten."

Actually she'd rather he didn't touch her—at least not in front of Benny. To her certain knowledge, the only man Benny had seen show her any affection since Mel's death had been her father. And there was a straightforward simplicity in Grandpa Johnson's hugs—not to mention his kisses—that was decidedly absent in the way Travis went about things. "You reckon right," she murmured, sliding from under his arm and putting the width of the kitchen between them.

"Show me where you keep your knives, then," he suggested, pushing back the sleeves of his shirt. He then endeared himself to her all the more by diverting all his attention to Benny without further argument.

Benny, raptly attentive, watched as his fish was skinned and deboned. "Wow!" he breathed, as Travis laid two neat fillets side by side on the chopping board. "How'd you cook them?"

Susannah knew, by the admiration in her son's tone, that he'd found himself a real live hero.

"Over a camp fire's the best way," Travis said, "but failing that, any kitchen stove will do the job."

"Yeah," Benny agreed. "Get the frying pan ready, Ma."

"Why don't we do that?" Travis suggested before Susannah could comply. "The first thing you have to learn, kiddo, is that if you're big enough to catch them, you're big enough to clean up after them and cook them, too."

"Can I cut them up, next time?"

Susannah opened her mouth to object. A seven-year-old was too young to handle a sharp knife.

Travis forestalled her. "You can start to learn how. Meanwhile, get cracking on the cleanup, and I'll start the cooking."

"Mom does the cooking."

"Your mom's got other things to do."

"I don't know about that." Susannah poked at the charred rhubarb pie, feeling like a fifth wheel. "I don't think this can be salvaged."

Benny spared her a glance. "You going to eat that stuff that's been soaking all night?"

The way he said it, he might have been talking about old socks. "I thought Travis and I might," she said, "but you're welcome to pass and make do with your fish."

"You can have some of my fish," Benny offered Travis in a low voice. "I've seen that other stuff." He rolled his eyes. "Gross!"

"I've got a big appetite," Travis replied, flinging an ambiguous glance Susannah's way. "I'll stick with whatever it is your mother has in mind."

"Marinated flank steak," Susannah said, and busied herself rummaging around in the refrigerator. It gave her an opportunity to collect her wits. She was beginning to see what made Travis different.

She knew he was interested in her as a woman—she'd have to be blind and stupid to believe otherwise—but it was his interest in Benny that made him so special. Travis really listened to him. He talked *with* him, not *at* him or *about* him. It was hard to resist a man like that.

Unused to sharing her child's attention with another, Susannah found herself sitting back and observing as the evening wore on. She discovered that, for all that the two of them were so close, there were things about Benny that even she had not fully realized before.

He was a boy in a predominantly female world. With the exception of his grandfather, he'd come into contact with virtually no men on a regular basis. His friends, as often as not, were the children of other single mothers or working couples. His teachers had all been women, and they had, without exception, done their best to make up for his not having a father. And in doing so, they had babied him.

Travis was treating him not as a child barely out of infancy, but as one on the brink of all the wonders of discovery to which a boy is heir. And Benny was responding to the challenge. Unconsciously he was imitating Travis: hunched forward in concentration, chin propped on one fist.

Too bad, Susannah thought with a smile, that his legs weren't long enough to rest under the table, ankles crossed, instead of having to dangle midway between chair and floor. It would have completed the image of man and boy cut from the same cloth.

It wasn't that anyone would readily mistake them for father and son—Benny was as dark as Mel had been, and Travis was blond—but a common bond united them that excluded her. It was something distinctly male, and Benny had been missing it, whether he or she realized it. It was difficult for her to accept that she had not succeeded in being all things to her son, but impossible for her to resent that someone else could make up for her lack. Benny was blossoming before her eyes.

"There are some who swear by lures, especially Tom Macks," Travis was saying, "but I always have the best luck with herring."

"Live?" Benny was all eyes.

"Of course live. Salmon are too smart to be taken in by something that's been dead so long it has to be kept in a freezer."

Susannah shuddered delicately. She preferred her fish on a plate, with a wedge of lemon and a sprig of parsley. The details of its demise she could well live without.

He had such a nice manner, she thought, watching the play of expressions flit across Travis's face. He wasn't bored, and he wasn't condescending; he was having as good a time as Benny. And that was what made him special. There were plenty of sexy men around, but nice, unattached sexy men were scarce.

"Time for bed," she told Benny, and refused to be swayed by his pleas to stay up another five minutes. She had to get Travis out of the house before he weakened her resistance any further.

THE EVENING wasn't turning out quite the way Travis had anticipated. No candles or wine, no soft music. And definitely no cosy intimacy between him and the lady, with the child out of sight and asleep. But he was having a good time anyway. He liked the kid, found him bright and up front.

If he were in the market for a son, Travis thought idly, Ben was the sort of kid he'd shop around for.

Son? Where had *that* thought sprung from? Not from Susannah, he decided, watching her as she came back down the stairs.

"Thank you for spending so much time with Benny. He had a wonderful evening," she said, "but we've kept you long enough, and I'm sure you'd like to get going now."

Not a chance, Travis thought, recognizing the tight voice she used to cover up uncertainty or nervousness. She wasn't getting rid of him that easily.

Apart from anything else, she intrigued him. He wanted to know what had happened to her husband, and he especially wanted to know what had triggered her reaction to Abe that afternoon. It had been more than simple shock at discovering him beside her when she awoke. "I wouldn't dream of it," he replied, "until I've helped you with the dishes first."

His mother would have dropped her teeth if she'd heard him. He'd bought her an automatic dishwasher with the money he'd earned pumping gas when he was in high school. It meant he wasn't able to afford his first car until his senior year, but it had been worth the sacrifice. When you were one of six kids, anything was better than kitchen duty.

"Oh," Susannah said, and he delighted in the way the lamplight played over her features, creating shadows that sent her cheekbones into relief and made secret pools of her eyes, "that's really not necessary. I can manage."

"Let's make a deal," he suggested. "I'll wash the dishes, if you'll make coffee."

She was still nervous and it was probably too soon, but he couldn't seem to help himself. He reached out and took her hand. It was as delicately fashioned as the rest of her: small-boned, soft-skinned. "Let's get the chores out of the way, then talk. I want to get to know more about you. Tell me why you were so afraid this afternoon."

"That man's strange," she said, evading the real question. "Anyone would be afraid, meeting him for the first time."

"That's not what I mean, Susannah, and you know it. Whatever happened to make you so nervous about Ben? He's a normal, healthy kid, not an invalid."

She pulled her hand away, defensive and withdrawn. "It's not Benny who makes me nervous, Travis. It's your Crazy Abe."

"Abe's harmless. He wouldn't hurt anyone."

"So you keep saying. Why do you feel you have to defend him? You're as protective of him as you claim I am of Benny."

She was piling up dishes as she spoke, half-turned away from him as she stacked them in the sink. When she saw that he was determined to help her, she managed to tie an apron around his waist and to place a dish towel in his hand without once actually touching him. She was visibly withdrawing from him, her message loud and clear: don't interfere.

"Because I hate for anyone to judge him without giving him a fair chance to prove himself."

She squirted Ivory Liquid into a stream of hot water. "What do you want me to say? That I'll wait until he hurts Benny before I make a fuss? That's like not putting a crosswalk on a busy street until someone's been hit by a car."

"Why do you assume anyone would want to hurt Ben?"

"Start drying," she ordered, rinsing plates and lining them up in the dish rack. Her face was closed, remote.

"Abe can't help the way he looks or acts," Travis felt compelled to explain. "He was in a car that hit a truck head-on. He was seriously injured, Susannah. He went through the windshield."

She flinched. "He's lucky to be alive."

"I think so, though not everyone would agree with me. We live in a society that worships youth, fitness, beauty. Too often, people like Abe are treated like an affront—something to be kept out of sight. Never mind that he can teach us something worthwhile about the quality of life."

Another grimace flitted across her face. If he hadn't learned long ago to trust his instincts, he might have concluded there wasn't a shred of charity or compassion in her. But instinct told him that what she felt was distress, not distaste. For a start, no woman could love a child as devotedly as she did and remain indifferent to a person like Abe.

"Still and all," she said, "I don't think many mothers of young children would feel particularly easy about someone like Abe running loose."

Travis opened his mouth to object, but she waved a handful of cutlery at him before depositing it in the dish rack. "I know what you're going to say—that he's got the mind of a child in a man's body. But to Benny, anyone who's big enough to look like a man is an adult, with an adult's sense of responsibility. He's far too young to understand that in terms of judgment and intellect, Abe's little more than a seven-year-old himself."

She hesitated, weighing her next words, then she decided to say everything she was thinking. "And besides, how does anyone know what really goes through a mind like that?"

"Don't be cruel, Susannah."

"I don't want to be," she cried, stung. "I want to be fair, but not at my child's expense. You can argue all you like, but that man makes me nervous."

The dishes were done. Travis untied his apron. "But don't you see? That's all it takes to make Ben nervous, too. You're smart enough to know that's not the way to teach him self-confidence."

The water gurgled down the drain, and he waited until she'd dried her hands before continuing. "At least say you won't make an issue of this with him. He's coping with a lot of new stuff, what with a new school and all. Don't put a damper on things."

So much unsought advice, and all for free! She resented it, though even a fool could see that Travis was as concerned about Benny as he was about Crazy Abe. "How do you take your coffee?" she asked coolly as she measured boiling water into the grounds in the filter and let it drip through to the carafe beneath.

"In a mug as a rule," he said, attempting a lighter touch. Did she know her face reflected her every emotion? Uncertainty, anxiety and annoyance chased across her features, creasing her brow and pinching her mouth with solemnity. "How old are you, Susannah?"

"Thirty-two," she replied without hesitation. "Old enough to form my own opinions and judgments."

He would not be deterred. "How long have you been widowed?"

Regret shafted through her. She'd thought he was different from the rest. Surely she hadn't been mistaken? "I don't need favors, if that's what you're really asking," she said cuttingly.

He turned his vivid blue eyes on her in mild reproach. She felt ashamed and fought the urge to go hide in the closet until he left. "Um...five years..." With an unsteady hand, she poured the coffee.

He took both mugs and carried them to the living room, placed them on the low table before the hearth and leaned against the tall stone fireplace that separated the kitchen from the rest of the main floor.

Moonlight flung his shadow across the pine floor, touching his hair with pewter and shadowing the expression in his eyes. Outside, Cameron's Landing resembled a collection of toy buildings nestled in the palm of a huge hand reaching down to trap the quiet inlet between its fingertips. Night had stolen down the mountain to close about the town, serene and undisturbed.

Until Travis spoke. "How did your husband die?" he asked without preamble.

The question left her open-mouthed with shock. Curiosity usually came cloaked in more subtlety. "He was shot in the face at close range with a .44 Magnum," she said baldly, and had the satisfaction of seeing his shock match her own.

Chapter Seven

Travis swore softly, and when he reached to pick up his coffee, his hand was as unsteady as hers had been a minute or two earlier. There couldn't have been much left of him. Certainly nothing recognizable.

Venturing a glance at her, he saw she was stretched taut as a bow, and knew he would have to finish what he'd started, even though just now he would have preferred to make as quiet and discreet an exit as his size would permit. "Why?" he asked, and the compassion in his voice threaded its way through her pain in a ribbon of warmth.

"Because he believed he could right all wrongs," she said, and felt a strange kind of relief take hold of her. The door to the memories was already ajar. She might as well confront them all now and have done with them, then maybe she could lock them away for ever. There'd be no going forward until she did. "He was a private investigator, hired by a family from down east to find their daughter who'd run away and was last seen in Seattle. She was twelve years old and living on the street. And Mel found her."

"Alive?"

"Oh yes, very much so. It was the other things he found that caused the trouble—child prostitution on a grand scale, run by people in high places who knew better and didn't care. Big, important names who'd go to any lengths to prevent being exposed."

"So they killed him." Disgust made his voice thick. It was a horrible, too-familiar tale of adult vice and child victims. "A decent man trying to make the world a decent place for a kid. No wonder you feel about Ben as you do."

She turned huge gray eyes on him, so full of pity that he quailed. "Do you really think it was that simple?"

He held up one hand, helplessly. "There's more?"

Her laugh was a hollow parody of mirth. "Travis," she said, speaking as one might to an untutored child, "heaven knows it was enough, but I'm afraid it wasn't nearly that clear-cut. When he realized what he'd unearthed, Mel began a one-man crusade to expose the names behind the operation. They sent their goons to convince him to leave well enough alone, but he was a man possessed, a father himself. The girl was one victim out of many—there were hundreds of others like her out there."

Travis took a mouthful of coffee. It tasted bitter. "So he had to be erased."

"He had to be taught a lesson. He had to learn who was really in charge." She stopped talking for a full minute, and turned to look up the darkened stairwell before going on, and when she did, her face was haunted in the moonlight. "They came in the night and took Benny," she said.

The coffee turned sour in Travis's stomach. "For the love of God!"

"We got a call. A voice that could have belonged to an uncle, or a grandparent. Educated, well modulated. 'Have you looked in the baby's crib recently?' was all he said."

Travis wasn't aware he'd moved, but he was close beside her suddenly, where she huddled in a corner of the couch, her hands clutched in her lap, and his arms went around her.

"I think my heart stopped. I don't remember how I got to the nursery door. I don't think I drew a single breath. I don't think my feet touched the floor. One minute the phone woke us, and I was listening to a stranger's voice, and the next, I was standing in the nursery doorway and Benny's crib was empty."

She covered her mouth with one hand and squeezed her eyes shut for a moment, trying to compose herself. "Do you know what I did then?" she asked.

"What?" Travis could hardly speak around the tightness in his throat. He was not a parent, but he was a decent man; the rage and sense of violation he experienced were no less real than if it had been his child taken.

"I saw the curtains flapping in the night breeze, and I went over and closed the window, so that the room wouldn't get too chilled. And then I went and felt the mattress, but I was too late. It was already cold. I think that was when I knew...here—" She placed her hand over her heart and spoke with difficulty. Her pain was a living presence that burned Travis's eyes with unshed tears. "—that Benny was really gone."

"Wouldn't you think," she ventured sadly, "that a good mother would have heard something? Would have known that someone was stealing her baby from the next room?"

"No." Travis spoke with absolute conviction. "I don't think a normal person can ever really understand the depths of evil to which a few can sink." He cradled her as tenderly as any parent. "What happened next?"

"We received another call, warning us not to go to the police, but I insisted. And when they came, they tapped our phone, certain we'd hear from the kidnappers again. And we did, from a woman this time. She sounded like someone's favorite aunt. Warm, loving. She was calling, she said, because she knew how anxious we must be to know that Benny was still alive, and then she brought him to the phone and slapped him or something. We could hear him start crying."

Her lashes drifted down over her eyes like mourning veils. This was more chilling than an Ira Levin script, Travis thought, feeling the sweat run between his shoulder blades. They were in the midst of horror, and he wished like hell he'd never asked her to relive any of it, but he knew there'd be no peace for either of them until she reached the end.

"The police traced the call and staked out the place where Benny was being held. They warned us not to interfere, promised that they had everything under control and that we'd have our baby back within twenty-four hours, but Mel didn't have the patience or the confidence in them to wait it out. He knew what it was doing to me, having Benny missing, and he blamed himself. He wanted to be the one to give me back our son. I suppose he saw that as a way to atone.

"I knew what he was going to do when I saw him take his revolver out of the locked drawer in his desk. I begged him to do things their way, because I was afraid for Benny. It never occurred to me that I should be afraid for Mel, too."

She wavered for a long minute, reliving the guilt of that omission. "Benny was already safe, but two of the kidnappers had managed to get away. Mel intercepted them in a back lane . . . and they blew his head off."

Because he was too horrified to speak, Travis pressed her face to his chest and held her against his heart. He didn't know what else to do. He liked this woman, very much. He admired her courage and resilience. And underlying all that, he still desired her. Yet at that moment, if it had been in his power to do so, he would have given her back her husband.

For perhaps a minute she rested against him, exhausted, then she pushed away from him and rose to her feet. "Please excuse me," she said. "I need to go upstairs for a moment."

She disappeared, and without invitation, he followed her. He knew where she was going, and why. From the landing he saw the glow of a night-light illuminating the child's room, and went toward it. Inside, Ben lay sleeping in a mate's bed, with the blankets hanging half on the floor. Bending low, she covered him, smoothed his hair, touched his cheek, then stood looking down at him, renewing herself with the sight of him peacefully asleep. To Travis, still raw from the experience of the last half hour, the silence seemed almost holy.

When she at last turned away, he saw that her face was calm and her ordeal had passed. He went to her, then, and took her in his arms again. Her chin only came to midway up his chest and for that he was grateful. He was able to bury his face in her hair so that she wouldn't see how moved he was. She had more courage than he thought he could ever hope to possess.

Intuitively she knew. "Don't be upset," she consoled him softly, winding her arms around his waist. "It's all in the past. Benny's safe. Let's go down now."

She made more coffee, and Travis promised himself he'd bring in a supply of brandy before he invited any more revelations. He felt depleted. "I guess I know why you decided to leave the city for a safer environment," he said, desperate to move onto less harrowing ground, "but what made you choose this place?"

"Economics and opportunity," she replied. "Did you know I'm the new traveling librarian? And that I live here practically rent free?"

It was on the tip of his tongue to ask her why Mel hadn't provided for her. In a business like his, surely the man had insurance? Instead, he pursued another avenue. "What about the rest of your family? Parents, brothers, sisters?" There must be someone else who cared about what happened to her.

"I'm an only child, but my parents are still alive. They live in Seattle, and they miss us terribly, but they understand that I had to make this move—sort of."

She threw him such a singularly sweet smile that he felt his heart lurch in his chest. "Actually my mother thinks I need my head examined. She'd like us to live with her and my dad indefinitely. We did for a while, but it's too easy to rely on other people when they love you so much. I have to learn to stand on my own two feet."

"Were you very young when you got married?"

"Young and inexperienced! My folks were horrified when they learned I wanted to marry a private investigator. They thought I should find an accountant or a banker. But I wouldn't listen to them. Mel was my first love, and I never dated any other man. Later, when they saw how well he took care of me, they relented."

She laughed. "My mother rates a husband by how many spare sets of sheets and towels his wife has in her linen closet, and my father looks at the sort of car a man owns. Mel drove a Porsche, and after our wedding, we had enough linens to open a shop. We lived in a penthouse apartment, with a three-hundred-and-sixty-degree view, and there was a mink coat under the tree for me our first Christmas together. That was enough for my parents. How could a man who did things like that for his wife be bad?"

Travis didn't have the brains or restraint to keep his mouth shut a moment longer. "How could a man who cared so much neglect to make sure his wife would be looked after, if anything happened to him?"

She turned a weary smile on him. "You sound just like my dad did, five years ago. Don't batter my memories with questions like that. I don't have any answers."

"I'm sorry. I just don't understand..."

"Do you expect to die tomorrow?"

Of course he didn't, but he was a pilot and never took life for granted. He didn't know a flyer who did. Too many other people depended on a pilot's judgment. But he didn't say so to her, not now. The same argument applied only too well to private investigators. To be fair, young men were often unable to comprehend that death touched people of all ages. He remembered well enough the first time he'd sat at the controls of a fighter jet and screamed across the sky. He'd been twenty-two, and so high on the experience he'd have thumbed his nose at any suggestion that his life hung by a thread. It hadn't mattered, he'd been so close to the heavens.

"You know something?" Susannah tucked her feet under her and looked through the moon-cast shadows to the years behind her. "I didn't really grow up until Mel died. Then, for the first time, there was no one to make it all better. It was just me and reality, face to face. I hadn't the first idea how to deal with either of us."

Yet she'd managed, Travis thought. There was steel under that porcelain exterior, dimensions that he'd never suspected. And now she'd moved away from the familiar crutch of parental support. He knew now why she'd chosen Cameron's Landing, why its isolation had appealed to her. He knew, too, why meeting Abe had unhinged her so completely.

"But you're learning," he said, getting up from the couch reluctantly. He didn't want to leave, but it was time. She looked worn out. "I want very much to see you again, Susannah."

He wasn't talking about accidentally running into her in town either, and he knew she knew that. He was talking about closeness, about spending time together and getting to know her. About intimacy. And for the first time, he didn't qualify that thought by adding *just for the summer*.

She walked with him to the door. Outside, the night was cool and the moon had slipped behind the trees, but the stars looked like daisies sewn on black velvet, close enough to pick. Below, beyond the harbor, the sea had a luminescence that spread to the horizon. The air was absolutely still.

He ought to have thanked her, and then had the decency to say good night and wait for another time. She had bared her soul to him, and he knew she had other loves who would never be displaced. He didn't care.

Her face was hidden in his shadow, but he found her mouth with his fingers and traced it with his thumb. At his touch, she started to tremble, whether from cold or fear or need, he did not know. He knew only that she uncovered something deep and private inside him that he had not shared before, and that it pushed him to test the limits of her forbearance.

It was too soon, too urgent, after all she'd told him, but he lowered his mouth and drew it over hers anyway and kissed her again. Not deeply, not intimately, but with feeling and sincerity and promise. He asked for nothing but that she accept it.

Her lips were warm and soft and unresisting. It was not a sister's kiss, and it was not a lover's, either. But for now, it was enough.

He was gone into the night before she had time to savor the moment. She stared into the darkness and raised an unsteady hand to her mouth. His touch was no longer on her lips, but the memory of it filled her with wonder.

All of a sudden, when she'd stopped looking and stopped being disappointed, a man had come along who made her unwilling to settle for half a dream. For the first time since Mel, she'd found a man she wanted to trust. And on the heels of that wanting came the uncertainty.

An outwardly straightforward man, Travis was a composite of subtle characteristics that provoked more complex responses in her than she'd ever experienced. He made her angry sometimes, and he made her laugh, but it was the hint of deeper passions stirring that alarmed her. She could fall in love with this man, and there were a number of very good reasons she should not allow that to happen.

The timing was off, for a start. She was looking to other goals. Their life-styles didn't mesh, either. He was professionally transient, and she wanted permanence, stability. And right at the top of the list was his work. He was a pilot, a fire fighter who put his life on the line every day.

She went to bed exhausted and slept like a child. Deeply, dreamlessly.

SQUINTING AGAINST THE LIGHT outside the next morning, she was captured by the memory of Travis's eyes, as unclouded and blue as the sky beyond her window. The sun, warm on her face, brought back the feel of his hands against her skin, the touch of his mouth on hers. She had never been kissed like that before, with such promise or such tenderness.

It didn't take insight or reason to recognize the effervescence that frothed inside her. It was easy enough to diagnose. Hope wasn't complex like love; it was simple and welcome. It made her feel, not like Superwoman, exactly—she supposed no one ever learned to clear all obstacles in a single leap—but hungry to discover what awaited her, with some degree of courage.

It was early May and even in the short time she'd lived in Cameron's Landing, Susannah could feel the change in the weather. There was a softness to the air, a gentleness that hinted of kinder days to come. It was as though the last stray remnants of winter had been blasted away in Thursday's storm.

After hurrying through her shower, she wrapped a towel turban-style around her wet hair and did something she hadn't done in a long time.

Not bad, she decided, squinting the length of her body. Not great, perhaps, but not bad, either. No saddle bags around the hips, no noticeable thickening around the middle, and only a couple of little stretch marks below her navel. No droopy breasts, either, but then, you had to grow them before they could sag and she had long ago reconciled herself to the fact that God decided these things, not man, or woman. Still and all, a cleavage would have been nice, even though higher minds might argue that inner growth was what mattered.

She made waffles from scratch for breakfast, humming along as she whisked eggs.

"You feeling okay, Mom?" Benny wanted to know, helping himself to orange juice.

She stopped just long enough between verses one and two of "Morning Has Broken" to smile fondly at his sweet little sleep-rumpled face. "Just fine, my lamb. Why?"

"You're making funny noises." He shrugged, slopping juice all over the place.

Susannah was the first to admit she could barely carry a tune, but that didn't mean she permitted her child to have a smart mouth. As a rule. This morning she found it impossible to take offense and giggled instead into the waffle batter. "I'm just singing, Benny."

"You hardly never sing," he pointed out, and made a big production of peering at the clock on the stove. "You hardly never even talk till the little hand's on the ten."

True enough until recently. "Don't you like having a cheerful mom, first thing in the morning?"

"Sure." He slid onto a chair and took immediate advantage of her good humor. "Can I go fishing again? You said it was okay, if it didn't rain."

Her glow faded a bit at that. Crazy Abe still hadn't been dealt with. She wanted to be fair, but she had to be careful, too. "We have to have our little talk from yesterday first, remember?"

Benny's mouth drooped. "Grown-ups aren't supposed to break promises, Mom, and you promised I could go."

"Who said anything about breaking promises? It's just that I want a promise from you, too."

"What?"

"That you won't speak to any...strangers." It was on the tip of her tongue to say "strange men," but Benny wasn't the only one to whom she'd given her word. She'd made a promise to Travis, too. She'd not condemn Abe out of hand.

Benny looked relieved. "Oh, that old stuff. You already made me promise that...every day when we lived near Grandma and Grandpa and I went to school." He knew by rote what was expected of him. Punctuating his recitation of the rules by stabbing his fork into his waffles, he gave a singsong parody of Susannah at her most maternal. "Don't take rides or candy from strangers. Don't forget your lunch. Do up your jacket. Look both ways before you cross the road. Only go when it's green."

He had a remarkable memory when it suited him. "Yes, well," she intervened, trying to get back to the point she wanted to make, "there aren't any traffic signals in Cameron's Landing."

"There aren't enough cars," he informed her, making inroads into his waffles. "Everybody I know walks—except for the kids who get the bus."

She tensed. "Who's 'everybody'?"

"Miss Basehart and Miss Evans."

They were both on the safe list. "I was thinking more about people you might meet in town...."

"This town's so little, Mom," he complained, shoveling more waffles into his mouth, "that I know all of them, too."

Her voice wavered just the slightest bit. "Oh? Like who?"

"The Turners and Joe and Travis. Everybody, even Larene." He made a face. "She's always pinching my cheeks and yelling to everybody that I'm a darling little leper corn, like I'm some sort of gross vegetable."

"Leprechaun, Benny."

"Whatever. I wish you'd talk to *her*, Mom."

"She means well."

"She's a wazoo. Can I—"

"You don't talk that way about grown-ups, Benny. Nor about anyone else, for that matter."

"Sorry." He wriggled on his chair, unrepentant. "Can I go now? Travis promised he'd show me how to stick a live herring on a hook."

She could hardly keep on stalling. "I guess so. How'd it be if I came down to the dock myself, later on? In case you catch a fish that you want me to cook?"

Halfway to the door already, he skidded to a stop and swung back to face her, the picture of outrage. "I'd hate it."

Her morning joy eroded a little. "Oh," she said hollowly, unable to offer much else by way of response at such short notice.

He scuffed his feet and watched her from under his brows. "Geez, Mom, you don't understand. It's just us guys down there. Moms don't belong."

He didn't mean to be ruthless, and she was crazy to feel hurt. This was independence with a capital I—just what she'd hoped he'd discover—and now it was time for him to explore it. Still and all, she had to swallow twice before she could answer him. "Well, but Benny..."

He lifted his head and she was reminded of Mel in the soft brown apology of his eyes. "Mom? You know what I mean?"

"No," she couldn't help replying. "I can't say I do. You say you don't really have any friends at school, but you're never likely to find any if you don't make an effort to get to know the other kids in your class."

"They already know each other," he argued, his expression stubborn. "They don't want me hanging around. The dock's the only place where no one bugs me. The guys down there don't care if I'm new—they aren't always trying to pick a fight about the way I talk or something dumb like that. They like me, Mom. You know what I mean?"

She knew exactly what he meant: he'd found a niche already, even if it wasn't ideal, whereas she was still not sure where she really fit in. It wasn't fair of her to expect him to keep her company until she found out. "Don't you miss having friends your own age?" she asked, wondering if he felt as displaced as she did.

He shrugged, far more accepting of his lot than she was of hers. "I got friends," he said. "That's what matters. I don't care how old they are. Can I go now?"

His wisdom boggled her mind. "Yes," she said, unable to come up with one good reason to detain him.

He raced off and that was the beginning of the new Benny. His quilt went into retirement again, and her misgivings were obliged to take a back seat as she watched him bloom. She saw barely anything of him the entire weekend and precious little of anyone else, for that matter.

BENNY WAS THRIVING, no doubt about it, but her own glow was wearing thin around the edges as the weekend passed with no word from Travis. She tried to be adult about it. He'd made her aware of a void in her life, but he hadn't exactly promised to fill it. Maybe she'd read more into his behavior than he'd intended. One thing, however, soon became clear: if she wasn't seeing much of Travis, Benny more than made up for it. From all accounts, the two of them were practically joined at the hip, and she grew thoroughly tired of listening to her son singing Travis's praises. She'd hoped for a more first-hand sort of contact with the man.

Monday arrived and still Travis didn't call.

"Travis says he'll take me out on his boat some day," Benny announced, breezing in the door just in time for dinner that night. "He knows all the good places to fish."

Susannah was tempted to say it was something Travis should have discussed with her first, but thought better of it. "Eat, Benny," she said instead.

"He's got a knife and he'll let me buy it from him for a dime."

But a knife wasn't a toy, Susannah thought. It was a tool that could turn into a weapon and inflict terrible wounds on its bearer—just like hope and dependency could, as she very well knew. So why was she running the same risks all over again with a man guaranteed to hurt her, one way or another?

"Don't gobble your food," she snapped at Benny. He could barely spare the time to show up for meals as it was. She was beginning to feel like a short-order cook who did laundry and windows on the side.

He beamed at her, the picture of apple-cheeked, happy boyhood. "Don't you want to know why I have to pay a dime?"

"Not particularly. It's your money," she muttered. He'd spent most of his allowance on fishing gear as it was. What was another dime?

"I'll tell you anyways." He paused long enough to fork in a mouthful of food. "It's because, if you give a knife, you cut a friendship, but if you sell it, you don't, so he selled me the knife and that's okay, see?"

She saw only one thing: she was regressing, fast. She was no longer sure she could handle romance. She was no longer sure about anything, in fact. Even her confidence in Benny was evaporating. Her next words proved it. "You're too young to handle a knife."

"No, I'm not. Travis said so. He knows everything."

No, he doesn't, Susannah decided bleakly. He doesn't know the first thing about women. Not this woman, at least. "How many times do I have to tell you not to talk with your mouth full?" she demanded irritably, and had the miserable pleasure of watching the animation seep from Benny's face.

He looked at her solemnly. "I guess you got over the singing, huh, Ma?"

Her own hamburger threatened to choke her. "I guess I did," she said glumly. It wasn't that she resented Benny finding his share of happiness. It was just that the evidence of it made her own emptiness more glaringly apparent, and she'd thought Travis might be the one to put an end to that. But what made her really angry was that she'd fallen into the trap of looking to someone else to fill her needs, when she knew better than anyone how susceptible that left a person. Not for the life of her could she fathom how she'd come to be so hung up on a man so fast.

"Travis showed me how...to...whistle...." Benny lapsed into silence, his face falling again as he caught sight of hers. "You want me to stuff it, Mom?"

She had the grace to feel remorseful. "I'm sorry. I don't mean to be so snarly."

"That's okay. It must be kind of boring, just being a mom all the time."

Not boring, Benny, she wanted to tell him. Just not enough.

Chapter Eight

On Tuesday her secret wish was granted. She accidentally ran into Travis at the store. Not literally, of course. He was using the radio telephone and didn't see her as she came in the door. But she saw him, and her response was alarming.

She didn't understand herself at all. She'd just spent three and a half days wishing she could see him. Now that she'd got what she thought she'd wanted, she was seized with an attack of nerves. Even though the reason she'd stopped by the store was to check on her mail, she swung away from the counter, made a swift right turn and bolted away between the aisles, determined to hide out until he'd gone.

The nice thing about the radio telephone was that everyone in the place could hear what was being said on both ends, so Susannah knew Travis was talking to a man, not a woman. That made her feel marginally better. The bad thing was that once the call was over, there was no telling where he'd gone from there, because the aisles in the Turner's store were too high for Susannah to see over.

The nice thing about the Turners' store, however, was that Henry Turner wasn't much taller than she was, so there were little stepladders all over the place. Susannah climbed up on the nearest one and established a little spy hole among the packages of cereal on the top shelf.

That was where Travis found her. "Whatever are you doing, Susannah?" he drawled at her back, his voice stroking up her spine. "Stalking moose?"

She tried to appear nonchalant, which was not easy with both arms wrapped around a sack of puffed wheat. "Oh, hi!" she said, hanging on to her balance by the skin of her teeth. "Imagine seeing you!"

He looked wonderful. In the subdued light of the store, his hair was the color of dandelion honey, a deep rich blond shot through with amber, and his eyes so dark they looked almost inky.

"How've you been?" he asked.

"Fine," she squeaked. She wanted to be charming and casual, to smile and make small talk, but her tongue seemed glued to the roof of her mouth, and her face felt as stiff as the back end of a bus.

"Larene's making her famous fish stew on Saturday. Just about everyone'll be there for supper."

"Really?" she croaked.

She appeared confused, Travis thought, as if she'd suddenly found her emotions were controlling her, instead of the other way around. He could sympathize with that. He felt the same way: outmaneuvered at his own game.

He'd always thought that if the right woman came along, well, that would be fine. He had nothing against marriage as such. But at the same time, he'd very carefully set himself up in a life-style that not only suited him just the way it was, but also precluded any serious threat of commitment. Lately he found himself not only reevaluating his priorities but actually thinking about ways to adapt his career along lines more convenient for a man with a wife and child.

Aware that the silence between them was growing strained, he tilted his head and looked at her. "Hey, talk to me, will you?" he said, when what he really meant was "Don't look so terrified."

"I'm busy shopping," she said, and squeezed the puffed wheat tighter. There was a little popping sound and a little sigh from the bag, as though it had grown tired of her manic embrace.

"Tell me," Travis murmured slyly, "are you planning to eat that stuff, or just decorate with it?"

Susannah ventured a glance down, and her face flamed scarlet as she saw that the bag had burst at the bottom and stray puffs of wheat had trickled out to cling like snowflakes to her corduroy-covered thighs and scatter on the floor. Travis was obviously intending to collect the escapees one at a time. "Um . . ." she gasped, swatting feebly at his hand, "don't . . . um . . . please don't do that."

It was more than she could endure. As she gripped the bag more tightly and prepared to step down off the ladder, the bag of cereal gave way entirely and sent puffed wheat kernels cascading about in forty different directions.

"Now see what you've gone and done!" Travis was so convulsed with laughter, he could barely get the words out. He tossed the puffed wheat he'd collected on top of the pile settling around his feet, and reached for her hands. "Look, get down from there and listen to me, will you?" he choked. "Or do you spend half your life climbing around on top of things?"

She clambered down, trying to keep a safe distance between them. She wasn't in any shape to cope with him being charming. "Well?" she demanded, puffed wheat crackling under her feet. "What is it you have to say that's so important?"

He raised his brows reproachfully, which left her feeling about as gracious as a cockroach. "How about 'Thank you for dinner on Friday'?"

"Well, it took you long enough," she retorted balefully. "Um, what I really mean is—"

"I planned to stop by your place before now, but I've been busy. On-site training, you know." He stopped and shrugged, his smile curving between his dimples. "Oh, hell," he confessed, linking his fingers with hers, "I've not been that busy. The fact of the matter is, I was a bit unsure of my welcome. I mean, I opened up some pretty deep wounds, after all." *And exposed a few cracks in my own armor, too.*

"Oh," she mumbled, striving to keep her intellect alive and well. Mesmerized by the way his mouth moved when he spoke, remembering the way it had settled so persuasively on hers, she felt her heart skip a beat. He looked down, his eyes smiling secrets at her. They told her things that should have been whispered in private and had her torn between confusion and impatience. "Well...what can I say?"

"That you'll go with me to Larene's fish supper on Saturday night." Damn it, he'd almost blown the whole thing with his stupid reticence! For a man who'd always prided himself on being reasonably brave in the face of danger, he was turning out to be a real chicken when confronted with a simple relationship. Except that this relationship wasn't that simple.

He ventured another smile. "Give me a chance to make up for being such a coward the last few days?"

"Well..."

Her answering smile gave him added courage. He held her so that her palms were together, and his were covering the backs of her hands. "I want you to come with me and promise not to sit next to anyone else but me. I want all sorts of things, but I'll settle for those two, for now."

She decided it would be smart to say no, after all he'd put her through, but his smile undid her. "Oh, yes," she breathed. "Please...thank you."

Very cool, Susannah, she thought, hearing herself gush like a groupie confronted by Don Johnson. Very sophisticated and independent indeed! What are you planning to do for an encore?

"My pleasure," he assured her. "What about Ben? Would he like to come, too? It might be difficult finding a sitter. No one likes to miss Larene's fish stew, and I think he'd have a good time. Anyhow, we can always leave early, if he gets bored."

His mouth was forming sentences, communicating clearly enough, but another kind of dialogue was taking place at another level. I've missed you, his eyes told her, and as though to confirm the message, he leaned down suddenly and stole a kiss, and took another little piece of her heart with it.

"It's very nice of you to ask." Her heart was singing an aria—in tune, no less! "I'm sure Larene's fish stew is excellent, she makes the best peanut butter cookies. I should try to get the recipe, Benny loves peanut butter," she babbled on joyfully, and didn't care a bit if she was making a fool of herself. "All of which means we'd love to come with you," she told him, laughter welling up to match his.

SHE DELIBERATED a long time over what to wear for Saturday night, which was something of an achievement, considering she had only three possible outfits from which to choose, once she'd discarded the idea of jeans and a fresh shirt. It wasn't just that this was her first real date with Travis. It felt more like her first real date since before she'd been married, and she was badly out of practice. She wanted to feel pretty and feminine without appearing overdressed. She finally settled on a full skirt and matching shawl in a green and blue Paisley pattern, with a white silk blouse that had been a going-away gift from her parents.

She slipped on jade hoop earrings, splurged with her precious supply of Diva perfume and secured her hair in a coil on top of her head with a long jade chopstick. She slipped on her only pair of sandals, decided they looked out of place, substituted a pair of leather boots with a bit of a heel, decided she looked like a cowboy in drag, and went downstairs to ask Benny's opinion.

"Heck, Ma," he said, running a critical eye over her, "what's wrong with jeans and sneakers, like me?"

"I should have known better than to expect you to be of any help," she complained, weighing the sandals in her hand and frowning at her feet.

Benny rolled his eyes and zipped up the electric-blue bomber jacket that was his idea of sartorial splendor. "Shake a leg, Ma," he suggested with unconscious irony, and went to lean over the railing of the deck to watch for Travis. "Us guys don't want to miss the food."

The way he spoke, it was obvious he considered that a decently perceptive mother would have recognized she was merely an extra and declined the invitation in the first place, leaving the food to the men. She removed one boot so that she could slip on a sandal for a side-by-side comparison.

"The boots, definitely," Travis offered, surprising her by coming quietly up from behind her and looping his arms around her waist so that she was leaning against him. "Then you can kick off the predators who try to steal you away from me."

She tipped back her head and laughed, a wonderful melody of sound as musical as a mountain stream.

He was enchanted. On top of that, she felt sensational, so slight and delicate that he could, he thought, have counted every last tiny bone, given enough time. "You smell delicious," he whispered, inhaling her fragrance. "Good enough to eat, in fact. Are you sure you want to go out?"

She didn't get the chance to be tempted. Benny was right behind him. "Yeah, she wants to come, Travis," he said, exasperation written all over his face. "Let's get going, before everything's been eaten."

The saloon in the hotel was fairly rocking with activity, packed with an assortment of tables, benches and chairs, not to mention people.

"Are you sure it's okay for Benny to be in here?" Susannah asked Travis. There weren't any other children that she could see. Not that that meant much, the way people were jammed together. Anyone under six feet tall tended to blend into the crowd unnoticed. In fact, she felt in danger of being stepped on at any minute. "It is a bar, after all."

"It's also the only restaurant in town," Travis told her, his eyes smiling down into hers. "Don't worry, we won't let anyone corrupt his morals. The closest he'll get to beer is the ginger ale I'm about to order for him. Look, we'd better grab a place while we can." He steered them toward an unclaimed table near the window. "You two stay here, and I'll go place our order."

"Where did all these people come from?" Susannah muttered to Benny, amazed at the number of new faces surrounding her. At least sixty people had shown up and the noise level was incredible. Everyone present seemed to be carrying on a conversation with someone at the opposite end of the room. Above the general hubbub, Larene cheerfully outbellowed them all, taking orders for drinks and directing traffic.

When she saw Susannah with Travis, she beamed at them in pleasure. "Well, well, dearies," she observed in carrying tones to the women helping her, "if our fair-haired darling hasn't finally grown brains to match his length! Would you look at the company he's taken to keeping these days?"

Marg Turner and Jan Hamilton were content to nod approval, but Vi Dawson openly cackled with satisfaction. Susannah ignored Benny's snort of disgust and smiled back.

"What do you think of the local social scene?" a voice at her shoulder inquired.

Glancing up, she met the amused gaze of yet another stranger. Tall and angular, with dark hair caught in a flame-red scarf at the nape of her neck, the woman looked to be in her forties. She was strikingly attractive, standing out from the rest of the crowd in her elegant deerskin skirt and hand knit sweater.

"I imagine you must be Susannah," she went on before Susannah had a chance to reply. "I'm Judith Petersen, Travis's landlady, and I've been meaning to call on you for the last two weeks."

Travis returned at that moment. "Judith, I thought you'd decided not to come tonight."

A smile touched her mouth. "I changed my mind, Travis. A woman's privilege, you know." She glanced around. "I seem to have left it rather late, though. There aren't many empty seats."

Travis cleared his throat and caught Susannah's eye, lifting his shoulders in a faint shrug, "Well, if you'd care to join us, Judith, I guess we've got plenty of room."

"Since you put it so nicely, I'd love to." She surveyed Susannah again, her smile gaining warmth.

Susannah restrained a grimace. Bad enough that Travis lived in her house. Landladies were meant to be fat and motherly. And old. Not svelte and exotic.

Or charming. Judith sank into the vacant chair, crossed her elegant ankles, and allowed Travis to bring her a gin and tonic. "Beer gives me heartburn," she explained to Susannah with a little laugh. "I'm always afraid I'll disgrace myself and burp in public."

Benny snickered, Judith obviously soaring in his estimation. She was one of those rare women, Susannah recognized, so utterly poised and in command of herself, everything she said or did sparkled with wit and sophistication. She made common gas seem like a prize social asset.

Susannah put down her own glass of beer, certain she'd disgrace herself if she took even the smallest sip. She was pea-green with jealousy, and the realization dismayed her. It was the last thing she'd expected when she'd so blithely embarked on the evening.

Vi's enraged squawk partially revived her. Surfacing out of the crowd, the old woman appeared at their table and glowered over Benny's shoulder. "Judith Petersen," she demanded, planting wizened fists on bony little hips, "what the Sam hell do you think you're doin', hornin' in on this feller's date with his gal? Didn't you never hear that three's a crowd?"

"Put a sock in it, Vi," Judith replied with the utmost composure. "If Travis and Susannah had been looking for privacy, they'd have gone somewhere else, as far from your prying eyes as they could get."

Oh, terrific! Susannah thought, Judith's words robbing the occasion of its last remaining shreds of glamour. She wished she'd stayed home and wrestled with chapter nine and the joys of subordinate adverbial clauses of cause as they pertained to sentence structure. At least she knew where she stood with them. She took a swig of beer for comfort, felt it gurgle unpleasantly all the way down to her stomach and experienced an immediate urge to burp, loudly.

The fish stew arrived. "How come you're not eating, Mom?" Benny wanted to know, wading through the contents of his bowl as if he hadn't seen decent food in a week.

Susannah gazed moodily at a chunk of halibut and took stock of her situation. She was in worse shape than she'd realized. For five years she'd kept men at a distance, but let one get close enough to call her darling, put his arms around her and kiss her a couple of times, and she promptly came unglued. Here she was, going into a decline in full view of the entire town, because Travis had an attractive landlady. A teenager would show more poise, for Pete's sake!

She was beginning to wonder about herself. She'd never questioned that she was suited to marriage or motherhood; she'd fallen into both roles without ever really having to try. She'd even accepted widowhood with a modicum of grace, once she'd come to terms with her grief and anger. But this business of falling in love again at thirty-two was something else. She couldn't function properly; the emotional roller-coaster rides were too trying. No wonder people past the first flush of youth settled for companionship. It might not be breathtaking, but at least it was comfortable.

Sublimely unaware of his effect on her, Travis lounged in his chair, bestowing charm as though he had enough to keep the whole world supplied, casting his smile carelessly on anyone who crossed his line of vision.

"So you've got a full house over the summer, Judith," he remarked.

"Fuller than I expected. Even the attic room's got a tenant this year." Judith sipped at her gin and tonic, deftly avoiding the wedge of lime floating near the rim of the glass. "I take it you're expecting a busy season?"

He leaned back, tilting his chair and extending his legs under the table practically to the other side. "Well, the weather patterns are changing," he said. "No doubt about it. Rainfall's down from what it was even five years ago and they've had what amounts to drought conditions, even in the Queen Charlottes. If this present dry spell keeps up, we could be in for a long summer."

He's lanky, Susannah reminded herself, eyeing him surreptitiously. Not sexy, not lean, not elegant and definitely not handsome. Just a long, lanky pilot who was also socially inept, if his idea of a date was to plunk a woman down in a noisy, smoke-filled bar and leave her to twiddle her thumbs while he made time with another woman right under her nose.

Suddenly Judith reached over and laid a hand on Susannah's arm. "You must think we're incredibly rude," she said, her voice full of warmth, "nattering on about people and things you know nothing about."

"That's right," Travis cut in, the smile he directed at Susannah so sweet, it blunted the edges of her resentment and had her smiling back. "I didn't get around to telling you, most of the rest of the crew flew in this afternoon. Their arrival always creates quite a stir around here."

Judith laughed. "Speaking of creating a stir, wait till they see Susannah. They're not going to be in nearly as much of a hurry to get back to civilization when they discover she's taken up residence in town."

As if on cue, the door flew open and four men burst into the saloon. Catching sight of Travis, they made a beeline for his table.

"Caught up with you at last, you old weasel," the largest and noisiest exclaimed, slapping Travis on the back. "Since when are you in such a hurry to start the season that you come up here two weeks ahead of the rest of us?"

"I wanted to do some quiet fishing before the rabble-rousers hit town," Travis replied.

A second man, so classically handsome he was almost beautiful, eyed Susannah admiringly. "And just look what he caught," he said with a pronounced Australian drawl, taking her hand as though it were the most priceless treasure in the world. "Since O'Connor is so lacking in the social graces, let me introduce us. We're the aviation brigade. This lump of lard is Fearless Freddy, so-called because he doesn't have the brains to know when to be scared, this is Steve, the kid over there is Jamie, and I, dear lady, am Dan and very much at your service."

"Shove off, Daniel," Travis advised good-naturedly, hooking one foot under the rung of Susannah's chair and drawing it snugly next to his. "I saw her first. Go do your own hunting."

Dan grinned. "Can't blame a man for trying," he said, and turned his attention to Larene who came plowing through the crowd with a tray full of food. "Larene, I've waited more than six months for this treat. How'd you know I'd be arriving today?"

"Lucky guess, dearie," Larene told him, her face wreathed in smiles. "If you boys'll push a couple more chairs around the table, you can all sit together and dig in."

Judith moved closer to Travis to make room for an extra chair next to hers. "Shift the other way," Larene ordered her with a marked lack of cordiality, "unless you're after having halibut cheeks down the back of your neck."

Susannah was appalled. Vi had been ungracious enough when *she'd* seen Judith arrive, but Larene was being outright rude. Not that it seemed to bother Judith. Unruffled, she deflected Larene's broadside with a slow smile. "Dear Larene," she chided, "I do hope you won't allow yourself to be clumsy. It would be such a waste of good food."

Larene shot her a look that would have withered a lesser woman on the spot. "Took the words right out my mouth," she said shortly and stamped off.

Susannah couldn't contain her curiosity. "Have you had a falling out or something with Larene and Vi?"

"Nothing new," Judith replied, quite unperturbed. "Larene doesn't like me, so as a matter of course, neither do any of the other crones."

Crones? Susannah's bite of dinner almost went down the wrong way at the collective name. "Why not, for heaven's sake?"

Just briefly, Susannah thought she saw something flicker in the woman's eye, then it was gone. "I offend them," she said, brushing an elegant hand down her deerskin skirt. "I don't join in their daily kaffeeklatsch, or trade recipes. I buy my clothes in the city instead of ordering through the catalog, and they consider that to be 'putting on airs.'" She leaned close and added in a confiding whisper, "I even paint my face. How much sin can one town be expected to tolerate?"

Susannah burst out laughing. "You're not serious!"

Judith laid a hand across her heart, the droll smile twitching at her mouth modifying the malice of what followed. "Certainly I'm serious. The way Larene and her cohorts see it, God meant for women to age rapidly and uncomplainingly. That's why He visited Vi Dawson on us—to serve as a reminder of what we should be striving for."

"How long have you lived with this state of armed truce?"

"Too long, let me tell you. I've been thinking lately that it might be time to move on, but it's not that easy, what with—"

Susannah was so engrossed in Judith's revelations, she hadn't noticed that Benny had eaten himself to a standstill until he tugged at her sleeve. "Mom," he complained, "I'm bored."

"Hush, Benny, you're interrupting. What were you going to say, Judith?"

"It can wait. Perhaps this isn't the best place to talk anyway."

"Can I go down to the dock?" Benny persisted. "There's nothing to do up here."

"There's nothing to do down there, either, Benny, so sit down and be quiet." Susannah was annoyed. She was just realizing not only how much she'd missed the company of a woman nearer her own age since she'd come to Cameron's Landing, but also that she'd almost missed the opportunity when it finally did arise. Judith was a much nicer person than she'd first thought. Travis was right, she did tend to judge people too quickly.

Benny tried again, garnering as much sympathetic attention from the others around the table as he possibly could. "There's people," he whined. "There's always somebody. I just want to go visit the guys."

Turning from his conversation with his buddies, Travis added, "Tony and Al Hamilton are down there working on an outboard engine. You can see them from the window here if you move this way a bit."

"I'm not sure . . . it's not very polite to run out like this, Benny."

"Travis doesn't mind, do you?"

"I don't mind, kiddo, as long as you promise your mom you'll behave."

"For sure." Benny was all smiles at the prospect of freedom.

"Wear your life vest," Susannah warned, "or you'll be back up here faster than you know."

"No probs, Ma."

Judith averted her face to hide a smile as Susannah rolled her eyes. "And be back here before it gets dark, Benny. I mean it."

"Sure, Mom." He was sidling toward the door, anxious to be gone before she found a good reason to change her mind.

She could think of several other vital instructions she ought to issue, but contented herself with peering through the window. She saw him run down the ramp and disappear inside the shed. Moments later he reappeared with his vest, and Tony Hamilton left his work on the outboard long enough to help him fasten the buckle.

Travis slid his arm over Susannah's chair and let his fingers trace a path up the back of her neck. "Don't worry so much, sweetheart. He won't come to any harm down there."

She toyed with her glass. "I know."

"Then why aren't you relaxing and finishing your beer?"

She made a face. "Because I hate the taste."

"Well, why didn't you say something sooner?" His eyes lingered on hers, drifted to her lips. "Let me get you something else. What would you like?"

The attraction was too potent to resist. "I'm afraid to tell you, in case someone overhears and labels me shameless," she murmured rashly.

"That mouth of yours ought to be outlawed," Travis told her, "for inciting an otherwise respectable man to indecent responses in a public place. When are you going to let me take you home?"

"When she's tasted my apple crumble," Larene bellowed at his back, and leaned over his shoulder to scoop up empty plates. "And don't you be rushing her into anything, my lad, or it's me you'll be answering to."

"Gee, thanks, Larene," Travis said wryly over a shout of laughter. "It's nice to know we all have Susannah's best interests so much at heart."

"And there's a line waiting to take his place," Dan added to Susannah, "so don't feel you're stuck with him."

How could she help but be warmed by their friendship? It had saved the evening from disaster and made her feel as if she really belonged. She craned her neck and saw her son, safe and happy, squatting down beside Tony and Al, absorbed in the mysteries of the outboard engine. All the pieces of her life seemed suddenly to be falling into place.

"It's not always easy being a single parent, is it?" Judith commiserated, noticing her checking on Benny.

"You're a mother, too?" Susannah swung round, surprised. Judith was so...impeccable.

Judith laughed outright. "Is that so hard to believe?"

"Well, no, not really. It's just hard to picture you wiping runny noses or bandaging scraped knees, but maybe that's because your children are grown up enough they don't need that kind of attention any longer."

Again, that enigmatic expression flitted over Judith's face, a blend of acceptance and resentment, almost.

"Some never outgrow that sort of need," she stated ambiguously.

Susannah felt as though she'd said something unforgivably insensitive and she was relieved when Dan engaged Judith's attention, leaving Travis free to devote himself to her. "Susannah," he murmured teasingly, "I'm the envy of every guy here tonight because you're with me and I want you to know I'm entirely sympathetic to their loss."

"Good," she said, and wished she could always be this happy and secure with her feelings.

He gave her the private smile that always rendered her brain inoperable. "I can think of a number of ways to pass the summer evenings, but for some reason, my mind keeps coming back to one thing in particular." His eyes caressed her outrageously. "Do you know how long the evenings last up here in July, Susannah? Have you ever spent the night in a boat, anchored in a fjord so far removed from the rest of the world that you can almost hear the moon rise?"

She shook her head, hypnotized. "Never."

"A good thing, too," he said. "I think I'd be very jealous of anyone other than me sharing that experience with you."

She lowered her eyes, glad he couldn't see the way she started to tremble from the inside out. It had been years since she'd had anything other than memories to remind her that she was still a woman, with a woman's needs and desires. Memories weren't enough anymore. She felt suspended on the edge of discovery. It was a wonderful feeling.

Larene dished up her dessert, generous helpings of apple crumble, warm and spicy, with dollops of homemade vanilla ice cream sliding down their sides. For a while, conversation took a back seat to eating again.

The atmosphere was mellow with contentment, time passing easily and unnoticed in a way that never seemed to happen in the city. There were no deadlines to meet, no morning rush hours to face. Tomorrow would happen at its appointed hour, and not a minute sooner. And meanwhile, there was now to be enjoyed.

It took Vi to shatter the mood. "Where's that boy of yours, Susannah?" she grumbled, wriggling between the tables until she was within earshot, a dish of apple crumble clutched in her gnarled little hands. "I can't keep this much longer. Folks here is worse than a pack of starving wolves. I reckon some of them ain't eaten in a month of Sundays, the way they go at it."

With a start Susannah realized the sun had set, and Benny hadn't come back to the hotel as he'd promised.

"I don't see him," she said, hurriedly pushing back her chair and peering out of the window. A rectangle of light shone from the open door of the shed, revealing nothing but evening shadows on the dock. "Travis, he's not there anymore."

Travis joined her at the window. "He has to be," he said. "Where else would he be?"

Apprehension clutched at her. "I don't know."

He heard the fear. "Don't panic, sweetheart. You know how kids forget the time when they're having fun."

"I have to find him, Travis."

He picked up her shawl and draped it around her shoulders. "We'll both go," he said, "but take this. It'll be chilly out."

"I'll come with you," Judith offered. "I know just how you feel, Susannah. You won't relax until you see for yourself that he's safe."

"Why don't you stay put, woman?" Vi demanded, fixing her beady little eyes on Judith. "It don't take three grown folk to find one lad."

"It won't hurt any, either," Judith answered dismissively. "And if he isn't where he's supposed to be, the more of us there are to search, the faster he'll be found."

"I hate to say it," Larene chimed in, "but she's right, Vi. That child shouldn't be wandering down by the water on his own at this time of night. Who's there to hear him if he falls in?"

The question galvanized Susannah. She raced out of the hotel and down the ramp, with Travis and Judith on her heels. She reached the dock in thirty seconds flat.

Benny was right there, oblivious to anything but his delight as he dangled mere inches from the dark water and swished a stick back and forth, creating swirls of phosphorescence.

Anchoring him to the dock, his giggle a high-pitched thread of sound on the still air, was Crazy Abe. The hulk of him cast a shadow over Benny so that it looked as if, with the slightest nudge, he could topple the child over the edge and into the bottomless water of the fjord.

Chapter Nine

Susannah's response was spontaneous and quite devastating. "You idiot!" she cried. "What on earth are you trying to do? Drown him?"

If it had been Albert Einstein dangling Benny over the water like that, she'd have said the same thing.

But it was Crazy Abe, and that made all the difference. Abe promptly let go of Benny and left him balanced precariously half off the edge of the dock. Benny teetered and let out a squeal that had Travis sprinting past Susannah to haul him to safety just inches short of a dunking.

The sight of Susannah bearing down on him sent Abe into further panic. Cowering against a pile of crab traps, he plucked agitatedly at the front of his gray flannel shirt, his giggles reduced to a soundless opening and closing of his lips. Judith came to a skidding halt next to Susannah, one hand pressed to her mouth.

Beyond the harbor, the desolate cry of a loon hung in the air, puncturing the sudden quiet. It acted like a signal, and everyone started to talk at once.

"Abe!" Judith was horrified. "What were you doing?"

"You aren't wearing your life vest, Benny," Susannah accused, shivering with reaction now that the immediate danger was past.

Benny scrambled to his feet, full of injured dignity. "It got in the way."

"That's no answer," Travis told him.

"I'm being good," Abe whined, inching closer to Benny. "I am. I am."

Travis tried to reassure him. "No one said you weren't, Abe."

"Stay away from my little boy," Susannah said, and tried to take Benny by the hand. "I don't want you anywhere near him, do you understand?"

Benny detached himself from her grasp. "Heck, Mom, why'd you have to come and spoil things?"

Susannah's anxiety, which had begun to level off just a little bit, flared into anger at this. "If I'd known what you were up to, or who you were with, I'd have been down here a lot sooner."

"We were only having fun." Umbrage in every line of his body, Benny moved closer to Abe who'd gone back to huddling up to the crab traps, and patted his shoulder consolingly. "It's okay, Abe. I won't let her hurt you."

It was a touching sight. Susannah swallowed her outrage and tried to be understanding. "Benny..."

He cut her off. "He was only showing me how to make sparkles in the water. We weren't doing nothing wrong." He flung her a resentful glare. "You can't yell at him like that. You hurt his feelings."

Susannah's patience vanished. It seemed everyone's feelings but hers were what mattered. "Don't you tell me how I should behave, young man," she snapped. "You promised you'd wear your life vest and you promised to come back inside before it got dark. It strikes me you've got a lot of explaining to do."

"I forgot. I told you, I was making sparkles with the water, and I didn't need my vest because Abe was holding on to me and he's my friend. He wouldn't let me fall in."

"I let you come down here in the first place because you said you were going to visit the Hamilton boys. If I'd known—"

"I never!" he argued. "I said I wanted to come visit the guys, that's all. Abe's a guy."

"Then what you meant and what you led me to believe were two different things," she retorted, "because never in a hundred years would I have let you come down here if I'd known who it was you really planned to meet.''

"Susannah." Travis laid a calming hand on her shoulder.

She shrugged him off. "Don't you interfere," she told him. "If I'd followed my own instincts in the first place, this never would have happened."

"Nothing actually did happen," he said mildly, "so let's not get too bent out of shape, okay?"

It struck Susannah as a classic case of men sticking together regardless of who was right or wrong. She didn't expect Abe to understand, and she supposed it was natural enough for Travis to side with someone he'd known longer, but that Benny's loyalty lay with strangers sadly undermined her composure. "Stop trying to make me look like some sort of hysterical woman!" she snarled, blinking furiously at the tears that suddenly swam in her eyes. She bloody well wouldn't give them the satisfaction of seeing her cry. "I'm not being unreasonable. Any normal person would be upset. We're just lucky that we got here when we did."

"I agree." Judith gave her arm a sympathetic squeeze. "Don't be so unfeeling, Travis."

He threw up his hands. "Hell, I'm not! I just don't think we're doing anyone any favors by carrying on like this now. Things get said that shouldn't."

"Yeah," Benny put in feelingly.

Judith took control of the situation. "All right, let's all calm down. Travis, do me a favor and take Abe home. I'd like to talk to Susannah alone for a moment."

Travis shrugged. "Come on, Abe. Time to go." He extended a hand, helped Abe to his feet and led him toward the ramp that connected with the road. To her absolute dismay, just as Abe drew abreast of Susannah he lifted his head and looked back at Benny, and she saw great silent tears roll out of his beautiful faded eyes and slide down his cheeks. Travis saw them, too. He angled a telling glance at her, slung an arm over Abe's shoulder and led him away.

She suddenly felt like the lowest worm on the face of the earth.

"This is partly my fault," Judith said, the moment they were alone. Shivering delicately, she turned up the collar of her sweater against the cool breeze coming in off the water. "I should have mentioned that Abe spends most evenings down here with the Hamilton boys. It's such a regular thing that I don't even think about it anymore."

"It's nice of you to try to make me feel better," Susannah sighed, feeling guilty without quite knowing how else she should have reacted, "but you aren't responsible for any of this, Judith."

"Well, in a way I am. At least, Abe is my responsibility. I started to tell you about him during supper, but we were interrupted. You see, he's my...child, I guess you'd say. My brother-in-law, actually, but he might as well be my son. You've obviously noticed he's not quite normal."

Susannah held both hands to her cheeks in embarrassment over her ill-chosen words earlier. She wished she'd called him something other than an idiot. "I really don't hold that against him, Judith. I mean, I know he doesn't intend Benny any harm. I just don't think he's a—"

"Suitable playmate for a boy of seven," Judith finished for her. "Well, frankly, neither do I, and that's why I wanted to have a moment with you. I do understand, Susannah, and I'm terribly sorry for what happened here tonight. I hope it won't stop our being friends."

Susannah felt like hugging her. Judith was the only one who seemed to have an inkling of how she felt. "Meeting you is the best thing that's happened to me all night," she said. And it was true. The rest of the evening was in a shambles, the delicate fabric of her relationship with Travis damaged by this latest confrontation over Abe.

"Then I'll sleep easier. Look, I hate to run off and leave you, but I ought to get back and check on—" she inclined her head in the direction Abe and Travis had taken "—things."

"Of course. Don't worry about us. We're fine."

"Good." Judith expelled a sigh of relief and reached over to smooth Benny's hair, which Susannah could have told her would not, even at the best of times, induce a favorable reaction from him. He glowered sullenly.

Judith remained unruffled. "Nice meeting you, Benny. Good night, Susannah. I'll be in touch soon."

Susannah watched her climb the ramp, envying the easy grace with which she conducted herself. It was hard to imagine Judith losing her cool. She'd rise above any situation, no matter how fraught with tension it might be, her emotions neatly in control.

"Let's go home, too, Benny," Susannah said dejectedly and held out her hand. "We'll talk some more tomorrow."

She was quite unprepared for his reaction. He'd been studiously ignoring her ever since Abe had left, gazing stonily out to sea, at his feet, at her feet—anywhere but at her face. Now he scowled directly at her. "I don't want to go home with you," he muttered sullenly. "I don't want to live with you anymore."

"Oh, come on, Benny," she sighed. "It's too late to get into this now. I'm tired, you're tired, and we'll both feel better in the morning."

"I won't!" he yelled, working himself into a fine old rage. Susannah was taken aback at the hostility emanating from her normally tractable child. "I'll never feel better again. You made Abe cry."

As if she needed to be reminded of that! "You're tired," she repeated, determined to deal with this latest development calmly.

She might as well have saved her breath. "He's my only friend," Benny lamented, angry tears filling his eyes. "The only one in the whole world."

"Well, you still have me," she offered lamely.

He soon disabused her of that notion. "I don't want you," he bellowed. "I hate you. I want Abe."

Susannah had read somewhere that sooner or later all children said they hated their parents and that rational people took such declarations in their stride, knowing they were words uttered without thought in the heat of the moment. But this wasn't a textbook case. This was her Benny, her son, the light of her life and the reason she hadn't crawled into a hole and died years ago. And there he stood, all the special times and the closeness they'd shared shoved to one side, telling her in no uncertain terms that he hated her. Her heart was breaking. "You don't really mean that, Benny."

"Yes I do," he raged. "I really do!"

It really defeated her. What did he think? That she enjoyed having to be the heavy? He was only seven, but old enough, surely, to understand that she held his welfare above all else. "Hate me all you like," she said, her voice wobbling dangerously, "but you're still coming home with me, so get used to the idea."

Something in her tone must have gotten through to him. He refused to hold her hand or walk with her, but he set off up the hill toward the house without another word, marching well ahead of her as though she were Typhoid Mary. They arrived home in silence and he went straight upstairs, brushed his teeth ostentatiously and got into bed without a word.

When she followed him ten minutes later to say goodnight, he turned to face the wall and pretended to be asleep. She kissed his ear and it was like embracing a chunk of rock. In the space of half an hour, he'd perfected the art of total rejection.

It was their first really big fight, and coming as it did at the end of an evening that had promised so much and delivered so little, it was the last straw. Damn it, he'd broken the rules and asked for trouble. Now that he'd got it, she wasn't going to let him dump his misery on her. She had enough of her own. She straightened up and marched back down the stairs and out to the deck, wondering what freak of imagination had earlier led her to think she was beginning to fit into this new setting, or that things were getting easier.

There were stars strung all over the sky, as brilliantly cold as Alaska in January. Snatches of laughter from the hotel wafted up the hill on the breeze, intermingled with the smell of springtime and growing things. The mountain loomed behind her, ancient and remote.

She belonged to none of it; not the country, not the people, not the way of life. And after the last half hour, she didn't know that she particularly wanted to; it was too much like living in a goldfish bowl.

So she'd said a few things that, in retrospect, were a bit hasty. People often did that when they were scared witless. Did that warrant Travis's unspoken disappointment in her, or Benny's outspoken disapproval? Was it reason, now, for her to be grappling with a feeling of such acute embarrassment that she was tempted to sneak onto the next ferry out of town and leave no forwarding address?

No, her rational mind declared. She'd been absolutely justified in reacting the way she had, and only a fool would knuckle under to the blackmailing tactics of her son. Or Travis.

Reason dictated that, by morning, hunger would displace hostility where Benny was concerned, especially if she made waffles—and she wasn't above a little blackmail of her own when push came to shove. But on the subject of Travis, her heart seemed indisposed to heed common sense. Grovel! it urged her. Apologize, atone, compromise! But don't walk away from romance, and don't let it walk away from you, not after all this time.

She was a mother first, she argued, and a woman in search of independence after that. Romance was nice, it made her feel good, but it ran a poor third to her other goals and there was a limit to how far she'd go to secure it.

It was a timely reminder, because at that moment she saw Travis loping up the hill to her house, all long lean elegance, and braced herself to withstand his magnetism, not to mention his criticism, which she was sure he'd offer, invited or not.

He climbed the steps and emerged from the shadows into the patch of light cast by the living room lamp, without saying a word. She examined the cuticle on her left thumb, stoking up on fortitude before raising her head—

and her eyebrows—and turning his way. She intended to wait until he'd finished everything he had to say before she opened her mouth. In the meantime, she'd marshal all her arguments so that she could decimate his.

He took a step closer, then another, until he was so near she could feel the warmth of him. "Sweetheart," he murmured, his eyes searching her face with unutterable tenderness, "don't look so tragic. Everything's going to be okay."

That completely undid her. Unpremeditated, the tears she'd contained down on the dock flooded her eyes and dribbled down her cheeks and off the end of her nose. "No, it's not. Benny hates me," she sobbed, and went into his arms so she could hide her face against him. She did not cry prettily.

He cradled her against his solid masculine chest. She could feel the steady thump of his heart through his sweater and burrowed closer, temporarily shutting out everything but the wonderful reassurance of being held this way by a man who was neither old enough to be her father, nor some sleaze pretending to be concerned when all he really wanted was to get her in the sack. Whatever his faults, Travis really did care about Benny.

"Ben loves you," he crooned now, his fingers finding all the knots of tension in her spine and massaging them away. "He's just mad because he wishes he didn't, then he wouldn't have to feel bad about disobeying you. He knows full well there's no excuse for what he did."

"You mean you're not on his side this time?" Surprise made her abandon her refuge. She stepped back and searched his face, amazed.

"If he were mine, I'd have been tempted to paddle his behind until he couldn't sit down for a week."

She couldn't believe her ears. Travis's tone had altered; he wasn't crooning now. "You're really ticked off with him, aren't you?" she asked.

"Him and me! I should have known better."

She was so discombobulated, she found herself defending the son she'd been ready to disown not ten minutes before. "Well, he can swim, you know, so don't feel bad."

"But Abe can't. Hardly anyone around here can, the water's too bloody cold."

She blanched. "I didn't know that."

"Well, I did, and I should have foreseen something like this. What if they'd both fallen in and we hadn't shown up when we did? Can you see Ben being able to fish himself and Abe out?"

If possible, she turned a shade paler. "I never thought about that."

He towered over her. "Well, think about it now, Susannah, and tell me what you plan to do about it."

Put a little distance between us for a start, she thought, moving away. Proximity was impairing her concentration. "I don't know. Ground Benny, I guess. From now on, the harbor's off limits."

"That makes a lot of sense," Travis replied, his usual confidence showing a few surface cracks, "especially when you consider the whole town's built around the harbor, which leaves him the choice of playing in the middle of the main street."

"Well, but—"

"Of course, he could always ride his bike up and down the airstrip. That should liven things up a bit, once the fire season gets underway."

As if she didn't have trouble enough, without him bringing that up! It made her move up here seem pointless. What had she gained by running away from old difficulties if new ones just took their place? "Don't keep throwing problems at me," she said irascibly, "unless you can offer solutions as well."

"Okay." He slumped and gestured toward the sliding glass door. "But do you think we could talk inside? Over a drink, perhaps, like civilized people? I don't know about you, but I'm a bit frazzled around the edges."

He was frazzled. Ha! "All I've got is a bottle of Arnie Swensen's home-made wine," she offered ungraciously.

Sudden amusement shimmered in Travis's eyes at that. Arnie's so-called wine had a kick that left overproof rum at the starting post. If *it* didn't chase away the cold lump of fear lingering in his stomach, nothing would. "I'll settle for that."

He waited until she'd poured two measures and was settled in the opposite corner of the couch from him, then he raised his glass. "Cheers, sweetheart. Here's to happy solutions."

Susannah took a sip and fire raced down her throat.

"My mother was just like you at one time," Travis said, blithely unaffected by Susannah's fight to draw breath. "Overprotective of her only child, certain he'd never survive the wicked world unless she kept him staked in the backyard where she could keep him under constant surveillance. My father soon cured her of that, though. He gave her five more where the first came from. He called it the Diversify and Delegate Method of Survival."

Susannah, on the verge of regaining control of herself, promptly succumbed to another choking fit. "You want me to get pregnant?" she gasped.

Chapter Ten

"Not just yet," Travis replied, calmly ignoring her asthmatic wheezings. "I have something else in mind first. After tonight's little escapade, I think we should concentrate first on *delegate* and deal with *diversify* and my long-term ambitions for us later."

Long term ambitions for us, he'd said, as though his future plans included her. Susannah took another sip of the wine. It left behind a subtle aftertaste of wild raspberries that was far from unpleasant. She hoped it was that, not the flickering excitement brought about by his oblique reference to a future she was almost afraid to let herself dream about, that was uncoiling a thread of delicious warmth deep inside her. "I'm listening," she said, her voice emerging so husky and uneven with anticipation that she hardly recognized it.

"Ben's got to learn to be accountable for his own actions," Travis said prosaically. "It's not in our power to make the whole world safe and that's something he'll learn a lot faster if he's got someone besides himself to look out for." He looked at her expectantly. "In other words, it's time for a little role reversal."

Disappointment had her practically snorting in his face. What sort of mind games was he playing, offering glimpses of wider horizons with his little hints, then withdrawing them before she had the chance to consider their potential? "What are you suggesting?" she asked with heavy sarcasm. "That I should start acting like a seven-year-old in the fond hope that it'll endow him with the maturity and wisdom of a grown man?"

Travis slumped lower in his corner of the couch. "I haven't had much practice at this sort of thing," he admitted sheepishly. "In fact, I usually make a point of not being around when my sisters' children act up. I guess I don't have any business telling you how you should be handling this. It's up to you to decide, not me."

There was a brief silence. Susannah stared into her glass and wished she hadn't snapped at him like that. It was her own fault for allowing her imagination to run riot over his teasing, offhand remark. She had both hands full dealing with Benny and the present. Fantasies about the future and having Travis's children were more than premature; they were preposterous. Apart from any other consideration, eligible bachelors didn't take on other men's children, no matter how attractive they might find the mothers.

"I really thought," she said on a sigh, "that I was teaching Benny to be accountable when I told him how important it was that he wear his life vest. Why would he defy me like that?"

"Perhaps," Travis said soberly, "because you didn't tell him why, and that is mostly my fault. I've been so busy spouting off all my theories about child raising that I forgot I don't have firsthand experience. I thought being an uncle fourteen times over entitled me to dish out advice, and it doesn't. I put Ben in jeopardy, and that scares me."

And not just because the boy could've drowned. The cramping fear Travis had experienced had brought him face to face with other feelings that he could no longer ignore.

He knew he liked kids; he was devoted to every last one of his sisters' children. But suddenly he realized that he'd really liked being able to walk away from them when he'd had enough. He was good old Uncle Trav, not Daddy, and that had suited him just fine.

Until tonight, when it had hit him with a blow that knocked the breath out of him that where Ben was concerned, he didn't want to be on the outside looking in. He wanted to be involved. Hell, he was involved, right here where it hurt. He wanted to play a part in Ben's future that included more than showing up for birthdays and Christmas with fancy gifts. He wanted to make sure he grew up right. He wanted to count for something in Ben's life. He wanted—and God knew this was the part that scared him—Ben to look on him as a father.

"What do you mean?" Susannah asked him fearfully.

"He's at risk here, Susannah, in a way he's never known before, and I'm not talking about his friendship with Abe. Ben's a city kid, and even though you think a city's full of dangers, it's also full of safety devices. He's grown up expecting those devices to be in place when he needs them."

"I still don't know what you mean."

He extended one arm along the back of the couch and let his fingers trace the delicate profile of her earlobe. She found it a hypnotic experience. "Well, take traffic, for instance," he suggested. "Because it's a potential threat to life and limb, you've taught him, quite rightly, to use the crosswalk and obey the traffic signals, which is fine and dandy except there aren't any of those safety devices in Cameron's Landing. Of course, there isn't much traffic, either, but it takes only one careless driver to teach Ben that he can't count on anyone but himself to get from one side of the road to the other safely."

Goose bumps of apprehension crawled over her skin. "He learned to swim," Travis continued, sliding his hand around her neck and smoothing them away, "probably in a pool or at a beach, under the supervision of a trained lifeguard. The Landing doesn't have any lifeguards, and the water out there might look inviting but it isn't a plaything. It's a vital source of income and food for people who work hard to carve out a living up here. What I'm saying, Susannah, is that everyone will keep an eye out for Ben, just as they do for Abe, but no one has the time to baby-sit him. He's got to understand that *he's* primarily responsible for his own safety, not you or anyone else."

"But he's only seven," she objected.

"Look around you, sweetheart. Younger kids than he have learned."

She sighed again, discouraged. "Oh, Travis, I feel so inadequate. I'm afraid of the dock and the ocean. I wish they weren't so close."

Travis raised his shoulders helplessly, wanting to thread his fingers through her wonderful red-gold hair and kiss away the shadows under her beautiful eyes, except that wouldn't solve anything. There was more at stake here than just teaching Benny how to deal with the realities of life. "Ignoring something because you're afraid of it won't make that thing go away."

He paused, choosing his next words with the utmost care. "The ocean is as much a fact of life around here as my being a pilot, and sooner or later you're going to have to come to terms with both of those things. Pretending they aren't there merely increases the risk."

"Pretending to have all the answers increases the risk, too. How do I teach Benny to face up to things when I'm not even sure I can do it myself?"

He drew her against him, propping his legs on the coffee table. "I think that's where the O'Connor Method comes into its own," he said. "It does more than diagnose the problem. It offers solutions that worked for my mom."

He just hoped his memories served him correctly, because they were all he had to go on. Susannah was uncertain enough without him doing anything to undermine her confidence. "This is just a suggestion, but I think you should get a dog."

She looked at him warily. "Why?" she asked, after a long moment of silence.

"Because looking out for something younger and smaller than himself is the fastest and surest way to teach a child responsibility. I'm the eldest of six. Trust me. I know what I'm talking about."

"A dog." Susannah rolled the idea around in her mind, remembering all the TV movie dogs she and Benny had fallen in love with over the years. She turned to Travis in dawning delight. "Why didn't I think of that? Benny's always wanted a dog and we could never have one while we lived in an apartment. Just think—" her voice grew all soft and fuzzy "—he'd have such fun looking after a sweet little puppy. It could sleep at the foot of his bed, and si—"

Travis sat up in alarm. "Hey, hold on a minute," he warned. "I'm not talking about a lap dog, Susannah." A pint-sized poodle would not only be hard to come by, it would pose more difficulties than it solved. "I mean a real dog. The sort with brawn as well as brains, that won't embarrass a growing boy when it tags along every place he goes. The sort with big powerful jaws that will clamp onto the seat of his pants if he shows signs of getting himself into trouble. Something big and fearless, with motherly inclinations, so that you can relax and enjoy the other parts of your life without worrying about your child every minute he's out of your sight. You know what I mean?"

She smiled at him. "I know what you mean, and I think it's a wonderful idea."

"Think of all the other benefits."

"I already am." She counted off on one finger. "A dog's never too tired to play."

"And it's the best and cheapest alarm system in the world. No one messes with a big dog."

"And it's loving and faithful."

Travis inched closer, if that was possible. "So are people, given half a chance," he murmured, captivated by the smile that curved her mouth.

The moment felt so right, and she was so sure he was going to kiss her anyway, that she reached up and pulled his head down until their lips met.

His eyes flared with pleasure, then he tightened both arms around her. "Do you think," he rumbled against her mouth, "that we could deal with one more issue before we get carried away?"

"What's that?" she whispered, her thoughts already becoming soft and unfocused.

"Abe," he murmured, teasing her lips with his. He knew he was pushing his luck, but there was still this last problem to be resolved before they could progress to *diversify*, where he hoped to play a more significant and active role.

"I might have known you'd take advantage of the moment," she sighed, pushing him away. "Why'd you have to bring him into things, just when they were going so well?"

"Because," he said, refusing to keep his distance, "like it or not, Abe's as much a fact of life around here as the ocean."

"So's Larene, but I don't see you suggesting—"

"And like Ben," Travis went on, "he's also something of a loner and a misfit. It's natural they should gravitate toward each other. And even you must've been moved by Abe's tears tonight. Hell, I thought I was going to start bawling myself, at one point."

She decided she hated it when he was right and stared mutinously past his left ear.

He wasn't deterred. "There's real affection there, Susannah, and a completely unself-conscious commitment to friendship. Does that happen so often in a person's life that you feel justified in depriving Ben of the experience now, when he most needs to feel he belongs?"

Susannah let her hands drop into her lap, the impact of his words making her forget all about fighting Travis. She'd learned the hard way that real friendship wasn't something to be squandered. It was too rare.

She'd known plenty of love. Her parents loved her, but they lacked the objectivity to be her friends; she was their little girl and always would be. Benny loved her, whether he wanted to or not, but she represented authority and security in his life. Being his friend didn't fit the job description. Mel had loved her, too, but his friends had all been men. She'd been his princess, something to drape in jewels and furs, to be spoiled and petted and adored.

She remembered the last five years, and the terrible emptiness of widowhood. When it had come right down to dealing with the loss and getting through the days, haunted as she was by the senseless violence of Mel's death, she'd been able to count on one hand the people who'd really been there for her when she'd most needed someone to lean on.

There was Linda Balfour, her best friend since grade school, who'd stuck by her through adolescence, acne and morning sickness, and who, though still grieving over the death of her own mother, had led Susannah by the hand through the rites and ceremonies of burying a husband. There was Megan Frost, her next-door neighbor, who'd sat up all night with her when Benny had the croup so badly that it was touch and go whether or not he'd have to be hospitalized. There was Beth Dalton and Jessie Whitehead, who'd joined forces to stop her from making a complete ass of herself over a professor, who'd been so anxious to get her between the sheets he'd neglected to mention he had a wife and three children at home. These were the people who'd taught her the real value of friendship.

And now there was Travis to add to the list.

She stared at him wordlessly, let her eyes examine him, feature by feature. So much of him showed in his face. The mouth was tender, bracketed by the dimples that betrayed his sense of humor. The jaw was firm, the gaze uncompromisingly direct. For the first time, she dared admit that she'd always seen beauty in his lean austerity, but now she recognized the strength and integrity that would make him enduringly handsome long after youth had faded, and her heart turned over.

"If Abe's welcome to come here," she said aloud, uttering the thoughts as if she were trying them on for size, "maybe Benny won't feel he has to spend all his time at the harbor, and I'll have a bit more control of where he is and what he's doing."

"I think you're right."

She chewed her lip consideringly. The idea made so much sense, she couldn't fathom why she hadn't thought of it sooner.

"What's the matter? Don't you trust my opinion?" Travis asked soberly, misunderstanding her silence.

She was absolutely terrified, less of him than of herself and what was happening to her. Emotions were unfolding: deep, powerful, disturbing emotions. She tried to smile and thought she might burst into tears instead. "I trust you," she said around the lump in her throat.

He took her hands in his own, turned them over and kissed first one palm, then the other. "Darling Susannah, I promise I'll never give you reason to regret saying that."

She looked at his bent head, with its thatch of wheat-gold hair, and wanted very badly to hold it next to her heart. "But what's the best way to go about things, I wonder?" she asked, before she made a complete fool of herself and poured out secrets she'd only just discovered. She needed time to examine them and be sure they were what they seemed to be. She didn't want to say things now that she might regret in the more clear-headed light of morning.

Gratitude, Travis found, lifting his head and drowning in the misty depths of her eyes, seemed to excite in him the same responses as desire. He shifted and took a deep breath. "Perhaps if you could make an effort to get to know Abe?" he suggested.

She nodded. "Okay. I'll try to give him a fair chance."

He held both her hands and hoped he knew what he was doing in encouraging her this way. Who was he, after all, to be offering advice when his main objective until recently had been to remain as uninvolved in other people's lives as possible? "Susannah, if, after you've done that, you still feel you don't want Ben spending time with Abe, I won't try to change your mind again."

At first she said nothing, immersed in thought. It had been a momentous evening, full of revelations. She'd learned a lot about the people around her and more about herself than she cared to admit. But was she really ready to make all these changes?

She looked up, saw the expectation in that utterly candid, devastatingly blue gaze, and was lost. "Okay."

He smiled at her then, releasing his dimples in all their heart-stopping glory. "Some time in the very immediate future," he promised, rising and pulling her to her feet also, "I plan to spirit you away some place where we'll be assured of privacy and leisure, so we can progress to *diversify*."

THE FOLLOWING THURSDAY, Susannah stopped in at the kennel on her way up to the logging camp and asked Elaine Sharp about choosing a puppy.

"A puppy?" Elaine's brows creased in thought at the request. "Today?"

"Yes. Is it a problem?" Susannah didn't know how it could be. They were surrounded by more dogs than she'd seen in one place since the time, two years ago, when she'd taken Benny to the SPCA's annual open house, a disastrous outing never to be repeated. They'd both been in tears when they'd left, haunted by the sad, betrayed eyes watching from inside the pens.

"If it's a newborn pup you're talking about," Elaine said, "it might be. The last litter won't be ready for adoption for another three weeks. You'd have to make do with a dog that's a bit older. If you really want to take one home today, that is."

"I really want to take one home today," Susannah confirmed. Things were going well with Benny. They'd had a long, serious talk on Sunday and reached a new level of understanding. They'd talked about Abe, and about shared trust. She'd explained why a more responsible attitude was mandatory if he was to retain his privileges. Then she'd grounded him for the next three days, to drive the message home, and because she didn't think he should get off scot-free for Saturday night's caper. He'd accepted his punishment with good grace.

Now it was time for a little reward. He didn't know what she had planned, and she could hardly wait to see his reaction when she climbed out of the bus that afternoon with a puppy in her arms.

Elaine indicated a compound on the other side of the house. "I've got a couple of kids over here that you might want to consider. I was just putting them through their paces when you arrived. Let's take a look."

She strode off in her knee-high rubber boots. Susannah followed, stepping more carefully. There was evidence of many well-fed dogs underfoot.

The "kids" pressed their noses to the fence and wailed a welcome. One was a stocky little male with mismatched ears and a tail that curved over his back like a fan. The other, a female, was big and black, with paws the size of snowshoes and the sort of tail that cleared a coffee table with a single swipe. When she saw that she had an audience, she rolled over on her back and waved her snowshoes in the air, offering herself shamelessly.

"If you want a fairly small dog," Elaine said, "Schnook's your best bet. He's eight months old and he won't get much bigger, but Ebony's still got a fair bit of growing to do."

Grief, she was already the size of a full-grown retriever, but, *Something big and strong . . . with powerful jaws . . .* Travis had said.

Susannah eyed the snow-shoe paws and abandoned any idea she might have had of placing a little furry bundle in Benny's welcoming arms. Ebony was big enough to haul a wagon. "I want a big dog," she said before she lost her nerve. "I'll take Ebony."

Elaine shrugged and opened the gate to the pen. Ebony galloped out with all the grace of an animated sack of potatoes and planted herself at Susannah's feet where she promptly rolled over again, displaying an astonishing length of black hairy undercarriage. Not sure what was expected of her, Susannah bent down and stroked the proffered ribs. "Nice dog," she muttered, and shied nervously when Ebony responded by displaying inch long canines. She might have been grinning. Or preparing to eat the hand that stroked.

Elaine watched, a distinctly skeptical expression on her weathered features. "You sure she's the one you want?"

Susannah nodded. There was no doubt this dog would be more than a match for anything short of a grizzly trespassing on the porch.

"Then I'll have her ready for you this afternoon. And I don't give my dogs away for free. People want a pet badly enough, they'll pay a bit for it. She'll cost you fifty dollars including collar, leash, and a week's supply of feed, but I won't take your money till you stop by next week. If she doesn't work out, bring her back. I don't want any of my kids winding up unloved."

"There's not the remotest chance that'll happen," Susannah said. Her shortcomings didn't extend to mistreating helpless animals. "My son would disown me."

"Nevertheless, the offer stands. She's housebroken—more or less—but she needs work on her obedience. Be patient with her. She's only a baby."

Susannah quailed. "How old is she, exactly?"

"Nine months. She'll be a year before she grows into those feet, so don't say I didn't warn you."

BENNY WAS WAITING in the school yard, hopping with impatience, when Susannah got back to town. The bus door hadn't properly swung open before he started jabbering. "Geez, Mom, I waited here, like I'm supposed to, but it's real boring. How long—?"

"Till dinner," she finished for him, resigned to the fact that it was going to be a while before she could put her feet up and relax. "At least half an hour."

"So can I go down and visit Abe? It's been five whole days already, and I'm not grounded anymore, right? You said I could, remember? You said—"

Smelling freedom, Ebony lunged for the open doorway, tripping over herself and Susannah in her bid to escape. She cleared the steps in one leap and hurled herself at Benny. Susannah, clutching the door frame to avoid being swept off her feet, watched with sudden misgivings as boy and dog rolled on the ground in a whirl of black fur and blue denim. It was hard to tell who was making the most noise.

"Mom! Geez, Mom!" Benny squealed, his face, split in a grin the width of a pie plate, periodically emerging from the fracas. "What a neat dog. Geez, Mom!"

Talk about instant bonding, Susannah thought. Her surprise was the success she'd hoped it would be and more. Ebony was howling with delight, in between washing Benny's face with a thoroughness Susannah hadn't achieved since his diaper days. "Her name's Ebony," she said, "but we don't have to keep her if you don't like her."

"Are you kidding!" Benny wrapped both arms around the dog's huge neck and hung on for dear life. "She's the best, Mom. The very best in the whole world. Wait till Abe sees her."

He stopped suddenly and shot his mother a nervous glance. "You didn't go change your mind, did you? I can still be friends with Abe and bring him home and stuff, even though I got a dog?"

Susannah almost blushed. It had occurred to her, in that mean, ungenerous portion of her mind she hoped no one else would ever find out about, that perhaps Ebony might displace Abe in Benny's affections, but she'd discarded the idea almost immediately. She detested people who gave with one hand only to take away with the other. It was time to honor her promise.

"Tell you what," she said, gathering up the supplies Elaine had provided, "don't bug me till we've finished dinner and you've helped me with the dishes, then we'll both go down and visit him. You can introduce him to Ebony at the same time. Think he'd like that?"

Benny scrunched his eyes closed as Ebony, apparently deciding she might have missed a few places, scrubbed his face a second time. "Sure he'd like it. Geez, Mom, anyone who doesn't like dogs is a real wazoo."

Chapter Eleven

Traditionally the bar was the place the crew congregated at the end of the day. Not that they were particularly heavy drinkers. Flying and hangovers weren't a good mix. It was the social aspect of the place that appealed, especially this early in the season when they had a lot of news to catch up on.

That afternoon, while Travis was checking chemicals in the supply shed, the twin engine Bird Dog Aerostar had joined the three Firecats at the base, its two-man crew bringing the fire team up to full strength. The new Bird Dog officer, a guy by the name of Chef Loomis, seemed like a decent enough guy and his pilot Charlie Ayres, a ten-year veteran of the fire circuit, had been greeted with a round of applause from the other pilots when he'd strolled through the door, for the very good reason that men like Charlie were the kind the other pilots liked to have around.

Charlie had the reputation of knowing his areas and his maps like the back of his hand, and of placing team coordination ahead of any personal likes and dislikes he might have. His first concern, always, was to effect a safe, efficient operation. The Bird Dog team did the reconnaissance, decided the risks involved in a drop, and made the initial assessment of the bombing run. A pilot taking off with a loaded tanker put his safety as much in the hands of the BD team as he did in his own aeronautical skills. Charlie refused to work with anyone but the best, so

Loomis must be topnotch, which meant the pilots were in good hands for the summer.

But while that probably accounted for the party atmosphere, it in no way explained why Travis felt so removed from it all. Everything was as it was supposed to be. Dan Ryder had come back with an endless fund of outrageous Aussie jokes that had Jamie the rookie turning bright red and pretending he wasn't listening. At the other end of the bar, Fred Hughes, the dispatcher, argued the merits of the Firecat over the old ocean-going DC6 with Steve Walinsky, the aircraft maintenance engineer. In the corner, Charlie banged out Scot Joplin ragtime on the old honky-tonk piano, while the new BDO nursed a beer and justified his bachelor status to Larene and Marg Turner.

It was the sort of scene Travis had often found himself missing between seasons, yet now that he was back in the middle of it he felt more like a captive spectator than a willing participant. Dan's jokes were suddenly boring, and his cynical views on what a woman wouldn't do to hog-tie a man to a mortgage struck a strangely hollow note. Fred's technical arguments were redundant, and if Charlie hit that tinny, off-key note one more time, Travis thought he might drown piano and player alike in the rest of his beer.

The plain truth was he was discontented, and for a guy who'd arranged his life to include all these thing—things he'd always thought he most wanted—it was disquieting to say the least. It was a bit like finding he'd been trapped somewhere out of time where nothing changed, then one day waking up to the fact that real life and opportunity were passing him by.

He'd long ago decided that personal commitment and his peripatetic life-style would make a poor mix. The last thing he'd expected was that the time would come when he'd reexamine his priorities and find them lacking. He'd thought they were too deeply rooted in conviction.

He'd seen enough of what having an absentee husband had done to his mother, with his father on the road seven months of the year and never there when she needed him. Not that Travis blamed his dad. Salesmen had to travel if they wanted to meet the bills, it was as simple as that. And when all was said and done, his parents' marriage had survived and so had the six children it produced, and only Travis, as the eldest, had known what it had cost his mother. He knew because he'd been the one who'd tried to ease the load for her when his dad wasn't there.

He'd decided years ago that inflicting that sort of responsibility and stress was unfair. He couldn't ask it of any woman, and he wouldn't let any woman ask him to give up flying. Instead, he'd convinced himself and everyone else whose opinion mattered that his professional commitment to making towns like Cam's Landing safe communities for their residents more than compensated for his lack of personal commitment to any one individual. The end result had been that no one expected anything more of him. Now, for the first time, he wondered if perhaps he shouldn't be expecting more of himself.

Discontented, hell! He felt deprived. And stupid. He was thirty-seven years old, and only in the last few weeks had it occurred to him that flying and the occasional brief romance weren't enough. He wanted something more in his life—commitment, sharing, a stab at immortality through children of his own, he didn't really know what all. It was a sobering realization that if he chickened out on a deeper personal investment now, he was likely to die an emotional pauper. Women like Susannah didn't grow on trees and he knew a summer fling was not what he wanted from her.

Bob Kelly's entrance from the back room, and the resultant commotion it produced, jarred Travis to the realization that he'd lost all track of the conversations around him. The noise level had risen to a dull roar, Larene's belly laugh rolling out above the male guffaws.

"...see, kid, a smart guy doesn't buy the cow till he's sure the cream is fresh, if you get my drift...."

"...salmon's running, and the tides'll be right for clamming in another week, if you don't mind getting up at dawn."

"...saw the look on her face. Saw the wrinkles, too, Marg. Sure and she won't see forty-five again...."

Draining his beer, Travis shoved back his stool and made a move toward the door, feeling claustrophobic. It wasn't worth the effort of joining in. He'd heard it all before.

In the middle of his best story yet, Dan didn't appreciate losing part of his audience. "Hey, mate, where's the fire?" he demanded.

Travis winced at the predictability of the question and wondered if the laughter that greeted it sounded as canned to everyone else's ears as it did to his.

"It's barely sunset," Dan persisted. "Stick around and I'll spring for another round."

"Thanks, pal, but I'll pass." Travis flexed his shoulders and stretched. "I need some exercise. Think I'll take a stroll before it gets dark."

Dan grinned knowingly and orchestrated a chorus of good-natured jeers with his next words. "Exercise, mate? That's not like the Travis we all know and love. What sort of exercise, I wonder?"

Travis suppressed his irritation, feeling so out of sorts that he wondered if he was developing ulcers or something. At the rate he was going, he could just see himself in another thirty years, shuffling into senility with every ache and pain known to man, too old to fly and so bloody lonely and bored with himself that he could hardly wait to die.

His irritation with everyone's interest in his affairs was nothing more than camouflage for the fact that he'd just discovered he was in a rut and didn't quite know how to climb out.

He wanted Susannah and Ben in his life. He was prepared to make changes to accommodate them, but he wasn't about to roll over and play dead. *If* he ever asked Susannah to marry him, and *if* she accepted, how would they reconcile their differences about his career? Even if they could live on his navy pension, he wasn't the type to settle happily into the role of house husband. He wasn't ready for retirement. New challenges in his chosen field were what he wanted, not just the removal of old ones. Flying was in his blood.

Dan was a pain but he meant no harm. And personal considerations aside, professionally the pilots had to get along, especially at the start of the season. Tempers would get frayed enough when August rolled around and the air was so thick with smoke a man wondered if he'd ever breathe normally again. "All I'm looking for is a nice, quiet evening constitutional."

"If it's up the hill you're thinking of heading, no one's home." She was at the other end of the bar, apparently embroiled in gossip with Marg Turner and Bob, but for all that they were small, Larene's ears missed nothing. "Susannah and the boy are down on the dock with Abe and the dog."

That stopped him. He'd hoped Susannah would follow through on Saturday night's discussion about mending fences with Abe and getting a dog for Ben, but he hadn't expected either to happen so soon. "You sure about that, Larene?"

"Dearie, what goes on in this town that I don't know about isn't worth the knowing in the first place. To be sure I'm sure. Heard it from my Bob not five minutes ago, and himself saw it with his own eyes not ten minutes before that."

"Bob, was down there, too?"

"Sure, and he took down a slab of meat pie for Abe, seeing as how herself that runs a fancy boarding establishment never cooks the poor man a decent meal." Larene shook her head wrathfully. "Wicked," she muttered. "Terribly wicked, when you think about it."

"And?" Were they getting along? Travis wanted to ask. Had Susannah bridged the gap of fear and mistrust that had sprung up between her and Abe? Had he given the right advice this time? Or had he pushed her into another confrontation that would turn into disaster? "Larene, tell me what else was happening!"

"The dog's going to need a new leash before long. Just about chewed right through the one it's got."

Travis ground his teeth. "What about Abe?"

"Sure and he doesn't have a leash, dearie. Herself lets him run free in the hopes he'll lose himself some place where no one'll ever find him."

Patience at an end, Travis let fly with a pungent oath that did little to alleviate his frustration, but provoked a roar of merriment from the others.

"Is it beer you'd be liking to wash out your wicked mouth?" Larene chortled, the rolls around her waist shaking. "Or are you still set on getting some exercise?"

"You and my mother," Travis grumbled sourly, "are two of a kind. The pair of you'd get along famously. Keep the beer for another time. The idea of a stroll to the harbor to watch the sunset gets more appealing by the minute."

"In that case—" Larene leaned as far over the bar as her height would permit, and lowered her voice by a couple of decibels to a rumbling facsimile of a murmur "—seeing as how you're so taken with nature all of a sudden, why don't you offer to take that sweet young woman and her boy out to the Point to see the sunrise, come next week?"

Travis's head snapped up in sudden interest and he caught sight of the gleam in Larene's eye. "Now there's an idea worth thinking about."

Larene's chins quivered. "Sure, and why would I waste breath mentioning it if it weren't? Any fool knows, what with the tide being so low and all, that the boy'd doubtless have the time of his life filling a pail or two with razor clams, and chasing all over them sand flats with his dog."

"And as any fool knows," Travis murmured, other ideas blossoming in his mind in glorious Technicolor, "it's also a great place for a picnic. If I were to take along some of your good home-cured bacon, I could build a fire and cook breakfast for Susannah and me. Could be that we'd have a fair amount of time on our hands. Alone... more or less."

"Don't be dimpling at me that way, my lad." Larene straightened up and threw him a severe glance. "And don't be confiding any sinful expectations. I'm long enough on my knees each night as it is, without having to pray for your salvation.''

TRAVIS COULDN'T BELIEVE the sight that met his eyes when he arrived on the dock a few minutes later. Ben and Abe sat together at the water's edge, chin deep in chocolate ice cream and conversation. Whatever else had been accomplished, it was plain that they were together with Susannah's consent.

She sat not far away and, despite its being a mild and balmy evening, was huddled under what looked like a large fur lap robe. What was even odder was that she appeared to be stuffing the lap robe with pink ice cream. Then he realized the lap robe was alive. At the sound of his footsteps, or perhaps because it was smart enough to recognize there was no more ice cream forthcoming, the thing stood up and swung its head toward him.

Chapter Twelve

"Good God, Susannah!" Travis was awestruck.

She looked up then, the somewhat frazzled expression that clouded her face lifting under the beginning of a smile. "Oh, Travis!" she exclaimed, fending off the beast with both hands and springing to her feet. "How'd you know I was thinking of you and wishing you were down here?"

"What *is* that thing you've got there?"

As a reply to what she considered a blatant invitation on her part, his response left something to be desired. "Well, it was my ice-cream cone," she said forlornly, "but Ebony was hungry. Again."

"I'm talking about the...ah...animal, Susannah."

"Oh, this is Ebony, our new dog."

It looked more like a cross between a bear cub and a cart horse to him. And with melted pink ice cream stuck all over its face, it might have escaped from a circus. Travis started to say so, then became aware of Susannah's expectant expression and buttoned his lip. He had four married sisters and a total of fourteen nieces and nephews. He knew better than to make fun of offspring, no matter how great the temptation. "Ebony, huh? That's a very...er... fancy name."

"It's a very dignified name," Susannah corrected him, "for what will be a very dignified dog. When she grows up."

Even then, he might have been able to contain himself if he hadn't looked at the animal again. Unfortunately it was staring him straight in the eye, and when it saw that it had his attention, it curled back its lips so that its teeth showed in what could only be described as a grin.

"Dignified?" Travis choked, convulsed with laughter. "Grown? You mean there's more of it to come?"

Offended, Susannah drew herself up to her full five feet two inches and tried to look regal. Ebony took this as permission to move and lunged toward Travis, trailing a length of frayed leash in her wake. "If you can't say something nice," Susannah suggested loftily, "then at least be sensitive enough to keep your voice down. You'll hurt her feelings."

"I'm sorry, Susannah. Really." The dog stretched out on her back at his feet, eyes rolling in ecstasy when he knelt to scratch her ribs, and he realized that, despite her size, she was little more than a pup. "But what made you choose her? She'll cost a small fortune to feed."

Susannah couldn't imagine what mental aberration had led her to believe her relationship with Travis was destined for great things. He was the most practical man alive. A boiled potato was more romantic. "Well, for heaven's sake, it was your suggestion in the first place."

"I know. But why not something a bit smaller?" Ill chosen words or not, he couldn't resist teasing her. "Like a Great Dane, maybe?"

"Because you said—" Susannah paused accusingly "—you *specifically* said I should get something big and strong."

Travis concluded from Susannah's sigh that she was nearing the end of her tether, and that perhaps he ought to be a bit more sympathetic. "So I did."

"And fierce. Once she's been properly trained, I think she'll do very well."

That did it. He took another look at the wanton creature sprawled at his feet, tried to envision her in the role of anything other than an overgrown lap dog, and started to laugh so hard that he lost his balance and landed on his behind with the dog doing her damnedest to sit on top of him. "Susannah, my darling," he spluttered around a mouthful of dog hair, "you've got to be kidding! This beast's got about as much potential for meanness as a butterfly. She's nothing but a brazen floozie."

Susannah sucked in an exasperated breath, as if it had been a particularly trying day. "Did you just come down here to give me grief?" she asked dangerously. "Or did you have something else in mind?"

The extent of what Travis had in mind encompassed a great deal more than he was prepared to deal with in the next few minutes, but he had to make a start somewhere. He noticed how the sigh threw her cheekbones into greater prominence, emphasizing the delicate hollows beneath them and drawing his attention to the soft pout of her lips, and decided he'd wasted enough time. He stood up and reached for her. "Come here," he said.

Susannah, hypnotized as usual by his eyes, saw the laughter in them chased away by something much more earthy and basic that persuaded her to forget her reservations about romantic involvement, so long as she remembered not to take anything Travis might say too seriously.

"Mom," Benny piped up at his mother's elbow, "we're still hungry."

The kid had a lot to learn about timing, Travis decided, and reached into his pocket. "Here," he growled, thrusting a five-dollar bill into Ben's eager little hand. "Go get yourselves another ice cream. Take the floozie with you and get one for her, too, while you're at it."

Benny saw the expression on Susannah's face and pocketed the money quick. "What's a floozie?"

"Never mind—" Susannah began.

"That wagtail slobbering at your feet," Travis said.

Abe, who hadn't spoken a word till then, started giggling. "Floozer," he amended. It sounded almost musical, the way he said it.

"Yeah, Abe!" Benny was sold. "Floozer's a much better name. Thanks, Travis!"

"Anytime, sport." He fished out another five-dollar bill. "Take this as well. You'll need it."

"Travis!" Susannah gasped, trying unsuccessfully to retrieve the bill. "That's way too much money. That much ice cream'll make them sick."

"It's a bribe," he said, closing in on her again. "I expect them to take a long time."

"You going to kiss my Mom again?" Benny wanted to know.

"Among other things," Travis said. "Spend a dollar on ice cream, and tell Henry you need to buy clamming gear with the rest. Now beat it."

"Travis—" She was flushed pinker than the sunset, and the pout had turned all dewy and inviting. It triggered quite an anatomical reaction in him. "What if someone sees . . . ?"

"What if they do," he rumbled, wrapping his arms around her waist and adjusting his legs so that she nested against him in all the places nature intended a woman to fit against a man. "I don't care. I'm tired of playing games. This is serious business we're getting into."

It wasn't his usual teasing tone. Or his usual restraint. The intensity of his voice was almost as disturbing as the knowledge of his arousal.

"I know," he went on, his voice sounding rather strangled, "that we have a lot to talk about, and that if we get into it now, the kids'll be back and you'll get all motherly and take Ben home to bed, so what I want to ask is this, can we please get away from here next week and just spend the day together."

"Alone? What about Benny?"

"We'll take him and the dog, but I warn you now, I'm not going to share you the whole day."

"Well, then," she said, before she lost all power of rational thought, "we'd better take Abe along as well. They can all keep each other entertained while you get whatever it is off your chest."

"Oh, sweetheart," Travis sighed with undisguised hunger, "it isn't exactly my chest I'm interested in."

Exactly what he meant by that made her heart falter. Maybe going off to some remote spot with him wasn't such a good idea, given her own predilection for throwing caution to the winds where Travis was concerned. On the other hand, it would be such a treat for Benny. Just because she had some doubts about the situation scarcely made it right to cheat him of the outing. And exactly how much trouble could she really get herself into with Benny and Abe as chaperones?

SUSANNAH WENT to make her weekly call home the next morning and took Floozer with her to the store with the idea of instilling a little leash training at the same time. Floozer, however, had her own ideas about who it was that required the training. She charged down the hill with ears and tail flying, and made it to the front door of the store with Susannah, practically airborne, bringing up the rear panting. It was a spectacular arrival, witnessed by half the people in town.

"That critter," Vi Dawson observed, picking up a broom and advancing on Floozer with retribution in her eye, "is a menace, Susannah. Whatever were you thinking of, girl, letting Elaine Sharp palm something that size off on you?"

Henry, hearing the commotion, poked his head around the door. "Why, Susannah, is that a dog you got there?"

"Well, it ain't a dancing girl," Vi cackled. "Tie the dad-blamed thing up, Henry, afore it destroys the store."

"She chews rope," Susannah said faintly, unwinding the remains of the leash from around her wrist and examining the grooves it had left in her flesh.

"If it were mine," Vi told her, "I'd slap a saddle on its back and ride it. Lord, girl, that thing's gonna grow till it won't fit through nothin' less than a stable door." Shaking her head in vexation, she trotted inside to make sure Henry was doing her bidding.

He reappeared with a length of yellow polypropylene rope. "This ought to hold her. It's the same as what they use to haul up the crab traps. You come to pick up your mail, girlie?"

"Use the phone, actually," Susannah replied, and eyed Floozer balefully, wondering if she wouldn't have been better off buying a leash for Benny, and a shotgun for protection. As though she sensed her tenure was far from secure, Floozer lolled against Susannah's thigh and ogled her ingratiatingly.

"Well, now!" Marg came out to see what was going on, and beamed at the sight. "If that isn't the biggest, blackest dog I ever laid eyes on. What's her name, Susannah?"

"Trouble," Vi declared with doleful satisfaction. "Trouble and nothin' but, you mark my words."

"Oh, hush, Vi." Marg stooped down and rubbed behind the dog's ears. "She's an overgrown baby, is all. Reckon Benny's just wild about her, eh Susannah? Come on in and talk to your mama while the line's still open. Judith Petersen's booked a call later on and there's no telling how long she'll be."

It took ten minutes to catch the dog, who apparently felt that being tied up was tantamount to being hanged from the nearest tree. Her whimpers followed Susannah inside the store and mingled with the clatter and burp of the long-distance static coming over the wires, distorting reception more than usual. It made conversation difficult.

"You sound all breathless, dear," Lois Johnson announced when she answered the phone in Seattle. "What's the matter?"

Susannah rolled her eyes as Floozer let fly with a particularly soulful howl. "Nothing much, mother. I just got a dog, that's all."

"What a pity," Lois said. "I was hoping that lanky young pilot you're so taken with was the reason. What are you planning to do with the hog, dear, eat it?"

"Dog, mother. I said *dog*."

"Well, that makes more sense than a pig, and I'm sure my grandson thinks so, too. By the way, we got his little letter, and the drawing of the house." There was a pregnant pause during which even the static diminished. "It looks very . . . primitive, dear."

Susannah heaved a sigh, aware that Vi, Marg and Henry were blatantly eavesdropping, as usual. Art had never been Benny's strong point, as his grandmother had pithily remarked the day he'd come home from school with a portrait of her that had sent his grandfather into noisy hysterics. "It's not primitive at all, mother. We're very happy here."

"Well, I'd be much happier if you were living closer to home, Susannah, but if burying yourself in the Arctic has led you to find a husband, it just might be worth every last tear I've shed."

Susannah ground her molars in frustration. Her mother knew full well that everyone in the store could hear what she said, because Susannah had written and explained why and how, but it hadn't prevented Lois Johnson from airing her opinions over the phone every chance she got. "Benny's doing so well," Susannah interjected loudly, "that if you could see how much he's grown and how independent he's becoming, you'd know it was worth it."

Her mother had a one-track mind as well as a loose tongue. "Does he like the pilot?"

Susannah flung a harried glance over her shoulder in the insane hope that, just this once, she didn't have an audience. She ought to have known better. Marg, Henry and Vi were lined up at the counter like sparrows on a tree limb, drinking in every word. "Yes," she whispered, practically swallowing the microphone in her attempt to preserve some privacy.

All three heard her, anyway. She could tell from the way Vi started to cackle and Marg tried to hush her up.

"Well, that's a relief," Lois said. "Finding a good man is hard when a woman's got a ready-made family."

Susannah decided she needed a muzzle, and not for the dog. "Mother, you don't know what you're talking about. Let's change the subject and—"

"What do you mean? For heaven's sake, child, surely the simple life hasn't affected your mind! You know better than anyone what it's like trying to find someone who'll take on another man's child. I say, if the pilot's willing, you shouldn't look a gift horse in the mouth.''

"Let me talk to Dad. Please." *Quick, before I die!*

"Well, all right. But tell me you'll at least think about what I've said.''

"Mother!"

"Is it asking so much?"

Susannah examined the cracks in the store floor, but they'd have to be at least a foot wider for her to crawl through and hide permanently, and closer to two feet before she could stuff her mother down one. "Okay, I'll think about it. Where's Dad?''

"What's all this your mother's twittering about?" Frank Johnson asked genially when he finally came on the line. "Here you had me fooled into thinking you went into the wilds to find yourself, and all the time you've been big-game hunting for a step-father for that grandson of mine. Have you really found someone, Susannah, or is it just another case of wishful thinking on your mother's part?''

Sagging with despair, Susannah looked over her shoulder again. Alive with anticipation, Marg and Henry were beaming, and Vi's lips had practically disappeared behind her snaggle-toothed grin. Just inside the door, Judith paused in the act of tucking sunglasses into her bag, and stood quite still, also waiting to hear Susannah's reply.

"Hurry up and answer your pa, like a good lass," Vi urged. "Madam Petersen's waiting on her call.''

"I have to go, Dad, someone else wants to use the phone, but I'll write a long letter and bring you up to date on all the news.''

"Well, hold on long enough to say goodbye to your mother, or I'll never hear the end of it. You look after yourselves, and don't wait too long to write that letter.''

"Susannah? Are you still there?"

Vi trotted by, pure enjoyment gleaming in her wicked black eyes. "She's still here, Mrs., but make it snappy," she ordered, with an earsplitting cackle. "You got this lass blushing like a rockfish. Reckon she's fit to be tied at the questions you ask her.''

Lois's voice came through the speaker, stiff with outrage. "Susannah," she said, "who *is* that person."

"I'm a friend," Vi replied, tilting her head to make sure her words were received loud and clear in Seattle. "A nice little old lady who ain't never been to the big city, but this little gal's like a daughter to me. Reckon you could say I stepped in where you left off. Take a real interest in her business, I do, and the way I see it, she's managing her life real well up here in the wilds."

There was an offended gasp and a clatter as the phone at the other end hit a table or something before the connection was severed.

"Your ma don't approve of us, do she? Pity about that," Vi observed with a marked lack of regret. "Good thing Travis ain't really one of us, Susannah, or she'd be getting her water into a real uproar at the idea of you getting yourself fixed up with a hick."

Judith, who'd remained rooted just inside the doorway up to then, suddenly stepped forward. "You . . . *crones*," she pronounced in a voice so enraged that it teetered on the edge of shrill, "have got a lot of nerve! And you . . ." She pointed a finger at Vi. "You must be senile if you think for one moment that—"

Trying to slink out of the store unnoticed, Susannah halted, taken aback by the red tide of anger that swept up Judith's neck. "They don't mean anything," she offered lamely, her own embarrassment fading under the heat of Judith's scorn.

Judith expelled a deep breath and turned commiserating eyes on Susannah. "I envy you your charity," she said, "but *I* resent their interference in your affairs, even if you don't."

"What you resent," Vi informed her cheerfully, "is that Susannie's gone and found herself a man already, and here you've been lookin' and advertisin' for years, with everything God ever give you and a few things He didn't, and you still ain't got any takers, not for all your fancy rags and city ways."

Judith dismissed Vi with a look that, personally, Susannah wouldn't have visited on a slug. Not wanting to get caught in the middle of what promised to be another round in the strange and continuing hostilities between Judith and just about every other woman in town, Susannah edged her way toward the door. "I have to go," she said. "That's my dog you hear howling outside."

Judith attempted a smile, but it emerged more as a baring of her well-flossed teeth. The composure she'd shown the night of the supper had slipped a bit. "Well, before you race off," she said tightly, "I wanted to ask if you and Benny would come down for dinner on Sunday. Travis brought me back a beautiful salmon from his last fishing trip, and I thought we might barbecue it."

He brought me back a bad case of infatuation, Susannah thought, remembering how after that same trip her feelings for him had become unmanageable. "That sounds nice, Judith. We'd love to."

"Come around four, so we have time for a visit before things get rowdy. My gentlemen will want to party—they always do," Judith said. "But I don't expect you to stay late, since Monday's a school day," she added firmly. Then she turned away, a distracted groove between her eyebrows.

Whether it was Vi's disgusted snort or the abrupt way Judith ended the conversation and went to the phone, Susannah couldn't quite decide, but she was left with the impression that she'd just been issued less of an invitation than an order to put in a late-afternoon appearance and then unobtrusively disappear before the real party got started.

She said as much when Vi and Marg came out to help her untie the dog. "That's her calculatin' face," Vi declared. "She's up to somethin'. I don't know as I'd want to eat anything she'd cooked, Susannie."

Larene, who'd waddled across the road just in time to catch the end of the conversation, nodded energetically. "Nor me, Vi," she puffed. "Herself's not the type to be wanting another woman on the scene when she's got her boarders around. Sure and it's up to something she is, no doubt about it."

Curiosity getting the better of discretion, Susannah opened her mouth to ask the reason the women were so united in their dislike of Judith. There had to be more to it than her so-called city ways. But at that precise moment, Larene made the mistake of bending over to pet Floozer. The dog reared up to plant her paws on Larene's well-padded shoulders and knocked her off balance. "Dearie!" Larene shrieked, flailing around on the ground like a beached whale, "call off your beast, before it eats me alive."

By the time they had Larene upright again, Judith had finished her call and joined Henry to see what was causing such a disturbance.

"Didn't I tell you," Vi felt prompted to remind Susannah, "that dog was trouble and nothing but? 'Course, if it was Madam Petersen she'd got by the throat, I might be inclined to see things differently."

Good grief, Susannah thought, wrestling Floozer up the hill, talk about getting caught in the cross fire! The scorching anger in the glare Judith had directed at Vi would have withered a lesser soul. One way or another, on Sunday Susannah planned to lead the conversation around to all this animosity and discover its cause.

Chapter Thirteen

Judith's house was the largest in town and as elegant as its mistress. Imported French sheers fluttered in the breeze coming through the open windows, and there was a large canopied swing set in the shade of the back garden.

"Let's sit outside," Judith suggested, leading the way. White and pink pelargoniums spilled over the rim of clay pots grouped on the cedar deck, and baskets of trailing sapphire lobelia hung from the lower branches of the young spruce trees lining the back of the property. A pitcher of chilled martinis stood on a white wicker patio table, with a smaller carafe of iced lemonade beside it.

Judith herself looked cool and sophisticated in a blue linen jumpsuit that enhanced her slender height. Apart from her strong hands, she looked more like a society hostess than a hard-working landlady. It was a scene light-years removed from fish suppers at the hotel in Cameron's Landing, though Larene and Vi would have had a fit at the thought.

"Would you like a glass of lemonade?" Judith asked Benny.

"No," he muttered.

Susannah glared at him and raised her eyebrows meaningfully.

"Thank you," he added so ungraciously that she almost wished he'd kept his mouth shut. He hadn't wanted to come visiting. To his way of thinking, Sunday afternoons were too precious to be wasted sitting around watching grown-ups at play, and it had taken some creative persuasion on Susannah's part to wipe the scowl off his face. It reappeared now as he looked around. "Where's everyone else?"

"Well, if you mean Travis, he's at work, of course. I assumed you knew that."

They did. The noise of low-flying aircraft had woken them and sent them both running to the bedroom windows in time to see the red and white Firecats clearing the trees and heading off north. It had become a daily occurrence in the last week as the crew honed their skills making dummy runs in preparation for the approaching season. But it still wasn't a routine Susannah could accept without qualms, and the only way she made it through the day without worrying herself sick was to work until she almost dropped.

That morning she'd roped Benny into helping her rake up the pile of weeds that had been collecting since the day she'd first gone out to the garden and tried to restore order to the honeysuckle. He hadn't been exactly thrilled about that, either, until she'd started to burn the heap. Then he'd suddenly become very officious and full of knowledge and treated her to a homily on fire safety precautions that had clearly come from a much higher authority on the subject. Travis would have been proud of his protegé.

She, on the other hand, was presently embarrassed by him. Benny's scowl had deepened to such thunderous proportions that she feared he was contemplating throwing another temper tantrum. She sincerely hoped he wouldn't. It wasn't a habit she wanted him to cultivate.

Judith, however, was very much in control of herself today and did not allow his behavior to perturb her. "As you wish. Susannah, what about a martini?"

Gin wasn't high on Susannah's list of alcoholic beverages, but she felt it would be ungracious to say so on the heels of Benny's response to the lemonade. "Lovely," she murmured. She could always take very small sips and make one drink last the entire afternoon.

Wonderful aromas were escaping from a covered barbecue, and the array of salads on the long picnic table under the nearest tree ought to have captured Benny's fascinated attention. It didn't. He shuffled restlessly in his seat and tossed his mother a frustrated look. "Where's Abe?" he asked truculently.

Judith shrugged. "Down at the docks, I believe. He wanted to check his crab traps, but he knew you were coming so I don't imagine he'll be gone very long."

Susannah decided that Benny was spending too much time around Larene and Vi, and picking up some very undesirable social attitudes toward Judith. Annoyed, she cast about for a neutral topic of conversation. "Your flowers are beautiful, Judith."

"Aren't they? I can't take credit for them, though. Abe's the one with the green thumb around here. He does everything in the garden and looks after all the houseplants, too."

"I've noticed how much he loves nature," Susannah remarked.

Judith sighed gently. "Yes, I'm told he's become an expert. What a pity he isn't as capable of learning other things."

Benny scowled. "He showed Mom how to hear a raven sing yesterday."

"Did he?" Judith looked amused. "I hadn't realized ravens knew how."

"They go 'kloo-klok' when they're flying," Benny informed her, his expression daring her to laugh.

Susannah knew that look. It spelled trouble. "They do," she said hastily. "It's really very melodious, Judith. I was surprised myself. Actually, we have a nice time with Abe."

"I wanted to talk to you about that," Judith said in a low voice as Benny slithered off his chair and slunk off to play under the trees. "I'm not sure it's such a good idea for you to invite Abe over so often, though I do appreciate your kindness.''

''But we really enjoy his company.''

''It's nice of you to say so, but gentle discouragement might be wiser, if you really want Benny to make other friends. Abe can be quite possessive, given half a chance.''

''Really?'' He hadn't struck Susannah as possessive so much as protective. He was the gentlest man she'd ever come across, which made her feel that much worse for having judged him so harshly to begin with.

''Well, he doesn't really have any other other friends,'' Judith said. ''The men around town are kind to him, but they've got more to do than keep him company all day long, and there aren't many children like Benny around.''

She hesitated and smoothed her linen pants over her knees, ''I don't want to be an alarmist, Susannah—I mean, Abe's never been violent or unpredictable or anything—but on the other hand, he can be stubborn. If he got the idea that Benny belonged to him, we might have a hard time convincing him otherwise.''

Judith liked her gin, Susannah thought, watching as the other woman poured herself a hefty refill after Susannah covered her own glass in refusal.

''When Howard, my husband, died ten years ago, I took on Abe's care,'' Judith continued, spearing an olive and regarding it contemplatively. ''Howard felt very strongly about family, and people looking after their own. I would never desecrate his memory by having Abe institutionalized unless I was convinced he'd become a danger to himself and others, so I hope you can see why I'm a bit concerned that his friendship with Benny doesn't get too out of hand.''

''I'll be sure to keep an eye on the situation,'' Susannah promised just as the front door flew open and the pilots came trooping home. Travis was first into the back garden. Ignoring the interested spectators, he pulled Susannah into his arms and planted a kiss on her mouth.

''Well, well.'' Judith was smiling as she tied a large vinyl chef's apron around Dan's waist. ''Now that we're all here, let's bring on the food. You're excused today, Travis, seeing that Susannah's with you, as it were, but I'll catch you next time. Dan, that salmon's ready to come off the coals. Jamie, there's a case of beer in the cooler under the table and a bottle of wine for the ladies. Help yourselves, everybody.''

"But Abe's not here," Benny pointed out, condescending to join the party now that Travis had arrived. "We can't start without him."

"I'll go look for him," Steve Walinsky offered, but Judith wouldn't hear of it.

"Absolutely not, you've been working since dawn."

"I'll go," Benny said, sounding agreeable for the first time that afternoon.

"No, you and your mother are guests. I'll go," Judith insisted. "I know just where to look. Go ahead and begin without us. We'll be back before you know it."

"Let's get in line," Travis murmured in Susannah's ear. "I'm starving. I haven't eaten since breakfast. And the sooner we're through here, the sooner we can leave and I can have you to myself."

He smelled of after-shave and shampoo, and his hair was damp. He wore a white cotton shirt that showed off his deepening tan, and dark blue jeans, which she decided didn't bear examination right there and then, considering the temptations that confronted her.

He ran a careless finger down her cheek and flashed those charming dimples. "Quit looking at me with your eyes," she scolded him, because they saw too much.

"What else would you like me to use?" he teased.

Oh, the wickedness he inspired! She'd decided it wasn't smart to rush headlong into intimacy, but while her resolution remained strong, various bits and pieces of her flesh were weakening by the minute.

"Tell me about your day," she said, thinking it was time to change the subject before she made a complete fool of herself in front of everyone else.

"My day, by Travis O'Connor," he recited, pushing her into line in front of him and handing her a plate. "Well, it began at dawn—again! I did my walk-around, took the Firecat up, and watched Jamie make an independent four doorstring drop. He's doing well for a rookie. We practiced another six runs with different targets and flew our final mission about two and half hours ago. Then I filled in my logbook, checked out the aircraft ready for tomorrow, showered and shaved and raced over here to be with my ladylove."

"Six times?" She was amazed. "I didn't realize you came and went so often."

"Each mission usually takes about forty-five minutes," he said, serving them both tossed green salad. "Take into account that reloading with goop takes another three minutes, and during red alert I could complete up to twenty flights a day. You want wine, sweetheart?"

"Please," she said. She felt like celebrating, and she'd watered Abe's pelargoniums with the remainder of her martini. Travis made his work sound so normal and straightforward, as safe as crossing the road, and for the first time she believed she might come to view it in that light, too.

Judith arrived back at that moment, alone.

"Where's Abe?" Benny demanded sourly.

"I don't know," she panted, looking rather less composed than she had when she left. "I didn't get as far as the dock."

She came up to where Susannah and Travis stood together, and when she looked at Susannah, her eyes were full of commiseration. "My dear," she said, "I'm afraid I have some rather unpleasant news. Your garden's on fire. I saw the smoke from the road."

All conversation promptly ceased. "That's impossible," Susannah said into the overwhelming silence, feeling accusation in every eye turned on her.

Then Benny dropped his plate on the table, splattering himself and Steve Walinsky with potato salad. "Floozer!" he yelled, and it might as well have been the password to panic.

Everyone moved at once, the pilots leading the way. Leaving plates half-filled, they rushed around the side of the house and out to the road that led up the hill to Susannah's place.

"Benny!" Susannah grabbed for him as he raced past.

He wriggled furiously. "Let me go, Mom. I got to get Floozer."

"You could get hurt."

"Your mother's right," Judith said, catching him by one flailing arm. "Let the men take care of things. They know what they're doing. You'll just be in the way."

"She'd be safe if you liked dogs and would've let me bring her with us," Benny accused, and turned imploring eyes on Susannah. "Please, Mom, let's go get her."

"Yes," Susannah said. This was not the time to insist on obedience. If anything happened to Floozer, it would break Benny's heart and destroy any hopes Susannah had that he'd settle down and accept his new life.

"I really think it would be better to leave it to the men, Susannah." Judith shook her head disapprovingly.

"Having a dog underfoot will only complicate things. This time I think Benny's right. Floozer's better off with us." Susannah grasped Benny's hand more securely and matched her steps with his, leaping the neat flowerbeds. "I'm sorry about spoiling the afternoon, Judith."

"Oh, well, I suppose it can't be helped." Grudgingly Judith followed at their heels. "If you're determined to go, I may as well come with you, I suppose."

They turned the corner at the bottom of the hill. Ahead, a thin column of black smoke rose up like a dark beacon against the afternoon sky. "We'll get Floozer, don't worry," Susannah reassured Benny.

They heard Floozer's howls over the shouts of the men. She was confined on the front deck, in no immediate danger, but unhappy at not being free to romp. Around the back of the house, Travis and the other pilots were stamping out runners of flame that streamed through the dry, overgrown grass toward the foundation of the house.

Someone had raised the alarm in town. The Hamiltons, Bob Kelly and Henry arrived with gunny sacks and extra pails. And from the fringes of the surrounding bush, Abe emerged with a length of rope.

"Abe!" Benny ran to meet him. "We got to get Floozer, okay?"

"I found a long leash," Abe said, "so I can look after her for you."

"How did you know the dog was in danger, Abe?" Judith asked.

His eyes slewed away. "I saw the fire," he said.

"How? What were you doing up here?"

"It doesn't matter," Benny declared. "Let's go get her down here, Abe."

Floozer was frantic with joy. She pranced around, tail thrashing, no more concerned about the fire than Benny, who clearly couldn't have cared if the whole house had burned to the ground as long as his dog was safe. Watching the pair of them, Susannah was inclined to feel the same.

Travis came over to where they were standing. "It's pretty well out," he said. "Tony's just hosing down your weed heap, Susannah, then that'll be it, so we might as well go back and get on with dinner. I don't know about you, but I'm starving."

"Good idea," Judith agreed as the other pilots joined them. "You can bring the dog with you this time, Benny, as long as you keep her outside and don't let her trample my flowers." She reached down to pat Floozer on the head.

"Thanks," Benny replied, his manner a trifle less sullen.

Susannah breathed a sigh of relief. She didn't know how the fire had started, but there'd been no real harm done and no one had been hurt. Perhaps the rest of the afternoon could be salvaged, and they'd all still be able to enjoy dinner without further crisis.

But Floozer, who Travis had denounced as being no more aggressive than a butterfly only a couple of days earlier, thought differently. She flattened her ears, rolled back her lips to expose her magnificent teeth, and snarled at Judith's proffered hand.

Chapter Fourteen

"I don't understand how the fire started up again," Susannah said, when everyone was settled in Judith's backyard, feasting on barbecued salmon and pretending Floozer hadn't really meant to snarl at the hostess. It was a case, they'd all decided, of the dog sensing that a human wasn't overly fond of animals. A minor slip of the lip, as Dan had put it.

"What do you mean, 'started up again'?" Travis asked, looking so stern that he had her tripping over her reply.

"Well...ah...I was—we were burning weeds this morning, but we watched the fire the whole time, and I hosed it down and shoveled dirt on the ashes when we finished. I was really very careful."

"You obviously weren't careful enough," he scolded. "When the weather's this dry, you don't fool around with fires at all."

"I wasn't fooling around," she said tartly. "I was trying to clean up my garden, and I couldn't think of any other way to get rid of the debris since this town doesn't offer garbage pick-up."

"It doesn't matter, Mom," Benny said, coming to support her for all the wrong reasons. "Floozer's okay, so we don't have to worry."

"That's not exactly the point, Ben," Travis began. "At this time of year—"

But Judith cut him off. "Enough said, for heaven's sake! Susannah's sure she put out the fire, and I think we should leave it at that." She laughed, giving Floozer a wide berth and indicating Abe, who was patting the dog with one hand and Benny with the other, doling out affection in the only way he knew how. "Anyone could have been responsible, even Abe. He was gone long enough, after all, and he'd obviously been at the house. Why else did he feel the need to find a rope for the dog?"

Sensing he was the new center of attention, Abe cringed. "No," he whispered, flapping his hands in front of his face, his eyes fixed beseechingly on Judith. For a moment, Susannah thought he seemed almost afraid of his sister-in-law, then decided she was being absurd.

"That was a completely unjustified remark, Judith," Travis observed critically. "Abe treats fire with the utmost respect. He's too fond of trees and wildlife to fool around with something that he knows could destroy both."

"Exactly," Judith replied, brushing the palms of her hands together with satisfaction. "And it's just as ridiculous to accuse Susannah. She's hardly likely to endanger either her child's pet or their home, so let's drop the whole subject and do justice to this food, or I'll feel I slaved all morning for nothing."

"Took the words right out my mouth," Dan said, and reeled off an outrageous story about asbestos undershorts for fire fighters that had almost everyone in stitches.

The party picked up again, the incident forgotten for everyone but Susannah. She was looking at the stubborn set of Travis's chin and deciding they had a few things to get straight, fast. She didn't like his attitude. She damned well *had* put out that fire, and while she could accept that he might have reacted so strongly out of concern for her welfare, she wasn't going to let him relegate her to the position of little-woman-in-need-of-a-keeper. She'd done enough of that with Mel, and look where it had landed her: about as able to cope on her own as a backward butterfly.

"If you think," she purred in her most dulcet tone, sidling up to him as he spooned more tomato aspic onto his plate, "that you can bully me, you're in for a rude awakening."

"You should have been more careful," he said.

"And you should give me credit for having some brains," she replied.

He had the grace to look embarrassed. "I do," he said mildly. "And I'm sorry if I misjudged you. I really didn't mean to give you a bad time."

The truth was he'd envisioned what could happen if she were sleeping in the house when a fire broke out, and had been assaulted by a cold wave of horror that was as unfamiliar as it was unpleasant. It provided a little insight into how she felt when she was worried about him and left him more amenable to the idea of compromising where his career was concerned. Maybe he could stick with aerial photography and leave the fire fighting to others. There were a number of advantages: good money, regular hours and stable conditions. It was worth thinking about.

"Apology accepted," she said. "Now all we have to figure out is how the fire got started again. What do you think happened?"

"I really don't know. It must just have been a freak accident. What matters is that you weren't hurt and no real damage was done, so let's forget it and hope it doesn't happen again." He reached one hand around her neck and pulled her to him in a quick hug. "After all, if I'm going to live to be a hundred, I expect you to do the same."

THE FOLLOWING WEDNESDAY, Travis nosed the Boston Whaler out of the harbor at five in the morning, just as the sun gilded the tips of the mountains to the east. In the shadow of the fjord, Cameron's Landing still slept.

The engine puttered softly, its crew huddled in sweaters against the dawn chill and half paralyzed with mirth. It was all Travis's fault.

"Don't make such a racket," he'd whispered as Benny and Abe came trooping down the ramp to meet him. "We might be up and about, but normal people are still asleep.

Disturb Bob Kelly at this hour and you'll be picking bird shot out of your bum for a week.''

Susannah could have told him that if he really wanted them to be quiet, he couldn't have come up with a more ill-chosen warning. Benny nurtured an ongoing and un-dimmed fascination for anything pertaining to anatomy, particularly if it happened to have a name not spoken in polite society.

He immediately succumbed to a fit of giggles in which Abe, after a second's hesitation and a nervous glance at Susannah, joined. "What's so funny?" Travis had growled, mystified.

Benny had been convulsed. "You said bum in front of Mum," he choked, and went into another paroxysm of laughter so contagious that it had them all in stitches.

Looking out over the stern, Susannah had marveled that they'd made such an inconspicuous escape, especially considering that, in addition to Benny, Abe, life vests, tackle boxes, coolers and hampers, they had Floozer on board, too.

She had tried, without much success, to dissuade Benny from bringing the dog along. He'd been aghast. "Ma! She'd be all alone the whole day, and you said yourself, she's just a baby. How's she ever going to learn, Ma, if we lock her up all by herself all the time?"

Staring down one pair of big brown eyes was tough enough; two had been out of the question, a fact Floozer seemed bred to understand. She'd rested her head on Susannah's knee and gazed meltingly at her. She couldn't have looked more tragic if she were about to be shot.

Recognizing she was out of her league, Susannah had given in, and the little tableau in front of her now convinced her that she had weakened for a good cause. The dog stood with forepaws braced on the side deck, facing into the breeze with an undeniable smile on her face, her ears streaming out like a taxicab with the doors flying open.

Hanging on to her tail in utter bliss, Benny had regained sufficient control of his mirth to make plans with

Abe for what he'd earlier described to Susannah as "absolutely the best day ever in my whole life." She didn't know when—or if—she'd ever seen him so radiant, but since Floozer had come into the picture, everything else in their lives had taken a turn for the better. And that made Floozer worth any amount of trouble, whether Vi thought so or not.

Travis opened up the throttle as they rounded the cliff that protected the harbor from open water, and the town slid from view. Pearly with mist, the waves lapped at the sides of the boat and flung the noise of the engine up into the still air of dawn. Cliffs rose sheer and black on either side but, ahead, the water reflected the soft pink of the new day. Far off to the left, Moses Point rose like a mirage out of the fading violet of the departing night.

Looking over his crew, Travis figured things were about as close to perfect as a man had a right to hope for in the real world. It was going to be hot again, and there was enough food on board for them to stay out till sunset if they wanted. Moses Point was a secret that Nature had kept to herself, as untouched as Eden and full of hidden treasures to delight boys of any age. Best of all, there'd be time alone, finally, with the woman who sat beside him now. Travis knew the smile on her face was not for him but for her son—and that was okay. What mattered was that when Abe's hand crept up to lie next to Benny's on the dog's back, Susannah saw it. And continued to smile.

The first chance he got, he was going to find out how the truce with Abe had been reached. Travis wanted all that out of the way so that when the opportunity arose for him to examine what was growing so strong between himself and Susannah that he was thinking about dumping the plans of a lifetime for her, there wouldn't be other things creeping in to muddy the issue. No problems with Abe, nor anyone else.

At high tide Moses Point was a rocky outcropping, topped by a clump of firs whose windward branches had been shaped and stripped bare by winter gales. At low tide a three-mile spit of sand arrowed out to sea, a rare and magical ribbon of beach protected from erosion by a low-lying island at its most westerly tip. To the east, cliffs cut back in the shape of a bow, protecting the bay on the other three sides.

Travis had barely nudged the boat up to a convenient slab of rock before Benny was ashore. "What a neat place," he breathed and, tearing off his life vest, headed for the spit as if he feared it might get washed away before he had a chance to imprint it with his footsteps.

"Hey—" Susannah began.

"I'll be okay, Ma. I'm just going to *explore*." His words were imbued with the zeal and reverence of a boy on a holy mission.

But she had instructions to give, rules to set, limits to impose. "Come back here," she said. "Wear your vest. Don't get your feet—"

"Save your breath," Travis advised, leaping ashore to secure the mooring lines around a convenient sapling. "There's a new world to be discovered out there, and it just can't wait."

Floozer thought so, too. She abandoned ship with a violence that practically tipped Susannah over backward. "Well, call him back," she said crossly. "He could get lost or fall in the water, or something."

Travis laughed. "When a guy's got to *explore*, his mom has to let him go to it. We wouldn't be here today if Mrs. Columbus had tried to tie little Chris to her apron strings. And Ben won't come to any harm out there. It's as safe as his own backyard." He flashed his dimples at her, endearingly.

She refused to be swayed by them. "I've heard that tale before."

"Benny's okay," Abe confirmed, climbing out of the boat with the utmost care and nodding his head sagely. "You see, lady. I stay with him. Me and Floozer."

The next thing she knew, he was loping away, too, an ungainly black shape silhouetted against the bright light of morning.

Travis reached down for her hand. "Relax, honey," he cajoled in his most winning tone. "This isn't Cam's Landing. The water's not more than a few inches deep. If he happens to get his feet wet, he'll find out fast enough that it's way too cold for swimming. Come on up here and see for yourself."

She climbed up beside him on the rock, and discovered he was right. The spit could have accommodated two football fields with ease, and she could see right past the end to the tide line. Benny and Abe were in heaven, racing around in circles trying to catch Floozer who seemed bent on proving that she was part race horse and part mountain goat. It was the perfect place for a boy and his dog to roll around, wrestle and chase each other.

"You're right," she said.

"Glad you realize it." Travis had the gear neatly piled on the rocks and rummaged around until he came up with a steel thermos. "Now, maybe you'll be able to relax enough to enjoy some coffee before we set up camp for the day."

She turned a suspicious gaze on him. "I hope you didn't bring me all the way out here to work. I sort of planned to lie back and take it easy."

"Patience, my darling. First we have to gather wood for our fire."

"Wood? Fire?" Susannah wasn't the hardy, outdoor type. Her idea of dining al fresco meant lighting a barbecue, preferably one fueled by gas, and seldom at this hour of the morning. "Grief, this is like playing caveman. Are you expecting us to be attacked by wild animals or something?"

He grinned. "You bet. In half an hour, those three'll be back and starving. We'd better have breakfast ready or there'll be trouble, so don't tempt me with any more talk of cavemen or I might develop an insatiable urge to drag you off by your hair."

She shuddered with delight. "You couldn't. It's not long enough."

He handed her a mug of coffee laced with something that tasted too good to be rum but which had the same warming effect. In the shadow of the cliffs the air hadn't yet shrugged off last night's chill. "Nothing about you's very long," he said, tucking his arm around her and standing much closer than was strictly necessary, "so I'd just throw you over my shoulder instead."

She hung on to him brazenly, his thigh brushing hers. Behind them the boat rocked quietly, Benny's screeches of joy and Floozer's ecstatic barks echoed over the sand flats reassuringly, and little bubbles of sheer happiness exploded within her.

"Do you come out here often?" she asked.

"Every chance I get," he said.

She wondered if he'd shared this magical place with any other woman; wondered how she could worm the information out of him; decided she might be better off not knowing, and promptly asked: "Have you ever brought anyone else out here? Besides me?"

"Would you be jealous if I had?"

Jealousy was entirely beneath her. "I'd rip their throats out."

"Thank God," he said, putting his mug on the ground and wrapping both arms around her. "I was beginning to worry that you weren't interested enough to succumb to anything so base."

If the frequency with which he occupied her thoughts, or the effect he was having on her now were anything to go by, he wasn't the one who should be worrying. She was. Given half a chance, he could end up shifting the focus of her life. Maybe he'd already succeeded if the question forming next in her mind was any indication. "Who else's been here with you?"

"Abe, nosy. Now tell me something. How did you overcome your difficulties with him? We haven't had a chance to talk since last week and I'm dying of curiosity."

"Travis!" Benny was heading for them, covering ground like a distance runner. "When are we going to get breakfast? We're starving."

As if in agreement, Susannah's stomach growled musically. "Me, too," she said. "Feed me first, then I'll tell you. It's a long story."

They packed all the gear out to where the sun was just beginning to warm the sand. While Abe gathered small pieces of driftwood, Travis started a fire from twigs and set out the supplies.

"It's a feast," Susannah marveled, when she saw what he'd brought. Larene had sent bacon and hash browns ready for the frying pan, Vi had parted with six new-laid eggs from the chickens she kept behind her house, and Henry had baked a loaf of bread and picked fresh mushrooms from a place only he knew about. There was orange juice and hot chocolate and coffee, and a bowl of water for Floozer, who soon discovered she liked hot chocolate better.

Benny was put to work toasting thick slices of bread on sticks over the fire, while Susannah unpacked the dishes in the hamper and Floozer tried to sit on the cloth. There was an outburst of dismay, and when Travis spilled forth words that kids weren't supposed to understand or hear, Benny went into seizures of merriment and dropped his bread in the fire. Nobody cared. Everything tasted delicious anyway, even if it was sprinkled with sand and ashes.

"I *like* this, Mom," Benny said, sharing his last piece of bacon with Floozer who was drooling with anticipation. "It's like playing at being a real family, with a dad and everything, you know?"

She knew. The only problem was, it seemed less like a game all the time. Travis had become part of their lives, whether she'd planned it that way or not. She shot him a glance to see if he realized this, too. She figured if he was pale and sweating, she'd know how he felt about it, and prepared herself to be disappointed.

He stood up and she thought her worst fears were about to be confirmed. "In that case," he said, reaching down and pulling her to her feet, also, "this dad is taking this mom for a walk while the kids do the dishes. There's hot water in the pot. Abe, put the fire out before you do anything else."

"Shouldn't we...?" Susannah began.

"No, lady," Abe said, in his longest speech to her yet. "I know fires. I look after it and Benny."

"Sure you will," Travis said. "Abe's no fool where fire's concerned, are you, Abe?"

"I'm no fool," Abe corrected him in his soft, high voice. "You teach me and I learn."

You and me both, Susannah thought, wondering if the extent of Abe's disabilities stemmed more from the limitations other people imposed on him than from his childhood accident.

"We'll be back in half an hour," Travis said. "And if everything's ship-shape, you guys can go clamming. Take off your shoes, Susannah, and roll up your pants. We've got to walk off this breakfast if we're going to do justice to the razor clam feast we're having for lunch."

The sand was smooth and hard and warm. Overhead the sky had deepened from amethyst to a blue that rivaled Travis's eyes. Susannah wondered if she'd ever again look at a summer sky and not be reminded of him. The tide, still receding, was a gentle line of silver far down the spit and only beyond the island gained the momentum and strength to roll away to Japan.

"Now that we're finally alone," Travis said, linking his fingers with hers and swinging their joined hands back and forth, "tell me what happened with Abe. What's all this 'lady' business?"

"I don't think he knows what else to call me," she said. "I still intimidate him too much for him to use 'Susannah,' and no one around here calls me Mrs. Boyd."

"I guess not. So? Go on. How'd you get to the point where he'd say anything at all, let alone share ice cream with you last Thursday?"

"With the utmost difficulty," Susannah replied, remembering. "If we'd had to depend on my skills as a peacemaker, we'd still be at war."

It had been a tense and awkward meeting. Abe had been fishing, a solitary figure hunched over and staring down at the point where his line disappeared into the water. Benny had run to him, leaving Susannah at the foot of the ramp with Floozer.

"Abe!" he'd yelled. "Hey, Abe, look what I got!"

But Abe hadn't cared. All that seemed to matter was that Benny was there. "You came back," he'd exclaimed in his strange, hushed voice. "You did! I thought you weren't my friend today, Benny." And his poor, ravaged face had been illuminated with a happiness and gratitude that had made Susannah's heart contract with pity.

"I'm always your friend," Benny had insisted. "I'm your *best* friend. And it's okay with my mom now. Isn't it, Mom?"

That's when Abe had appeared to notice her for the first time, and the elation had been wiped from his face to be replaced by abject uncertainty. He'd cowered behind Benny and hidden his face. Floozer couldn't have looked more like a whipped puppy than Abe did at that moment.

"Tell him, Mom," Benny had muttered urgently. "Tell him he doesn't have to be scared."

And she'd tried. And failed. "Well, Abe...um...don't be..." He'd been shaking like a leaf, and her words had petered away. She'd taken a breath and tried again. "I mean, it's okay...that you're here...."

Grief, she'd sounded as if she was giving royal consent to his being alive! "With Benny," she'd added lamely.

"She's smartened up," Benny had explained, cutting through all the garbage and getting to the heart of the matter. He'd flung a pitying glance at his stammering excuse for a mother, and enunciated his next words carefully, as though she were the one with brain damage. "Haven't you, Mom?"

That's when Floozer had come into her own. Huge feet splayed on the wooden boards, she'd nosed her way around Benny until she could plant herself down before Abe, with Susannah, on the other end of the leash, forced to follow. The dog had known what Susannah hadn't: that you couldn't make peace—or contact, even—from a distance.

Abe hadn't said a word; he'd just kept his head down and continued to stare at his feet.

"Abe, I'm so sorry if I misjudged you."

He'd looked at her then, bewildered, and something in those beautiful vague eyes called out to the mother in her. Travis had been absolutely right. Abe was a child in the best, most innocent sense of the word, trapped forever in an aging body. And for that, she'd condemned him.

Floundering, she'd said the only thing that came to mind, because when he was very little it had been the one thing that would comfort Benny when his feelings had been dreadfully hurt. "How would it be if I went and got us all ice-cream cones? Would you like that?"

Still no direct response, but she'd noticed that his hand had stolen up to caress the dog's ears, and the tremors that had gripped him were lessening. Taking a chance, she'd lifted his chin so that his eyes were level with hers. He'd flinched, but only slightly. "*I'd* really like it," she'd said.

Near transparent lashes had fluttered down, hiding whatever expression his eyes might have revealed. She'd sighed and stood up, about ready to give up, as well. She'd given it her best shot, and she didn't know what else to say or do.

She hadn't dared look at Benny, for fear of the disappointment she'd see in his eyes. Most of his life he'd believed she was the next best thing to God and could do just about anything. She'd done more to disabuse him of that in the past month than in the previous seven years. That her disappointment in herself was even greater than his didn't help matters. "I'll go get the ice cream," she'd said.

She had been almost at the foot of the ramp when she'd heard him.

"Chocolate..."

It was a whisper carried on the breeze, so light she thought she might have imagined it. But when she'd looked over her shoulder, a question in her eyes, Abe had met her glance and answered it, dipping his head in a touchingly timid gesture of acquiescence. "I like chocolate," he'd said softly, and that had bridged the awful yawning gap she'd unwittingly created between them.

"Then you came," she said to Travis, and blinked. Tears were sparkling on her lashes, blinding as crystal in the morning sun. "And now I'm crying again."

They'd stopped walking some time ago and turned so that they were facing each other. He looked at her, and his heart swelled until it seemed to fill his entire chest. He opened his mouth to tell her that he was proud of her, that she was generous and good and that she'd worked a miracle.

"I think I love you," he said instead, and then he went hot and cold. He'd never said that before in all his life.

Chapter Fifteen

She stared at him, stricken. She'd suspected she wanted to hear him say that, but now that he had, she was terrified. His admission knocked down all the protective barriers they'd both erected and exposed the only issue of any lasting worth between them.

Infatuation she could deal with, chemistry she understood, hormonal stirrings she could accept as nature taking its course. But she considered love, the kind Travis was talking about, to be something reserved for the very few and fortunate. She'd told herself so a million times in the past five years, because nothing she'd experienced since Mel's death had led her to suppose she could expect to know that kind of love again. She wanted to believe she'd been wrong, and didn't quite dare.

Her thoughts skittered around the idea, afraid to settle, in case she found that once she entertained it she wouldn't be able to let it go.

Travis watched her, his unwavering gaze relentless. Evasive tactics weren't going to work. He was waiting for a response. "How do you know?" she asked.

He took her hand again and resumed walking. "Search me," he shrugged. "I only thought I knew when I didn't. And I didn't until now."

They were almost at the water's edge. It was a blue and gold day, the cry of seabirds and the distant boom of surf beyond the island somehow isolating the two of them from the rest of the world. He fastened his attention on the gulls swooping overhead, their wings iridescent with sunlight, because he was afraid to go on looking at her for fear she'd read in his eyes the insecurity he was experiencing in his heart. *She hadn't said she loved him back.*

She reminded him of a kid in high school, with her hair flying loose around her face and her feet crusted with sand. But she was a woman who'd already known a man's love and had it snatched away from her. He wished he could be the first man in her life because he was afraid she might always compare him to Mel and find him lacking. And how could he compete with a dead man?

She seemed ready for flight, perilously uncertain of him and herself. Because he wanted to impress on her the complexity of his feelings—that they weren't inspired by a passing urge like sex or loneliness, and that for once in his life they weren't prompted by selfishness—he tried another approach. "I keep thinking," he told the wheeling gulls, "about what Ben said back there, about being a real family."

Her throat went dry. Was that what had induced him to make his declaration? Pity for a boy growing up without a father? "He didn't mean anything."

"Perhaps not. But I keep thinking about it anyway."

"Is that what made you say... what you said? Did you feel it was expected of you?"

Her question left him hurt and angry. "If I did and said what I thought was expected of me, sweet thing, we wouldn't be here together like this, now. I'd have married Jessica Bailey when I was twenty-three, because she and her mother thought she'd like to be married to a navy pilot at Pensacola with the prospect of a good pension and early retirement. I'd have teenage sons and daughters, two cars in the garage and a lawn to mow every Saturday."

She tried to take refuge in anger. "You make it sound like such purgatory," she retorted pithily, "that I can't imagine why you're now giving so much thought to a little boy's offhand remarks about being part of a real family."

"I'll tell you why. Because it's only since I met you that I've come to see what I've been missing."

He was in love with a dream, she thought sadly. He thought teaching a boy how to fish and handle a boat was all there was to it. That it was something out of a Disney movie. He hadn't considered what taking on a stepson would do to his free-wheeling life-style. He hadn't the first idea of how he would feel if, after giving up so much for an ideal, he were one day to be faced by Benny reminding him that Travis wasn't his real father. And he hadn't given the least thought to how she would feel if she let him into her life and he found he didn't like it and left her. "You don't know the half of it," she said.

"Maybe not, and maybe I never will. All I know is that I think love you."

And if he did, and she did, what then? Would it be something that would endure, or just a lovely interlude that ended with summer? There were those who claimed that loving was a risk worth taking, but she was too vulnerable to be philosophical about it. Love between a man and woman was a double-edged sword: enchantment and despair, agony and ecstasy, riches and poverty. There was a measure of contentment in being emotionally self-sufficient. But after having known love and lost it, it seemed she had nothing left without it.

Susannah wasn't certain she could survive the loss of love a second time. "I don't know if I want that. Love is too... insatiable. It takes everything and leaves you wanting all the time. Wanting tonight and tomorrow, and afraid all you might have is yesterday."

"I only know how to deal with the present, Susannah."

"But I want the future, too," she cried passionately, and it might as well have been pouring rain for all the sunshine left in the day.

He wanted to promise her tomorrow, next month, next year; tell her she'd never cry again, and that he'd outlive her just to spare her the grief of widowhood a second time. But he was afraid. He was only a man—more courageous than many perhaps, but not God. "Susannah," he muttered, ''the only thing I can tell you is that if all I wanted was an affair, I'd have grown tired of waiting weeks ago.''

Well that much at least was the truth, she knew. He'd shown sensitivity and restraint. There'd even been times when she'd wished he hadn't been quite so circumspect.

She was worse than a kid, always wanting what she didn't have, always looking for easy answers, always hoping for instant solutions, and most of all, always asking for guarantees. Which, in a woman of her experience, was just plain foolishness. She knew better than anyone that growing up was more than a matter of taking control of your own life. It was accepting that no one ever had complete control over anything, and learning to live with that knowledge.

The bottom line here was, she wasn't sure she could trust her feelings for Travis. They were so physical. Take away his blue eyes and honey-gold hair and his dimples, and all that lean and lovely body that she itched to discover, and what was left? A vagabond pilot who was nice to her child, but whose first commitment was to a dangerous job.

He was such an unsuitable man, and even if he weren't, she hadn't planned on his appearing in her life now, if ever. She struggled to control herself. ''I'm not sure this is the best time to be in love,'' she said. ''It really isn't very appropriate.''

For a moment he looked thunderstruck. ''Susannah, if you could hear yourself! If you could see your face…you sound like a Sunday school teacher, confronted by a little boy wanting to play doctor behind the pews!''

''Shut up,'' she said.

''What's the matter, sweet thing? Afraid you've maybe fallen in love with me, too?''

''Don't call me sweet thing,'' she said. If plain old Susannah wasn't enough, the least he could do was put his mind where he claimed his heart was, and come up with some more romantic endearment. ''And I'm not in love with you.''

''Couldn't you pretend to be, just for today?'' he asked, maneuvering her into his arms before she had time to plot a counter-strategy. His gaze was deep and disconcerting and so full of knowledge that she quaked.

She twirled a lock of hair frantically around one finger. He was encroaching again, robbing the air of oxygen and tempting her to abandon her dignity and good sense. "I . . . don't think so . . ."

"Are you sure?" he murmured softly, and coiled one arm around her waist until she was pressed up against him. Released, the lock of hair sprang free and fell across her left eye. Her heart, not the most reliable of organs since she'd met him, cartwheeled around behind her ribs.

"Yes," she whispered desperately.

She closed her eyes and sank against him, feeling the tension and disappointment in him. When she opened her eyes again, the world was all fuzzy around the edges, except for Benny's face staring up at her. "Heck, you guys," he moaned, wide-eyed with frustration, "me 'n' Abe're waiting."

For what? The complete seduction? Susannah wondered.

"It's been hours," Benny went on. "The clams'll be all gone at this rate. Heck, you can do mush anyplace."

"It's been," Travis replied, with a precision Susannah could only envy since she wasn't sure she even knew what day it was any longer, let alone what time, "exactly twenty-five minutes. We have five minutes still to go."

Oh, wrong! she thought. It had been another lifetime ago that they'd set off for their little walk. The earth had slipped a notch on its axis since then.

Benny looked mournful. "You going to stay kissy-faced with my mom all that time? Geez, Travis, clams're funner."

Although he loosened her enough so that he could face Benny, Travis didn't let her go completely. His palm rested at the indentation of her waist, his fingers tracing the pattern of her ribs and laying siege to her with subtle messages that dealt death blows to her fine determination.

"You promised . . ." Benny began.

"Yes, you did," Susannah said, uncoiling herself from the temptation of his touch.

Travis sighed and scowled. "Never let it be said I'm not a man of my word," he grumbled, then flung her a telling look. "Especially where women and small children are concerned."

During the time it took him to organize Ben and Abe for clamming, she enjoyed a respite, but the minute they were alone again, he picked up where he'd left off. "The conversation we started back there was merely halted by an untimely interruption," he warned her as they wandered up the beach to the picnic site.

It was just before ten. The sun had risen clear of the mountains and the cliffs, and the entire spit was awash with summer. At the tide line, Benny and Abe were waging a losing battle trying to keep pace with Floozer, whose paws were working like bulldozers. Sand flew in twenty different directions, though how many clams were being uncovered remained to be seen.

Susannah searched for another scintillating topic with which to distract him, unwilling to have the magic of the day spoiled by too much reckoning with reality. "Such a beautiful day," she murmured, endowing the words with more meaning than he could ever guess. Tomorrow in all its brutal practicality would come soon enough.

They'd arrived back at the picnic site. Everything was ship-shape, the dishes done, the fire out, the cushions from the cockpit of the boat spread out like a mattress.

Damn! Travis thought vehemently. The way she had her mouth pursed up reminded him of the drawstring bag he used to keep marbles in when he was a kid. He hung on to his patience by a very slender thread. "May I ask how you feel about me?"

She looked at him, consideringly. "You're tall," she hedged. "Nice and tall."

His eyes shot sparks, and the breath whistled past his lips in exasperation. Couldn't she tell how insecure he was without him having to spell it out for her? "I'm getting crabby," he said. "I think it's time for my nap." And he flung himself down on the cushions and covered his forehead with one arm.

The silence between them lengthened. Suspicious that he was only pretending to be asleep, she circled him warily. The only movement she could detect was his chest, rising and falling in even and unperturbed rhythm. Crabby or not, he appeared to have dropped off as easily as a baby.

Stealthily, she sat down beside him, positioning herself so that she could watch him without having to move a muscle. She had some serious thinking to do. He hadn't seemed to understand that when he'd told her he loved her, he'd uncovered everything she'd been trying to hide. She wished she could go back to being the girl who'd once believed that the words ''I love you'' were a sort of talisman that would make everything else right; that she could take a moment that was precious and treasure it without having to search out the flaws. Flaws were always there, lurking under the surface and waiting to spoil the moment.

Travis didn't know how much she expected in a relationship. She wasn't as certain or strong as he. She'd come to Cameron's Landing, made a better life for herself and Benny, and quite by accident had learned to love again. But she knew now that she would never forget what it felt like to have love taken away. Part of her was still afraid. It wouldn't be fair to hold him to his words until she'd learned to be less needy. It would be so easy to let her own feelings loose, and take whatever he had to offer, without looking at whether or not what she had to give back was enough. If he was capable of unfettered generosity in love, he deserved something other than timidity in return.

Would it be easier to follow her heart if he were a plumber instead of a pilot? Was it really his work that made her hold back, or was she looking for excuses where none existed? She looked at him, sprawled out before her. His arm had slipped enough that she could see the line of his lashes, surprisingly dark and dense against his cheek. His mouth had fallen slightly open revealing the glint of his teeth. He was not quite snoring.

She thought about running her tongue over his lower lip, and slid her eyes away in an attempt to control the hot flash of desire that ran through her. But he'd loosened his shirt enough that she could see more firm golden skin than was good for her, and she found herself losing interest in his lip and wondering instead if his skin felt as smooth as it looked. Did he have a hairy chest waiting to be discovered, and if he did, was the hair honey blond like that on his head, or dark like his eyelashes? And did it stop at his chest, or wander until it joined up with other places?

Mel, she remembered distantly, had been very hairy.

Travis's belt buckle gleamed in the sun. Beneath it, his stomach was as flat and hard as a board. Susannah suppressed a sudden and outrageous urge to take off all his clothes so that she could see all of him, and wondered if she'd had a touch too much sun. Not once in all the time she was married to Mel had she taken the initiative in their lovemaking. It had never occurred to her. She'd had a very formal upbringing in that respect.

Travis would be the type to parade around stark naked, she just knew it. And the next thing, Benny would think it was hilarious, and start doing the same. But Travis would be fun, too. He made her laugh the way no one else could.

She sank back on the cushions, stared up at the dome of sky overhead and allowed herself the luxury of playing What If.... What if they were married? What if they lived in a little house on a quiet street, in a nice neighborhood? Would they live happily ever after?

It could happen so easily, she thought, her fingers sliding across the distance that separated them to entwine with his. Because he loved her and she loved him, and because that was the most important thing, it ought to be enough.

The sun beat down, so dazzling it pushed all her uncertainty and anxiety to one side. For a little while, she would hold perfection in her hands, enjoy a little taste of heaven that was never meant to last. Just for today, she would pretend that tomorrow wouldn't come.

"Travis," she said quietly, and knew he hadn't really been sleeping when his fingers tightened around hers, "I love you, too."

He lifted his other arm from his face and looked through her to her soul. "What about—?"

"No," she said, and leaned over to kiss him, stopping the question. "Don't spoil things, not yet. Let love be enough, just for today."

THEY MOTORED BACK TO TOWN, tanned and sated with clams. No one talked much. Travis let Abe steer the boat, propped his feet on the seat and pulled Susannah into the cradle of his bent legs. She could feel his heart beating against her back, strong and steady. Benny and Floozer curled around each other making a heap of black fur and little boy, and fell asleep.

To the west, the sun slid into the sea and left the sky raspberry pink shot through with peach. The dock was deserted when Travis took over the helm and eased into the mooring, but there were two strange boats rocking at anchor in the harbor, and snatches of laughter and piano music coming from the hotel.

"Tourists," Travis rumbled. "The season is upon us."

Abe nudged his elbow and pointed to the pole outside the store. Earlier in the month, Henry had run up a green flag denoting low forest fire hazard. Now, a yellow one hung limply in its place. Abe opened his mouth to speak, then changed his mind when Travis frowned and shook his head.

A chill settled on Susannah that had nothing to do with approaching night. She had the premonition that more than just a perfect day had come to an end. "What's the matter?"

Travis became very busy mooring the boat. "Nothing."

Abe, unaccountably nervous, didn't want to look her way. He fumbled with the lines on the bow, staying as far away from her as possible.

"Tell me," she said.

Benny was awake and grumpy, and Floozer needed to find a patch of grass. "We're on yellow alert," Travis said tersely, securing the last line, and hauling Benny into his arms he headed for the ramp. "Come on, sport, bedtime for you."

Abe still wore a hang-dog expression and Travis slowed down long enough to reassure him. "You haven't done anything wrong, Abe," he said. "She'd have seen it for herself, sooner or later. Get started on the cleanup, and I'll be back down to give you a hand soon, okay?"

Susannah grabbed her tote and Benny's sneakers, gave Abe a quick pat of farewell and raced to catch up with Travis's long stride. "What's yellow alert?"

He looked at her, then shrugged and slowed his pace. "The first fires have been spotted," he said, and although he tried to play them down for her sake, she saw the light in his eyes and heard the note of suppressed excitement in his voice. "I'm a working man again."

Chapter Sixteen

He wasn't going to make it easy for her, she realized, and there was no escape in make-believe, after all. Whether she liked it or not, she was involved with this man, and everything that affected him touched her, too. She'd arrived at an emotional milestone, and there was no turning back now.

They had reached the house. While Travis carried Benny upstairs and put him to bed, Susannah fed Floozer then stood by the kitchen table, twisting her wedding ring around her finger and praying for the fortitude to accept what it was too late to change. Once again, she had fallen in love with a man who thrived on danger.

The gold band slipped toward her knuckle and revealed a narrow strip of pale skin which, like her heart, had been well-armored against exposure. She'd continued to wear the ring for protection, as though it would keep her safe from future entanglements, but it hadn't worked. Memories, along with resolve, were wilting under the heat of her feelings for Travis. Deliberately she slid the ring from her finger and placed it on the table.

SHE AND TRAVIS hadn't discussed the future, but he had made it plain enough that he wasn't opposed to the idea of being a father to Benny. All things considered, it was logical to suppose that the question of marriage would arise sooner or later. If he was brave and generous enough to take on another man's child, the least she could do was scrape together the courage and faith to meet him halfway. He deserved better than having to settle for commitment turned lukewarm by caution. And so did she. To have been a wife, and to be a mother, weren't enough. She wanted more, for herself and for Benny, too.

She'd been kidding herself to think she could open her heart to Travis for just one day. Once done, there was no turning back on it. Truth could be denied to the rest of the world, but only a fool lied to herself.

She didn't know Travis was in the kitchen until he came up quietly behind her and locked his arms around her waist. "Tell me what you're thinking," he said.

He felt so good, so strong, that she was terribly tempted again to immerse herself in the here and now, and let tomorrow go hang itself. It was so easy to push away the difficulties when there were two to share the load; so easy to pass the responsibility to broader shoulders. But she knew better than anybody that, ultimately, every person had to build her own strength. Two halves making a whole were good, but two wholes coming together, in love and trust, were better. "I'm scared," she said.

"I know. What can I do?"

She shook her head. What answer could she give that wasn't unrealistic or unreasonable. *I love you, but I'm not willing to entrust my happiness or my son's to a man who puts his life on the line every day?* What sort of love was that?

"I want to be able to accept your work, because it's an extension of you, and I love you," she said, "but I keep thinking…Travis, I don't want to hold dinner for you and have Dan or Charlie show up instead, and tell me you're never coming back. I don't think I could live through that a second time."

Little alarms sounded in the back of his mind. If it came down to a choice between her or his work, he didn't know which way he'd jump. He'd loved flying since he'd found his first model airplane in his stocking at Christmas when he was nine. Flying was all he'd ever really wanted to do well. Now she'd come into his life and turned everything upside down, snaring him forever with her tenderness and courage. If he chose, he could turn in his resignation tomorrow, and there were hundreds of men who could do his job. Somehow that disturbed him less than the idea of some bozo waltzing in to replace him in Susannah's life and usurping his place with her and Ben.

On the other hand, he'd seen enough to know that a relationship stood or fell on the two people involved accepting each other for what they really were, not for what they'd like each other to be. "I'm a good pilot, Susannah," he said quietly, "and this isn't war. I'm not making enemies, and no one's out there gunning for me."

"But accidents happen. What if you crashed, or the chemicals exploded, or you were—"

He spun her around to face him. "What about the danger of self-fulfilling prophecies?" he asked savagely. "I could be a plumber or an accountant and get killed crossing the street. If all you want to see are disaster and death, they're waiting for you at every turn. But I want to live, Susannah, and I set my sights accordingly." His gaze softened, and his hands grew gentle at her waist. "And I could make myself crazy every time you take that rattletrap old bus up the logging roads, wondering if you've run off the edge of the cliff, or been attacked by bears. So I don't allow myself to think that way."

She opened her mouth to defend herself, but he stopped the words with a finger across her lips. "No, let me finish. I take reasonable precautions to ensure my safety and I expect you to do the same. And instead of praying for your daily deliverance from possible death and destruction every time you're out of my sight, I thank God that I found you while we're both still young enough to contemplate a future together."

She leaned her forehead against his chest and felt terribly envious of his confidence and his ability to focus on all that could be good and beautiful between them. "I'm not ready to talk about the future," she said miserably. "I have to deal with the present first. I don't want to be the weak half in a relationship.''

He didn't want her that way, either. Left to fester, her anxiety about the work he loved would generate a mutual guilt that would eat at both of them and come full circle to resentment. And for all the flaws he thought he'd detected in his parents' marriage, the one thing he'd never seen was resentment. They'd accepted each other for what they were. He wanted at least that much for him and Susannah.

"I've got to go and help Abe," he said, knowing that it would take more than verbal reassurances from him to allay her fears and assure her that he wasn't going to fly into the side of a mountain, blinded by smoke and bravado. She'd have to discover for herself what his work really consisted of, and hopefully realize that her fears were miles removed from actuality. "I'll see you later on tomorrow and that's a promise you can count on. Do I get a kiss to sustain me till then?"

"Of course," she said, and wished trust and faith were as easily bestowed.

She offered her lips, but first he kissed her eyelids then her forehead and jawline and cheekbones with scrupulous tenderness, and only after that did he take her mouth in a kiss that was full of promise of wondrous things to come. "I have two burning ambitions," he whispered. "One is to love you for the rest of my life. The other is to live until I'm a hundred. Remember that."

THE TRIP TO MOSES POINT marked the end of lazy days in the sun. By Friday morning a more serious outbreak of fire had been spotted north-east of town. The peaceful calm of morning was broken by the honk of the air horn summoning the pilots to their tankers, and the recurring sound of low-flying aircraft. From then on, the fire fighters were on call seven days a week, from daybreak to sunset.

Susannah tried not to let her entire life revolve around what Travis was doing each day, but it took mammoth discipline and a rigid work schedule of her own to prevent her from making hourly checks on the sun's decline, and waiting for the sound of the Firecats droning safely back to base at the end of the day.

The weather, especially the lack of rain, was the chief topic of conversation around town. In the space of one week, fourteen fires were reported within a two-hundred-and-fifty-mile radius, and there was speculation that the logging camps would soon close down operations for the summer. Tourists, in the area for the salmon fishing, were advised that open fires were banned until conditions improved. The sense of community that had first impressed Susannah was reinforced by the united concern of all the residents to keep the town safe and the immediate area green. Larene and Vi even went so far as to halt their attacks on Judith, though their tongues wagged freely on the topic of the strange inability of tourists to comprehend that cool and wet was preferable to hot and dry when it came to vacation weather.

"Dad-blamed fools," Vi complained, "don't know nothin' about nothin'."

"It's all that pollution," Larene declared sagely. "It rots the brains in city folk."

Despite the ominous threat of fire, somewhere in the orderly passing of the days Susannah's anxiety began to level off, diminished in part by the routine she and Travis established. They saw each other every evening. She would make dinner, and he would stop by Judith's long enough to grab a change of clothes, then head on up to Susannah's.

Sometimes they'd carry the meal up the hill behind the house, and watch the colors in the west fade into dusky purple as the first stars came out. Once, they took a picnic down to the harbor where an off-shore breeze made the heat more bearable, and sat on the edge of a dock with their feet dangling in the water while they ate. Abe often joined them, and one time he brought up a pail of crab that they steamed in wine, then ate with their fingers, throwing the discarded shells into the dried-up garden on the theory that, when they decomposed, they'd make great fertilizer.

They talked about everything: the things they believed in, their memories of childhood, what kinds of things they wanted in the future. They laughed a lot, and discovered new things about each other, and through it all, the love grew stronger, the feelings surer.

But two things remained constant: they never discussed marriage, and it got harder each night for Travis to leave Susannah to sleep alone. It was her choice. Travis had made it perfectly clear that he wasn't prepared to disrupt their new harmony by being the one to bring up the future, nor pressure her into intimacy with Benny no further away than the next room. Any changes would have to come from her.

Susannah started to have erotic dreams, and Travis began to follow Henry's habit of swimming in the frigid ocean on a regular basis, as water rationing prevented him from taking long, cold showers.

The school year wound down to a close. Benny chose forest fires as his last project for the term. Because he was only in grade two, he wasn't expected to do much writing, but he hit on the idea of taping conversations with the pilots and anyone else who could give him information on the subject. He elected himself a kind of roving reporter, and *interviewing* became as integral a part of his vocabulary as *exploring*. Naturally his chief source was Travis, and he abandoned the dock in favor of hanging around the airstrip, waiting for the crew to fly home.

Susannah felt a little sorry for Abe during this time. He'd show up after school, looking for Benny and Floozer, and wander off stoop-shouldered with disappointment when he found that they weren't around. Occasionally he'd sit at the foot of the steps to the deck and sort his fishing gear, just passing time until they came home. If she wasn't too busy, Susannah would take down iced tea or lemonade and visit with him for a little while. Whenever that happened he'd bring a wild flower or a handful of dried grasses, or some other little thing he'd found and leave them outside her door. She laughed to herself when she remembered her reaction the first time he'd done that; it was hard to believe she'd ever been so mistrustful of him.

The night before Benny's project was due to be completed, Travis arrived with a large manila envelope and emptied it on the dining room table. "Here's some more stuff you might be able to use, Ben."

Benny's shriek of glee brought Susannah running out of the kitchen. Scattered over the growing heap of Benny's sketches and diagrams were a dozen or more aerial photographs of the serrated west-coast shoreline with its thousands of islands. There were shots of canopy fires, where only the tops of trees were burning, and candle fires where a single tree stood sheathed in flames. They were spectacular shots, the kind people framed and hung in dens and libraries.

"Who took these?" Susannah asked, impressed.

"I did, except for this one here," he replied offhandedly, and pointed to a five-by-seven color print of the familiar red and white Firecat, with a bright orange cloud streaming from its undercarriage as it flew over a stretch of forest partially obscured by smoke. "That's me doing the flying, and Dan took the picture."

Susannah's heart dropped about six inches, but she struggled to remain calm. "You're on fire!" she said shakily, staring in horror at the photograph.

"Geez, Ma," Benny complained, grabbing it away from her. "That's not fire, that's goop."

"What do you know?" She could hear her voice breaking. "It looks like fire to me."

Travis looped his arms around her and planted a kiss on her nose, his expression so smug a person would've thought he'd hand-raised Benny from the cradle. "The kid's a fast learner," he boasted. "He knows his stuff."

"What's goop? And when did this get taken?" she demanded, sinking against his warm chest and winding her arms around his waist. She'd come a fair distance toward controlling her fears, but the sight of the aircraft, tiny against the vast and burning landscape, set her back some.

"Last year," he murmured, and followed up the first kiss with another.

Benny rolled his eyes. "Goop's the stuff they dump on the fires to make them go out," he informed the room at large. "It's like your spaghetti sauce, Ma."

Susannah straightened up. "Don't be sassy," she reproved him and, noticing Travis's smothered grin, shuffled through the stack of papers Benny had compiled. Laying aside an out-of-scale diagram of the air base, she picked up his latest artistic effort. "Why don't you show Travis this?"

Benny turned pink with pride. "Yeah, I forgot. Look, Trav, it's a picture of you."

Travis took the paper and tried to keep his smile pinned in place as he examined the drawing. Something bearing a close resemblance to E.T. was crammed into a sort of elongated goldfish bowl with fins, and the only thing that distinguished the creature on the paper from the Spielberg original was the bright yellow hair sticking out of the top of its head. To add insult to injury, Floozer had wiped a dirty paw over one corner of the paper as though to indicate what she thought it should be used for.

"That's me?" Travis asked, trying valiantly to maintain his grin which was shrinking visibly. "Holy cow!"

"Maybe you should get a haircut," Susannah sniggered.

His mouth twitched. "Don't *you* be sassy, either, madam."

"I'm not very good at drawing," Benny said matter-of-factly, "but Miss Evans guessed right off that it was you."

"Holy cow," Travis said again, a shade more weakly than before, then examined the drawing more closely. Damn, but it wasn't so bad! Ben was an observant little guy, and he'd included all sorts of things that showed he had a real eye for detail. He might never be a great artist, but he'd make a hell of a good photographer some day. He'd be ready for a camera by the time he was ten—a Kodak, maybe, or better yet, that little SLR Canon that had been sitting in the bottom of a drawer ever since the day Travis had bought his new rig.

Whoa there! he thought. Two years down the road was a fair distance from where they stood now. Any number of things could happen. Then he glanced down at Ben's eager little face, and knew that whatever else changed, Susannah and her child were in his life to stay.

He knelt down and wrapped Ben in a bear hug. "You know something, son? No one's ever drawn a picture of me before. It makes a guy feel kind of special."

The two of them grinned at each other in pure, unabashed affection. Susannah swallowed, blinked to clear the mist from her eyes and seriously doubted she'd ever loved a man this much before. Son, he'd said. Not Ben, or kid, or sport, but *son*.

THE NEXT EVENING, Travis didn't show up. Susannah had made almond chicken with orange sauce and tried to keep it warm in the oven, but by the time nine o'clock rolled around, the poultry looked more like a fibrous hen that had managed to escape the hatchet in its youth and, many years later, finally keeled over from old age.

She pulled it out of the oven, wrapped it in foil and kept a tight rein on her imagination. Travis had warned her this might happen, and that all the crew kept packed suitcases in their airplanes for just such an eventuality. Still and all, when Fred Hughes, the dispatcher, arrived on her doorstep, a sense of déjà vu overtook her. Her heart lurched, and every ugly possibility that memory and imagination could conjure up to push a person to the brink of despair crowded to the forefront of her mind.

Chapter Seventeen

"Where is he?" she asked in a whisper that sounded as thin and frail as dried leaves. Her heart was lodged so tightly in her throat that it was all she could do to speak at all.

"There's been a fire in the Fairbanks zone, Susannah, and one of our aircraft has been sent up there until things are under control. It was Travis's turn, I'm afraid, and the odds are he won't be back for a few days."

She practically sagged with relief. "Oh," she said. Her heart returned to where it belonged but was still galloping like a race horse. "That's okay. If he knew what he was missing, he'd be glad he wasn't here."

Fred seemed a bit taken aback at that. "He didn't give me that impression when he heard he'd been dispatched out of the area. In fact, he stated his objections in rather colorful language."

"My mom's a real wazoo sometimes," Benny explained helpfully. "She burned the chicken, and she was going to blame it on Travis. She did the same thing with a rhubarb pie once, and it was all his fault then, too."

IT WAS FOUR DAYS before Travis came back, which was enough time for Susannah to complete the last chapter of her textbook and to arrive at some rather disturbing conclusions. It was one thing to be in love with a man, but another thing entirely to discover that he'd woven himself so thoroughly into the tapestry of her life that there were permanent gaps left when he was gone.

On top of that, Benny missed him and harped on about him the whole four days. It was "Travis this," and "Travis that," every other breath. His end of term report card and his project, marked with a big red A, were left out where Travis couldn't fail to notice them. A snapshot of Travis, standing beside his Firecat and squinting into the sun, was pinned to the wall by Benny's bed.

Belatedly Susannah realized that the decision of whether or not she dared entrust her child's happiness to this man had been taken out of her hands. Benny had chosen in its favor without asking her opinion.

The Kellys were the only people in town with a video machine, and every time Bob went into the city, he brought back a couple of movies. On the evening of the fourth day of Travis's absence, Benny and Abe were invited to go down to the hotel to watch the latest Superman movie. Susannah had made an early dinner and planned to catch up on her correspondence while she had the chance, but within ten minutes of leaving, Benny was back at the house, yelling that Travis's Firecat had just landed. "He's home!" he beamed.

"Did you actually see him, or just his plane?" All Firecats looked the same to her, and there was more than one stationed at the base. She didn't want to get her hopes up then be disappointed.

"Oh, Ma," Benny replied condescendingly, "you mean aircraft. Real pilots never say plane. Everybody knows that."

"Never mind the technicalities," she replied a trifle testily. "Just answer the question."

"I saw him."

Oh grief, she thought, dizzy with happiness. She'd taken a shower and shampooed her hair earlier, but did she have time to fix her nails before he arrived on her doorstep?

"He was filing his report and then he had to talk to Steve about getting the Firecat serviced," Benny went on blithely. "Dan says that sort of thing is a real pain in the butt when you've got a heavy date, but it's part of the job."

Her child was a regular little mine of information and profanity lately, Susannah thought, bringing a reproving glare to bear on his cheerful little face. He'd be spending less time at the air base if this was the sort of thing he was learning. Her mother's hair would turn blue if she heard her precious grandson uttering such vulgarities. "That is not a term we use in polite society," she said severely.

"Travis says it all the time," Benny argued. "And he says—"

"Hi, too, and what does a guy have to do around here to get a proper welcome home?"

She spun around, and there he was in the doorway, beeper clipped to his belt, at the beck and call of danger whenever or wherever it arose, and she didn't care. He was there, and he was alive, and that's all she'd asked for.

"You're home!" she breathed, her mouth curving into a smile. She loved the color of him, tones of gold on gold except for his forget-me-not eyes which rested on her face with driving hunger. She loved him and was helpless to do anything about it. He was not Mel. He didn't pretend or try to be, yet she loved him in ways she hadn't known about when she'd been married to Mel.

His eyes never left her face. "Ben," he said, "I passed by the hotel on my way up, and Bob's wondering what's keeping you."

"Oh, wow, the movie!" Benny clapped a hand to his head and started off at a run. "Gotta go, you guys. See ya."

At first they didn't move or say anything to disturb the silence he'd left behind. Then Travis stepped right into the room and carefully pulled the drapes across the glass doors. "Come here," he said, his voice edged with that same sandpaper roughness that she'd heard so often lately.

There was intent in his gaze and a hunger that wasn't going to be appeased by kisses. She knew that if she went to him now, she'd wake up tomorrow with a part of her bound to him for the rest of her life. The choice lay with her.

She moved toward him, transfixed by his loose-limbed grace, lured by the desire in his eyes, driven by a need that left her weak and aching, the need to reassure herself that he was here. He scooped her into his arms and she ran her hands up his chest and into his hair, tugging him down until he tasted her lips, all sweet and giving.

"I have...missed you..." he whispered in heartfelt tones, between kisses that rediscovered every feature of her face. "I don't ever...want to be away from you...like that again."

She could feel the full-fledged urgency of him against her, at odds with the exquisite delicacy of his kisses, and wished he'd forget that she'd once been too frail and unready. But he was leaving the choice up to her, the way he always would.

Her fingers found the buttons on his shirt, slipped one free, and then another. She touched his warm, smooth skin wonderingly, and knew exactly when the tempo of the heart beneath it shifted to a faster rhythm. He tore his mouth free and buried his face in her hair. "Careful," he muttered.

But she'd been careful long enough. Fantasies of a perfect future were for children and she was a woman, ready to focus on the reality of today. "No," she said, and loosened the rest of the buttons until his shirt hung loose except where it was caught in the belt at his waist. Impatient as much with his restraint as her own timidity, she pulled it free. "I love you," she said and swept her mouth over the solid planes of his chest. He smelled of soap and aftershave, tasted of lemons and sunshine.

His question emerged taut with desire. "Enough?"

She met his gaze, and what she saw there took her breath away. "Enough," she whispered.

He reached back, slid the glass door shut and clicked the lock in place.

The bedroom was full of dusk, washing the plain white walls with tones of muted lilac. Outdoors, the air hung quiet and still; within, the sound of her breathing, light and rapid, underscored the tattoo of his heart as it labored to contain itself.

He had desired her for weeks, but nothing had prepared him for the onslaught of passion that gripped him now. She was a contradiction of everything he thought he knew about women, the trust of a child and the innocence of a girl overlaid with a power and knowledge inherited from Eve.

They undressed each other haphazardly, his attention trapped by glimpses of flesh beneath scraps of silk and lace, hers skimming the length of him before her lashes fluttered down to shield her eyes from the evidence of the havoc she was wreaking with her feather-light caresses.

He could not believe how lovely he found her. Her skin was like satin, like velvet, like ivory; like all of those things, and like none of them. Luminous as moonlight, cool as marble—and more, and better. She had curves that were full of promise, hollows that beckoned, slender arcs that led to deep and secret enclaves of the flesh. They left him blind with desire and burningly conscious of a tight, expectant arousal that begged for release.

He sought out parts of her she'd forgotten existed, his every touch inviting little spasms of ecstasy. She tried to preserve each moment in memory against the time when he'd be gone again, but the tide of passion ran too swiftly between them, and all she could do was cling to him, and not care if she drowned, as long as he was with her.

Time slowed to a crawl, the seconds strung out like pearls, each one perfect, priceless, matchless. His fingertips touched her throat, then slid from the shadowed triangle of her collar bone, lured by the gentle slope of her breast. He leaned forward to rest his mouth against her neck where her pulse beat savagely, his hand shaping the curve of her hip and holding her against him in shattering temptation.

Heat rushed through her, searching for an outlet and pooling heavily between her thighs. If the whole town burst through the door at that moment, she didn't think she'd care. Consciousness narrowed until it focused on nothing but the tiny, pulsing eternity of space that prevented her from becoming joined with him.

When she could bear it no longer, and she was swaying and uttering urgent little pleas, they fell together onto the bed.

Battered by a passion like nothing he'd every known and bewildered by the tearing loneliness of being away from her, he sank into her as though, with his heart already so unalterably hers, he sought to lose the rest of him in her dark and complete possession.

That was when she froze, uncertain not of him but of herself. Shedding her clothes had revealed more than just her body. Travis seemed so comfortable with himself, with the situation; so utterly graceful and secure. Fear that he'd find her clumsy and inept fractured her thoughts. She'd been alone too long, been misled too often, to trust either of them enough to take the pleasure he was so willing to bestow.

Those books written by men, they said every woman should.... She never had...she hadn't known, back then, that she was entitled.... It had never occurred to her to demand anything, only to accept the homage of an adoring husband.

She closed her eyes and cooperated, wanting the closeness to last and waiting for it to be over both at the same time. Most of all, she didn't want him to be disappointed.

But he wouldn't let her get away with that, any more than he'd let her leave all the decisions up to him. He murmured little words of love in her ear, his tongue swirling over the lobe. His hands beseeched her, promising immortality if only she would leap the final hurdle.

"I can't," she sighed, breathless.

He urged and cajoled and would not relinquish the goal. "You can," he whispered against her mouth.

And when she allowed herself to shed the inhibitions that had confined her passions, he met her and raced with her beyond the farthest horizons, past the ultimate ecstasy of two mortals in union to a single, perfect place she'd never known before.

Travis stirred and looked down at her, his eyes heavy with spent passion. "If this is what loving is all about, my Susannah," he said, pulling the sheet over them against the creeping chill of night, "then don't you think we should get married?"

She had been lying there, reliving the wonder of their lovemaking and permitting herself the dangerous indulgence of living for the moment without any thought for tomorrow. When he spoke, she closed her eyes, abruptly shutting him and the question out.

He felt her withdrawal and tried to hide his dismay in a feeble attempt at humor. "Before you turn me down," he said, catching her hand and holding it against his chest, "bear in mind what I said the other week at Moses Point— I don't do things because I feel I have to. You can safely assume any proposal I make is motivated by desire, not duty."

There it was, the safety net she'd vowed never again to depend on, spread out for the taking. It would be so easy to leap into it and never mind if it was full of holes and weak spots. She could almost hate him for offering it when her resistance was at its lowest.

"I don't think it would work," she said.

"Why not?"

"We have different priorities. With you, your work comes first, and with me, it's Benny."

He shook his head at that. "First of all my work doesn't exactly come first. I admit flying's been my first love until now, but there's room at the top for you, Susannah, if that's where you want to be. I think," he said carefully, aware that he was on dangerous ground, "that a man and woman have to put their marriage first, if it's to stand a chance."

"Where does that leave Benny?" she asked, staring out of the window at the stars.

"In the middle, between a mother and a father, which is where he really belongs."

"He's managed without a father for a long time now. We've had to learn to make do with just each other."

"And you think that's enough?"

She turned her head on the pillow and looked at him. "It's not perfect," she said, "but it's better than having to cope with losing you. What if you die? What if you find that marriage with a ready-made family isn't what you thought it would be?"

He turned on his side and propped his head on one hand. "Let's not confuse the issues here," he said grimly. "We're not talking about me getting killed or walking out on my commitment. I'm not a complete fool, Susannah. I've got fourteen nieces and nephews and one more on the way. I know what kids are like, and I'm not ashamed to admit that there was a time when I thought having my sisters' pack of rug rats around was enough to satisfy my domestic urges."

"That's different," she pointed out. "When you've had enough of them, you can send them home. Benny's not going anywhere without me."

"And how long do you expect that to continue?" he asked, running a finger down her cheek. "You're kidding yourself if you think you're all he needs. He's got his own life to live and although he'll always love you, you're not going to stay number one in his life very much longer, whether you marry me or not."

As if she didn't know! "He's only a baby," she said feebly.

"He'll always be your baby, your Benny, long after he starts shaving and everyone but his mama calls him Ben."

"It'll be another fifteen years before he's ready to shave!"

"And how old before he's allowed to date?" Travis wondered aloud. "Forty-six, perhaps?"

She giggled weakly. "Sounds good to me. He could get married when he's fifty—to someone still young enough to bear him sons."

Travis broke out into laughter that was not entirely kind. "In that case, don't hold me to my proposal, my darling. I'm not sure I can promise to be patient that long."

Her giggles died into the night. "The fact of the matter is, you can't really promise me anything with any certainty."

"I love you. Doesn't that amount to something you can count on?"

"It isn't enough."

He tossed back the sheet and started climbing into his clothes. "Funny," he sighed tiredly, "I'd've said it was the most important thing, and all the rest didn't amount to a row of beans without it."

"They don't," she said. "I just don't think I'm ready for 'all the rest.' Not yet."

"What does that mean? That you don't love me, after all?"

"Oh, I love you," she sighed.

He came back and sat beside her. "Well then, what's the problem, sweetheart? What did I say or do to turn this lovely evening into such a disaster?"

"Loving you isn't all there is to think about. I have to know that I can live with the consequences of those feelings before I can think about marriage."

"And how do you propose to do that?"

"I guess I just need more time," she said miserably, because she didn't know how long she could ask him to be patient or how long it would take. "I came too close to the edge of despair when Mel died, and the only thing that kept me going was knowing that Benny needed me. What if something happened to you? I owe it to myself to be sure I can cope with that possibility, and I owe it to Benny, too. He might not need me forever, but he's still just a little boy and you have to know how important you are to him. I need to know I'm strong enough for both of us, if I have to be."

She was asking for guarantees that no man could offer. She wanted perfection in a world that she already knew was often ugly and cruel, and she seemed willing to relegate the love they shared to some indefinite back burner. How long could he stand it?

Chapter Eighteen

July came in hot and oppressive. The leaves on the alders hung listless with dust, and when lightning strikes caused a rash of fires to break out within thirty miles of town, logging operations closed down until the weather changed.

"Wonderful," her mother crowed, when Susannah braved the local eavesdroppers once again to call her folks. "If they don't need you up there, you can come home for the summer. Seattle's a much nicer place to be."

That was an unbridled fib if ever she'd heard one, Susannah thought. The entire West Coast, from the tip of the panhandle down to southern California, was parching in the drought. No city was pleasant in that sort of heat, and even if it were, she wouldn't have left Cameron's Landing now, with the town on red alert and Travis on call around the clock. Every day that she survived his leaving in the morning and coming safely home in the evening pushed her a little closer to being able to live with his work on a permanent basis. And nothing would induce her to forsake the few precious hours that they were able to steal alone together.

"I couldn't do that, Mother. I'm being paid to be here."

"But if they've laid you off, dear . . . ? Oh, I see. It's the pilot that's keeping you there, isn't it?"

"Among other things," Susannah admitted, turning her back on Vi's gappy grin which blossomed over the top of the ten pound sack of flour she was toting to the counter.

"Is this getting serious, Susannah?" her mother persisted.

"Yes, but we're safe enough," she replied, deliberately misconstruing the question without much hope of fooling her mother or Vi.

"I meant you and Travis," Lois said, as Vi emitted a malicious little cackle, "not the forest fires."

"He's a pilot, Mother," Susannah replied evasively.

"Well at least he's not out of work. Think about that."

She thought about it all the time. He was a good pilot and he loved what he did. She could never ask him to settle for what he'd once scathingly referred to as "flying a desk." It would be as cruel as trying to cage one of Abe's beloved bald eagles.

"No one's out of work up here," she said. "Every able-bodied man has been recruited to patrol the logging roads and run supplies, or relieve the men in the look-out towers so that someone's on the job around the clock."

In fact it was a bit like a town at war, with the women taking over in town while the men were out fighting the common enemy that was just over the next ridge and threatening to destroy their homes and way of life if it wasn't stopped. The only difference was that most of the troops came home at least every two days, and there hadn't been any casualties to date.

For safety's sake Susannah had had to curtail some of Benny's activities. With the end of school, he was free all day, and now that he could spend all his time there, the dock had lost some of its appeal. The air base was off limits, personnel there too busy to have time for a seven-year-old underfoot.

"Why can't I explore up the mountain?" he complained to Susannah, impatient to discover wider horizons and irritable with the heat. "There's paths up there under the trees. I saw them."

"Because," she explained patiently, "if you should get lost, there just aren't enough people to go looking for you."

"I won't get lost. I'm not a baby."

He was right on that score. He'd be eight in another few days and was a changed person from the homesick little boy he'd been when they'd first arrived in town. He was independent almost to a fault. For the first time, she recognized one of the drawbacks of such an isolated existence. This was where parks and day camps would be a help and there weren't any of either in Cameron's Landing.

The final straw came when Travis, who'd promised to take Benny and Abe on an overnight fishing trip to a nearby lake, had to postpone the whole idea. "Sorry, son," he said. "It just can't be done right now."

"You promised," Benny scowled. "You're not supposed to break your promise."

Travis looked unhappy. "I know that, but you know I'm on Code 2, and you know what that means."

The beeper codes had fascinated Benny at first, but like everything else that denoted restriction, they'd soon lost their charm. "You've got to be able to get to the base and be ready to go within ten minutes," he muttered, unappeased, "but what about my birthday treat?"

"There's no way I'd forget your birthday, and I'm not trying to weasel out of taking you and Abe fishing. We just have to put it off for a while, that's all. You know what it means, if I'm not there to do my job."

They'd talked about that at length, weeks ago. Fire wasn't something that Benny had devoted much thought to before meeting Travis, but Travis's account of what happened to animals trapped in a blazing forest, coupled with Abe's distress at their plight, had brought the lesson home to Benny in a very real way.

Travis reminded him of that, now. "Think how you'd feel if Floozer got caught in a fire, and I wasn't there to put it out and save her."

Floozer was the dearest thing on earth to Benny. She followed him everywhere, but she loved all of them and was never happier than when her whole family, including Travis and Abe, were gathered in one place where she could keep a proper eye on them.

"I don't want anything to happen to Floozer," Benny muttered, and Susannah made the mistake of thinking he'd accepted the situation and would make the best of it.

She was down at the store the next day when Alan Hamilton came running to find her. "You'd better get to the airfield quick, Susannah. That dog of yours is running wild on the tarmac and raising merry hell with take-offs and landings."

They left the store at a run. "I thought she was with Benny," Susannah panted, her T-shirt sticking to her from the heat.

"Not according to the dispatcher. It looks as if the dog was tied up and broken loose, but Benny's nowhere around."

By the time they arrived at the base, Travis had caught Floozer and shut her up in the office. Her howls soared above the roar of the Firecats' engines as the three aircraft stood in line, ready for reloading prior to receiving clearance for take-off.

"Where's Ben?" Travis yelled, ducking down and running over to her. "That bloody dog's got no business running loose here. She's going to get herself killed."

Susannah shook her head helplessly. "I don't know. He said he was going fishing."

Travis wiped the sweat from his forehead and shook his head. "Something's up," he said. "There's no way Floozer would be here if Ben was where he said he'd be, doing what he said he'd be doing. I don't like this."

Neither did she. "Travis, I'm worried. Benny's been pretty hard to handle this past week, really resentful that he can't just come and go as he pleases. Do you think he's run away or something?"

"Of course not. Where would he go?"

Dan Ryder signaled, pointing both hands toward the waiting aircraft. "Susannah," Travis said, planting a swift, hard kiss on her mouth, "I'm sorry but I've got to go. There's trouble along the south-east sector. We've radioed for reinforcements from below the border, but until they get here, we're needed in the air. We can't do any good down here.''

"Go," she said. "I understand."

He'd been intolerably hurt and frightened by her strength the night she'd turned down his marriage proposal. He'd felt that he'd offered her the best he had to give and that it hadn't been enough. Now he welcomed her stamina, even as he cursed his inability to take all her worries on himself and spare her. "I hate leaving you. I'm worried about Ben, too."

His eyes were ringed with fatigue, his mouth bracketed with lines of tension and anxiety. He'd been in the air since five that morning and it had been weeks since he'd been able to sleep late or take a day off. Over to the east, the sky was filmed with gray smoke, and the sun had a peculiar copper haze around it.

He was being pulled in two opposing directions with very little real choice about which way he had to go. She cupped his jaw in both hands, smoothing her fingertips over the roughness of overnight beard, and knew this was one time when she couldn't burden him with her own problems, no matter how pressing they might be. She didn't want him distracted by worry about Benny or Floozer or anything else that might make him careless of his own safety. She was going to have to deal with this alone. "I'll handle it," she said. "Don't worry about us."

He covered her hands with his. "How can I not?" he asked. "I love you."

"Hey, Travis!" Steve Walinsky came racing over. "Look, man, either load up or move that heap out of the way so someone else can."

Travis flung her one last apologetic look, then turned and ran to the waiting Firecat. Filler hoses were clamped to the coupler on the right side of the aircraft, and there was a rushing gurgle as over seven hundred gallons of chemical retardant poured into the four storage compartments. Halfway through loading, the fuselage sagged with a distinct thump, then settled lower to the ground.

"Oh, God!" Susannah whispered, clutching Steve by the arm and digging in her nails.

"It's okay," he said, unpeeling her fingers and examining the dents in his skin. "That's just the goop filling the tanks. The chemicals are mixed with clay or mud to give them weight. It's easier to make an accurate drop that way."

Within seconds, Travis had taxied the Firecat down the tarmac and was airborne. Susannah shaded her eyes and watched him bank to the south then skim over the trees and out of sight.

Someone brought Floozer to her, a length of rope attached to her collar. Susannah sank to her knees and wrapped her arms around the big black neck. "Floozer," she whispered, face to face with her fears for Benny and with nothing to distract her any longer, "why aren't you and Benny fishing down on the dock?"

Floozer leaned against her and licked her hand, then turned back to the airstrip and whined. "He's not there," Susannah said, tugging on the rope, and she decided to start her search at the harbor and work backward from there. Maybe Benny had gone home with Abe, which would explain why Floozer was running wild around town. Judith was not one of her fans. On the other hand, Abe didn't spend much time around home and Benny wouldn't be at the boarding house without him.

Floozer remained where she was. She sat down, planted her paws in front of her, braced herself and refused to budge. "Come *on*, Flooze," Susannah begged, knowing that only a very slim margin of control separated her from unhindered panic. "Find Benny, okay?"

Those were words that had meaning for the dog. Susannah uttered them every school day at three o'clock in the afternoon. They were the signal that sent Floozer racing down the steps from the deck and along the path to the road that wound down to town. This time, they had quite a different effect.

Floozer leaped to her feet and galloped determinedly back toward the airstrip, dragging Susannah willy-nilly on the other end of the rope.

"Damn it, Susannah," Steve yelled from the loading bay, "will you get that animal out of here? The airplanes will be back in fifteen minutes for refill, and we've wasted enough time already chasing after her."

"We're looking for Benny," Susannah shouted back furiously, in no mood to be harassed. If the man had two neurons to rub together, he must realize sprinting up and down a landing strip was scarcely any sane person's idea of a pleasant way to pass the morning.

"Well, he obviously isn't here."

Floozer came to a precipitate halt and sat down on Susannah's foot, anchoring her firmly in place. Her big black nose, activated by some ancient ancestral hunting instinct, twitched in the direction of the loading bay.

Like a bolt out of the blue, enlightenment struck Susannah. Benny wasn't here now, but he had been, and that's what the dog was trying to tell her. "Where is he, Floozer?"

Floozer shifted her expectant gaze from the empty tarmac to the equally empty sky.

"Oh, my sainted aunts!" Susannah blanched, suddenly recalling a conversation she'd had with Benny before the end of the school term. They'd been discussing his project.

"I oughta go for a ride with the guys," he'd decided. "It'd make things realer, Mom. Then I could make a recording of what it's like and play it for the class. Don't you think that'd be neat?"

"No," she'd said, squelching the idea without mincing words. She had enough on her plate learning to accept Travis's addiction to flying, without having her son catch the bug, too.

Benny had appeared to accept her decision at the time, but that was before he'd become mad at the whole world. In his present frame of mind, it made sense that he'd rebel, and lying about going fishing when he had some other plan to explore, followed his old pattern of behavior when confronted by restrictions he didn't want to accept.

"I know where Benny is," she told Steve. "He's gone with Travis."

"Lady, you've got to be kidding! Travis wouldn't take a kid up there in these conditions."

A cold lump of fear rose in her throat. "Why not? Is it more dangerous today than it was yesterday?"

"That's not what I mean. But you've got to understand, those guys aren't up there worrying about giving passengers a smooth ride. They race for the target, dump their load and get out of there as fast as they can. They're not conducting guided tours."

"But he'd know by now that Benny's with him, and he'd . . . make allowances, wouldn't he? Maybe?"

Steve shook his head. "Not a chance. If Ben's there, he's stowed away in the rear compartment, and let me tell you, it's a far cry from first class. He's going to be one sore and airsick little kid when he gets home."

Sore in more places than one, Susannah vowed. She'd be plucking gray hairs out of her head for the next month after this.

The BDO Aerostar was the first airplane back. Chef Loomis climbed down from the cockpit with Charlie Ayres and headed for the trailer that served as office and coffee shop. When Steve told them what Susannah suspected, they came over to her shaking their heads in disbelief.

"Are you sure?" Charlie asked her.

"Not exactly, but I think so," she said. "It's the only explanation that makes sense."

The men looked at each other, appalled. "Not to us, it doesn't," Chef said. "And it won't to him by now, either."

Travis flew in directly after Dan, with Jamie the rookie coming in close behind. The Firecats screamed to the end of the tarmac, slowed for the turn, then taxied to the loading bay. Before Dan had come to a complete stop, Steve and the Bird Dog crew were running out, with Susannah and Floozer at their heels.

"Keep your head low," Chef yelled, falling back beside her and shoving her down until she was running bent almost double. Floozer stayed close, her ears flattened to her head, hating the noise of the engines.

Travis taxied up behind Dan and immediately opened the door to the cockpit to lower his ladder over the side. "What's happened?" he shouted, coming down the rungs three at a time. His face was gray with fear.

"Susannah thinks the boy's with you," Charlie yelled back.

Travis turned a despairing look on her. "He isn't, sweetheart."

But Floozer knew better. Whining, she nosed up to the belly of the aircraft to where a small retractable panel was set near the tail.

Curious about the commotion below, Dan had come down from his aircraft in time to hear the end of the conversation. "Want to lay money on it, mate?"

Travis cursed, and squatted down so that he could push the panel up into the body of the fuselage. Benny came tumbling out, pea green and bawling. He had been very ill, and was terrified and humiliated.

He made a beeline for Susannah, but Travis caught him by the collar. He was absolutely livid. "If you *ever* pull a stunt like this again, you little devil," he promised with a certainty that stopped Benny in mid-howl, "I'll shake you till your head spins."

Benny believed him.

THAT EVENING, Judith came up to the house. "I heard what happened to Benny," she exclaimed. "Heavens, Susannah, you must have been frantic."

Benny sat in the corner of the couch and tried to look tiny. He'd gone from being humiliated and airsick to being extremely embarrassed, something he'd decided to hide under a rather unattractive show of belligerence. Floozer lay on the floor at his feet, eyes open a crack to make sure he didn't pull another disappearing act.

Susannah hoped Judith wouldn't make the mistake of mussing up Benny's hair. Floozer wouldn't bite, but Benny just might, in the mood he was in. "I think it's safe to say no one had fun," she said dryly, pouring iced tea. "Did Abe come with you?"

"No, he's sulking, too," Judith replied airily, accepting the glass. "Apparently he and this young man here had plans to go crabbing this morning."

"Well, that's something that'll have to wait a couple of days. Benny's grounded and he won't be going anywhere without me, which means the high spot of his socializing for the next little while will be trips to the store for groceries. Tell Abe I'm sorry."

Travis arrived just as they were finishing their iced tea. Judith immediately stood up to leave. "I'm sure you'd rather be alone," she said, smiling. "I'll see myself out."

After she'd gone, Travis approached Benny, and Susannah pretended to be busy in the kitchen so that they could have some privacy. In reality, she hid behind the corner and listened unashamedly.

"You know, son," Travis began, "I don't enjoy having to come down hard on you the way I did this morning."

"You don't like me anymore," Benny muttered.

"If I didn't like you a whole lot, I wouldn't give a hoot what you did."

"You don't have to give a hoot. You're not my dad."

On the other side of the wall, Susannah clapped a hand over her mouth and closed her eyes in dread. Here it came, the big confrontation she'd feared, and it was shaping up to be a doozie.

"No, I'm not your dad, but that doesn't make me love you any the less. And I sort of hoped you might let me stand in, in your dad's place, since he's not around to look out for you or your mom. I guess I thought we got along so well, it was something you'd want, too."

"If you really liked me," Benny whined pathetically, "you wouldn't've yelled at me that way. Mom never yells at me when I throw up like that."

"I was worried about you, and scared that you'd been hurt or lost."

Benny chewed on that for a while. "Dad's aren't supposed to get scared," he accused in a slightly mollified tone. "They're supposed to be brave."

"Sometimes it's smart to be a little afraid. That way, you learn to be careful, too."

Susannah leaned her head against the wall, caught between the knowledge that if only Mel had understood that, he'd be alive today, and the realization that if he were, she wouldn't be here now with Travis.

"I guess," Benny said in a more conversational tone, "that's how come you're the best pilot in the whole wide world."

"I try to be, Ben, just like I'd try to be the best dad in the whole wide world, if you'd let me."

"I guess that'd be okay," Benny conceded.

"It might mean I'd get mad with you sometimes," Travis warned.

"I guess that'd be okay, too," Benny agreed magnanimously, "but only if I did dumb things, right?"

"If you did things that made your mom or me worry. Like not being where you say you'll be, or breaking the rules."

"And if I did," Benny said with relish, "I'd be picking birdshot out of my bum for a week, right?"

Travis gave a snort of laughter. "You can count on it, kiddo. Are we pals again, or what?"

"Yeah," Benny said. "Do I have to call you Dad?"

"Why don't we just stick to Travis for now, and you think about it for a while."

The weasel! Susannah thought indignantly, feeling the matrimonial net tightening around her with tender and alluring strength whether she was ready for it or not. Since when was a proposal a three-way decision?

Since one of the parties comes with a child by a previous marriage, a little voice inside her piped up. *Count your blessings, woman. You could've fallen for a man who*

*took one look at Benny and hot-footed it in the other
direction.*

THE NEXT AFTERNOON, another fire broke out in Susannah's back garden, this one near the old toolshed. She and
Benny were at the store picking up ice cream and milk
when Abe came rushing down the hill to raise the alarm.

Henry happened to be in town that day, and so was Tony
Hamilton. The two of them raced back to the house with
gunny sacks and a hose, while Larene ran out into the road
and fired a shotgun in the air three times, which was the
signal to alert every other able-bodied person within hearing that a fire in town had been reported.

By the time Susannah and The Crones arrived at the
house, the fire was more or less out, though the shed walls
were pretty badly scorched.

"Girlie," Henry scolded, wiping eyes that were teary
from smoke, "you got to be a durn sight more careful
what you do with them weeds you been raking up. You just
can't go burning till this here weather breaks."

"I didn't," Susannah protested, mystified and mortified. "I haven't burned anything since the last time I . . ."

"Set fire to your yard," Henry finished for her. "That's
what I mean, Susannah. You got to be more careful."

Vi hoisted up her skirt and tramped over to the steaming heap of weeds. "Listen to what the gal's saying, y'old
fool," she snapped. "She didn't start no fire, and it didn't
start itself. T'ain't reasonable to say it did."

Larene threw in her two bits' worth at that "Sure and
Vi's right," she wheezed, inspecting the charred walls of
the shed. "A body knows better than to be lighting
matches this close to a building, and you'd be realizing it
for yourself, Henry Turner, if all that cold water you're so
fond of swimming around in hadn't turned you soft in the
head."

Henry shoved back his baseball cap and scratched his
bald spot. "Reckon you're right at that," he agreed.

"Sure and when is it that you've ever known us to be
wrong?" Larene inquired loftily.

Henry muttered to himself and poked around among the weeds. "It don't take much...a bit of broken glass that you might not even notice could do it, or a pile of wet sawdust. Spontaneous combustion, you know." He peered at her. "You got anything like that lying around the place, girlie?"

Susannah shook her head. "Not that I'm aware of, but I've never spent much time in the shed. It's full of spiderwebs. Benny plays in there sometimes, though."

"Then I reckon you got some questions for the little whippersnapper," Vi declared. "Seems like he mighta been playin' with matches."

Susannah hated to admit it, but Vi might be right. "I'll go see what I can find out," she said, and went looking for him.

He and Floozer had run back to the house with her. She remembered that quite distinctly, because she'd grabbed hold of Benny to stop him from getting in the way of the hose Tony had been wielding with such amazing accuracy. But that had been a good fifteen minutes earlier. Now, Benny was nowhere to be found, and neither was Floozer.

Chapter Nineteen

Dusk was a long time arriving. By the time the Firecats flew in for the last time after sunset, Benny was still missing, and Susannah was verging on hysteria.

"Sweetheart, I came as soon as I heard," Travis said, holding her hard against him. He hadn't seen that dazed and terrified look on her face since the day she'd first met Abe, and it struck arrows of fear into his own heart now. "Tell me what happened."

Larene and Vi had taken her to their collective bosom and stayed with her, forcing her to swallow half a sandwich and several cups of strong coffee. "It don't make no sense," Vi maintained, mixing up the potato salad she'd concocted. "Henry and Tony looked everyplace they could think of, and the boy plain ain't around town."

"At first we thought he might have started the fire by accident and hid because he knew he'd be in trouble. But he couldn't have been the one. He was with me when the fire broke out." Susannah shivered with eloquent terror. "He's just disappeared into thin air, Travis."

"Hush, darling," he murmured. "He can't be far away."

"Here's the menfolk now, and Marg," Vi said, peering out of the kitchen window. "Henry's rounded up a posse, looks like. Don't you fret, Susannie, we'll find your boy afore it gets dark."

"Keep her here while I deal with this," Travis muttered to Vi, passing Susannah to Larene who enfolded her in a motherly embrace and crooned softly to her.

He was worried. The fires were creeping ominously close to town, and if Ben hadn't been found after all this time, the odds were, for whatever reason, that he'd headed east, right into danger.

Out on the deck, the men waited for him to take charge. "I don't like this," he said quietly.

Henry acted as a spokesman for the group. "Neither do we. The whole thing's a mystery, Travis, starting with that fire. We can't figure out how the thing got a hold so fast."

"If someone deliberately set it, that would explain it," Travis said, and could have cut out his tongue when Susannah uttered a choking little cry behind him.

"Are you saying it was arson?" she whispered. "Who would do such a thing? Who would try to burn down my shed, and then take my little boy? Travis, what have I done to make someone hate me enough for that?"

"Larene!" Travis shouted, his own fears erupting in annoyance. "I thought I told you to keep her inside."

Larene hovered behind Susannah, for the first time in her life uncertain what to do. "Sure and it's her boy that's gone missing, Travis O'Connor. Don't be asking her to sit inside and darn socks while other people take up the cause on her behalf."

He was a man used to dealing with crises, and experience told him Susannah's panic was spreading to the rest of the group and gaining momentum. A lost child might not create a ripple in Seattle, but in a town this size it touched the lives of every last resident. "Let's not waste valuable time arguing," he said calmly. "There's not much daylight left. Susannah, sweetheart, have you talked to Abe at all?"

She shook her head, still bewildered by the return of a nightmare she'd always believed too horrible to strike the same victim twice in a lifetime. "He hasn't been around."

"He was the one what found the fire," Vi recalled, wiping her hands on her apron and shoving her way past the crowd gathering around Travis, "but we ain't seen hide nor hair of him since."

"Well, he'd be the logical place to start asking questions. Let's go find him."

"He's not on the dock," Tony Hamilton said. "No one's down there but a couple of tourists cleaning fish."

"Maybe he's at home." Travis cast a worried glance at the sky. To the west it was still rosy, but overhead the stars were beginning to peak through. "We'll check there first."

Judith was understandably surprised to see almost the entire town congregated outside when Travis burst through the front door. "Abe?" she echoed in response to his question and shook her head. "I haven't seen him since earlier this afternoon. Why? What's he done now?"

"Nothing that we know of," Travis hastened to explain. "We just hoped he might know where Ben is."

Judith's eyes flew to Susannah, wide with shock. "He's missing?" she breathed. "Oh, God, Susannah, when? Why didn't you send for me?"

"Where do you think Abe might be, Judith?" Travis asked brusquely, conscious of losing the race against nightfall with every passing minute.

"Usually he's home by now, but he's been acting strange lately." She lifted her hands, palms up, perplexed. "I don't know what's got into him. He's usually so docile, but he's been—I don't know, furtive, I guess. More than usual, that is. I caught him stealing food, for heaven's sake, and going through drawers! I scolded him about it, so he's been keeping clear of me ever since. He just goes up to his room when he comes home and doesn't even bother to say goodnight."

Vi made a rude noise, but Travis overrode her intended outburst as a possibility occurred to him. "So he could be up there now, and for all we know, Ben could be with him. Do you mind if we check?"

Judith waved him toward the stairs. "You know you don't have to ask," she said, and stepped back hurriedly as everyone else trooped uninvited over her polished floors and followed Travis.

Abe's room was empty, but it was such a Spartan little cell it didn't take much time to see that some of his things were missing. "His sleeping bag's gone, and his fishing tackle," Travis said, scanning the contents of the closet.

"He don't never go nowhere without his fishin' tackle," Vi noted dolefully. "Looks like he's up and run away, too."

Susannah winced and clung to the doorjamb, wondering how a loving God could put her through this again. "With my baby," she cried in a voice grown thin with dread. "Travis, he's taken my baby."

Judith took her in her arms and rocked her back and forth. "No, my dear, he wouldn't do that."

Henry's perturbed voice underscored her optimism with foreboding. "Travis," he said quietly. "Look what we found."

They flocked around, shielding Susannah from the view, their silent observation sending fresh alarm streaming through her.

"What?" She struggled free of Judith's hold and fought her way to the front. Henry was holding up a corner of the mattress, revealing a stash of matches hidden underneath, and Tony reached under the bed and came up with a small can of kerosene. It was empty.

"Reckon you were right, Travis," Henry said in a low voice. "Maybe we do have someone setting fires on purpose around here."

"Let's not jump to unfounded conclusions, Henry."

"Don't let your fondness for Abe blind you to the obvious, Travis," Judith said dully. "There's no denying the evidence, and it all ties in with what I was telling you. Abe's out of control."

She swung toward Susannah and taking her hands, chafed them between her own. "I should have seen this coming," she said brokenly. "I guess I just didn't want to face it."

"Face what?" Vi demanded. "That you're not fit to keep fleas, let alone a poor benighted creature like Abe?"

"If I have been remiss," Judith replied with dignity, "it is out of respect for my late husband, but I can promise all of you that when we find him, I shall send Abe someplace where he cannot jeopardize the safety of this town or its inhabitants again. I just pray that we aren't too late to prevent a tragedy this time."

Susannah gave a thin wail and would have sunk to the floor if Travis hadn't caught her to him. "Hold on, Judith," he protested. "There's nothing here to prove that Abe's dangerous or that he's done anything wrong."

"'Course there ain't," Vi asserted. "The day that man turns bad'll be the day that pigs ain't pork."

"Really?" Judith's mouth curved grimly. "Then where is he, and where is Benny?"

"Travis." Susannah reached blindly for his hand. "Why would he kidnap Benny?"

"He wouldn't, darling."

She drew in a ragged breath. "He might," she said, wondering why hindsight could be so cruelly perceptive, "if he thought he was losing his only friend."

"I warned you he could be possessive," Judith said, "but I had no idea he'd go this far."

"He would never deliberately hurt Ben, Susannah," Travis said firmly. "I just know it."

"He might not mean to, but if he's taken Benny away, he could hurt him anyway. It's dangerous out there. You said so yourself, Travis."

"I don't believe Abe would mess with fire, or go anywhere near it," Travis maintained, and knew that he was stating only half the truth. The town was trapped in an ever-tightening noose of flames. All he could do was trust that Ben and Abe would be found before the crisis became more acute.

"And wherever Ben is," he said on a sudden burst of inspiration, damming with gentle fingers the tears that clustered along her lower lashes, "Floozer's with him, and she's one smart dog. We found that out yesterday. She won't let him anywhere near a fire. As long as he's got her, he'll be okay."

Susannah's eyes were huge, haunted by memory. "What do we do now?"

Her courage was all that was holding her together, and he loved her for it, almost as much as he hated what he had to tell her next. "We wait until it gets light tomorrow, darling."

"I can't!" She was so stricken by his words, he thought it might have been easier to hit her—and he'd no more think of lifting his hand to a woman than he would to a baby.

"Stay here with me," Judith urged. "We'll wait together."

"Sure, and why would she be doing that," Larene scoffed, "when it's to his own hearth the boy'll turn when he comes home?"

Judith flung a dismissive glance Larene's way. "She shouldn't be alone."

"She ain't goin' to be," Vi announced. "She's got her man by her side. Don't make sense she'd need you, too, Judith Petersen."

TRAVIS TOOK HER BACK to her house and lay beside her on the bed, holding her for hours, and asking only that she'd let him share the agony of the night. Then, somewhere between two and three in the morning, fatigue claimed him and he dozed. It took the moon, riding high over the spruce trees and shining full on his face, to rouse him to the awareness that she was no longer in his arms.

She stood at the window, staring down on the empty garden and the silent town. Quietly, he rose and went to stand beside her. "Are you okay, Susannah?"

"No," she said. "I keep thinking about death."

The last thing he'd have asked or expected was that she'd turn to him for more than comfort. When he'd brought her home and taken her upstairs, he'd removed only his shirt so that he'd be ready to leave at the first hint of daylight. But he'd made her take off all her clothes and put on a light cotton nightgown for the relief it offered from the cloying heat that hung in the bedroom. He'd seen how exhausted she was and knew she needed rest; surcease, however brief, from the unremitting treadmill of her anguish, if she was to deal with what still lay ahead.

Now, she reached for his hands and guided them inside the gown until they covered her bare breasts. "Make me believe in life again," she begged.

"Are you sure, Susannah?"

"Yes," she said. "I am empty."

She didn't know how else to describe the terrifying feeling inside her—the smothering fear that if she didn't make contact with reality in its most elemental form, she might lose herself forever in the mists of madness. "Travis?" she whispered, groping for him.

He closed his arms around her, shocked to discover that grief and fear had reduced her to a distraught handful of bones wired together with such tension that the merest extension of misery would splinter her.

He wanted to tell her how much he would always love her, that he would die for her if she asked him to; that she was the most courageous and desirable woman in the world to him. And he could say none of these things, any more than he could see for himself the pale beauty of her in the moonlight, because tears choked off his words and blinded his eyes.

Even in the urgency of the moment, he was careful to leave his clothes ready where he could find them quickly and easily, because he knew that when the time came to leave her, the seconds would count. Naked at last, he pulled her into the shelter of his body, pressed his lips to her hair and her face and gathered her against flesh that was aching and willing to give her the renewal she craved. Then he carried her to the bed and covered her with the broad protection of his body.

She sighed and felt a flicker of warmth stir in the frozen wastes of her soul. She was starving and hollow, echoing with need. To have him there, answering her needs, filling her with power and passion and life, gave her the strength to shove aside the negative forces of doubt that crowded the threshold of her pain, and to know that whatever tomorrow might bring, she would face it and she would survive.

At five o'clock he rose from the bed and left her. Within fifteen minutes, he was airborne, skimming the treetops to search the fire breaks cut through the forest, on the off chance that he might spot some clue to Ben's whereabouts. All he discovered was that the brush fire circling north of town had leaped over a mile to form another link with those to the south, tightening the net closing in on Cameron's Landing. And added to that, the sky was a dull copper and had the heavy, brooding feel that was the forerunner of a storm. It made him very anxious indeed.

When he returned to base, Susannah was waiting and she knew without asking that he'd found nothing to comfort her. He walked up to her and buried her face against him just as the first round of thunder rattled distantly behind the mountains.

Charlie Ayres joined them. He was a man of few words, but his hand on Susannah's shoulder was compassionate. "It's bad out there, Travis. The crew's loading." He knew as well as anybody what lightning could do in this already critical situation.

"It's best that I do what I can to hold the line on the fire," Travis said, lifting her chin and letting his eyes roam her face. "You do understand that, don't you, sweetheart?"

She wondered if perhaps time had gone crazy, flying backward five years, but the faces around her were different, the actions changed. Travis was bleak-faced with frustration, this golden man of hers, but there were no rash promises of a miracle in his steady gaze, only purpose and resolution and willingness to give of his expertise where it would do the most good.

She'd switched roles, too. Instead of begging him to find her son, she gave him her blessing in the silent pressure of her lips against his.

Ten minutes after the crew disappeared over the ridge, Tony Hamilton found Floozer in the bush, not half a mile from the house. She was chained to a tree, the silky black fur behind her right ear matted with blood from an ugly gash that could only have been caused by a blow to the head.

Bob Kelly carried Floozer home. He was the only man in town big enough for the job. Susannah spread a blanket on the deck and brought a bowl of warm water and disinfectant. Floozer wasn't feeling so swift, but she managed to thump her tail a couple of times and lick Susannah's hand.

"This was no accident, dearie," Bob muttered, inspecting the wound. "Someone's deliberately set out to hurt this animal, and it's my guess that if we find that someone, we'd be after knowing who it was that tried to burn down your shed yesterday."

"And it ain't Abe's name you're goin' to come up with," Vi declared darkly. "He'd no more hurt this beast than he'd hurt young Benny. There's a power of evil at work here that's beyond that poor man's figurin' capabilities."

Dread gathered inside Susannah, so corrosive she doubted she'd ever heal. Benny would be eight in three days. The makings of a birthday cake waited in the kitchen, and she had his gifts wrapped and stacked in the top of her closet. His dog lay injured, the listless droop of her head as much a symptom of her failure to keep Ben safe as of her physical discomfort. Would Benny be found soon enough to appreciate any of these things?

AFTER THE FLYING was done for the day, Travis called a strategy meeting at the hotel. Fred Hughes, the dispatcher, had requisitioned extra crew from the Campbell River base south of the border so that as much manpower as possible could be utilized in a wide-scale search for Benny and Abe.

Alone at the house, Susannah fought off a persistent drowsiness born of anxiety and fatigue. The nightmares hovering on the brink of consciousness were more terrifying than reality, filled with loud voices and violence that jerked her awake and back to the oppressive stillness of the night. The sound of footsteps behind the house brought her fully alert because they were too stealthy either to be part of her dreams or to belong to Travis. His staying with her the previous night was an open secret that made clandestine arrivals redundant. She knew immediately that someone was outside, and that whoever it was did not want to be discovered.

Hope raced beside her as she flew to the glass doors and flung back the drapes, praying for the simple miracle of a little boy grown tired of playing runaway and stealing back home under cover of darkness. There was no one there.

Behind her, Floozer whined softly. Spinning around, Susannah saw that she was pawing at the small door that led out to the back garden. "What is it, girl?" she whispered. "What do you hear?"

Logic dictated that it was unlikely to be Benny trying to sneak in unobtrusively, since he knew that door was always locked from the inside. Panic, increasingly predatory, screamed that it could be the arsonist, returning to finish what he'd started the day before, but Floozer's tail waved gently back and forth, and gave Susannah the courage to open the door a crack.

Abe rushed out of the brush toward her, a wild-eyed apparition more deranged looking than he'd been the first time she'd seen him hovering over her a lifetime ago, when Benny was safe and the world was still fresh and green. "Lady!" he whispered hoarsely, his big uncoordinated body weaving closer, his hands reaching for her. His clothes were scorched in places and reeked of smoke.

Out of control, Judith had said, and she'd been right. Of all the people in town, she was the only one who understood how fine a line he trod between normality and confusion.

They call him Crazy Abe, Travis had said. A cruel name, born out of ignorance, but conceived in truth, perhaps? Susannah tasted fear.

She slammed the door just as Abe reached it, slid the bolt home seconds before the knob rattled under his grip and raced to lock the glass doors, too.

"Floozer," she whispered, reaching for the comforting touch of the dog, not caring that there were other dangers greater than Abe converging on the house. She could hear the burning crackle of tinder-dry grass, see the leaping orange flames illuminating the garden where all the other fires had started, where Abe waited.

"Lady...!" He was beating on the door wildly, his words hoarse as the smoke choked him.

He'd taken Benny. He'd set fire to her house. What else did he want? "Leave me alone," she shouted, taking Floozer by the collar and backing to the glass doors. Why had she locked them, when they offered the only other route to escape?

She tried to release the lock and slide back the heavy doors. They fit snugly to keep out the winter storms, and she, all thumbs, needed both hands. At last she got them open just enough to allow her and Floozer to squeeze through. She reached for the dog and found nothing, spun around, frantic, just as the back door splintered under Abe's assault.

He was in the house, was lunging for her again, and this time his hands closed on her.

Chapter Twenty

"Floozer!" she screamed. "Go find Travis! Quick!"

The dog shot by her, through the glass doors and onto the deck.

"You, too, lady." With his enormous strength, Abe picked Susannah up and flung her over his shoulders. Awkwardly he hurtled after Floozer, while behind him a dull rumble seemed to fill the house, shaking the foundations. Clearing the steps, he stumbled for the protection of the nearest spruce.

"Down!" he panted, tossing her on the dusty ground and flinging himself on top of her just as a ball of orange flame rolled toward the back of the house.

His hand pushed her face down in the dirt, the weight of his body pinning her there when she tried to struggle up again. "Stay, lady," he whispered hoarsely.

Around the corner of the house, another explosion tore through the night, showering him with debris, and suddenly his actions made a different kind of sense to her. She tried to say something, but he yanked her to her feet and took her hand.

"Run," he begged, and together they raced at an angle between the trees, down toward the road, Floozer at their heels. Above them, the fire settled in like a hungry beast finding a meal.

They stopped at the edge of the property, and Susannah saw Abe's distress and the way he reached for Floozer to keep her from wandering into danger, and she remembered this was the man who loved animals and hated fire. He wasn't the one she had to fear, any more than he was the one who'd hurt Floozer. "What's going on, Abe? Who did this, and where's Benny?"

"Benny's safe," he said, tugging at her with his free hand, "but not you, lady. You come with me, then you're safe, too."

People from the town were hurrying up the road. She could see Travis leading the pack. "I'm safe here," she said, hanging onto Abe's sleeve and running to meet the crowd. "Look, Abe, they're coming. Travis will help us. So will Judith."

But Abe dug in his heels, breaking her grip with a flick of his wrist. "No," he breathed, and melted into the bush, looking around to see if he was being followed, his actions those of a furtive and frightened man.

"Wait—!" Susannah began, but before she could go after him, someone materialized out of the dark and a hand closed around her arm. She'd thought they were still alone and yelped in alarm.

"Susannah!" Judith cried, for once anything but calm and controlled. Her hair had escaped the white scarf holding it back and her blouse was streaked with dirt. "I saw the explosion from my window and got here as fast as I could. Thank God you're all right."

"I—Abe—"

"I know. I saw him."

"He's not—"

"Over here, Travis." Judith waved her scarf. "She's safe."

Travis raced toward them, and Susannah ran to meet him, sobbing all at once when she saw the absolute dread on his face. He swept her into a bone-crushing embrace while the rest of the town milled about. Every last person had come to the rescue, men and women alike flinging pails of chemical retardant onto the flames and hooking hoses to the two outside faucets. Heavy boots tramped through the downstairs rooms of the house, the old shed succumbed to the fire and collapsed, but by some sort of miracle, most of the damage was confined to the rear wall of the house.

"I should never have left you alone," Travis lamented when the worst was over, his voice breaking and his eyes begging Susannah's forgiveness. "I'm supposed to be looking out for you."

"I'm a grown woman." She hiccuped on a dying sob. "I shouldn't need someone to look out for me."

"It was Abe. I saw him myself," Judith announced to the assembled group. "God knows what he'd have done if we hadn't all arrived when we did."

"Well, whoever it was would've burned the whole house down if he hadn't been interrupted," Dan said somberly, and held up a tin can. "It wasn't kerosene this time, Travis, it was gasoline. My guess is he'd soaked the grass around the shed and was about to do the same under the deck."

"Gasoline's lethal," Travis said. "It's highly combustible, much more so than kerosene. Abe knows that."

"He's also crazy," Judith said. "Crazy enough not to know or care that he might have killed Susannah and himself."

"I don't hear Susannah laying no blame on Abe," Vi put in. "I reckon it's a mite strange that you should be so sure, Judith Petersen, when she don't seem to agree with you."

"Especially," Larene added, promptly taking up where Vi left off, "seeing as how it's Susannah who was here the whole time, and yourself as arrived after the damage was done."

Bob Kelly disagreed. "Well, now, dearie, there's no use denying the facts. If herself saw Abe, then I'm after agreeing with her that he had a hand in this mess."

"It wasn't Abe," Susannah insisted, fearing a lynch mob would be out searching if she didn't speak fast.

"Then who was it?" Judith demanded.

"I don't know. But it wasn't Abe."

"Well, why did he run off when he saw me? And where is he now?"

"I don't know."

Travis looked around. "Where's Floozer, Susannah?"

"She was here with us."

"Well, she ain't here now," Vi said. "Reckon you'll be accusing her next, Judith Petersen."

"Maybe she followed Abe," Travis said. "Look, folks, there's not a lot more we can do here tonight. Let's not lose sight of the fact that a child is still missing, and that's our first priority. We haven't finalized our plan of action, so I suggest we go back to the hotel and get on with it."

"And I'll take Susannah home with me," Judith said. "She obviously can't stay here."

"She can stay with me," Vi said. "Or with Larene or Marg. She don't have to sleep under your roof, madam."

"But she'd rather," Judith replied with a return of her usual composure, "if only because that's where Travis will come when he's finished at the hotel, and I'm sure they'd rather wait out the night together."

Vi harrumphed, which was as close as she'd come to admitting defeat, and stamped off with Larene and Marg. The men rounded up the hoses and pails and started down the hill also.

Susannah sagged wearily against Travis, wondering how their lives could have become so complicated in so short a time.

Judith eyed her sympathetically. "You poor little thing," she said, and held out her arms. "Hand her over, Travis, and go to your meeting with an easy mind. I'll look after her for you, and you can be sure I'll keep an eye out for Abe, though I doubt he'll try anything else tonight."

"Susannah?" Travis hesitated as the rest of the men turned the corner at the foot of the road.

"I'll be fine," she said.

"You sure?"

"Really. Just hurry back."

"You know it." He pulled her close again and kissed her. "We'll find Ben tomorrow," he promised, then hurried to catch up with the others.

Judith's house was just around the corner, and they were there within minutes. "I'm going to run a bath for you, then make you something to eat and drink," she said, "so don't bother arguing. Go sit down while I look out some towels and a nightgown."

"You're so kind to me, Judith."

"That's what friends are for, Susannah."

Judith climbed the stairs, and Susannah sank onto the chair that stood beside the small table next to the front door. She leaned her head on her arm. The week's mail lay piled on a silver tray and quite by accident Susannah's eyes fell on a letter that had been set aside and opened. It had come from a private mental institution.

Susannah had the letter in her hand and was blatantly reading it when she heard Judith coming back down the stairs. She had plenty of time to stuff it under the other mail and pretend she didn't know what was going on.

"Your bath's ready, Susannah. Why don't you go soak while I fix you something to eat?"

"Why are you trying to have Abe put away?" Susannah asked, waving the letter under Judith's nose and deciding that when it came to being a discreet and clever spy, she was about as much use as a plumber's apprentice.

"You of all people should know the answer to that," Judith replied calmly, seeming not at all put out that her guest had overstepped the boundary of good manners so far as to snoop through her private correspondence. "He's obviously become a menace to society and I simply cannot allow him to run wild any longer."

The envelope was postmarked Detroit. Susannah tried to envision a haven for the disturbed and came up with thoughts of iron bars and red brick surrounded by high wire fences and city streets. No bald eagles or ravens or little wild creatures; no towering mountains or sweeping sunsets. "Abe doesn't belong in a place like that. He'll die."

Judith shrugged. "Look, the rate he's going, he'll die here unless I take steps to have him protected. I've done my best, but it's out of my hands now, and frankly, I can't say

I'm not relieved." She paused on her way to the kitchen. "I'm surprised you'd see it any differently, Susannah, after all he's put you through."

"He hasn't put me through anything."

"My dear, your child is missing and there seems little doubt that Abe is responsible for his disappearance. You came up here to this miserable little outpost—where culture is a dirty word and anything approaching sophistication is regarded as the worst of the seven deadly sins—because you thought the safety the place had to offer was worth the sacrifice, and what happens? One of the locals is a forty-year-old man with the brain of a backward six-year-old, and he takes it into his head to burn down your house and kidnap your son."

She threw up her hands in disgust. "I'm sure you can't wait to shake the dust of Cameron's Landing from your heels, the minute Benny is found."

Susannah reminded herself that she considered Judith a friend, and she tried to hold on to that thought when she spoke. "I like it here. I like the people, and so does Benny."

She stopped for a moment and took a deep breath because anger was growing inside her, and when she became very angry she always ran out of breath and started to cry and it didn't seem the right time to do either; not if she wanted to make the right sort of impression on Judith. "I don't think Abe set any of the fires, and I'm sure that tonight he was trying to get me out of the house because he wanted to protect me. I think he knows who *has* been setting the fires and he's scared to come forward and say anything."

Judith's laugh was a screech of contempt. "Susannah, you're coming unstrung! Abe is not made of the stuff of heroes. If he's scared, it's because he's done something bad, and his reaction is always the same—to run away where no one can find him so that he can't be punished. Trust me. I'm right."

You're also a callous bitch, Susannah decided, feeling her control slip a notch. "He's not capable of being deliberately bad. He's the most gentle person I've ever come across . . . and he's kind . . ." Blast the tears that were blurring her vision! "And he's Benny's best friend. He wouldn't hurt him, or me, or Floozer, or anyone he loved—"

"All right, Susannah," Judith's hand was at the base of her spine, urging her up the stairs. "Whatever you say, dear. It's time for a little rest now."

"I don't want to rest!" Susannah heard the shrill note creeping into her voice and clamped her mouth shut. Grief, she thought, she'll be having me put away next.

"Yes, you do." Judith cooed. They were on the landing and beside the door of a neat little room where cool cotton sheets had already been turned back on the bed. "Just lie down now and close your eyes, and before you know it, Travis will be back and everything will work out." Big, efficient hands urged Susannah down, removed her shoes, while the serene voice continued to soothe. "Benny will be found, and you'll forget any of this ever happened."

Outside, thunder grumbled over the mountain. "I'm not sleepy."

"You're overwrought, Susannah, not yourself at all. Just lie quietly, like a good girl, and I'll bring you something to make you relax."

Susannah heard the door close softly, and waited for the sound of Judith's footsteps receding down the stairs before she popped up in bed, swung her feet over the side, and pulled on her shoes. Her anger had diminished, displaced by something else. The more she thought about it, the more certain she became that Abe was afraid, and the longer she remained in this house, the more afraid she became, too.

She opened the door a crack and listened. Judith was clattering dishes in the kitchen, running water. The front door stood open at the foot of the stairs. She might not get another opportunity to make an escape.

Ridiculous, she thought, scuttling down the stairs and out into the blessed cover of night, *to be thinking about escape as if I were a prisoner!* Yet there was something about that house, something about Judith's inflexible, unemotional determination, that made Susannah's blood run cold. First she had to get away, and then she had to try to find Abe's trail through the bush and hope it would lead her to Benny.

"Lady!" The whisper traveled on the air light as a breath of wind. He was there, crouched under the trees at the side of the garden, beckoning frantically.

Ducking down, she ran over to him. "Abe, we have to—"

"Run," he finished for her, and grabbing her hand, made off through the bush, surefooted in the dark, despite his awkwardness. And with every yard they put between themselves and Judith's house, Susannah's fear diminished a little.

Finally they stopped in a small clearing where the grass was trampled as though someone had been squatting there for some time. Through the branches they had a clear view of the front and back of the house. "We have to go, lady." Abe panted, and pointed to the lights twinkling from Judith's kitchen windows, his lips working loosely with agitation. "She'll hurt you. She makes fires."

"*Judith* makes fires?" Judith's calm and smiling exterior had a cold, unfeeling heart, but arson? Susannah couldn't quite believe she'd go that far. "Why would she do that, Abe?"

"She's bad," he said, with simple honesty.

But what if Judith were right and Abe was deranged to the point that he didn't know what he was saying or doing? Look at him now, drooling with fear, his hands flexing and clenching in a mindless rhythm. What if those hands had hurt Benny? What if they hurt her?

Stop it! she told herself, but she couldn't help scanning the road for any sign of Travis in case she needed to scream for help. She could see clear down to the hotel, and the lights streaming from the windows and open door showed the street was empty. Surely the meeting would be over by now? Travis hadn't come home, but what if he'd gone back to her house first, to check that the fire was completely out?

She swung around and craned her neck, but the road curved too far to the left. She couldn't see her house from here.

Nobody could see her house from here.

I saw the fire from my window, Judith had said.

Abe touched her arm, gentle even in his urgency. "I tell the truth," he said.

"I know, Abe." But Judith told lies. There was no way she could have arrived so quickly on the scene of the fire, unless she'd been there when it started.

"Why would Judith want to hurt me or Benny?" Susannah asked, and knew the answer because Judith herself had spelled it out quite clearly not fifteen minutes before. Judith wanted an excuse to get rid of Abe, so that she could leave this "outpost of civilization" and go back to the city, unencumbered by the social stigma of "a forty-year-old man with the brain of a backward six-year-old." Judith didn't particularly want to hurt Susannah, but she didn't particularly care if she did, either, as long as she achieved her end, which was to place the blame for the fires on Abe and give herself the excuse she needed to be rid of him.

A twig snapped behind them, and something cold and damp nudged at Susannah's hand, startling her into a squeak of terror.

"It's okay, lady," Abe said, and he bent down to pat Floozer gently on the back. "Good girl," he crooned softly. "Now we go to Benny."

Susannah dropped down on her knees beside Abe and wrapped both arms around Floozer's neck, mindful of the gash healing behind her ear. The dog trusted Abe. She needed to do the same. "You do know where he is, don't you, Abe?"

Abe nodded solemnly. "I took him."

"Where? Where did you take him?"

"To the cabin," Abe said, lifting his shoulders as though he couldn't understand why she hadn't figured that out for herself. "It's safe there. There's water, so he won't be thirsty, and there's fish so he won't be hungry. Now I take you and Floozer and me there, and we'll all be safe."

He gave her his gentle sweet smile that knew nothing of guile or deceit. In compensation for his other limitations, his thoughts traveled in straight and simple lines instead of complicated circles, ignoring irrelevant tangents and going directly to the heart of any matter. He had seen that Benny was in danger, and he had taken him out of reach of the source of it, simple as that. Now he would do the same for her.

Judith had a lot to learn about the stuff heroes were made of, but then Judith had a lot to learn about many things, and would doubtless have plenty of time in which to do so. Arson was a felony.

"We go now, lady," Abe said, "then we'll be safe."

From Judith, perhaps, Susannah thought with a sinking dread, but even as she and Abe crouched in the shadow of the trees with help not more than half a mile away, Benny was alone in an area that had been on red alert for days. They couldn't afford the time it would take to go for reinforcements and make lengthy explanations. Hadn't Travis postponed the fishing trip because the lake was too close to the brush fires?

"Let's go," she said. "We have to hurry, Abe. The fires are coming close to the lake. It isn't going to be safe there very much longer."

The trail was indistinct even in daylight. Susannah would never have found it without Abe and the narrow beam of his flashlight. The path wound up the hill then dropped down into a ravine, meandered through a stand of aspens and eventually followed the bed of a small stream that trickled over flat rocks.

They were climbing higher, the scent of the ocean lost in the pervasive smell of smoke from the encroaching fires. Smoke carried for miles on the wind, which had picked up sometime during the evening and blew hot against their faces. In the distance, thunder growled restlessly.

Floozer, nose to the ground, seemed to pick up Benny's scent and bounded ahead, turning back every few yards to make sure they were following. Abe stayed close beside Susannah, helping her over the stumps of old trees and the chunks of rock that littered the path. Once he lifted her clean off her feet and carried her through a patch of thorny brush.

For almost an hour they plodded through the dark, with tiny blackflies tormenting them every step of the way, and the ever-present odor of smoke filling their lungs, but at last Abe came to a halt. "The lake," he said, pointing.

Ahead, Susannah caught the gleam of water. As they emerged from the shelter of the trees, a tongue of jagged lightning forked across the sky. In the brief moment before it buried itself in the dark on the far side of the lake, it lit up the landscape as bright as day, revealing a little cabin perched on the near shore.

Between one breath and the next, Susannah grabbed the flashlight, crossed the open stretch of ground and was through the door. Benny was there, huddled on a sleeping bag, crying softly.

"Benny, sweetheart, don't cry! Mommy's here."

At the sound of her voice, he catapulted into her arms and clung to her, burrowing his face into her neck. "It's dark, Mommy," he sobbed. "I can't see the bogeymen coming."

"Hush," she soothed him, kissing his hair which smelled of smoke laced with a faint trace of shampoo. "There aren't any bogeymen, just me and Floozer and Abe." To hell with grammar!

"I want to go home."

"That's what we're going to do, right away."

Another drumroll of thunder echoed over the mountain, closer this time. "In the morning when it's light, Mommy," he whimpered tearfully.

"We can't wait that long, honey."

Floozer nosed anxiously around them, whining softly. Lightning flung its eerie light across the tiny window, slithered over the sky and struck a mortal blow. Somewhere across the lake, a tree crashed to the ground, taking others with it, its death throes reverberating over the water.

"Lady!" Abe stood in the doorway, a tall black figure silhouetted in dull red. "Come quick!"

Susannah scrambled to her feet, Benny clinging to her like a limpet. "What is it, Abe? What's that light?"

She saw as soon as she reached the door. Across the lake to the south, about ten miles from them, red sparks shot clear of the trees to shower down on the surface of the water. Even as they stood there watching nature's pyrotechnics at their beautiful and destructive best, a column of flame roman-candled into the sky, then leaped to embrace everything within its deadly grasp.

Chapter Twenty-one

"We have to hurry," Susannah said, shouting to be heard over the ominous crackling of dried timber submitting to the voracious demands of fire. The trail back to town led northwest of the lake and it was downhill most of the way, but it was only a matter of time before their escape would be cut off. Already, hot ashes were floating down on them, carried by the wind, and the air was suffocatingly close, pungent with smoke.

"You carry the sleeping bag," Abe decided, "and I carry Benny."

"Never mind the sleeping bag, Abe. We'll buy a new one."

"No, lady," he said firmly. "We go to the water and get all wet and the sleeping bag, too. Then we go home."

Benny perked up at that. A midnight swim was his idea of high living, and Susannah gave thanks to the Almighty that he was too young to understand the gravity of the situation. "Floozer too," Benny insisted.

"Yes," Abe said solemnly. "Floozer too."

"Why?" Susannah muttered as he hurried them to the lake's edge.

"So we don't burn," he replied with that familiar lifting of the shoulders that left her wondering why she hadn't thought of it herself.

A blast of wind swept over them like a furnace, the smoke a hot, foul breath searing their throats and constricting their lungs. "Oh!" Benny wailed. "My chest hurts."

"No more talking." Abe's tone brooked no argument. "Save your breath now."

The lake was glacier fed, ice-cold against their heated bodies. They dunked their heads, and Susannah helped Abe push the down sleeping bag under the surface until it was sodden, while Benny scooped handfuls of water over Floozer. They were a sorry looking crew when they'd finished.

The trip down the trail was horrendous. If it hadn't been for Abe's incredible physical strength and his unerring sense of direction, they never would have made it. He hitched Benny onto his back, told him to hang on, and forged ahead of Susannah, holding back branches and lending a hand over the rough spots. Floozer circled them like a sheepdog with a wayward flock, sometimes running ahead and uttering anxious little barks, but mostly nagging at their heels to make sure none of them strayed.

The sleeping bag weighed a ton. It slowed Susannah down time and again, dragging on the ground, catching on low-hanging tree limbs, snarling in bushes. She would have dumped it after the first twenty minutes, but when she suggested it, Abe pointed above the trees behind them. A ring of sky glowed red as the yawning mouth of hell. The fires were creeping closer, even though the sound of them was muffled by rolling thunder. All around, the night was full of hidden movement, tiny creatures fleeing to safer ground. Once, a black-tailed deer bounded past, fear of the holocaust behind overriding its wariness of people.

An eternity later, as they straggled across an open stretch of ground, Susannah went sprawling, her knees buckling under her, sheer exhaustion leaving her limp with defeat. The rocks beneath her were sharp and unforgiving, but it was the rain of ashes carried by the wind that terrified her.

Floozer's sharp yap of alarm brought Abe racing back. "Get up," he begged, his hands flailing aimlessly over her, unsure whether or not he dared touch her. "Please, lady, don't be hurt."

"I'm tired," she said feebly. "Just go on ahead. Get Benny to safety, and I'll come later."

It was a damn fool thing to say as Benny was quick to point out. "Don't be a wazoo, Mom," he said. "We're almost there. You can see the harbor from up here."

But she felt like a rag doll with half the stuffing falling out. Her legs and her chest hurt. I'm going to die in this forsaken wilderness without even telling Travis how much I really love him, she thought, as gritty little tears of self-pity oozed down her cheeks. I'll die and he'll marry someone else.

That thought mobilized her where Benny's insult had failed. She struggled to her feet, clutched the soggy sleeping bag to her bosom and pushed the hair out of her eyes. "No way!" she threatened ambiguously.

Benny exchanged mystified looks with Abe. "Maybe she hurt her head," he muttered.

Abe took the sleeping bag from her arms and draped it over her like a shawl, covering her hair. "This will help," he said kindly.

It insulated her against the heat enough to give her the strength to stumble the last half mile. One minute they were in the smothering darkness of the forest, and the next they were coming to the clearing where Abe had sat and watched Judith's house, waiting for the chance to warn Susannah of the menace lurking there.

They straggled through the trees, out into the open, and ran smack into a search party out looking for them. Dazed with fatigue, Susannah experienced a kaleidoscope of impressions: Travis's hard warm body crushing her close, his mouth whispering a mixture of endearments and profanities in her ear; the voices of the other men raised in relief; Larene and Vi and Marg clucking with concern. And Judith, calm and smiling, with not a trace of remorse or fear or guilt in her eyes.

It was that indomitable assurance of Judith's that made Susannah try to disengage herself from Travis. She wanted the record set straight in front of everyone so that there were plenty of witnesses to vouch for him should Abe require them.

"I think you should all know..." she began, pushing Travis away so that she could be seen.

He was not disposed to be cooperative. "I could wring your neck," he interrupted, taking hold of her shoulders in a grip that was distinctly unloverlike and giving her a little shake that made her teeth snap together with a click. "Where were your brains, woman, to go traipsing off like that without a word to anyone?"

"I had to rescue Benny before it was too late," she said, a little testy that he was behaving this way when there were more important issues at stake. "In case you aren't aware, *sweetheart*, there's a fire out there and it's coming closer by the minute."

"Precisely, *darling*, and I'm the one trained to deal with it, not you."

"You folks gonna fight," Vi suggested, "you'd be better off doin' it in the hotel. I'd feel a whole lot easier down by the water than I do up here. I don't aim to get myself fried to death while you two sort each other out."

"That's fine, as long as you all come," Susannah said. "I have something I want everyone to hear."

"It's all damp and dirty you are, dearie," Larene fussed, lifting a strand of Susannah's hair dubiously. "Sure and whatever it is can wait until you've all three had a bath and a bite to eat. Bob, go heat up the clam chowder and fill the coffeepot, and take Henry Turner with you. He's neither use nor ornament, standing here gaping as if he'd never before seen a woman walk out of the bush with all her faculties intact."

"I'm hungry," Benny informed them. "We didn't eat much while we were camping, did we, Abe?"

Judith shot Susannah a triumphant glance and turned to Abe. "So," she purred, "it *was* you who kidnapped Benny, after all. That was a very bad thing to do, Abe."

He positively shrank behind Travis. "I was good," he whimpered. "I didn't hurt Benny."

Vi marched up to Abe, minute beside his great size, and yanked him out of hiding. "Folks'd have to be daft to think you would," she scolded, leading him to where Bob and Henry still waited, then she faced Judith, her fists planted on her hips in a fighting stance. "If you can't do nothing but give the poor man the whim-whams, Judith Petersen, you'd better keep your mouth shut."

"Listen," Susannah said. "Maybe we should get this sorted out now—Travis, please stop swearing."

"That's right. You can hold your fire, too," Vi declared, intending no pun. "There ain't nobody sayin' nothin' till these folks smells clean again. The rate them fires is moving, we could all be on tomorrow morning's ferry, and foreigners'll think we ain't got no pride if you three goes aboard like this."

"Abe can get cleaned up here. It's still his home," Judith put in, and something in her tone set off warning bells in Susannah's head.

"We all stay together," she insisted.

Travis couldn't contain himself a minute longer. "Never mind all this!" he fumed. "You could have been killed, Susannah. Did that ever occur to you?"

"Yes," she said.

"And how the hell was I supposed to deal with it if you had, or didn't that matter?"

"Stop the hysterics," she ordered him sharply, part of her delighting in the role reversal taking place. It was nice to discover she wasn't the only one who lost control when the going got rough. "There are more important things to be getting upset about."

"Really?" His blue eyes sparked dangerously. "Such as?"

"Such as the fact that Judith's planning to have Abe committed to an institution," Susannah announced in a voice loud enough for everyone to hear. "She's already picked a place and made a booking."

Abe's wail of fear rose over the general hum of anger this information produced. "How'd you know this, girlie?" Henry asked.

"I saw the letter only a couple of hours ago."

"She ain't got no cause," Vi declared, patting Abe briskly on the backside. "Don't you fret, Abe, she ain't sending you no place."

"I'm not bad," Abe whimpered plaintively, his hands setting up a distraught rhythm.

"Course you ain't, child," Vi consoled him and fixed a malicious glare on Judith. "Judith Petersen, if you was a dog, Bob Kelly'd take you out back and shoot you to put you out of your misery. Since you ain't a dog, he probably won't do that, but I ain't so sure I won't."

"And I'd help her," Larene snapped, "so don't be pushing your luck."

"Be quiet, you silly old crones," Judith said scathingly. "You're defending the man who almost burnt Susannah's house to the ground, with her still inside. Do you really want someone like that running free in your community?"

"That's not true," Susannah said. "You're the one who started the fire, Judith, and you tried to set Abe up to take the blame."

It all came out then, and as Susannah expected, Judith was quick to deny all the accusations. But the evidence was conclusive, given weight by Abe's abject fear when Judith advanced on him in fury as all her fine plans crumbled.

"You pathetic half-wit!" she raged. "I've suffered you hanging around my neck like some great clumsy albatross for the past fifteen years! You've cost me everything I ever wanted and deserved, and now when I come this close to being rid of you—" her hand shot out, thumb and index finger pressed together "—you're costing me again."

Judith's composure cracked, revealing depths of unbelievable ugliness.

"Shame!" someone chided, and was greeted by a rumble of support from the rest.

Judith swung around, eyes blazing, mouth twisted. "Don't you dare judge me, you ignorant louts. Not unless you've lived with an inheritance like mine. I was married to a rich man, and I was still a young woman when he died. Young and beautiful with most of my life still to be lived. And what did I inherit? All the money, a place in society, a cosmopolitan life in the style to which I was accustomed...*provided that* I play keeper to his idiot brother."

"So why weren't you after staying in the city where you belong instead of saddling us with your face?" Larene asked sourly.

"For what?" Judith shrieked. "To go to the opera and attend balls on the arm of my dear demented brother-in-law?"

"You could've put him away," Vi suggestd. "It might've been kinder than him having to live with you all these years."

"But I couldn't," Judith explained in a voice made all the more venomous by its syrupy tone. "Not if I wanted to keep the money—unless I could prove he was unfit to be allowed loose. I tried every way I could find to lose him."

"The Lord looks after his own," Larene declared piously.

Travis reached out for Susannah and Benny and pulled them close. Vi held Abe by the hand and clucked comfortingly to him. Dan Ryder, who'd said not a word, looked physically ill.

"You always did treat him cold, and I never could figure out why when he's as harmless as a body can be," Henry observed, shaking his head dolefully.

"Why should I have had to put my life on hold for someone who isn't even aware of what's going on half the time?" Judith defended herself. "What about what I gave up?"

"You could've had a good life here, and we'd all have helped you if you'd let us," Marg said. "We're a friendly town."

Judith seemed to sag, as though she knew she was looking down a one-way street leading nowhere. "Do you think I give a rap about you or your town?" she asked wearily. "The only reason I came here at all was in the hope that he'd wander off in the bush and never come back. I should have known I'd be stuck with Nature Boy reborn.''

"None of that explains what you've got against Susannie or her boy," Vi said.

Judith sighed. "I'm so tired of hearing about Susannah and her boy. So tired of the sympathy she earns for her misfortunes, when she's got her youth and her child's got his wits. I knew that if either of them seemed to be threatened by Abe, you'd all climb on the bandwagon and rush to see that she was protected."

"So you resorted to arson," Travis finished quietly. "I could almost pity you for your warped idea of justice."

"I do believe," Judith said defiantly, "I'd have resorted to murder if I'd had to."

"There's some as'd say you came pretty damn close," Vi accused. "Bob Kelly, you're the nearest thing we got to a sheriff around here. Reckon you got a job to do."

The crowd parted to let him walk his prisoner down to the store. "You'd better be coming with me, Henry," he said. "I'll be needing to use the phone, and that storeroom you got at the back, till tomorrow."

After they'd gone, the town closed ranks around Abe who was truly one of their own. "You're staying here with us where you belong," Larene said. "There's room to spare at the hotel."

"He's staying with me," Vi intervened. "You got your hands full as it is, Larene Kelly, and I ain't got nobody's business to mind but my own since I buried George."

"We'll argue about it later," Larene decided. "After we've cleaned these folks up and fed them."

THE HOTEL'S BATHTUB was a huge cast-iron affair, sitting on ornate claw feet and deep enough to drown in. Susannah could almost float. She soaked away her aches and pains along with her grime, listened to the sound of the tinny old piano in the bar, inhaled the aroma of clam chowder and accustomed herself with the idea that she'd come very close to losing Benny, and to losing Travis, too.

It could happen again. People were sometimes the victims of circumstances they couldn't control. But if there were no guarantees in life, she finally recognized, neither was there any life worth living without love. Love was what gave a person the strength to accept the possibility of loss; it was what brought pleasure from memories and what gave hope for the future. It was what made the present worthwhile.

People had rounded up clean clothes for them; sensible things like underwear and a pair of shorts and a shirt for Benny. But Vi had given Susannah a white cotton dress that she'd made when she was a bride. It had a full skirt and long demure sleeves. Embroidered forget-me-nots decorated the hem.

Susannah brushed her red-gold hair until it gleamed, then opened the door and went to find Travis. If he still wanted her after all she'd put him through today, she'd marry him and accept whatever the future held, stronger because of the love they shared.

He was at a table in the bar, Benny sitting across from him with Floozer at his feet. Larene was ladling clam chowder into bowls, and Henry, his baseball cap dripping, had just come in the door with a basket of fresh rolls.

"The wind's changed," he told them. "And it's raining to beat the band. Looks like you might get to sleep late tomorrow, Travis."

Vi looked up from the pie she was slicing. "Reckon the old town ain't ready to burn down after all," she decided sagely.

Benny caught sight of Susannah. "Mom," he said, "you look pretty."

Travis turned then, and saw her in the doorway. He pushed back his chair and went to her. "I've been thinking," he said.

She nodded. "So have I."

"About getting married."

"I think we should. If you're sure you still want to."

His heart lurched with relief and joy. It had seemed hours that she'd been missing, and he'd never be able to tell anyone how he'd felt when she'd walked out from under the trees, looking like something no self-respecting cat would drag in, and started giving him grief.

He'd realized then that marriage was a combination of strength, not just a man taking responsibility for a woman and their children. He'd remembered how as a boy he'd resented his father's being away so much, because he felt it was too hard on his mother, but he'd forgotten until tonight the look on his mother's face when his dad walked in the door. He saw the same radiance on Susannah's face now. "I still want to," he said.

He kissed her then, a beautiful, deep, healing kiss that tore away all the devices by which they'd tried to protect themselves, and revealed a capacity for loving neither one had dared believe existed.

I want to be beside this man, Susannah thought. *I want to live with him, with all his hazards, and bear his children.* And if it should be demanded of her that he, too, should be taken from her, it was worth the price for the breathtaking joy he brought to her in the swift passing of his smile, his gentleness when he touched her son, his humor and zest and compassion.

She loved him not sedately or tranquilly, not securely or reasonably, but with ecstasy and unfettered generosity and a deep, abiding passion that owed nothing to youth or beauty, and had everything to do with eternity. And it was time she told him so.

"Reckon we've got a weddin' on our hands," Vi observed to the enthralled audience. "Pity you ain't a girl, Benny. You could be a bridesmaid."

"Geez, Mrs. Dawson," Benny complained, horrified. "Don't say that. Girls are wazoos."

Floozer rolled over and waved her snowshoe paws in the air, showing anyone who was interested that she could use a little attention and affection, too.

"Except for Floozer," Benny amended, and submitted to having his hair mussed up by Larene, because he didn't want to draw his mother's attention to the fact that it was way past his bedtime. There were a lot of side benefits for a guy when his ma and pa got all kissy-faced.

What the press says about Harlequin romance fiction...

"When it comes to romantic novels...
Harlequin is the indisputable king."
   —*New York Times*

"...always with an upbeat, happy ending."
   —*San Francisco Chronicle*

"Women have come to trust these
stories about contemporary people,
set in exciting foreign places."
   —*Best Sellers*, New York

"The most popular reading matter of
American women today."
   —*Detroit News*

"...a work of art."
   —*Globe & Mail*, Toronto

Six exciting series for you every month... from Harlequin

Harlequin Romance
The series that started it all

Tender, captivating and heartwarming...
love stories that sweep you off to faraway places
and delight you with the magic of love.

◆

Harlequin Presents
Powerful contemporary love stories...as individual as the women who read them

The No. 1 romance series...
exciting love stories for you, the woman of today...
a rare blend of passion and dramatic realism.

◆

Harlequin Superromance®
It's more than romance...
it's Harlequin Superromance

A sophisticated, contemporary romance-fiction
series, providing you with a longer,
more involving read...a richer mix of complex plots,
realism and adventure.

"I Wasn't Interested in Women."

"Of course not."

"Well," he admitted as he released her hand and sat forward a little, "there may have been a few, but none of them had a background as interesting as yours." His blue eyes captured hers and held them for a long, searching moment. "You know, Suzy, this 'Christina' thing might be the turning point of your life. Have you thought about that?"

"Yes," she admitted. Suzy tried to ignore the rush of sensations beneath her skin and appear only mildly concerned—not an easy task with him so near and so disturbingly attractive. She cleared her throat. "Frankly, I'm not sure I'm ready to handle a turning point."

"Really?" He seemed surprised, and then he surprised her by adding, "I am."

Dear Reader:

Nora Roberts, Tracy Sinclair, Jeanne Stephens, Carole Halston, Linda Howard. Are these authors familiar to you? We hope so, because they are just a few of our most popular authors who publish with Silhouette Special Edition each and every month. And the Special Edition list is changing to include new writers with fresh stories. It has been said that discovering a new author is like making a new friend. So during these next few months, be sure to look for books by Sandi Shane, Dorothy Glenn and other authors who have just written their first and second Special Editions, stories we hope you enjoy.

Choosing which Special Editions to publish each month is a pleasurable task, but not an easy one. We look for stories that are sophisticated, sensuous, touching, and great love stories, as well. These are the elements that make Silhouette Special Editions more romantic... and unique.

So we hope you'll find this Silhouette Special Edition just that—*Special*—and that the story finds a special place in your heart.

The Editors at Silhouette

JEAN
KENT
Memories
of the Heart

Silhouette Special Edition

Published by Silhouette Books New York

America's Publisher of Contemporary Romance

To Lois Bayless

SILHOUETTE BOOKS
300 E. 42nd St., New York, N.Y. 10017

Copyright © 1985 by Jean Kent

Distributed by Pocket Books

ISBN: 0-373-09268-7

First Silhouette Books printing October 1985

10 9 8 7 6 5 4 3 2 1

America's Publisher of Contemporary Romance

Printed in the U.S.A.

Silhouette Books by Jean Kent

Silhouette Special Editions

Love's Advocate #237
Memories of the Heart #268

JEAN KENT

was an accountant as well as a self-employed businesswoman until four years ago, when she decided to make a change of career. After enrolling in a creative-writing class, she dusted off her typewriter and went to work. A resident of Uniontown, Ohio, she has three grown children who lend her encouragement and much-needed support.

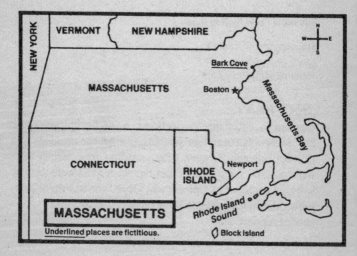

Prologue

Since Suzy was a new patient at the dental offices of Brenhen and Brenhen, she was asked to fill out an information card. She wrote down her name: Suzy Yoder; her age: twenty-five; occupation: real estate saleswoman; address: Windland, Pa.; and so on down to the bottom of the card, where the last question made her pause.

Name of parents: _____

Suzy realized this was for children who weren't responsible for their dental bills, but she was feeling a little zany that day, so just for the heck of it, she proceeded to fill in the blank.

Name of parents: <u>Unknown</u>

Chapter One

Boston's Logan Airport was teeming with activity as travelers hurried across the wide expansive areas dragging children, clutching carry-on bags, checking their tickets, their watches, their gate numbers. Rich Link, however, barely noticed the activity around him as he waited to pass through the metal detector arch. He had no luggage to put on the conveyor belt, no book or newspaper in his hand.

He was a tall man with black wavy hair that was cut short and combed straight back, but stubborn wayward strands kept falling forward. Though they covered his hairline, however, they didn't conceal his brow. In fact, the contrast of his tousled hair, the wide smooth forehead, the bushy black eyebrows and the penetrating blue eyes were startling...and innately captivating.

Walking slowly, Rich kept to the far right of the concourse, his gaze sweeping over the heads of the passengers walking toward him. He was looking for a young woman, twenty-five years old to be exact, of medium height, probably nice-looking, even beautiful; he couldn't be sure. The only thing he was sure of was that she'd have red hair, and, if her voice on the phone meant anything, she'd be walking straight and tall and at a brisk pace. Though Rich had only spoken to Suzy Yoder twice, both times briefly, she'd come across as a no-nonsense type of person who was meeting him more out of a sense of duty than expectation. Odd, he thought, it was usually the other way around.

At gate 12, the crew of flight 709 were bidding their passengers farewell and wishing them a good day. Impatiently Suzy Yoder pushed a strand of tawny red hair back from her face, checked to make sure her white blouse was tucked into her tight-fitting khaki pants and zipped up her quince loafer jacket. Then, sliding her feet back into her high-heeled Italian sandals, she hoisted the straps of her bulky handbag over her shoulder and, bidding the flight crew a cheery good-bye, stepped off the plane.

As she followed the signs to the baggage pickup area where she was supposed to meet Mr. Link, she tucked her hands into the pockets of her jacket and tried to look calm and collected. *If you look composed, you are composed,* she told herself, hoping her façade of casual indifference was convincing. Actually, every nerve in her body was taut with apprehension.

Over the phone, Rich Link had sounded a little brusque, but pleasant enough. His voice had been somewhat guarded, of course, but that was understandable. As the late David Hepburn's lawyer, it was only natural that he'd be skeptical of a woman who showed up twenty-two years after the Hepburn child had been kidnapped and calmly stated that there was a possibility she could be the missing Christina Hepburn. Even Suzy, who loved fantasy as much as anyone, would have found that hard to believe. Nevertheless, she promised herself to look into it and settle the question once and for all. Evidently she wasn't the only one who felt this way. Since the Hepburn estate was paying her fare, someone out there was just as anxious to clear this up as she was. Suzy smiled to herself. Gawd! Wouldn't it be a riot if she really did turn out to be the kidnapped child? Would that ever shake the barn roof!

Walking with a long, firm stride, Suzy wended her way past fellow travelers and kept looking ahead for signs to the baggage claim area. Finally she spotted one at the end of the concourse and was just about to increase her speed when, suddenly, a strong hand grasped her arm in a grip that was so powerful and so possessive that it sent shafts of strange vibrations straight up to her shoulder. For a moment Suzy blinked, a little confused, but not for a minute was she alarmed. She knew right away who it was. The unexpected gesture as well as the firm grip had to belong to the man she'd spoken to on the phone. He'd come across as aggressive, boldly self-confident and tremendously persuasive. After all, hadn't he talked her into coming here to meet the Hepburns?

"Rich Link," came the familiar voice beside her. "I hope to God you're Suzy Yoder."

With a quick laugh Suzy turned toward him and was pleasantly surprised to find herself looking into the face of a young and very handsome man. She'd always thought of lawyers as pompous and stuffy, but not this one. He had a pair of sparkling sea-blue eyes and a wide mouth that tipped upward at the corners in a slightly devilish grin. Using her knowledge of horses as a yardstick, Suzy sensed right away that Rich Link was good stock...trim, neat, confident and just cocky enough to attract attention, but intelligent enough not to be a troublemaker. She liked him instantly.

Suzy rewarded him with a wide sunny smile and extended her hand. "I'm Suzy all right. It's nice meeting you."

"The pleasure is all mine," he assured her, and, still holding her hand, he stepped back a little and deliberately let his gaze sweep up and down her well-proportioned body. He tipped his head slightly to one side. "Hmmm," he murmured, lifting his eyes to her face. He admired her thick auburn-red hair. It was straight and layer-cut to brush down over her forehead and back at the ears with enough length at the nape of her neck to disappear under her collar. His gaze then went to her oval gray-green eyes that were clear and steady and slightly impatient. "Mmmm," he murmured again, and this time he leaned forward and peered closely at her upturned nose. "No freckles?" he asked, squinting to see better.

"A few," Suzy confessed, "but I manage to hide them with makeup." Jauntily she tipped her head to one side. "Well? What do you think? Do I pass?"

"As far as I'm concerned you do."

"Do you think I look like either Joanne or David Hepburn?" she pressed anxiously.

Rich shook his head. "No, not really, but that doesn't mean anything. I don't look like either of my parents, either. Besides," he said as he tucked her arm under his and started toward the baggage claim area, "looks aren't as important as getting these time segments pieced together. We've got a lot of notes to compare before I announce your arrival to the Hepburn family."

With a blink of astonishment, Suzy stopped in midstride. "Do you mean to tell me they don't even know I'm coming?"

"No, not yet. I'm not going to throw everyone at Thrushmore into a state of hysteria until I'm reasonably sure of my facts."

"What facts?" Suzy demanded. "I've already explained everything that pertains to my visit here and you know it." Was he setting himself up as judge and jury? Was she supposed to pass his screening test before he'd allow her to meet Mrs. Hepburn?

He gave her a maddening look of sublime patience. "I don't mean to offend you, Suzy, but you have to realize that over the years we've had almost a dozen young women come here claiming to be Christina Hepburn, and this is always a trauma for Joanne. Until David died three weeks ago, he did all the initial interviewing himself, but now that he's gone, and I'm the executor of the estate, the task has fallen to me."

Without waiting for her response, he took her arm and started down the concourse again.

"I can see where it wouldn't be easy for you," Suzy murmured, wishing now that she'd asked a few more questions before she'd agreed to come out here. She didn't like the inference that she was just another candidate in a long list of contestants. Glancing up at Rich, she was surprised to catch him looking at her. His expression was an odd mixture of boldness and humor. Fascinating.

Deliberately she squared her shoulders and drew herself up to her full height. It was time to look assertive. "I think we'd better get something straight right now, Mr. Link. I didn't come here trying to worm my way into a family where I don't belong. If I happen to be the missing Hepburn child, wonderful, but if not, I have no intention of hanging around. My plans for the weekend are very simple. I'd like to meet Mrs. Hepburn, talk to her for an hour if possible, and leave. If she wants to pursue it further, that's up to her. As for myself"—proudly she lifted her chin—"I am twenty-five years old. I own my own home, and I have a nice job. I'm not seeking crumbs from a stranger's table." *There, mull that over for a while,* she thought as she swung her eyes back to the concourse and started looking for baggage signs again.

Rich expelled an exaggerated sigh. "Well, you're certainly independent, I'll say that, and I apologize if I sounded as if I thought you were here under false pretenses. Needless to say, if I suspected that, you and I wouldn't be standing here at this very moment arguing." Without waiting for a reply, he took her arm and practically shoved her toward the baggage area.

"Come on, let's get out of here. How many bags do you have?"

"Just one. I'm only going to be here until day after tomorrow, remember."

Flattening his mouth into a straight line, Rich shook his head and put a hand on Suzy's shoulders, a large hand with long sensuous fingers and a firm grip. "We need a nice long talk, Suzy. I'm afraid things aren't going to be as cut and dried as you think they are."

There was a note of warning in Rich's voice that made her pause. She glanced up at him, looking him straight in the eyes. "Are you trying to tell me there are strings attached to my meeting with Joanna?"

"No, of course not, but I'm afraid this whole thing goes a little deeper than you realize. Unfortunately, I seem to be caught in the middle."

"Then why doesn't Mrs. Hepburn step in and handle this situation? Why should she leave everything to you?"

Lowering his voice, Rich leaned forward so only Suzy could hear. "Because Mrs. Hepburn hasn't made a decision in twenty-two years. I'll tell you about it later. Right now, let's get your bag and get out of here."

Suzy agreed. The sooner the better. "Over there. The blue one with the orange tag."

In what seeemed like one fluid motion, Rich grabbed the suitcase, took Suzy's arm and marched her through the exit and out into the parking lot. As they hurried along, their arms brushing against each other, Suzy couldn't resist taking a deep breath of the clear air of early spring. This was her favorite time of the year—planting time—at least it used to be her favorite time.

Swallowing a rising ache in her throat, Suzy walked in silence, and, as if sensing her mood, so did Rich. He was really a very thoughtful person, she decided, casting him a sideways glance. Professional-looking, too, in his blue-gray slacks, white shirt and the standard muted print tie. He seemed to typify the successful businessman, tall, straight, athletic. Impressive. The sort of man one could depend on, confide in, draw strength from.... Suddenly Suzy brought herself up short. Why couldn't she ever learn? That was exactly why she'd gotten involved with Roger Mayer.

When Abby Yoder, the woman who had raised her from a child of three, died, there was such a void in Suzy's life that she didn't think she could possibly face it alone. She was in college at the time and dating Roger, a classmate and a pleasant man, but not an outstanding one. Yet with the gnawing loneliness that closed in around her, she turned to Roger for comfort, for strength. Unfortunately he interpreted her need for him as a friend as an invitation for a more permanent relationship. When Suzy refused to let him move in with her, he simply walked out of her life, making her loss twofold. Suzy learned a hard lesson from that experience: If you lean on someone, be prepared to fall.

Rich's car was a sleek black Trans Am, a far cry from the conservative four-door sedan she'd expected. Except for the amused tilt of his mouth and the blue lights that seemed to dance in his eyes, Rich Link came off as a typical lawyer, well groomed, conventionally dressed, efficient, persuasive and friendly.

Yet Suzy couldn't help but wonder just how friendly he really was. So far, he seemed to be genuinely interested in putting the Hepburn family back together again, but obviously there were a few missing pieces and Suzy couldn't help but wonder if, since Rich had been so anxious for her to come, he was using her to solve some other family problem. He certainly didn't look like the conniving type, but who knew what lay beneath the exterior? It was an intriguing thought, but not a worrisome one for Suzy. She prided herself on being a graduate of the school of hard knocks. If Rich Link had any intention of exploiting her, he was in for a few surprises.

With her self-confidence back in place, Suzy found herself relaxing. Idly she watched as Rich wove his way out of the airport parking lot and headed south toward Plymouth. He hadn't gone far before he turned off the expressway.

"Since this is your first trip to Massachusetts, I thought we'd take the scenic route," he explained. "Have you ever been east before?"

"No," she said, pleased that he was going out of his way for her. She knew local residents never took the scenic routes. "I've never seen the Atlantic Ocean, either."

"You'll get a few glimpses of it from the road, but to really appreciate the ocean you have to be so close to the water that you can feel it on your face."

Suzy knew she'd never get that close, but at Rich's suggestion, she rolled down her window and let the rush of sea-clean air blow across her face. Its salty snap felt refreshing on her skin, and turning toward the window, she inhaled deeply. "Mmm, that feels good," she marveled. "Smells good, too."

"There's nothing like it anywhere in the world," he boasted proudly.

Though it was still early May, it was warm, and new leaves were on the trees. All along the side of the road, blue gentians and buttercups kept peeking through the weeds as their colorful blossoms stretched toward the sun. Occasionally Suzy caught a glimpse of the ocean where sailboats slipped effortlessly through the water like flags in the wind. How different this was from the rolling hills of Pennsylvania, she thought as she resettled herself in her seat.

Rich caught the movement. "Comfortable?" he asked.

"Yes, perfect, and the view is spectacular. I hope my hotel room overlooks the bay."

"I'm afraid not," he said with a shake of his head. "As a matter of fact, I haven't booked you into a hotel. I thought it would be better if you stayed at my place."

"Your place?" Suzy cast him a dark, suspicious glance.

His response was a quick grin. "Don't worry. It's all neat and proper. I have a big old house just west of Plymouth and not too far from the Hepburns. I also have a live-in couple who've been there for years, and believe me, Mrs. Slingluff will make sure you're very safe."

"Well! I should hope so!" Suzy huffed playfully. Though she pretended to be shocked, it was impossible not to conceal her delight. She'd dreaded being alone facing the walls of a hotel room for two days.

Besides, the prospect of spending the whole weekend with the vibrantly attractive Rich Link was a temptation no woman in her right mind could resist.

"There aren't any hotels in the immediate area," Rich was saying. "Besides, you and I have a lot of talking to do before you meet the family."

"Before I meet the family or before you allow me to meet the family?"

He shook his head. "I wish you'd realize that I'm not trying to keep you from seeing Joanne, but I *am* trying to piece together some background information."

"It seems to me you should have asked for that before I got here."

"I realize that now," he admitted, "but I thought if I just took it up where David left off, I'd end up with the same results." He flipped his hand out, palm up. "But it's not turning out to be that easy and frankly, I need your help."

"All right," Suzy agreed. It was a reasonable request. "Tell me what you want to know and I'll fill in where I can."

"Fine." Instead of starting with a stream of questions, however, Rich paused for a moment. Was he trying to decide where to begin, she wondered, or how much to tell her? Finally he expelled a deep breath. "Three days before David died, he came into my office and said he wanted to change his will. No problem, it's done every day, but David wanted it done right that minute. He even sat around until it was typed and signed."

"Do you think he knew he had heart trouble?"

"Dr. Hilton swears he didn't, but that's beside the point. Previously he'd left the bulk of his money to his brother, Wayne, who has been his business manager for twenty-five years."

"Didn't he leave anything to his wife?"

"A little property, that's all, but Joanne doesn't need it. She has money in her own right."

Oh, that must be nice, Suzy thought. "It doesn't sound as if the Hepburn family is exactly scrounging around for their next meal."

Rich slid her a long, searching look and then continued. "David changed his will to read that his brother would get the inheritance *unless* his daughter Christina showed up within a year of David's death, in which case half the estate would go directly to her."

"That sounds fair enough," Suzy said, barely aware of Rich's sharp glance.

His voice was low, almost mysterious. "There's a lot of money involved here, Suzy."

"Oh, really? And what do you call a lot?"

"Approximately one hundred million."

"One hundred million dollars? Oh, my God!" she gasped, falling back into her seat. "That's a heap of hay."

"Yes, it certainly is." His voice was no longer teasing, but hard and skeptical. Suzy didn't like it.

"Just for the record," she informed him coolly, "I would like to remind you that I came here to meet Joanne, period. I have no intention of getting involved in a family dispute over money. And furthermore," she added meaningfully, "I wouldn't take the damn inheritance if you handed it to me. I don't need that kind of hassle."

Crossing her arms, she turned to look out the side window. She was aware of Rich watching her, probably trying to analyze her reactions. Well, let him. She wasn't getting embroiled in this one. Money meant trouble and she'd had enough of that in her life, so why ask for more? She felt like telling Rich to make a U-turn and take her right back to the airport, but something about his silence made her pause. Had he accepted her or dismissed her? she wondered, and then immediately answered her own question. If he had dismissed her, she'd have felt it, and if he'd accepted her, he'd have said so. Evidently she was somewhere in between, in limbo. It wasn't the ideal spot to be, but it did make Suzy pause. Since there wasn't open warfare between them, why should she rush back to Pennsylvania? She didn't have anything to lose by staying the weekend. As long as she was here, she might as well stay. She was due a vacation. She needed a change of scenery. The fact that she'd be spending most of her time with the devilishly handsome Rich Link had nothing to do with it. *And if you believe that, Suzy Yoder, why don't you try walking on water sometime?*

Rich's gaze didn't remain long on her face, however. Without turning her head, Suzy knew his eyes were skimming the length of her body, checking her out. If she'd known him better, she'd have asked him how she scored.

Evidently satisfied that she wasn't some ogress out to swindle the Hepburns, he turned his eyes back to the road and, ultimately, returned to the subject at hand. "I don't mean to be insulting, Suzy, but you have to realize that this is a big responsibility for me and I have very little to work from. When David died, the only clue that he'd been in touch with you was a note on his appointment pad. Fortunately, he'd jotted down your phone number. Otherwise I'd have had no idea who you were or why he was going to meet you."

"I'm glad you called," she said, mellowing a little. "Otherwise, I'd have driven up to Harrisburg for nothing. But who knows? He might not have shown up anyway. Even I have to admit the whole idea was a little farfetched."

"Evidently David didn't think so. In all the years I've known him, he's never agreed to go out of his way to meet anyone as he did with you, so there must be something there. I don't know what it is, but"—turning, he gave her a broad wink—"maybe we can figure it out."

The combination of his slow lopsided smile and his curiously expectant expression was irresistible. Suzy found herself wondering if she could do enough for him. "I'll help all I can," she promised.

"I'm sure you will." He gave her hand a gentle pat. "Why don't you start by telling me exactly how you contacted David? That's still a little fuzzy."

When he put his hand back on the wheel, Suzy's skin still tingled from his touch, and she found herself wishing they'd met under other circumstances. But that was ridiculous, she scolded herself, and settling back in her seat, she tried to decide where to begin. "Let's see," she mused, "I guess you could say the whole thing started about two months ago when I went to the dentist. Since I was a new patient, I was asked to fill out a card and in the space marked 'Name of parents' I wrote down 'Unknown.' Don't ask me why I did that. I guess I was just in a kooky mood that day. Anyway, when the dentist read the card and came to that last line, he looked at me and then the card and then leaned closer to inspect my two front teeth.'' She turned to Rich. ''In case you haven't noticed, they're slightly separated. Then he rubbed his chin as if he were trying to remember something. Suddenly he snapped his fingers. Several months ago, he'd seen an article in one of the dental journals about a family in the east looking for a lost child. Since this separation of the two front teeth was a family trait, they were hoping to find this child through the dental association.''

Rich shook his head. ''Oh, God, what a long shot.''

''Yes, I agree. At any rate, Dr. Brenhen found the article and let me take it home to mull over. It read that a New England family was looking for a girl who had disappeared—they **did**n't use the word 'kidnapped'—twenty-two years ago at the age of three. She'd be twenty-five now, my age. The child had red hair and a possible separation of the two front teeth. At the bottom of the ad was a P.O. box number where anyone having information could write.''

''So you wrote?''

''Eventually. I had to think about it for several days, though. I didn't want to get involved in a situation that could backfire.'' She didn't add that after Abby's death plus her blowup with Roger, she wasn't in any mood to chance another disappointment. ''But,'' she added, ''I finally sent the letter off. Why, I don't know.''

"Because it's a natural instinct to want to know who your parents are."

"Maybe," Suzy murmured, not at all convinced. Abby had been the only parent she'd ever had or ever wanted to have. "Anyway," she went on, "I gave whatever information I could, which wasn't much. Needless to say, I was a little surprised when I got a call from David Hepburn about five days later. We talked a few minutes and made arrangements to meet at Harrisburg International Airport a week from the following Saturday." She gave him a sudden grin. "I figured if he was some kind of a kook, I'd be safe enough there. As it was, two days before I was supposed to meet him, you called and told me not to come."

"I see," Rich said. "Now things are beginning to fall into place. When I found the note in David's papers, I assumed you were another woman who thought she might be Christina. Normally, I would have just canceled the appointment and forgotten it, but in view of the new will, I thought the least I could do was check it out." He gave her a warm, spontaneous smile. "And believe me, I have no regrets."

Suzy returned the smile. "I don't, either," she managed to say, wishing the fluttery feeling inside her would settle down. If Rich could accelerate her pulse with a mere grin, what would happen if he really decided to turn on the heat? She'd probably disintegrate.

Rich turned his attention back to the road, as if trying to hide a satisfied smile. Was he having the same trouble with his body's responses as she was? she wondered, cherishing the thought. Then, as if to confirm her suspicions, she could almost feel him forcing himself to keep his mind on the immediate subject.

He cleared his throat. "It's odd that David agreed to go to Harrisburg to meet you," he went on doggedly. "Why didn't you come here? Everyone else did."

Suzy was almost sorry to be back on the same old subject, but then, that's why she was here, she reminded herself. "He did ask me to come here, but I'm a realtor and sometimes I work seven days a week. I just couldn't take the time off."

Rich laughed. "That alone would have impressed David. He was a workaholic himself, though I always blamed that on Joanne."

"What's she like?"

"Oh, that's a long story," he said, dismissing the whole subject as something too wearisome to go into at this time. Instead, he concentrated on the driving.

They turned off the main road and headed west, away from the coast. The countryside was magnificent. Occasionally Suzy caught glimpses of large, spacious homes screened from the road by towering trees and heavy foliage. As they sped past the manicured lawns and curving driveways, her interest quickened. Did the Hepburns live in a place like this? she wondered. Did Rich?

Her answer wasn't long in coming.

"Here we are," Rich announced as the car slowed. Turning into a drive almost completely hidden by shrubbery, he started up a steep hill. When they crested the rise, Suzy drew in a deep breath. She didn't need a guidebook to tell her she was looking at one of the most outstanding country homes in America, probably built at the turn of the century. Rich cruised around a wide circular drive before stopping under a magnificent portico. It was supported by four gigantic Corinthian pillars that stood like sentinels, tall, white, dazzling in the afternoon sun.

Chapter Two

Suzy was so enthralled with the spectacular landscape that she was only vaguely aware of Rich helping her out of the car. With a firm hand at the small of her back, he started leading her up the stairway, but Suzy refused to be hurried. She stopped to look around her at the beautifully kept lawns, the neat hedges, the newly planted gardens, all of which testified to the existence of a conscientious gardener as well as a very proud owner.

"Magnificent," she whispered as her eyes swept past the gardens and up to the large Colonial-style house before her. "Is this your family home?"

"Yes. It's called Link Hall. My grandfather built it in 1910. Eventually it was passed down to my father and he kept it because he and my mother were planning on having a big family. Unfortunately, she died of polio when I was two years old."

"Oh, I'm sorry to hear that. Then you and your dad lived here alone?"

"Right. As a matter of fact, he and David Hepburn were very close friends. My dad was his lawyer. Unfortunately, Dad died two years ago and Link Hall was passed down to me."

"Are you planning on keeping it?"

"I don't know." He shrugged. "I haven't decided yet."

"You're very fortunate to own such a lovely piece of property." She paused, then added, "Of course, it's a lot of house for a bachelor."

Rich nudged her in the arm. "What makes you think I'm single?"

"Oh, just a guess," she equivocated. How could she explain that her responses to him were dead giveaways? If he'd been married, his vibes would have been entirely different and her body wouldn't be thudding with strange pleasurable sensations that refused to go away.

"You're a good guesser," he said quickly, dispelling any shadows of doubt. "I'm a grumpy thirty-two-year-old bachelor who, at this moment, is tired of standing on the front porch and would like to go inside and share a drink with one of the most beautiful women to ever enter Link Hall." The hand at her back that had been so gently guiding her suddenly pushed her forward. "Let's go."

Suzy proceeded to ignore the shove, preferring instead to remember the tenderness of his first touch. Just the same, an unruly tingle of excitement ran down her spine and she found herself wondering if perhaps her initial doubts about him hadn't been a little premature. Why would anyone with his looks, personality and money want to exploit her?

Suddenly the door opened and a tall, thin, grayhaired man nodded a brief welcome. Immediately he took possession of Suzy's suitcase.

Rich introduced him as "Albert, the man who keeps things running around here. He's also the husband of the best cook in New England who"—he sniffed the air thoughtfully "—is making cherry cobbler, right?"

Albert's face broke into a wide smile. "Right again."

The comfortable friendship between the two men made Suzy wonder just how long Albert had been there, but before she could ask, a plump little woman in her late fifties bustled across the spacious hallway, her face wreathed in a smile.

"Mrs. Slingluff has been waiting all day for this hour," Rich joshed. "If there's two things she likes, it's company and gossip."

The older woman obviously enjoyed his teasing and shook her head good-naturedly. "If you didn't have me to torment, you'd die of boredom." She turned to Suzy. "He's been that way ever since he was two years old, but don't let him hurry you. I know you want to freshen up. He can find something to do until you get back."

Rich glanced at his watch, then at Suzy. "You've got five minutes."

Instantly, Mrs. Slingluff rallied to Suzy's defense. "Stop being so impatient. She wants to unpack and settle in. It won't hurt you to wait a minute. Read the mail or something."

"Oh, all right," he conceded reluctantly. "Where is it?"

Mrs. Slingluff exhaled a patient sigh. "It's on the hall table in the same spot I've been putting it for thirty years."

"Well, you can never be too sure," he teased, then gave Suzy a conspiratorial wink. "You've got two minutes."

"She does not," Mrs. Slingluff stated firmly, and turning to Suzy, she added, "Don't listen to him. He just likes to hear himself talk. That's why he's a lawyer."

Rich made some comment, but Suzy didn't hear it as she and Mrs. Slingluff crossed the spacious hall and started up the sweeping staircase that curved in a wide arc to the second floor. Though Suzy was listening to Mrs. Slingluff's bright chatter, she had trouble giving it her full attention. She knew instinctively that Rich was watching her ascent, but she didn't dare turn his way. She didn't want him to know that his mere presence was enough to upset her concentration.

Halfway down the hall, Mrs. Slingluff turned into one of the bedrooms. Suzy stepped across the threshold and immediately fell in love with the room. It was pure femininity from the starched curtains to the soft floral pattern of the wallpaper to the muted moss green of the carpet. "This is the most beautiful room I've ever seen," she exclaimed. "It's like a garden of flowers."

Mrs. Slingluff beamed with pride at Suzy's enthusiasm. "Thank you," she said, straightening a fold of the dust ruffle. "All of the bedrooms here are beautiful. Rich had Miss Tolbert redecorate the whole second floor last year. She has such elegant taste. She was nice to work with, too. Not at all like the grouch we had last time."

"It sounds like you've been here quite a while."

"Oh, I have." She smiled lovingly. "Rich was only two years old when we came and a real demon, too. Albert and I had a terrible time keeping him in line, but he grew up to be a wonderful boy, don't you think?" Her eyes twinkled expectantly.

"Oh, definitely." Suzy smiled. Then, for Mrs. Slingluff's benefit, she added, "And very polite, too. He has beautiful manners."

She couldn't have said anything more flattering. Mrs. Slingluff absolutely beamed. "Yes, he turned out pretty good."

"He sure did." Suzy knew that Mrs. Slingluff and Albert were, in all likelihood, solely responsible for Rich's upbringing. He was probably closer to them than he'd been to his father, just as she'd been closer to Abby than...than who?

Shaking herself, she walked over to the antique dresser. She couldn't resist running her hand across its satin-smooth finish and inspecting a bowl of early spring roses. "Did these flowers come from your garden?" she asked.

Mrs. Slingluff nodded, pleased that Suzy had noticed them. "My husband has a way with roses. He built a little greenhouse off the south porch. Do you like flowers?"

"Oh, I love them. In fact, I like anything that has to do with the outdoors."

"That's grand. I wish Rich was more like that. He's such a bookworm. Maybe you can get him out in the fresh air. I've tried, but no luck."

"I'd like to, but I'll be going home on Sunday."

"Oh?" she asked, surprised. "From the way Rich talked, I thought you were going to be here a week or more."

Suzy shook her head. "Oh, no, Rich must have misunderstood me."

Mrs. Slingluff looked decidedly disappointed. "Oh, that's too bad. It's always nice to have young people here, but since Mr. Link died, Rich hasn't had much time for entertaining. Miss Tolbert comes over once in a while, but that's all."

Suzy couldn't help but wonder just how involved Rich was with Miss Tolbert, but immediately she chastised herself for being so sophomoric. Of course there'd be a woman in Rich's life, lots of them, perhaps even a fiancée. His looks and personality would almost automatically make him the most sought-after bachelor in Massachusetts. Still, Suzy found herself wondering just who this Miss Tolbert was and was even tempted to pump Mrs. Slingluff. But why? she asked herself. What difference did it make to her? She wasn't in the running. In two days she'd be back in Windland and out of his life forever.

Mrs. Slingluff had turned back toward the door. "If you don't need anything, I think I'll go back to my kitchen." She gave Suzy a broad wink. "I'm preparing a surprise for Rich."

"You go right ahead." Suzy smiled and waved her off. "I'll be just fine."

When the door closed behind her, however, Suzy felt a strange cloud of disappointment settle over her. Just tension, she told herself. Maybe if she took a long, soaking bath and changed into something dressy for dinner, she'd feel better; but then, Rich was expecting her downstairs right away. No guest should keep her host waiting, right? Hurriedly Suzy took off her jacket, freshened up her makeup and brushed her hair. As she stood before the mirror and fussed unnecessarily with her blouse, she began to wonder if she'd done the right thing in coming here. It would have been different if David Hepburn were still alive. He'd been her only contact, and with that gone, she stood alone. Or did she? Suzy wondered. Her thought flitted back to the boldly handsome face with the mischievous light blue eyes....

"Two minutes," he'd said.

She found Rich in the library sitting in a big chair, reading. It was a room filled with treasures: a collection of jade figurines, a porcelain vase full of greens, a detailed replica of an old sailing ship and shelves and shelves of books. At the far end of the room was a huge oak desk and beyond that were French doors. They stood open, now, letting the amber tones of late afternoon sunlight cast shadows on the floor.

As Rich stood up, his appreciative glance swept over Suzy's slim figure with unabashed admiration. Suzy knew he was being deliberately provocative, so she, in turn, did a little reviewing herself. First she noted the certain boldness in the way he stood, feet apart, arms thrust forward, shoulders broad and square, head up, one eyebrow lifted in amused scrutiny. His gaze was a veiled challenge, but Suzy met it steadily, fully aware of the effect his male vigor was having on her but confident that she could handle it. No problem.

With a quirk of his eyebrow, Rich motioned her to one of the deep-cushioned sofas. It wasn't hard to guess that he planned to settle down beside her, so Suzy opted for one of the other chairs. She was finding his nearness more disturbing than their brief friendship warranted. And since their relationship had nowhere to go, why fan the fire?

Rich, obviously disappointed that she'd taken the chair beside his, flattened his mouth into a straight line. "Do you have something against couches?"

"Not at all, but they always make me feel sleepy, and it's too early for that."

As soon as she said it, she could tell that Rich was making a note of her last statement, but he made no further comment and crossed over to a small built-in bar near the bookcase. "What'll it be?" he asked.

"Wine if you have it, please."

"And we do. How about a light Beaujolais?"

"Sounds wonderful."

"I thought you'd like it," he murmured as he busied himself with the drinks. "Most women do."

Suzy ground her teeth, sorry now she hadn't asked for a straight shot of whiskey. Not that she wanted it, but she just felt like shocking someone.

Rich handed her a glass and, touching it with his own, proposed a toast. "Here's to a successful tomorrow." His eyes met hers with a look of curious amusement that was as challenging as it was tantalizing.

Suzy met his gaze steadily. "I hope so," she said, taking a sip of wine. "But don't make it sound so ominous."

"I didn't mean to." Sinking down into his chair again, Rich set his glass on the table between them and turned his full attention to Suzy. "While you were upstairs, I phoned Thrushmore, that's the name of the Hepburn home, and talked to Wayne."

Her eyes gazed expectantly at his. "And?" she prodded, slightly wary now.

"I told him we'd be over to visit them tomorrow. Needless to say, he wasn't exactly overjoyed to hear there was another prospective Christina on the horizon, let alone that she was staying at my place."

"No," Suzy agreed, "I don't imagine he'd like that at all, and frankly, I don't blame him." Absently she turned the glass in her hand, staring, unseeing, at its contents. "I hope I didn't make a mistake in coming here."

"Of course you didn't," he stated emphatically. "Who knows? Maybe you really are Christina, in which case you owe it to Joanne as well as yourself to hang in there until you find out."

"But if I'm not, then I'm putting a lot of stress on the family unnecessarily."

Rich squared his jaw. "Well, it's too late to worry about that now. You've come too far to turn back." The stern tone of his voice surprised her. "Now that everyone at Thrushmore, except Joanne, of course, knows that you're here, you can hardly sneak back to Windland, Pennsylvania, and pretend nothing has happened. At this point, I'd say you were committed to seeing the thing through."

Thoughtfully, Suzy brushed a strand of hair back into place. He was right, of course. She couldn't turn back now even if she wanted to. "All right," she conceded, "I guess I can handle it for a few days." Her face eased into a sudden smile. "We Amish are made of pretty stern stuff."

"And so are we New Englanders," he assured her, giving her foot a gentle nudge with the tip of his shoe. Suzy slid him a warning glance, but he wasn't even looking, or so it seemed. Nevertheless, she recrossed her legs and swung them away from him.

As if entirely unconscious of the meaningful shift of her body, Rich leaned back in his chair. "Well," he said, slapping his hands together, "what do you say we get back to filling me in on the details? Let's see, why don't you start with Abby? She seems to be a key person in this thing."

"Okay, well…"

"Why don't we get comfortable first?" Before Suzy could even open her mouth to reply, Rich was on his feet and pulling her out of the chair. In one swift movement, he'd seated her on the couch and eased down beside her. Then, turning toward her, he stretched his arm across the back of the sofa in a pose of rapt attention. "There, that's better," he said. "Go on."

His maneuvering didn't fool Suzy for a minute, but she did enjoy his nearness, and why make an issue of something so trivial? "Well, Abby—"

"Comfortable?"

"Yes, fine."

"Good." Rich resettled himself. This time he seemed a little closer, but Suzy didn't make any at-

tempt to move away from him. After all, if this was
going to be story hour, why not get comfortable?

Oddly, it was Rich who got the story going again.
"Why don't you start by telling me what Abby was
like?"

"Well, needless to say, she was everything I had, but
you already know that." Rich nodded but made no
comment. "She'd been born and raised on an Amish
farm near Windland, Pennsylvania. She had one
brother, but he died when he was very young, so the
responsibility of caring for her aging parents rested
squarely on Abby. She never married, you know, and
had a minimal education. She only went through the
fifth grade, but don't misunderstand me, Abby was no
dummy."

"I'm sure of that," Rich agreed.

"After her parents died, she inherited their small
farm and proceeded to eke out a living from it the best
she could. Unfortunately, Abby was no farmer. She
had to work so hard to get so little that she became
something of a recluse. The only bright spot in her
week was Monday, when she went into town to sell her
produce." Suzy tipped her face up to Rich's. "Windland was a small farming community then, and once
a week they had a farmers' market where everyone for
miles around gathered to sell their fruits and vegeta-
bles as well as any secondhand stuff they had."

"You mean a flea market sort of thing?"

"Yes," Suzy answered, "but not like the ones they
have today. Twenty-two years ago they were very ru-
dimentary and strictly for farmers only, especially
small ones like Abby. She had an old pickup truck and
every Monday she'd load it up with produce and

chickens and eggs. If there was any room left over, and there usually was, she'd toss in old books, hardware, broken furniture, you name it.'' Fondly, Suzy shook her head. ''Abby had a whole barn full of junk. In fact, she had so much stuff that she didn't know half of what was there. Anyway, come Monday morning, she'd fill up the truck, tie a tarp over it and head for town. When she got to the market, she'd back the truck up to her stall, unload her produce and set up a chair. She sold whatever she could at whatever price she could get. Abby had no system of markups, you understand, or anything as sophisticated as inventory control.''

''I know the type well.''

''When it came time to go home, she'd just reverse the process, tossing everything back into the truck at random, never really knowing what she'd sold and what she was taking back.'' Again Suzy raised her face to Rich's. ''I'm telling you this because it's important that you know how disorganized Abby was.''

Rich nodded, understanding. ''I think I'm beginning to get the picture.''

Suzy went on, determined not to let her growing awareness of him interfere with her story. This was business. ''One Monday, July seventh to be exact—''

''July seventh? That was four days after Christina was kidnapped.''

''I know. That's what Mr. Hepburn said on the phone.''

''Sorry, I didn't mean to interrupt.'' His fingers tapped against the back of the couch. ''Carry on.''

She nodded. ''Abby stayed at the market later than usual. It had been a scorcher of a day and she was in a hurry to pack up and get out of there. So she tossed everything in the truck, hooked up the tailgate and headed down the road. She was about halfway home when her eye caught a movement of some kind in the rearview mirror. At first she thought one of the ropes on the tarp had blown loose, but she was in a hurry and didn't bother to stop and fix it. The next time she looked in the mirror, however, she saw a face staring back at her.

"Oh, my God!" Rich whistled. "That must have been a shock."

Suzy couldn't help but laugh. "To hear Abby tell it, her hair stood on end. She slammed on the brakes and pulled off the road. It wasn't until then that she realized the face peering at her through the window was that of a child."

"Ahh," Rich exclaimed, nodding. "Now the pieces are beginning to fall into place."

"I hope so."

"Go on. What happened?"

"She went around to the back of the truck and called. When no one answered, she hauled herself up onto the truck bed and started shoving stuff out of the way. When she got to me, I was soaked with perspiration, stark naked, and had a deathly white pallor. She knew right away I'd been 'grogged,' as she put it."

"Doped?"

"Yes, but that didn't alarm Abby. She just put me on the front seat beside her and drove home." Suzy threw up her hands. "That was it."

Rich's brow creased in a deep frown. "What do you mean? That was it? She didn't call the police?"

"No." Suzy shook her head insistently. "I know it sounds ridiculous, but if you knew Abby you'd understand. You have to remember that she'd lived alone for almost twenty years and was a very suspicious person who distrusted strangers. All the while I was growing up, she'd have a fit if anyone came onto the property."

"But this could hardly be considered a normal event," he insisted.

"I know, and so did Abby. She decided it was getting late and she'd just wait until morning to call. She didn't have a phone, so she'd either have to drive into town or go to the neighbors. Time wasn't important to Abby."

"I guess not! But the police were called the next day, weren't they?"

Again the answer was negative. "By that time she'd changed her mind." Suzy shrugged. "When we got home the first thing she did was give me a bath, and it was while she was bathing me that she recognized the smell of chloroform in my hair."

"Chloroform?" Rich repeated. "How would Abby know anything about that?"

"In the old days it was used all the time to anesthetize farm animals. In any case, she recognized the smell and it made her realize that some farmer had left me in her care deliberately...and that made me her property. You have to remember, Abby wasn't a worldly person. She didn't even have a radio, let alone a TV, and the only magazines she read were a year old. So if there'd been a kidnapping anyplace except next door to her, she'd never have known about it."

Rich kept shaking his head, incredulous. "But surely she must have at least suspected foul play."

Suzy straightened, pulling away from him a little. "You'd think so, and frankly, I'm not sure she didn't suspect something...."

"But why, then...?"

"Because she was in her late fifties and had spent most of her life alone. When she found this child it was like a whole new world to her, don't you see? She wasn't a criminal. She was a very honest person who convinced herself that my mother had put me in that truck knowing Abby would take care of me. I doubt if kidnapping ever crossed her mind. If it did, she chose to ignore it."

"Oh, my God," Rich murmured, half to himself. "I can't believe this. It sounds like something out of the Dark Ages."

Suzy smiled. "Sometimes I find it hard to believe myself."

"What happened the next day?"

"Well..." Suzy shrugged. "There isn't much to tell. Abby went out to the barn the next morning and brought in some used clothing she had out there. The things that fit me were size three, so she assumed I was three years old. She'd asked me several times what my name was, and I always answered 'Suzy,' so she named me Suzy. Suzy Yoder, age three. She told everyone I was her cousin's child from Nebraska. No one thought anything about it."

Closing his eyes, Rich shook his head with disbelief. "Wow, what a TV show this would make," he exclaimed, gazing at her with a sort of wonder. "It's incredible that you not only survived this thing, but that you turned out to be such a beautiful, intelligent woman with a great deal of poise and flawless grammar. How in hell did you manage all this, anyway?"

Suzy had to clear her throat. There was a strange throbbing tightness there that seemed to be getting worse by the minute. Darn her nerves anyway. "Abby had good grammar," she went on to explain. "She was poor but she wasn't illiterate, and of course I went to public school through the twelfth grade and then into college."

"Did you graduate?"

"Yes. In fact, it was just before my graduation that Abby died."

"And then what did you do?"

It was a natural question, but one Suzy was hoping he wouldn't ask. She tried circling around it. "Well, I stayed there awhile, then I sold the house and bought a co-op apartment." That sounded normal enough, didn't it? But she'd underestimated the prodding of the legal mind.

"Did you live there alone?" he pressed.

Okay, that's enough, Suzy decided, and turning, she met his bright, inquisitive eyes with her calm gray ones. "That has nothing to do with the Hepburn child."

"Of course not." He nodded quickly, pretending to be chagrined. "I understand. I didn't mean to pry.... Did you have a boyfriend?"

"I was dating a classmate of mine."

"After Abby died, did he move in with you?"

Suzy couldn't help but smile. "Boy, you sure are nosy."

"I know, but I want to get the whole picture. It's important." He leaned toward her until he was so close that Suzy felt she should back away a little. "Well, did he?"

Suzy imagined she could feel the warmth of his breath on her cheek. It was a nice feeling, like a breeze that was so soft nothing moved, but you could still feel its coolness. It was also mesmerizing. Before Suzy realized it, she was sharing her innermost secrets. "As a matter of fact, right after Abby died, I turned to Roger for support and solace. Unfortunately, he wasn't thinking along those lines, so he walked out."

To her amazement, Rich wasn't surprised at all. "I can understand that. You were grieving, you were very lonely and you sought out a companion."

"I know." She grimaced. "But this one didn't last long."

"Some people can't handle responsibility"—he shrugged matter-of-factly—"but in the long run, you were better off without him." He gave her hand a teasing pat. "I hope you ran him off the property with a shotgun."

"Believe me, I was tempted to." She laughed, loving his humor, but he'd delved into her past long enough. Time to change the focus. "And what about you? What kind of growing-up years did you have?"

Resting his head back against the cushions, Rich stretched out his long legs. "Well, frankly, Suzy, after your story, I feel like I've spent my whole life in a pencil box. Nothing exciting ever happened to me."

"Oh, I can't believe that."

"Well, there may have been a few fracases at college, but nothing serious. Unfortunately, my father didn't think so. He was a stickler for the rules."

"Most parents are, especially when they're footing the bill."

"His opinion exactly. I went to a college that absolutely forbade the consumption of alcoholic beverages in the dorm."

"And you sneaked in a six-pack of beer?"

"No, I sneaked in a small refrigerator and sold cold beer to my classmates. I had a nice little business going until some jerko squealed on me."

"You weren't surprised, were you?"

Rich tipped his head slightly to one side. "As a matter of fact, I was. It never occurred to me that my little enterprise wouldn't go on forever." Again he leaned forward, and this time Suzy did, too. "Which all goes to prove how naive I was. I even tried to blame my father for raising me in a sheltered environment."

"And how did that go over?"

"Not well at all."

Suzy grinned. "What happened? Were you suspended?"

"No, my dad talked them out of that. I was put on probation for one term, but that turned out to be kind of fun, since all the guys I'd sold the beer to were also put on probation."

"That must have endeared you to your classmates."

"Well, it made us quite a status symbol. All the girls thought we were real macho. Of course," he added with a nonchalant shrug, "I wasn't interested in women."

"Of course not."

"Well," he admitted as he released her hand and sat forward a little, "there may have been a few, but none of them had a background as interesting as yours." His blue eyes captured hers and held them for a long, searching moment. "You know, Suzy, this Christina thing might be the turning point of your life. Have you thought about that?"

"Yes," she admitted. Suzy tried to ignore the rush of sensations beneath her skin and to appear only mildly concerned, not an easy task with him so near and so disturbingly attractive. She cleared her throat. "Frankly, I'm not sure I'm ready to handle a turning point."

"Really?" He seemed surprised and then he surprised her by adding, "I am."

Suzy couldn't imagine how anyone as secure as Rich would want to change a thing, but then she barely knew him. "I suppose anyone could turn his life around if he really worked at it."

"I wouldn't know where to start."

Suzy grinned impishly. "Why don't you start by spending more time outside? Jog or something."

"Mmm, you've been talking to Mrs. Slingluff, I can see that. She absolutely refuses to believe that working out in a gym is as healthy as jogging through the woods." He gave her a jaunty look. "Of course, if you'd like to get up early in the morning and go with me..."

"Not on your life," Suzy stated. "I'm on vacation."

"That's the best time to start." Getting to his feet, he extended a hand and pulled her up beside him. For a moment their faces were so close together that Suzy could feel the warmth of his breath on her cheek. For a moment she wondered if he was going to take her in his arms, but the thought was quickly dispelled as he dropped her hands. It wasn't until then that she heard the footsteps crossing the hall.

It was Albert. "Dinner's ready," he announced, and quickly turned and left. His departure was so expeditious that Suzy suspected he was accustomed to interrupting amorous scenes. She wasn't surprised; Rich wasn't the sort of man who remained inoperative for long. He probably had a whole book full of phone numbers he could have called, would have called, if she hadn't been there.

Chapter Three

The table in the smaller of the two dining rooms was set with soft green linen mats and sprigs of spring flowers in a long crystal bowl. Short tapered candles flickering in the fading twilight gave the room a warm and welcoming air. Suzy felt comfortable and relaxed and, admittedly, protected. Despite Rich's light bantering, he was a very assured person who had himself well under control. When Suzy was with him, her anxieties about the morrow, as well as her resolves of yesterday, seemed to melt like butter on a warm day. She had the feeling that with Rich on her side, she could tackle anything.

Sitting opposite her, Rich put his arms on the table and, leaning forward, proceeded to indulge in his favorite occupation—studying Suzy Yoder. His gaze roved over her neck and shoulders and then upward to her hair, where copper highlights danced in the flickering light.

He shook his head. "I'll say one thing for you, Suzy. You do have red hair."

She smiled good-naturedly. "Candlelight seems to make it redder."

"It makes it glow like a sunset," he said. "Maybe you should dine by candlelight all the time."

"As a matter of fact, I used to do it quite often, though not by choice. In rural areas, electricity isn't very dependable. Abby and I got very accustomed to eating by candlelight."

"I know what you mean. We have the same problem out here when a storm comes in from the east."

"I think it's fun once in a while," Suzy admitted. "In fact, I kind of miss it since I've been living in an apartment."

"Well, maybe we can conjure up a big old-fashioned storm for you while you're here. Then you'll feel right at home."

"I feel at home already," she assured him. "It doesn't seem possible I've only been here a few hours."

"Seems to me you've only been here two minutes...."

Mrs. Slingluff came bustling into the room, her face the typical picture of a happy cook. Her big surprise was beef Wellington with béarnaise sauce, one of Rich's favorites. He made a big fuss over it, which delighted Mrs. Slingluff, but when he suggested that she should have made a cherry cobbler for dessert, he went too far.

"That Albert," she scolded. "He can't keep anything to himself."

Rich insisted that Albert hadn't said one word. "It's my sixth sense," he whispered mysteriously.

"Oh, posh!" She laughed and started out of the room. "You don't have any sixth sense."

Grinning, Rich glanced across the table at Suzy, who was looking at him with a relaxed, open smile. He tipped his head to one side. "Something tells me I'm beginning to develop one, though, because right now, you remind me of someone."

"Joanne?"

"No, not Joanne, and not David... I just can't place it now." He smiled quickly. "But I'll work on it. What do you say we concentrate on the beef Wellington? If you eat very fast, Mrs. Slingluff will hustle out here with seconds."

Suzy looked down at her plate. "I'm afraid I have all I can handle with this."

"Not me," he exclaimed, picking up his fork. "Besides, she'd be disappointed if I didn't complain about the meager portions she serves."

"It's very loyal of you to eat enough for two just to make her happy."

"It's the least I can do."

Suzy smiled and shook her head. "You and the Slingluffs seem to get along very well."

"They're like second parents to me."

"So I see. But why do you still call her Mrs. Slingluff? Doesn't she have a first name?"

"Yes." He grimaced. "It's Hermione, and as a child I couldn't pronounce it. Yet strangely enough, I could handle Mrs. Slingluff, so it's been that ever since."

"Were the Slingluffs in charge of your upbringing?" Suzy couldn't resist prying into Rich's background. Why, she didn't know; but then, why not? After all, he'd been prying into hers all afternoon.

"More or less. My dad usually took over on the weekends, though."

"Were you and your dad very close?"

"Not so much when I was growing up, but as I got older and took an interest in law, we spent a lot of time together." He glanced up at Suzy. "That's not saying we agreed on everything, you understand, but," he hurried on, "basically we hit it off pretty well, especially when it came to leisure time. He and David Hepburn owned a small sailboat and very often the three of us would spend a whole weekend at Newport Bay."

"Sounds like wonderful times." Suzy sighed wistfully. "You must have known David Hepburn pretty well, then."

Rich mulled this over for a minute. "As much as anyone, I suppose. He wasn't one to confide in people. Sometimes I think my dad and his brother, Wayne, were the only people David really knew well."

"Did Wayne ever go sailing with you?"

"Oh, God, no. He's the most unathletic person I've ever known, and he's the opposite of David. But they seemed to have gotten on very well. David hired Wayne to manage the Hepburn business enterprises about twenty-five years ago. He's invaluable as a consultant and adviser, but I'm afraid he's also penurious." He cocked Suzy a warning brow. "I can tell you right now he's going to put up one hell of a fight before he lets any of the Hepburn assets out of his hands.''

Suzy wasn't at all intimidated. "As I told you, I'm not here for the money. I came to see Joanne." Why was it so hard to make him understand this?

Rich slanted her a guarded look. "Don't be surprised if Wayne tries to stop you."

"Why would he do that? As long as I don't want the Hepburn money, what does he have to lose?"

Rich leaned forward, his expression calm but serious. "Wayne doesn't think that Joanne is emotionally capable of making any sort of a decision at this time, and frankly, I have to agree with him."

"So what's there to decide?" Suzy asked. "No one could look at a twenty-five-year-old woman and say, 'Yes, that's my three-year-old baby all right.'"

Rich expelled a long breath. "Suzy, that's just the point. Do you realize what the consequences would be if she really did say that? Legally, if a mother and daughter both decide they belong together, that's it! Who's to dispute it? The brother-in-law? He'd be thrown out of court. He wouldn't have a leg to stand on."

"But I'm not arguing about the money," Suzy retorted. "Why can't you understand that?"

"I do understand it, but it's out of your hands. Legally, if you are Christina Hepburn, the money is yours whether you want it or not. Of course," he added, "you could give it all back later, but I'm sure Wayne isn't going to hang his hopes on that."

"Then what's he going to do?" Suzy asked, worried. The conversation was getting a little more involved than she'd bargained for.

"The only thing he can do." Rich flung his hands outward. "He's got to try to get Joanne declared mentally incompetent and claim that you have swooped in here and are coercing Joanne into believing you're her child."

"Why, I'd never do that!" Suzy declared.

"I know you wouldn't, Suzy, but try convincing Wayne of that."

"He must be a real worm," she said irritably.

Rich gave her a wise nod. "Now you're catching on."

Dejected, Suzy sat back in her seat. "*Now* what am I supposed to do? All I need is a legal battle."

Rich gave her a broad, reassuring smile. "Don't start worrying about something that may never happen. Besides"—gently his foot nudged hers—"I'll be there to make sure you get a fair shake."

To Suzy, his words were like a balm on an aching wound, and almost immediately her confidence level went up one notch. With Rich on her side, how could she lose? He was on her side, wasn't he?

Raising her head, she faced him squarely, her gray-green gaze boldly searching the depths of his dark blue eyes. "Are you going to represent me?"

Rich looked at her with such a magnetic gaze that for a brief moment Suzy stopped breathing. Then, to her disappointment, he slowly shook his head. "I'm sorry, Suzy, but I can't be your lawyer. God knows I'd like to, but technically I represent David Hepburn. It's up to me to see that his wishes are carried out. This means that if you are Christina Hepburn, I must see that you get half the estate. But if you aren't, then it's my duty to see that Wayne gets it."

"I understand," Suzy said quickly, but despite her concurrence, she felt a sudden stab of disappointment. Somehow she'd just assumed Rich would be on her side, but she could see the error in her thinking. Rich's job was to remain objective, and he couldn't very well do that if he was representing her. It would have been nice to have a teammate, Suzy thought, but the realization that she'd be standing alone didn't throw her into a panic. She'd been in this position before many times and she'd learned to take it easy, not expect too much, stand tall and hang in there like a bulldog. She intended to do all of the above. Her goal was to see Joanne and talk to her, and to hell with Wayne and his mercenary objections.

With her objectives firm, Suzy decided to guide the conversation back to neutral ground, and by the time the meal was over, it was as if the Hepburn family never existed. After dinner, however, when they took their coffee into the living room, Rich hauled out a thick law book and started looking for something on the rights of alleged heirs. Suzy sat on the couch, her feet tucked under her, and listened to some of the short passages that Rich read aloud. It was hard for her to concentrate on the complex legal language, though, and she found her mind and her eyes drifting to the tall, handsomely muscled man beside her. Silently she studied his tousled dark hair, his strong neck and shoulders, his tapered fingers as they leafed through the book. Even when he was motionless, he had a commanding presence, and it was hard for her not to feel disappointed that he wasn't on her side one hundred percent. Trying to regain her confidence, she reminded herself that if it hadn't been for Rich, she'd have never gotten this far in the first place. What more did she want, for heaven's sake?

As if in answer to her question, Rich gripped her ankle with his broad hand and set the book aside. When he looked at her, his mouth was parted slightly in a half smile. "That's enough homework for one night. What do you say we take a walk? It's still warm out, and I know a lot of secret paths we can explore."

"In the dark?"

"Of course, that's the best time." Without waiting for a possible protest, he pulled Suzy to her feet, and putting his broad hand across her back, he walked her outside, where the sweet scent of spring blossoms hung in the warm night air. The sky was clear and spattered with a myriad glittering stars. It was easy for Suzy to forget herself and her problems and just enjoy the moment.

"Mmm," she murmured, inhaling deeply. "I smell apple blossoms."

"Yes, there's an orchard over here on the hill. Let's take a walk that way." Sliding his arm up to her shoulders, Rich led her to a path behind the house and past Link Hall's well-tended gardens to a leveled area at the top of a hill where one could see for miles.

Suzy's eyes swept appreciatively across the panorama before her. "I'll bet this was one of your favorite spots when you were growing up."

Smiling, he nodded and squeezed her shoulder. "You're right. Did you have one?"

"Oh, definitely. Mine was on the top of a hill, too, but all I could see were acres and acres of cornfields."

"Well, I hate to brag, but from my secret spot, you can locate almost every high point in the area. You can even see Thrushmore from here."

"Oh, really? Where?"

Instead of pointing, Rich took her chin in his hand and turned her head toward a cluster of lights on an adjoining hill. It was an obvious intimate gesture, and, though the temptation was great, Suzy knew better than to let her throbbing responses have their own way. Turning, she freed her chin from his grasp and pretended to be so lost in the mysteries of Thrushmore that she was barely aware of his presence.

"Do you remember the kidnapping?" she asked nonchalantly.

She could sense his reaction, amused but not discouraged. Evidently deciding to play it her way, however, he, too, turned toward Thrushmore. "No, not really. I was just ten at the time, and all the parents in the neighborhood decided to protect their children from the travails of reality. Besides, they didn't want to encourage a second kidnapping. Their reasoning was that if the abductors got away with the money once, they might try it again."

Suzy was surprised. "I didn't know they got the ransom. In fact, I really don't know much about the kidnapping. How did it happen, anyway?"

Rich looked at her, slightly amazed. "You really must have been isolated out on that farm. It was one of the most famous kidnappings since the Lindbergh case. In fact, the two were even compared. The Hepburns didn't get as much attention, though, because the family refused to be interviewed by reporters."

"And I don't blame them." When Rich didn't respond, Suzy glanced up at him. "Well, go on. What happened?"

He took her by the arm. "Come over here where we can be more comfortable and I'll tell you." His voice was deliberately seductive and Suzy knew he had other things on his mind besides the Hepburns, but then, so did she. Being human, it was impossible not to be aware of the setting: a handsome man, a moonlit night, the top of a grassy hill. No one could resist that.

As Rich eased himself to the ground, he pulled Suzy down beside him and together they leaned back against a smooth boulder, stretched their legs out before them and gazed silently into the starry night. It was like home, Suzy thought, something she hadn't allowed herself to think of since she'd sold Abby's farm four years before.

As if sensing her nostalgic mood, Rich covered her hand with his in a warm and reassuring grip. She knew he was watching her, waiting for her to turn her face to his, but Suzy pretended to be more interested in the landscape than in his nearness. She wasn't fooling anyone, she knew that. Just the quickening of her breath would give her away, but Rich seemed to be in no hurry. Instead of pressing his advantage, he settled comfortably beside her and let his gaze sweep across the countryside.

He pointed to Thrushmore. "See those lights over there on the right? That's where Christina's room was. Her parents' room was right next to it, then farther down the hall was Mae Voght's room. She was Christina's nurse."

"Oh? She had a nurse? That's the first I've heard of her."

"Well, it won't be the last, I assure you. She's still there."

"For heaven's sake, why?"

Lifting their hands, he rested them on his thigh. "I'll get back to that later. Let me start with a July morning twenty-two years ago when Mae went into the nursery to see if Christina was awake. When she found her bed empty, she thought Joanne had gotten up with her in the middle of the night and had taken her back to bed with her. She did this often, I understand. But when a couple of hours went by, Mae started to worry that maybe Christina was sick. It wasn't like her to sleep past eight o'clock. So Mae tapped on the Hepburns' bedroom door and asked if Christina was all right. Needless to say, all hell broke loose."

"Whew! I would say so."

"Unfortunately, kidnapping was the last thing they thought of. Their first assumption was that she'd gotten up early and had decided to wander around the house. Within minutes, David, Joanne, Mae and all the rest of the servants started tearing that house apart from one end to the other. Then someone went out into the yard and, eventually, the garage. They didn't find Christina, but they did find a note stuck under the windshield wiper of David's car. Though I've never seen the note, I understand it didn't say much, just that the child had been taken and that the kidnappers would get in touch with David later. It also warned him about calling the police. If he did, he'd never see his child again."

"Oh, how awful! What'd he do?"

"Well, at first he didn't believe it and went back up to Christina's room, and sure enough, the screen had been cut and there were scratches on the windowsill. Later they found the ladder, but it didn't prove anything." Rich glanced at Suzy. "The ladder belonged to the Hepburns. It'd been in their garage for years."

"Oh, my God."

"That's what David thought, I'm sure. He didn't know what to do. Joanne wanted to call the police right away, but David thought they should at least wait until they got a ransom note. He felt they had a better chance if they dealt with the kidnappers on their own terms. He and Joanne had a terrible argument, I understand, but David finally convinced her to wait."

"You mean he didn't call the police? God," Suzy said, "he was as bad as Abby."

"I'm beginning to think you're right." Putting his arm around her shoulders, he nestled her head against his chest as if protecting her from the unknown. It was a nice feeling, comforting and warm....

"Anyway," Rich went on, "the next day they got a note in the mail with specific instructions. David carried out each detail to the letter. He was supposed to put the money in a certain wayside trash barrel and return an hour later and Christina would be there. An hour later, the money was gone, but there was no Christina. It wasn't until then that David called the police."

"By that time it was too late."

"Right. The trail was cold. They never did find her."

Suzy rubbed her eyes with her hand. "Damn, I can't remember anything that happened to me before Abby found me. But don't you think a child of three would have some vague recollection of an experience as traumatic as that?''

"It might be that the shock was so great she got amnesia.''

"Hmm, I never thought of that. I suppose it's possible. But if I'm Christina, how did I end up in Pennsylvania?''

"Who knows?'' Rich shrugged. "Maybe the kidnappers were from that area. Maybe they thought if they dropped you off somewhere, whoever found you would call the police. God knows the child's picture was on every TV news show for weeks.''

Leaning her head back, Suzy rested it against Rich's arm and sighed tiredly. "This is too much. We'll never find out who took the child.''

"But we're not interested in who took her,'' Rich reminded her. "We'll never solve that one. What we're concerned with now is—''

"Who's who,'' Suzy finished wryly.

Smiling, Rich brushed a kiss across her forehead. "I'll say one thing for you, you have a good sense of humor.''

A smile touched the corners of her mouth, and tipping her head back, she looked up at him. She couldn't resist touching the cleft in his chin with the tip of her finger. "Yours is pretty good, too. Have you always been this pleasant?''

"Always,'' he answered quickly.

"Mmm,'' Suzy mused. "Maybe I'd better check this out with Mrs. Slingluff.''

Playfully, Rich pressed Suzy's hand tight against his muscled thigh. "If, perchance, there was a slight flaw in my character, she'd never admit it. She's like Joanne in that respect. She believes in suffering in silence."

"Whatever happened to Joanne, anyway? You started to tell me...."

"Actually, there isn't much to tell," he said, settling back again. "Suffice it to say that the kidnapping was her undoing. At first she was very bitter because David hadn't called the police, and then she felt guilty because she hadn't done it herself. As the days of waiting dragged on, she went straight downhill. Dr. Hilton told her to try to assume the child was dead and not suffering somewhere. But since there was no body, no funeral, no casket to bury in the family plot, there was nothing Joanne could hang on to."

"What a terrible thing to live with."

"I agree with you on that. To this day, Joanne has never conceded that Christina is dead. She lives with the eternal hope that someday she'll be found alive."

"What about David? How did he feel?"

"He learned to live with it, but it was hard for him. Several days after the kidnapping, Joanne started getting terrible headaches. Dr. Hilton called on her every day, but as the weeks went by, she became confused and vague. She could hardly carry on a conversation. Finally, they got her into Sunlight Sanitarium. I think she was there about six weeks or so, but there was no improvement, so they decided to send her home. Before they released her, they told David to get rid of anything and everything that would remind her of Christina."

Suzy sat straight up. "Why in the world would they do a thing like that?"

"I guess it seemed to be the right thing at the time, and David just blindly followed orders. He threw out everything—clothes, toys, books, you name it. By the time Joanne came home, there wasn't a scrap of evidence that there'd ever been a child in that house."

"No wonder she took to her bed for the rest of her life," Suzy fumed indignantly. "I'd have done the same thing. That David Hepburn must have had his head screwed on backward."

Rich nudged her gently in the ribs. "Quit blaming the poor guy, will you? He did as he was told."

"And the result was he had a double loss, his daughter and his wife."

"I know, I know. It was a botched-up mess from beginning to end. Fortunately the baby's nurse stayed on to look after Joanne."

"And she's the one who's still there...."

"That's right. If it hadn't been for her, Joanne probably would have died years ago. But Mae keeps her moving and sees that she eats and gets some exercise and takes walks. But beyond that, Joanne is an empty shell." He paused thoughtfully for a long moment. "It's too bad. My dad used to say she was the most beautiful woman he'd ever known. As a matter of fact," he said, shifting his weight a little, "she's still very attractive. I only see her occasionally, of course. David handled all the business transactions."

"It sounds as if you don't know Joanne very well."

"I don't. In fact," he said, turning his head so that he was looking into her upturned face, "I know you better than I do her."

"But we just met this afternoon."

"Which all goes to prove that our chemistries are very compatible." His hand trailed up her arm and tightened over her shoulder in a tantalizing grip that sent an immediate and dangerous shaft of arousal racing through her bloodstream. She thought of protesting, but when she felt the warmth of Rich's breath as he pressed a soft kiss against her temple, her common sense took off like a filly in a field of clover.

"Do you have the feeling that we're being pulled together?" Rich whispered, his voice teasingly husky.

"Yes." Suzy's mouth tipped up in a mischievous smile as she slid her arm around his waist and spread her hand across the muscled hardness of his rib cage. "In fact, we seem to be getting closer by the minute."

"And I like it." Tightening his arm, Rich snuggled even closer and buried his face in the softness of her hair. He held her in the circle of his embrace for several long moments, giving the smoldering embers within them time to grow and spread until suddenly they ignited into a burst of fiery sensations that created responses from Suzy she'd forgotten she had.

As Rich cupped his hand at the nape of her neck and tipped her face up to his, Suzy forgot about controlling the pulsing demands of her body and met his lips in a questing kiss that sent wild tremors of desire down her spine and into her thighs. Slowly Rich's mouth moved temptingly across hers in such a mesmerizing massage that Suzy found herself willingly parting her lips to let his seeking tongue enter her mouth. He explored the inner depths with such languorous ease that Suzy's mind blocked out everything but the moist insistence of his searching tongue and the deep inner restlessness that was beginning to grow in the pit of her stomach. A tiny sigh escaped her.

Though her heart still throbbed with pure longing, she forced herself to remember that everything she was feeling at the moment was temporary, and though she had to admit she'd been completely caught up in the enchantment of Rich's kiss, the moment was over. It was time to go back to being Suzy Yoder, the girl from Pennsylvania who had just dropped in for a few days. Reluctantly, she twisted her head away from him.

Pressing his face against her cheek, Rich exhaled a long breath. Then, wordlessly, he cradled her head into the folds of his shirt and held her with his large, gentle hands. Suzy could feel his breathing. It was almost as ragged as hers—an exciting thought, but a sobering one, too. Her feelings toward him were far more intense than the circumstances warranted. Hadn't she turned to the arms of a man for solace and comfort once before? And hadn't it ended in a disastrous breakup? What she'd thought was love had really been a temporary need that ended when she'd finally cried herself out and decided it was time to get on with her life. God, what a fool she'd been, she thought with a slight shiver.

Rich's arms tightened a little. "Cold?" he asked, his voice a husky whisper.

When she raised her head slightly, Rich met her gaze. His features were blurred in the shadows of the moon, but the virile pulse of his body was still there, clear and tempting.

"I think we'd better get back," she murmured as, reluctantly, she pulled out of his arms.

He wasn't one to give up so easily. Though his arms loosened around her, they didn't free her. "I think I deserve an encore."

His presumptuousness brought a smile to Suzy's face. The grass would never grow under his feet. "Wrong," she said, and pushing away from him, she got to her feet. "Encores are for theatrical productions."

He stood up beside her. "You kiss like a movie star."

Suzy burst out laughing. "How would you know?"

"I spent my adolescent years watching movies on TV."

"And that's all the experience you've had?" she asked teasingly.

"Well..." Rich shrugged elaborately, but he didn't answer her question. He didn't have to. He was a man very experienced in handling a woman, and Suzy knew he hadn't learned that watching TV.

"In any case," Suzy hurried on, "I think you'll have to agree we've carried this relationship far enough."

"Hmm," Rich murmured, but he made no reply. Instead he took her arm and helped her up the path to the grassy slope above. Suzy couldn't resist stealing a look at his face. His features were only vaguely outlined against the moonlit sky, but his bright eyes glittered like the stars. They rested on hers for a long, thoughtful moment.

"Maybe you're right," he conceded, his voice low and serious. "We both have commitments, and to pretend they don't exist is as unreasonable as it is unjust." Gently he ran his fingers through her bangs.

"But I want you to know that I think you're a very special person, Suzy."

"Thank you," she murmured. As she accepted his arm and they started toward the house, she felt as if the magic of the evening had suddenly slipped away forever.

He didn't have to agree with everything she suggested, did he?

Chapter Four

When Suzy awoke the next morning, she was disappointed to find that the sunny warmth of the previous day had been replaced by gray clouds and a high wind. In a way, it matched her mood, but she refused to let herself think negatively. She and Rich had agreed to keep their relationship on an impersonal level, a gloomy thought, but at least there was one bright spot: she'd be spending the whole day with him.

She had a little trouble deciding what to wear and finally settled on a simple skirt and blouse. If she wore the slacks and modish tops that she preferred, she might come off as too casual, and why put her worst foot forward? On the other hand, she mused, Joanne might like to see something trendy for a change. Maybe it would make her realize how long she'd been cooped up. In spite of all her theories, however, Suzy wore the skirt and blouse. But as she put on her makeup and brushed her bangs across her forehead, she realized that, now that she knew a little more about Joanne, it was getting harder and harder for her to remain detached. The woman had been through so much, was it really fair to press her any further?

Suzy knew it wouldn't do any good to consult Rich. He had already expressed his opinion on the subject, and if he was like most men, he probably didn't realize the anguish a mother went through when she lost a child. Suzy stared at her reflection in the mirror, at her pointed chin, her small mouth, her reddish eyebrows, and she could almost hear Abby's voice of caution when they went into the barn to collect eggs: "Careful, Suzy, once they're broken that's the end of them forever."

She would walk carefully, Suzy promised herself as she went downstairs to the dining room. She'd step with caution and not allow anyone to hurt her, not even Rich.

He was sitting at the dining room table devouring a cinnamon sweet roll. "Hurry up before I eat everything in sight." He started to get up, but Suzy motioned for him to stay seated and took a chair opposite him. "You look great," he said appreciatively, "like a schoolgirl."

"I'm trying to project the image of a cool-headed businesswoman."

His eyes traveled up and down her body before resting on her face. "All I know is, I like what I see."

Suzy did a little appraising of her own. "You look pretty good yourself." In truth, he looked terrific in his white crewneck sweater over a blue shirt. It emphasized the well-proportioned contours of his physique. He was a handsome man, no disputing that. Observant, too....

"You look like you had a good night's sleep," he mused. "Must be the sea air. It makes you drowsy if you're not used to it."

"That's all I need," she said as she poured herself a cup of coffee. "I'm going to need all the concentration I can get today."

"You make it sound like you're going to a funeral. Try to think of it as a challenge."

"I'm thinking of it as an ordeal I have to get through somehow."

Mrs. Slingluff, who was one of those people blessed with eternal happiness, bustled in from the kitchen. "Do you eat breakfast, Suzy?" she asked, obviously hoping the answer would be in the affirmative.

Suzy was not one to disappoint her. "I sure do—big ones."

Mrs. Slingluff's face spread into a big smile. "Oh, good," she exclaimed as she hurried back to her kitchen to conjure up some epicurean delight.

Leaning forward, Rich lowered his voice to a confidential tone. "You have just made her day."

"Good," she declared. "Now if I could just do as much for myself..."

"Don't worry, you'll come through with shining colors." He looked at his watch. "But you'd better hurry. I told Wayne we'd be there in thirty minutes."

Slowly Suzy replaced her cup on the saucer and took a deep breath. "Today, I refuse to be hurried either physically or emotionally."

"Translate that, would you?"

"I'm going to approach my visit to Thrushmore one step at a time and cautiously feel my way without being hassled by anyone to speed it up."

"Good idea," Rich agreed, glancing at his watch again. "You have ten minutes to eat your breakfast and fifteen minutes to drive over there...."

Thrushmore stood majestically on the top of a long green hill hidden from the road by stands of pine and cedar. Huge oaks and maples served to further conceal the house, making it look formidable and uninviting. Only the early spring daisies growing along the side of the road and in the brush next to the driveway softened the look.

As Rich's Trans Am moved swiftly up the long drive to the house, Suzy leaned forward in her seat, hoping for a flashback, a fleeting sign of recognition, a familiar feeling; but she remembered nothing. Even the house looked strange and cold and uninviting, not at all what she'd expected. Discouraged, she sat back in her seat.

"The place looks like a mausoleum."

"That's because it's a gray day. Everything looks gloomy," Rich assured her, trying to bolster her spirits. Then, a little more anxiously, "Do you remember anything?"

Slowly Suzy shook her head. "Nothing."

"Well, I don't suppose three-year-olds remember the outsides of buildings anyway. Wait until we get inside." Pulling to a stop at the front of the house, he parked his car next to another. "I see Wayne got here ahead of us."

"Oh?" Suzy sat up. "You mean he doesn't live here?"

"No. He and his wife have a big home just south of Plymouth. The only people left at Thrushmore now are Joanne and Mae and the two servants." Getting out, he helped Suzy and, with a firm grip on her elbow, led her across the brick terrace to the door and rang the bell. The door was opened almost immediately by a stout, square man whom Rich called Frank. He didn't, Suzy noticed, introduce her to him.

Frank told them Wayne was waiting for them in the office, and Rich led the way. Once again Suzy felt the firm pressure of his hand at the small of her back; it was a little thing, but at the moment it was just the touch of encouragement she needed as they walked down the hallway. It was high and narrow and dimly lighted. Several rooms seemed to open off of it, but the doors were all shut, giving the place a somber, drafty atmosphere. Only at the far end of the hall was a door standing open.

Wayne rose when they entered and greeted them cordially, though unenthusiastically. He was a small man with thin gray hair and thick horn-rimmed glasses. His demeanor was as dolorous as his appearance. His eyes flicked quickly over Suzy's face and hair. Almost begrudgingly he offered her a weak, lukewarm handshake. "Well," he said, motioning Suzy to a leather chair, "Rich tells me you think you're the Hepburns' daughter."

Suzy was quick to clarify her position. "I think there's a possibility I could be. I'm not sure."

"I understand you were in touch with David Hepburn before he died. How did you happen to meet him?"

"I don't think Suzy has anything to add to what we already know," Rich cut in quickly. "But you might fill Wayne in on how you reached David in the first place, Suzy."

"Oh, of course." As Suzy retold her experiences, she drew the ad from the dental journal out of her purse and handed it to Wayne. Instead of reading it, however, he leaned back in his swivel chair and studied Suzy as if he were trying to decide if she looked like either of the Hepburns. Evidently satisfied that she didn't, he seemed to relax and listen with a detached attitude that Suzy found very annoying.

When she'd covered every detail of the story up to the present moment, Wayne merely nodded politely. "I don't suppose you have any pictures taken of you just after you were found," Wayne surmised, making no attempt to hide the suspicion in his voice.

"No. Abby didn't own a camera. Besides, she was Amish, and they don't approve of photographs of themselves."

"Well, do you have any other proof? Clothes or blankets or something?"

Rich cast him a derisive look. "Oh, come on, Wayne. You know very well Christina had nothing on but her pajamas when she was taken. Quit trying to play games. We're all fully aware of the identity complications."

Wayne shot Rich a cold, level look that clearly indicated he was doing his best to control his irritation at Rich's intrusion and apparent support of Suzy's claim. Coolly he shifted his gaze to Suzy. "Frankly, Miss Yoder, I'm not at all surprised at your appearance here. We've interviewed many young women like you through the years and, needless to say, they've all turned out to be imposters. Even you must admit you don't have much to go on, and since Christina's fingerprints aren't on her birth certificate, I don't see how you or anyone else can prove they're the missing child."

"Evidently David didn't think so," Rich reminded him.

"That doesn't prove a thing," Wayne maintained, "He probably put the ad in the journal just to appease Joanne."

"But that's not why he agreed to meet Suzy," Rich argued. "Because Joanne doesn't know anything about it."

"My brother was a very compassionate man," Wayne said. "He didn't want to raise Joanne's hopes and then have to disappoint her again." He peered at Rich from over the tops of his glasses. "And I'm sure he didn't intend to have you meddling in this. It's none of your affair."

"Oh, yes, it is," Rich was quick to counter. "As the executor, it's my duty to see that the terms of the will are carried out, and that's exactly what I intend to do." His statement left no room for doubt.

Irritably, Wayne shoved his chair back and stood up. "Just how do you plan to do this?" he demanded. "Are you planning on dragging Joanne into this?"

"She would certainly have to be consulted."

"But that's impossible. She isn't well enough to grasp what you're saying, even you should know that."

"No, I don't know that." Leaning comfortably back in his chair, he rested his left ankle on his right knee, not once letting Wayne out of his line of vision. "Joanne certainly didn't look non compos mentis at David's funeral. She was upset, of course, but that was only natural."

"That's just the trouble," Wayne railed defensively. "You never know how she's going to be from one day to the next. Even Mae can tell you that."

"Then maybe that's where we should start," Rich decided. "Not that I think Mae could remember Christina any more clearly than Joanne could, but I think her opinion should be voiced."

To Suzy's surprise, Wayne seemed almost relieved. "Why not?" he asked. "It seems to me if anyone could recognize Christina, it would be her nurse. At least," he added sarcastically, "she has her wits about her."

Suzy felt a sudden defensive ripple of anger at Wayne's snide insinuation. To hear him talk, Joanne was ready for the psychiatric ward, not at all the impression she'd gotten from Rich, who to her disappointment offered no rebuttal.

"Then if it's all right with you," Rich went on, "I'll ask Frank to call Mae down here." Without waiting for a response, he disappeared into the hall, leaving Suzy alone with Wayne.

Strangely, she felt more relaxed than she'd been all day. Despite Rich's intention to remain neutral, it was quite plain that he wasn't going to let anyone try to bully her around. Part of her wanted to assure him that she was perfectly capable of taking care of herself, but another part of her basked in the feeling of being protected, even if it wasn't in the warm shelter of his arms.

Rich returned to the office to report that Mae was on her way. As they waited in silence, Suzy kept hoping Rich would try to catch her eye to give her a look of encouragement. When he kept his gaze averted, however, she decided he was either very worried or he was trying to appear indifferent. Suzy, optimist that she was, chose the latter. Behind that beguiling smile of his was a quick, decisive, tough-minded man who could be as stubborn as he was captivating, an unbeatable combination and one that would make him a very powerful opponent if he chose to be. *A very powerful lover, too,* she thought, savoring the memory of the previous night's kisses.

The door banged open and Mae Voght strode into the room and stood there, feet apart, just inside the door. She was exactly what Suzy had expected even to the navy-blue skirt and white blouse of a companion-nurse. Her iron-gray hair was cropped short, emphasizing her broad face and heavy chin. Stolid and mulelike, she glanced about irritably, making it quite clear that her routine had been rudely interrupted.

Her eyes settled on Wayne. "Well, what is it?" she demanded in a harsh voice.

Wayne exhaled an exaggerated sigh of strained patience. Obviously this wasn't the first time these two had clashed, nor would it be the last, and if Suzy had to make a bet, she'd put her money on Mae. She was a very formidable person, whose conduct implied that

Wayne was the intruder here and she'd appreciate it if he'd leave and take his friends with him. Evidently Thrushmore wasn't as serene as it appeared to be.

Rich, instantly sensing the controversy, got to his feet. "We won't keep you a minute, Mae. I know you're busy. But we wanted you to meet Suzy Yoder."

Mae's gaze turned to Suzy, taking in her trim figure with a quick impatient glance. Suzy started to extend her hand, but just as she did, Mae turned back to Rich.

"Do you recognize her?" he asked.

Without answering, Mae looked at Suzy again, this time at her face. Her scrutiny took in the gray-green eyes, the smattering of freckles across her nose, the high cheekbones and, lastly, the reddish-rust hair. As if sensing the purpose of this visit, she flattened her mouth into an irritable line and turned back to Rich. "No, I do not!"

"Look again, Mae," Rich urged, using all his charm now. "We have reason to believe she's Christina Hepburn."

"I thought so!" she scoffed, but just the same, she turned her glance back to Suzy. This time she stared for many long, hard moments before swinging her gaze back to Rich. "She's an imposter," she retorted icily.

Suzy felt her spirits plummet at the realization that this whole trip was going to turn out to be a fiasco. It didn't help to see Wayne's smug expression of triumph, either. Flipping his pencil across the desk, he stood up. "That does it for me," he announced.

But Rich wasn't easy to bulldoze. "Now let's just wait a minute. I'd hardly call this a fair determination. It'd be virtually impossible for Mae to recognize Christina after all these years."

Immediately Wayne objected, and as they argued back and forth, Suzy studied Mae, hoping to find a shadow of remembrance in the stern face before her. Suddenly, Mae turned to face Suzy. Instantly their eyes locked in a frank and assessing interchange as each tried to place the other in the puzzle of missing pieces.

Suzy was the first to break the standoff. "Did Christina have a space between her teeth when she was a baby?" she asked quietly.

With a resolute lift of her chin, Mae shook her head. "No more than any other child of three."

"Look at my teeth," Suzy urged. "Are they like Joanne's?"

The old woman winced at the name "Joanne." Evidently she wasn't accustomed to such familiarity from a stranger. But Suzy sensed there was something else there, too, something deeper, something unexplained.

For a fleeting moment, Suzy thought she saw Mae's face soften just a little, but the expression vanished almost as quickly as it had appeared. She gave Suzy one last, long look, then, straightening, she stepped back a little and faced Rich. "No," she announced firmly. "This is not Christina Hepburn."

Her words were so final that Suzy had to struggle to keep her head up, her shoulders straight. Then, as if he'd reached across the room and put a hand on her shoulder, she felt Rich's closeness. It was a strange feeling, communicating across space, but it gave her the confidence and encouragement she needed at that moment. And it was very special. In fact, everything about Rich was beginning to feel very special.

Wayne had given Mae a nod of dismissal, and without another word or even a backward glance, she turned and walked stiffly out of the room. Suzy didn't realize how tense she'd been until she started to sit down and found that her knees were ready to buckle out from under her. As she eased herself into the chair, she caught Rich's eye. Since his back was to Wayne, he could, and did, give her a big wink. He seemed to be very pleased with the way things were going. *God, he'd better know something I don't,* Suzy thought.

Evidently he was just getting warmed up. ''Mae's testimony bears considerable weight,'' he admitted, ''but it isn't conclusive. I think we should take the next step and let Suzy meet Joanne.''

Wayne immediately jumped to his feet. ''No way,'' he protested. ''She's not strong enough to go through another trauma at this time.''

Rich faced him directly. ''Why don't we let Dr. Hilton decide that? He knows Joanne better than anyone.''

''He won't allow it, I can tell you that right now.''

''All right.'' Rich nodded, agreeing. ''If that's the case, we'll let the whole issue drop. Now, you can't ask for more cooperation than that.''

Wayne hesitated, not sure he liked the decision, but finally he agreed. Before he changed his mind, Rich picked up the phone and called Dr. Hilton's home. It turned out he was just on his way over to the hospital, but he promised to stop by in about two hours. He'd planned to look in on Joanne anyway, he said, and this would give him a chance to meet Suzy, too.

Rich thanked him and put the phone down. ''Since we have a few hours to spare,'' he explained to Wayne,

"I think I'll take Suzy down to see Bark Cove." Without waiting for assent from either one of them, he took Suzy by the arm, nodded a brief good-bye to Wayne and hurried her out of the office, down the hall and into the clean air of midmorning. The weather had cleared, the sky was lighter and Suzy's spirits were headed straight up.

"Where did you say we were going?" she asked, not really caring.

"Bark Cove. It's a little village about three miles from here. They have an ice-cream shop that serves the best hot-fudge sundaes in Massachusetts."

"But it's only ten o'clock in the morning...."

"With whole pecans and real whipped cream."

"Oh, well, it's never too early for that," she said as she got into the car and settled back in her seat.

Rich got behind the wheel and slammed the door. "I think someone's watching us," he commented, sotto voce.

"Oh? Mae?"

"Probably." Starting the engine, he coasted down the drive. When he stopped at the road, he glanced at Suzy. "Did you have any feelings that you'd known her before?"

Suzy shook her head in a firm negative. "None whatever. She's a tyrant, the sort of person any kid in their right mind would like to forget. Unless..." She raised her brows. "Do you think that was all just an act to get me out of there?"

"Naw," he said as he pulled out onto the road. "She's like that with everyone, except Joanne, of course."

"You don't think she and Wayne could be cooking something up between them?"

"Not a chance. Besides, Mae has nothing to gain financially. David set up a retirement fund for her, but he didn't leave her anything in his will. He was afraid if he left her a nest egg, she'd leave Joanne and go back to England. Joanne, however, has left Mae a very tidy sum." He gave Suzy a mischievous grin. "That way, if Joanne died first, Mae *would* go back to England."

"You men are horrible," Suzy denounced but she couldn't repress a smile; Mae wasn't exactly the sort of person one enjoyed having around.

"Maybe you didn't recognize Mae," Rich mused reflectively, "but I had the feeling that she might have seen something in you."

"For a moment there, I felt the same way, but if she did, why didn't she say something?"

"Because that would jeopardize her position as Joanne's nurse and constant companion. After all," he rationalized, "if the reason for Joanne's illness is because her daughter is lost, wouldn't finding that daughter cure her? And if she were cured, would she need a nurse?"

"Hmm, I see what you mean." Dejected, Suzy slumped back in her seat.

Rich reached over to give her an affectionate pat on the knee. "But don't worry. We'll get to the bottom of this thing if we have to shake the timbers right out from under them."

"Oh, no, we won't!" Deftly Suzy removed his hand and replaced it on the steering wheel. "I'm planning to see Joanne, talk to her once and then leave. Any decision she and you and Wayne and Mae want to make is strictly out of my hands. I refuse to interfere."

Rich slid her a surprised glance. "What are you talking about? Suppose you really are Christina? Are you going to let Mae and Wayne rob you and Joanne of your rights?"

"I didn't come here to make trouble," Suzy retorted. "I told you that from the beginning."

"You're here to claim your rightful heritage," he stated, "and if that involves a little trouble, that's just too bad."

"Well!" she railed defensively. "You certainly don't mind butting into my business!" Suzy could feel her anger rising, but she was in no mood to rein it in. As much as she appreciated Rich's help and advice, she wasn't going to let him make decisions for her. "I have no intention of forcing my way into someone's life until I know I belong there."

"And just how do you expect to find out if you turn tail and run?"

Suzy crossed her arms and looked straight ahead. "If it's meant to be, it's meant to be, that's all," she stated simply.

"Oh, God," Rich lamented. "If that isn't the most illogical statement I've ever heard in my life! When are you going to learn you have to fight for what you want in this world?" They'd reached the small village of Bark Cove, and Rich was turning the car into a parking space. "No one is going to walk up and just hand it to you, you know."

"Hand me what?" she demanded hotly. "A fifty-year-old woman who is slightly deranged, a crabbed old nurse and an obnoxious brother-in-law? Thanks a lot!''

Rich had parked and gotten out of the car. He slammed the door behind him with a thunderous crash and, stomping around to Suzy's side, yanked open the door. As she stepped out of the car, she eyed him coolly. ''If you don't watch that temper of yours, you're going to break a window.''

His answer was to slam Suzy's door—not quite so hard, she noticed—grab her by the arm and march her into the ice-cream parlor. They were seated at a small round table near the front and handed menus. Rich waved them aside.

''Just bring us two hot-fudge sundaes with pecans and whipped cream.''

''Oh, I'm sorry,'' the waitress said apologetically, ''we're all out of hot fudge. Would butterscotch do?''

Rich expelled a long, impatient breath. ''No, just bring two coffees and two Danish.''

''And I'll have the butterscotch sundae with whipped cream,'' Suzy ordered; then, leaning back in her chair, she proceeded to ignore her partner. But that didn't last long, not with Rich staring at her like a bull at a red flag.

''You sure are independent,'' he observed wryly.

Suzy gave him her sweetest smile. ''Thank you.''

''Persuasive, too,'' he added, and signaling the waitress, he ordered a butterscotch sundae ''to wash down the coffee and sweet rolls.''

''Of course....''

As they drove back to Thrushmore, Rich's spirits were much improved. Though he disagreed with Suzy's come-what-may attitude, he was pleased that she was more interested in seeing Joanne than in trying to gain a foothold in the Hepburn household. At least that's what he wanted to think. But he also knew that her blasé attitude toward the possibility of cashing in on a large inheritance could be a deceptive ruse to throw him off guard. Realistically, her story did have the familiar ring of an old movie—the long-lost daughter returning to the arms of her loved ones and picking up her life, and her bank account, and forging onward. As much as Rich liked Suzy, and he was finding her more fascinating by the minute, he was grateful that he had to remain neutral. He'd misjudged a woman before with disastrous results. He wasn't ready to risk that again.

Their timing was perfect. Just as Rich approached the drive to Thrushmore, another car from the opposite direction turned in ahead of them. "There's Dr. Hilton now," Rich announced, following the car up to the top of the hill.

Suzy leaned forward. "Am I supposed to know him?"

"It's possible. He's been the Hepburn doctor since before you were born."

"Mmm." To his surprise, Suzy settled back and inhaled deeply. "I'll go as far as crossing my fingers," she said.

Smiling, Rich shook his head. "Where's your fighting spirit?"

"Oh, it's here all right, but I don't think I'm going to need it." Suzy indicated Dr. Hilton, who had just gotten out of his car. He was a tall, muscular man in his mid-fifties whose graying hair was almost white at the temples, emphasizing the heavy black brows and flat mouth and set jaw. He was a determined person, not the sort who could be manipulated by Wayne or anyone else.

After brief introductions, Dr. Hilton took Suzy's hand in his large, firm grasp. "Now, what's all this I hear? Rich tells me you might be Christina." Pausing, he took a closer look at her. "You don't resemble either of the Hepburns, but that's not conclusive. Tell me," he said, turning to Rich, "how did you manage to get such a beautiful young woman to come down here and visit you?" He winked at Suzy. "He's a real terror to get along with."

"Really?" Suzy laughed. "I hadn't noticed."

"That's because you don't know him as I do. I suppose he forgot to tell you he was almost kicked out of college for inciting a riot, or about the time he spent the whole summer defending a beautiful woman saboteur."

"She was not a saboteur," Rich reminded him. "She was an innocent victim of—"

"Never mind, never mind." Hilton smiled, satisfied that he'd gotten a rise out of Rich and, not so incidentally, had broken the ice with Suzy. "Right now I'm interested in Suzy here. Would you care to fill me in?"

"Sure," Rich agreed. "Shall we go inside?"

Dr. Hilton waved the suggestion aside. "No, it's too nice a day to sit inside. Why don't we walk around here to the patio? I want to hear this without Wayne's intervention. Besides, if we stand here any longer, Mae just might fall out the window."

Glancing up at the window of Joanne's bedroom, Rich caught the subtle movement of a curtain. "I think you're right. In fact, I think Mae's been at the window all morning. She was here when we left about an hour ago."

Taking her arm, Dr. Hilton led Suzy toward the flagstone path that led around the side of the house. "You can't blame her for wondering what's going on down here. This is probably the most activity Thrush-more has seen in years."

"Is that how long it's been since the last Christina was here?" Suzy asked.

Hilton grinned and shook his head. "We haven't had as many as all that. A few looked promising, but David was quick to screen them. He seemed to have a secret system, but I don't know what it was." He glanced over at Rich. "Am I to understand that David made plans to meet Suzy? He wasn't the sort of person to jump to conclusions. Suzy, you must have told him something about yourself that rang a bell with him. Any idea what it could be?"

"None at all. In fact, we didn't even discuss the past. We just talked about the dentist."

"The dentist?" Hilton repeated vaguely. Then, with a shake of his head he motioned to the lounge chairs on the patio. They were made of sturdy redwood with bright blue cushions and plaid throw pillows, the first spark of color Suzy had seen since she'd arrived at Thrushmore. "Let's get comfortable and pool our thoughts. I need to catch up."

It was Rich who did the explaining while Hilton and Suzy listened. Occasionally, Hilton would interrupt with a question or a comment, but for the most part, he was a rapt listener. Rich realized that the more often he retold the story, the less phenomenal it became. Actually, many things fitted together: the timing of Christina's disappearance with that of the day Suzy was found, Suzy's age, her hair and teeth and, most important, David's response to her. As Rich explained the facts to Hilton, he glanced occasionally at Suzy. She looked very young and lovely as she sat quietly under the shade of the towering oaks, at home in the outdoor surroundings. Rich wondered what she was thinking about, another oak tree long ago? a sleepy town in Pennsylvania? Abby? or, possibly, how to win Dr. Hilton over to her side?

Chapter Five

The sun was high and warm by the time they finished talking. Putting a fatherly arm around Suzy, Dr.
Hilton led them all back into the house where Wayne
still waited in the office. If Suzy had been in his place,
she would have worn a path in the rug by now, but
Wayne had papers on the desk and appeared to have
gotten some work done, not an easy task under the
circumstances. For some unexplained reason, Suzy
found herself feeling sorry for Wayne. He and his
brother had been close for years, and to see the rewards of his work handed over to a total stranger
would be hard for anyone to take, especially since that
stranger could pick up the purse and leave without
ever a look back. Then who would take care of
Joanne? Wayne, of course, who else?

Dr. Hilton gave Wayne a warm handshake and, motioning for everyone to take a seat, wasted no time in getting to the point. Suzy glanced over to Rich, who gave her an encouraging wink, but he seemed strangely quiet. Maybe it was because Dr. Hilton and Wayne had know him since he was a child, and he felt subordinate to them. But no, she thought, that wasn't Rich's style. He was too forceful for that. He was probably just biding his time, sizing things up, maybe even wondering why he'd ever gotten involved in this thing in the first place and how he was going to remain neutral. Maybe, Suzy wondered dolefully, he was regretting the kiss they had shared in the moonlight and the—

Dr. Hilton's deep voice broke into her thoughts. "Rich has filled me in on all the details so far and, frankly, I don't think there's much more we can do but let Suzy meet Joanne."

Wayne objected instantly. "Don't you think Joanne's been through enough without throwing this outlandish situation at her and saying, 'Here, handle it the best way you can'?"

"I understand how you feel, Wayne," Hilton said sympathetically, "but I don't think Joanne is as incompetent as David led us all to believe. She may be a little disoriented at times, but there's nothing wrong with her reasoning powers. She's a very intelligent conversationalist on subject matters that concern her, and I'm thoroughly convinced that she'd not only be interested in meeting Suzy here, but that she'd be furious if we didn't ask her opinion."

"Regardless of the consequences?" Wayne demanded angrily.

Dr. Hilton paused to look at each of them. "I'm afraid I have an ulterior motive. My job is to get Joanne well, and I think this will be accomplished by treating her as a well person, something David always refused to do." He sat back in his chair. "I'll bet my diploma that if we give Joanne a problem and expect her to solve it, she'll do just that."

"Aren't you expecting a little too much?" Wayne argued. "There isn't a woman in the world who can identify a child she hasn't seen in twenty-two years."

"Maybe not," Hilton agreed, "but who's to know? There's the possibility that Suzy is Christina and Joanne won't know her. There is also the possibility that she isn't Christina and Joanne will swear that she is."

"Then this whole thing is absolutely ridiculous!" Wayne blustered.

But Dr. Hilton stayed him with a raised hand. "No, it isn't. There is also a third possibility...that she is Christina and that Joanne will recognize her. Does everyone agree?" he asked suddenly, his eyes darting from one to the other.

"Certainly sounds reasonable to me," Rich agreed. "How about you, Suzy?" His voice was warm with concern, and immediatly Suzy's confidence increased. Despite his pretense to remain neutral, she knew Rich was on her side one hundred percent, a delightful thought and one she realized she'd been hoping for ever since she met him.

"Of course I agree," she said. "That's why I'm here."

Wayne shot her a stony glare. "I doubt if that's all you came for," he snapped.

Immediately Rich was on his feet. "Hey, hold the accusations," he said. "Right now we're all just trying to feel our way. We're not in court."

"Something tells me we will be," Wayne replied defensively.

Dr. Hilton dismissed Wayne's threat with an impatient wave of his hand. "Well, until then I'm taking Suzy upstairs to meet Joanne."

When Wayne and Rich made a move to follow, Dr. Hilton gave them both a stern look. "You two stay down here. If Joanne feels up to it, I'll ask her to come down and join our discussion group."

"Not likely," Wayne scoffed. "The only time Joanne leaves her room is when she and Mae go for their afternoon walk."

Hilton didn't bother to reply, and tucking Suzy's hand under his arm, he sallied her out of the office and down the hallway. When they were out of earshot he asked, "Nervous?"

Suzy shook her head. "No. I figure if she's a perfect stranger, what difference does it make? And if she's my mother, she'll understand."

He gave her hand a reassuring squeeze. "I like your attitude, Suzy. Too bad some of it doesn't rub off on Wayne."

"Still, I can see how he feels...."

"Don't worry about Wayne," he assured her. "He's a big boy now and very capable of taking care of himself. You just worry about Suzy."

"And Joanne...."

Leaning his head toward her a little, Dr. Hilton lowered his voice. "I hate to say this, but just between you and me, I think Joanne's improved a great deal since David's death. They were always locked in a dispute of some kind," he confided as they started up the stairs. "David never let Joanne take over any responsibilities, not even household ones, but now that he's gone, she's faced with some big decisions, among them what she's going to do with Thrushmore and where she's going to go from here."

"Those are two hard questions for anyone to answer."

"You bet they are, but frankly, I think Joanne is having a ball trying to make up her mind. This is something new to her."

"Do you think she suddenly feels free?"

"I'd say that would be a normal reaction."

Suzy gave him a quick glance. "Then you think she's normal?"

"Of course I do. I wouldn't be taking you up these stairs if I didn't."

"I suppose not," she murmured. She liked Dr. Hilton. He was straightforward and to the point. No dallying around with this man.

As they reached the top of the stairs and started toward Joanne's room, Mae stepped into the hall, closing Joanne's door firmly behind her. Dr. Hilton greeted her with a professional nod and started into the room, but Mae barred his way.

"Isn't Mrs. Hepburn dressed?" he asked, surprised.

"Of course she is," was the cold reply, "but you can't go in there. She's resting."

"Oh?" Dr. Hilton's amazement was superseded only by his irritation. "Well, I'm sure she won't mind being disturbed for a few minutes to meet Suzy." He started for the door, but still Mae refused to budge.

"Since when," Hilton demanded in a loud voice, "is your authority greater than mine?"

Mae's defenses started to wobble, but she managed to rally. "It is in most things, but a shock like this could bring on convulsions."

"Oh, for God's sake, Mae, shut up," he flared. "Joanne never had a convulsion in her life and you know it. Now go on down to the kitchen or something. I don't want you hovering around here. This is strictly between the three of us." Pushing Mae aside, he opened the door and stalked into the room with Suzy beside him. Then he closed the door with a decisive click.

Joanne was wearing a soft white robe with a corded tie and was sitting in a wicker rocker looking out at the lawns and gardens that were just starting to bud with color. A book lay open in her lap. She looked up when she heard them. Suzy's first impression was that she was a very pretty woman with brown hair tinged with gray, a small oval face and large, luminous eyes. As they crossed toward her, her face widened into a very lovely smile.

"Why, Paul," she said, surprised. "I didn't expect to see you here today."

He strode over and took her hand firmly in his own. "I just keep popping up, you know. I can't have my favorite patient feeling neglected." He turned to Suzy and, taking her hand, drew her closer to Joanne. "I've brought a lovely young lady to see you."

Joanne's glance swung to Suzy's face and rested there for a long minute, then lifted to the copper-red hair, dropping back again to the gray-green eyes, so clear and steady. Suzy stared back, hoping to recognize Joanne's features or her expression or even the set of her shoulders or the long, narrow fingers. But nothing was familiar.

A vague frown crossed Joanne's face as she leaned forward a little more and peered intently into Suzy's eyes. Finally she looked up at Dr. Hilton. "Are you asking me if I think this is Christina?"

"It's a possibility," he answered quietly.

Once again Joanne's eyes swung to Suzy, her expression one of mild surprise, not at all what Suzy had expected. From what she'd heard, she was prepared for almost anything—fright, belligerence, denial or even gushy acceptance. But Joanne showed none of these emotions. In fact, if Suzy had to sum it up in one word, she'd have said that Joanne was interested, intensely interested, but then, so was Suzy. The woman before her was about her size and build, but there the similarity ended. Joanne had pale blue eyes, where Suzy's were a deep gray green. Joanne's coloring was much lighter, too, and her skin was more delicate than Suzy's, but the difference in their ages as well as their life-styles could have contributed to that.

Reaching out, Joanne took Suzy's hand and held it in hers. Then she smiled, a delightful smile, friendly and welcoming. "You don't look like either David or me, but then Christina didn't, either. You do remind me of my mother, though. She was the redhead in the family and"—she cocked a brow at Suzy—"had the temper to go with it."

Suzy grinned. She was beginning to like Joanne. "I've been known to boil over a few times in my life," she admitted.

"I'll bet you have," Joanne teased, "but I don't think you hold grudges. You have too lovely a smile for that."

"She also has a slight separation between her front teeth," Dr. Hilton pointed out.

Joanne nodded. "I noticed that. My mother had the same thing. So did I, but my separation was much more noticeable than yours, so I had to wear braces when I was a teenager." Releasing Suzy's hand, she glanced up at Dr. Hilton. "It's too bad David isn't here, isn't it?"

"We can't turn back the clock," Hilton stated firmly. "But David did talk to Suzy on the phone just a few days before he died. He'd planned on meeting her before he brought her here to see you."

"He never mentioned it."

"He didn't want to get your hopes up."

Joanne's brow furrowed into a slight frown. "I don't know why not. I have a right to hopes and dreams, too."

"Oh, hell," Hilton swore, sighing elaborately. "Who knows what David was thinking? I'm sure he did what he thought was right, though, so don't hold it against him."

"Oh, I don't. I'd never do that. He was a stern man, but in his own way a loving one, too." She turned to Suzy. "But enough of this reminiscing. Tell me how you contacted David."

"Oh, that's a long story. It begins way back."

"That's all right," Joanne assured her. "I have nothing to do all day, and I'd love to hear it."

"I might as well listen, too, since it's Saturday, my day to relax." Dr. Hilton pulled up a chair and sat down on the edge as if poised for flight. He turned to Suzy. "Go ahead. Start with when Abby found you."

As Suzy told the story again, Joanne and Dr. Hilton leaned back in their chairs and listened. Her voice had a pleasant lilt and her story was laced with amusing incidents and Amish colloquialisms that captivated her listeners.

"Tell me what Abby was like," Joanne urged when Suzy had finished.

"No, no, no," Hilton objected. "You and Suzy can go into all these little details later. Right now, we have two rambunctious males downstairs waiting for our appearance." He glanced at Joanne, his eyes bright and questioning. "Would you like to go down with us?"

Almost automatically, she shook her head and started to decline, then paused for a moment. She looked at Suzy, who was watching her with wide, inquisitive eyes. "Well, maybe I will." To Suzy's surprise and Dr. Hilton's utter amazement, Joanne got to her feet, straightened out her robe and, taking Dr. Hilton by one arm and Suzy by the other, started toward the door.

Dr. Hilton grinned. "You realize, of course, that Wayne is going to faint when he sees you."

"Well, he'll just have to get used to that," Suzy piped up. "Joanne can't spend the rest of her life in her room."

Joanne shot Suzy a quick look of surprise, then suddenly her face widened into a warm smile. "You're right, Suzy. It's about time Thrushmore got some fresh air in it."

Dr. Hilton slapped his hand to the side of his face. "My God, if I hadn't heard this with my own ears, I'd never have believed it."

Suzy and Joanne burst out laughing at his droll humor, and Dr. Hilton, ham that he was, positively beamed. Suzy wondered how long it had been since he'd heard Joanne laugh.

Rich met them at the bottom of the stairs, and though he was surprised to see Joanne, he was delighted to see Suzy. He went right over to her and, taking her by the arm, fell in step behind Dr. Hilton and Joanne. "You've been gone so long, we were beginning to think you'd been asphyxiated or something. Wayne and I were about to come up and investigate."

"Joanne wanted to hear the whole story, and it seems to be getting longer every time I tell it."

"But more interesting," he assured her. "In fact, fascinating." His eyes held hers for a long moment. There was a look of silent approval there, something she hadn't noticed before.

As they entered the office, Wayne was trying to pull some chairs together without appearing too stunned at Joanne's presence. Joanne took a seat near the door, and within moments, to Suzy's disappointment, Mae appeared and stood behind Joanne's chair, arms crossed like a guard at the door of a bank.

Rich began. "If everyone's settled, what do you say we pool our thoughts and see what we can come up with. Paul, how do you feel about this?"

Paul Hilton was very firm. "It's not up to me to decide. I think it's strictly between Joanne and Suzy."

"Well, I don't," Wayne objected. "I think the whole thing is too unrealistic from start to finish. To begin with, a child of three would certainly know her own name."

"Who knows?" Rich shrugged. "Maybe Abby just assigned the name to her and that was it."

Suzy shook her head. "No, that's not what happened. When she asked me what my name was, I said, 'Suzy.'"

Suddenly Joanne sat straight up. "Why, Christina named all of her dolls Suzy," she exclaimed. "Remember, Mae?"

Fidgeting, Mae mumbled something about "she couldn't exactly recall." Suzy couldn't hear the rest of the sentence.

But Joanne did. "Well, I recall," she insisted. "When anyone asked Christina what her name was, she thought they wanted to know the name of her doll and always answered 'Suzy.'" Turning all the way around in her chair, she looked at Mae. "I'm surprised you don't remember that."

Mae dismissed the whole thing with a nonchalant shrug, as if coincidences like this were mere trivia.

Suzy swung her glance to Rich and realized he was aware of Mae's reaction, but for some reason he chose to gloss over it. When his eyes met Suzy's they were dark and steady, as if he were trying to warn her off. What the hell was going on? she wondered.

Rich focused on Suzy. "Did you have any dolls when you were with Abby?" he asked.

"Sure, I had one. It was a soft rag doll that Abby made from old scraps of cloth the first day I was there."

"Did you name it Suzy?" he probed hopefully.

She hated to disappoint him. "No, I named it Lucky."

"Hmm, Lucky," Wayne repeated, but as he was making a note on his paper, Suzy heard a slight gasp behind her. Turning, she saw that Mae's mouth was slightly open, her eyes wide with disbelief.

"Does that name ring a bell with you?" Suzy asked anxiously.

Instantly Mae got herself under control. "No," she snapped sullenly. "Of course not." Then, pressing her lips into a thin line, she straightened her shoulders and stared directly ahead.

Confused, Suzy swung her glance back to Rich, but he was talking to Wayne and Dr. Hilton in a low, undemonstrative tone; evidently he'd missed her fleeting interchange with Mae. Disappointed, Suzy settled back in her chair and tried to convince herself it was probably nothing anyway. She was just overreacting.

Joanne had little to add to the conversation, but she listened with interest and an occasional nod or shake of her head. It wasn't long, however, before her shoulders started to droop with fatigue.

Dr. Hilton was the first to notice it. "Why don't we knock this off for today? We're not getting anywhere anyway, and Joanne's tired. Besides, I have to go back to the hospital and"—he glanced from Wayne to Rich—"I'm sure you two have other plans for the day. Let's leave it this way. Before we jump into anything, I think Joanne and Suzy should spend more time together. They've barely met and haven't had a chance to talk. Who knows?" he said. "Given time, they might even discover a few ties to the past." He looked from one to the other. "Well, what do you say?"

"I say it's a waste of time." Wayne retorted.

Rich disagreed. "I think it's a good idea. The decision is going to be up to them anyway."

Wayne started to object, but Dr. Hilton cut him off. "Good, let's leave it that way." Getting up, he strode over to Joanne and took her hand in his for a long moment. She looked up at him, her eyes unusually bright. "I don't know if Suzy is Christina or not," he said, "but I want you to spend a few days with her. She's good therapy for you. You've improved more in the last hour than you have in months." Giving her hand a final squeeze, he nodded a brief good-bye to everybody and left the room.

Immediately Rich walked over to stand beside Suzy as if protecting her from any possible verbal abuse from Wayne or Mae. It was a nice feeling, like the sun coming out from behind the clouds at the end of a rainy day.

Joanne stood up. "You're coming back tomorrow, aren't you, Suzy?" she asked. Her voice sounded confident, but Suzy detected a slight hesitation there, as if she were wondering what disappointment would be next. Suzy's heart went out to her, and she found herself wishing fervently that there were something about Joanne she recognized.

"Yes, of course I will," Suzy assured her.

"I'll bring her myself," Rich promised.

Joanne's eyes sought Suzy's as if she needed further confirmation, so Suzy nodded again. She realized that she was getting more involved than she'd counted on, but then, if Joanne really was her mother, it was worth risking a few bumps to find out for sure. Wasn't that the purpose of the trip?

Joanne appeared to have gotten her emotions back under control, and taking Suzy's face between her hands, she looked deep into her eyes and smiled. "We have a lot of catching up to do, don't we?"

Suzy nodded wordlessly, not quite sure what that meant, but if she looked perplexed, Joanne didn't notice it. Instead she ran her hand lightly over Suzy's hair for a moment before kissing her on the cheek. "I'll see you tomorrow," she said brightly, and with a nod to Rich she started toward the door with Mae right behind her. She paused for a moment to give Suzy a smile...a soft lovely smile...a smile that tugged at something deep in Suzy's memory....

As Rich pulled out of the drive and headed in the opposite direction of Link Hall, he glanced at Suzy. She was unusually quiet and pensive, and well she should be, he thought. She had some big decisions to make, among them whether or not she should pursue this ruse, if indeed that's what it was.

But he wasn't as dubious as he'd been earlier in the day. She hadn't snatched at the few suggestions he'd thrown her way, as he'd expected. When he'd hinted that Abby had probably named her Suzy just because she liked the name, she had refuted that, and when he'd implied that her doll was probably named Suzy, too, she'd corrected him. This puzzled Rich. It was possible that Suzy was clever enough to realize that by forfeiting a few minor advantages she could enhance her status as an innocent young woman who was honestly seeking knowledge of her heritage. Yet somehow, that didn't fit the image of the Suzy he knew. Rich couldn't imagine her as a conniver. The role just didn't fit. But then, he'd been wrong before.

Reaching over, he covered her knee with his hand. "I'm going to buy you the best shellfish lunch you've ever had. On the other side of the shore road, right on the ocean, is one of the finest seafood restaurants in the state."

"Sounds wonderful," Suzy murmured. "I never get much fish at home. It's supposed to be good brain food."

Gently his fingers tightened. "What's the matter? Are you upset because you don't have total recall?"

"No, not upset," she mused, "but a little puzzled. When Joanne left and said, 'I'll see you tomorrow,' I had the feeling that I'd been there before. Do you know what I mean?"

"I certainly do. And maybe you have. After all, that's the name of the game, isn't it?"

"This is not a game!" Suzy reminded him tersely. "At least not to me it isn't. Nor to Joanne, either, I'm sure." Recrossing her legs, she moved away from him.

Her pique surprised him. "I'm sorry, it's just a figure of speech. I didn't mean to insult you."

"I know. I guess I'm a little jumpy."

"And who wouldn't be after what you've been through?" Teasingly he nudged her with his elbow. "What do you say we forget about Thrushmore for the rest of the day and just enjoy?"

Her mouth curved in a grateful smile. "Sounds good to me. There's nothing worse than trying to chase a faded dream. If it's going to come back, it'll come back."

Rich nodded appreciatively. "I like your attitude, Suzy. It shows a lot of self-confidence."

Glancing over at him, Suzy tipped her head slightly to one side and smiled a silent "thank you." She looked as beautiful as the backdrop of flowering trees behind her. Suzy was a person who shined in the daylight because she was so much a part of it. Even her eyes were the color of the sea, but at night, Rich recalled, they sparkled with reflections of the moon, a fact he intended to investigate further.

"After lunch would you like to walk down to the beach and watch the waves come in?" he asked.

"Oh, I'd love it," was her eager response, "but I'm afraid I'm not dressed for it." She glanced down at her nylons and high heels.

"Take them off."

"Well," she demurred, "I would hate to miss wading in the Atlantic Ocean. I might never have another chance."

Rich swung her a quick glance. "Are you still planning on going home tomorrow afternoon?"

"Sure," she answered, but her voice wasn't as positive as it had been before. "That was my plan."

"But you haven't solved anything," he protested, "and a few hours with Joanne isn't going to be enough to convince you that you are or are not Christina Hepburn. But two days could make all the difference." When Suzy didn't reply, Rich knew he had the advantage and, not one to take chances, he pressed it further. "As long as you're here, you might as well settle this thing once and for all. Would it be too inconvenient for you to take a few days away from your work?"

Suzy pursed her lips thoughtfully. "No, not really. I work on straight commission, so my time is pretty much my own, but I don't know...." Her voice trailed off uncertainly.

"Why don't you give it some thought?" he suggested. "Right now we're in need of nourishment, and just around the next bend is where we're going to get it. Captain Jonah's Ocean Eats."

"Eats?"

Rich laughed at Suzy's cynical frown. "Horrible name, isn't it? But the food's terrific."

"With a name like that, it'd have to be." Laughing, she turned to face him. A swath of hair had fallen across her cheek, and Rich found himself aching to reach over and smooth it back, to rest his palm on her cheek; but he forced himself to keep his hands on the wheel. Her nearness was beginning to cause some disturbing quakes in his reserves, not exactly what he'd counted on. But then, he'd never met anyone exactly like Suzy before. The women he'd dated, like Marcia Tolbert, had a brittle crispness about them due in large part to their auspicious social standing, something Rich had never found especially alluring. He was more attracted to women who were natural and straightforward with an openness about them that showed that, though they could be vulnerable, they'd never be defenseless wimps.

Admittedly, this had gotten him in trouble before. Ratonia Zinsky was, seemingly, as straightforward as you could get. He'd met her at the close of his senior year in law school when one of his classmates, Morgan Arnold, had sought his advice. Ratonia had come to this country from a small town in Poland as the wife of an American businessman. Shortly after they married, her husband died, and she tried to make a life for herself in Boston where his family had been ensconced for generations. They not only looked down their noses at this strange foreigner, they even refused to accept her as an American, let alone a relative. They used all the legal tricks they knew to separate her from the family fortunes.

Rich and his friend Morgan Arnold took it upon themselves to defend her and burst upon the courtroom scene with all the zeal and freshness of young, enthusiastic lawyers. After three months of intensive litigation, however, Ratonia broke down and admitted that her marriage certificate was a forgery and that she was, in fact, still married to a man in Poland. The news media immediately dubbed her as an embezzler and a swindler, and some even went so far as to imply that she was trying to sabotage the family's drug research lab. These allegations were unfounded and unproven, but Ratonia Zinsky had had enough. Tearfully kissing Rich and Morgan good-bye, she returned to her homeland to recuperate from the rigors of the trial. That was the last Rich heard of her.

The havoc she left behind was devastating to the two young lawyers. The news media ripped them up one side and down the other. A few journalists tried to be kind by putting the blame on their inexperience. One even ventured to admire them, claiming they had at least fought for what they'd thought was right. This was small consolation, however, and one that made Rich's father cringe every time he heard it. It was because of this that Rich decided not to go into practice with his father as planned. He and Morgan Arnold made plans to start their own practice. Morgan had daringly suggested they specialize in defending immigrants, since they were so experienced, but Rich insisted they only take wealthy old hags and small children. He'd had enough of the homespun little girl from the country.

Chapter Six

Despite the unsophisticated name of the restaurant, Captain Jonah's Ocean Eats was well staffed and tastefully decorated with a breathtaking view of the ocean. The food was even better than Rich had promised, and both he and Suzy took their sweet time savoring every morsel of lobster with drawn butter, bread custard and fresh-picked raspberries with thick cream.

"I've just gained twenty pounds," Suzy proclaimed as she consumed the last raspberry and sat back with a satisfied sigh.

Resting his arms on the table, Rich nodded in agreement. "It wasn't exactly a no-cal meal, but if you feel guilty, you can justify your indulgence by taking a brisk walk on the beach."

"Somehow the word 'brisk' doesn't sound too appealing."

"All right, make it 'languid.' In which case," he added, "I might even go with you."

Suzy looked up at him and laughed, and Rich winked back. He reminded Suzy of a pirate with his dark curly hair and bright blue eyes and rakish grin. That, combined with his sense of humor, was a tantalizing combination and one Suzy knew she was going to miss terribly when she returned to Windland the following day. Of course, she reminded herself, she didn't have to leave so soon. If she called Terri at the office and explained the circumstances, Terri would be the first to insist that Suzy stay and settle this thing once and for all.

It would be a reasonable solution. Suzy wanted to spend more time with Joanne and, not incidentally, with Rich, too. In the short time she'd known him, she'd found him easier to talk to than any man she'd ever met, including Roger Mayer. Suzy didn't even pretend not to be aware of Rich's physical attractiveness, but, though her insides tingled with delight every time she was near him, there was also a fluttering of apprehension. Was she just a cynical old fool? she wondered. Or was Rich something other than he appeared to be? But if that were true, why was it every time she was with him her uneasiness would start to slip away? Because he exuded an aura of sureness that had a way of dissolving doubts and uncertainties and replacing them with steaming hope...that's why.

Maybe she was being too investigative, she decided as she watched Rich start the car and head down the road to his "secret" beach. When he pulled the car off the road into an area of overgrown weeds, however, Suzy pursed her lips and frowned.

"Strange, I thought beaches had sand."

"We have to climb down a slight incline first," he explained, giving her thigh an encouraging pat. "When I say hidden, I mean hidden."

"I just hope it's not out of this world."

"You can see for yourself as soon as you get out of those hose." Twisting his body toward her, he stretched his arm across the back of her seat and settled in for the show.

Suzy flattened her mouth into a grim line. "I presume," she said loftily, "that you are going to be a gentleman and turn your back."

"Oh." He thought about that. "Actually, I had presumed you were going to be a good sport and let me help."

"Sorry, but I'm not the sporty type. Now do you want to get out of this car while I take off my panty hose, or do you want to just sit here all day?"

"Did anyone ever tell you you were a hard woman to reason with?"

"Yes. Often. Now, are you getting out or—"

"All right. I can take a hint." Before he turned to open the door, though, he gave her a playful knuckle on the cheek. "However, if you should decide to change the game plan..."

"I'll blow the whistle," she promised.

A few minute later, Rich and Suzy, both barefoot and laughing and holding hands like kids, wove their way down a narrow path that curved erratically around the rocks to a small patch of sandy beach below—a very small patch of sandy beach, smaller than anything Suzy had ever seen before.

"This is a beach?" she questioned skeptically.

"Certainly," was Rich's quick response. "In this part of the country, huge sandy beaches are hard to come by."

"But this isn't as big as a barn."

"But it's hidden," he whispered mysteriously. "If you sit back there against those rocks, no one can see you from up above."

Suzy's glance swung from the rocks at the base of the hill to Rich. She didn't pretend naiveté. She knew very well why he'd brought her down here, and he knew she knew. As she turned her face up to his, her eyes locked with his. He looked so devastatingly handsome against the background of the sea and the sand and the sun that she had an almost uncontrollable desire to throw her arms around him and hug him to her. Fortunately, she still had a few shreds of common sense left, and despite the invisible warmth racing through her, she knew it was time to rein in her horse.

"Look," she reasoned, trying to sound as matter-of-fact and coolly reserved as possible, "we both know our relationship is a temporary one, so let's not spoil it by getting ourselves involved in an impossible situation." She cocked her head to one side. "What do you say?"

Putting his hands on Suzy's shoulders, Rich looked deep into her eyes. "I disagree with you on one vital point, and that is that our situation has to be a temporary one. But if you feel that it does, then I'll not pursue a personal relationship if it's against your wishes.''

If he'd clicked his heels and bowed, Suzy wouldn't have been surprised. He was a perfect gentleman, almost too perfect, in fact, but even though his eyes flashed with a mischievous glint, at least his voice rang with sincerity, and that meant something, didn't it?

Suddenly Rich smiled, his face bright with an inner happiness that always seemed to be there, just under the surface. ''Come on,'' he urged, taking Suzy by the hand, ''let's test the water. Too bad you didn't bring a bathing suit.''

''Yes, it is,'' Suzy quipped as she skipped across the sand beside him, grateful that he wasn't the resentful, pouting type. He was as reasonable and understanding as she knew he would be.

When Suzy reached the shoreline she was disappointed to find so many rocks, not at all what she'd expected. Releasing her hand, Rich stopped to roll his pants up to his knees while Suzy strode confidently into the glistening blue waters of the great Atlantic Ocean.

''Oh, my God!'' she screamed as she jumped back to the sand. ''It's like ice!''

''Of course it is, but you'll get used to that. Come on, try it again,'' he urged, but Suzy had already had enough. With a firm shake of her head, she sat down on the warm sand and proceeded to watch Rich as he bravely waded into the surf.

Within minutes he was on the beach beside her. ''The water's like ice, Suzy. You'd better not go in.''

She laughed at him, loving his humor, his boyish face, his wind-tossed hair...

"But at least the sun's warm," he continued, unaware of her examination and the look of silent approval that crossed her face. Instead, he took off his sweater and arranged it on the sand behind them. Then, curving an arm around Suzy's shoulders, he tumbled them both back onto the sand, turning Suzy slightly so that she faced him.

His eyes roved intimately over her face, her neck, her shoulders and down to her breasts. Then once again they swept back to her face and rested provocatively on her lips. As Suzy looked up at him, she was suddenly aware of the sensual flare of his nostrils, and instantly every nerve in her body tensed with an ache of hunger that couldn't be denied. She realized the time to pull away was now, but she couldn't, wouldn't. Her longing to be close to him, to touch him, to hold him was turning out to be greater than her self-discipline.

Forgetting all her resolves, Suzy framed Rich's face with her hands and placed delicate kisses on his temple, the hollow below his cheekbone, the square ridge of his jaw. She was only vaguely aware of his hand curving around the back of her head until he drew her closer and, with an intoxicating sweetness, covered her mouth with his. With a soft "Mmm," Suzy sank into his embrace and parted her lips. Eagerly Rich's tongue met hers in a delicious tangle of fiery sensations that reached deep into the lower regions of Suzy's body.

Rich shifted slightly and then his hands, hungry to feel the smoothness of her skin, burrowed under her blouse and moved upward to curve around the warm swell of her breasts. The sudden delectable sensation made her breath catch in her throat as desire overcame her like a summer storm, unexpected and uncontrollable. As Suzy's awareness heightened, she found herself enjoying the restless seeking of Rich's hands, the firmness of his warm body, and she yearned to return his sensuous stroking. But a sense of caution reminded her that they were on a public beach and that someone could come along at any minute.

Straightening, Suzy leaned back, her mouth parting from the kiss reluctantly. Lazily Rich opened one eye and exhaled a long, satisfied sigh. Then, smiling gently, he patted her cheek. "That wasn't bad, considering...."

Suzy straightened. "What do you mean?"

"Considering we're not going to get personally involved."

"That's not what I meant," she said, holding his face in the palm of her hand. "I was referring to the 'that wasn't bad' part. Frankly, I thought we did pretty well."

"Oh, so do I," he replied quickly, "but remember, we don't want to get in over our heads." He gave her an affectionate pat on the back. "We'll start our new leaf tomorrow," he promised.

"That's fine," Suzy agreed, fully aware that his promise didn't include tonight. She tried to slant him a knowing glance, but he was so engrossed in shaking the sand out of his sweater that he didn't see it. It was probably just as well, she thought. She could handle the problem later if it should arise. Right now she was still having trouble getting her pulse to stop thumping, an all but impossible task.

Suzy would have been content to stay there for hours huddled next to Rich, watching the ships on the horizon, listening to the waves splashing up on the beach, but as the sun started to go down, the air turned chilly. Reluctantly, they decided to go home.

As Suzy stood up, she patted her stomach. "I hope Mrs. Slingluff hasn't fixed dinner for us. I couldn't eat a bite."

"She hasn't," Rich assured her. "Saturday is their day off. They usually go down to New Bedford to visit relatives, but you can be sure she's left a snack for us in the fridge. She always does."

"That's certainly nice of her," Suzy commented. "You're very lucky to have someone taking such good care of you."

"She's the nearest thing to a mother I have," he said, brushing the sand off his hands. "In fact, that's probably one of the main reasons I haven't sold Link Hall. It's really too big just for me, but the Slingluffs have a nice apartment in the east wing and to them, that's their home. How can I kick my own mother out of her home?"

"I guess you can't," she murmured, wondering if the Slingluffs realized how lucky they were to have Rich take care of them. "You know, you surprise me," Suzy said as they started up the beach to the path. "Most businessmen would have sold the old homestead, invested the money in business property and moved into a swank apartment in Boston and to hell with the old folks who had taken care of them since childhood."

Rich shook his head. "Oh, I don't know. You're a businesswoman. Would you have kicked Abby out?"

"Good heavens, no!"

"There you are," he said, nudging her in the ribs. "We're both just a couple of sentimental fools."

"And proud of it," Suzy added.

Rich couldn't resist pressing his point. "Does that sentimentality extend to Joanne? At least she's a possible mother, and if you stayed over a few more days, you might find out for sure."

"As a matter of fact," Suzy said, pausing on the hill to catch her breath, "I've decided that if it wouldn't put you out too much, I might stay over a few days."

Rich grinned, delighted. "That's the best news I've had all week. You can spend a few hours with Joanne tomorrow and all day Monday if you want."

"Why only a few hours tomorrow?"

"Because she'll probably tire very quickly. She's not used to so much excitement. Besides..." He paused to nudge Suzy up the hill again with an encouraging pat on the fanny. "I have a few plans myself."

"Oh, really? What?"

"I thought we could drive down to Newport tomorrow and watch the ships in the harbor and have lunch and just laze around. Have you ever been there?"

"No, but it sounds exciting."

"It's a fascinating place. You'll love it. It's the only city I've ever known that's been able to resist the rigors of gross modernization. They still have cobblestone streets and old buildings and schooners and yawls and yachts..."

Suzy's mouth curved in a smile. She loved his romanticizing. "It sounds as if Newport is a favorite haunt of yours."

"Oh, it is. And one of these days I'm going to get a boat, but at the moment, it's not high on my priority list."

He didn't go on to explain what was high on his list, and Suzy didn't ask. It could very well be Miss Tolbert, and if it was, she didn't want to know about it. Why spoil a beautiful day?

It was after nine when they raided the refrigerator to see what goodies Mrs. Slingluff had left for them. They decided on corned-beef sandwiches on rye. While Rich made the sandwiches, one inch thick, Suzy got out corn chips, pickles and beer. "And if this doesn't give you nightmares, nothing will," she announced as they carried the fare into the library, which, inadvertently, had become their favorite place to be together.

After dinner, Suzy suggested they play a game of cards, but Rich was less than enthusiastic. "I don't think I could handle anything more mind-boggling than a game of Old Maid. Besides," he said as he stretched his arm across the back of the couch and settled in comfortably beside her, "don't we have some unfinished business to attend to?"

"No, we don't," she stated firmly. "I've already explained my position and you've already agreed that under the circumstances"— Rich blew a moist kiss into her hair, soft and tantalizing—"under the circumstances we both have little to gain by extending our relationship any further." His arm slid down across her shoulders, his hand folded over her arm, bringing her closer, pressing her against him, beckoning, tempting. "Our relationship, ah, further, ah...

Oh, hell!'' Casting all of her self-imposed restrictions aside, Suzy circled her arms around Rich's neck and turned his face so that it was just inches from hers. One little kiss, that was all.

Her promises were quickly forgotten, however, as Rich's arms closed around her and his lips captured hers in a devouring kiss. The intoxicating warmth that had been throbbing inside her all afternoon began to bubble and swell until it suddenly burst to the surface. As a ragged breath caught in her throat, Rich answered her body's surging response by once again exploring her mouth with his tongue, restlessly seeking, consuming, demanding more.

At first Suzy was powerless to keep her body from arching into him, from responding to his sensuality with a fervor that almost equaled his. Her fingers tunneled into his hair, then paused to massage the base of his neck before trailing down his spine in a slow, provocative motion that brought a hot shiver of response from him, delightful in its intensity but more than she'd counted on.

Separating his mouth from hers, Rich took a deep, ragged breath. "Let's go to bed," he whispered, his voice sexy and inviting...and irresistible.

Almost. Suzy had a few fragments of caution left. It wasn't that she didn't want to spend the night with Rich; she couldn't think of anything she'd like better. It was facing the hurt of the morning after that stopped her. She dreaded waking up knowing that to Rich lovemaking was merely a form of physical exercise, while to her it was the first step on the path to a long and lasting love affair.

Suzy swallowed a large, uncomfortable lump in her throat. Though she didn't want to get hurt herself, she didn't want to hurt Rich, either. "I'm sorry," she murmured, striving to discipline her voice, "but as much as I find you a very fascinating person to be with, I'm just not ready to share my bed with you." She wanted to add "and my heart," but men didn't understand things like that.

"I see," Rich replied. Suddenly releasing her, he sat back. There was disappointment in his face, she'd expected that, but she wasn't prepared for the pain that scorched his eyes or the inexplicable feeling of emptiness she felt.

Rich stood up and, jamming his hands into his pockets, strode toward the windows and stared out into the night. He didn't speak or motion for her to come and stand beside him or even cast a glance at her over his shoulder. She was dismissed.

Straightening her legs, Suzy smoothed down her skirt before she, too, got to her feet. She yearned to walk over to him, to wrap her arms around him, press her cheek against his broad back, but why start something she'd just ended?

"It's getting late," she said. "I think I'll go upstairs."

"Good night," he answered in a dull, inflectionless voice. "See you tomorrow, Suzy."

Suzy started to turn toward the door and suddenly stopped. She'd heard those words before today. Joanne! The words had a strangely familiar ring. She'd heard them many times in her life, but today at Thrushmore... Echoes of the past began to tug at her, and she forced herself to delve deep into her memory, to retrieve that one fleeting thread that might connect her to her past. Suddenly it exploded all around her.

"Oh, no!" she cried, covering her eyes with her hands. "I've got it all mixed up."

Rich swiveled around. "What's wrong?"

"This afternoon when we left Thrushmore, Joanne said, 'I'll see you tomorrow, Suzy.' At the time it sounded so familiar that for a moment..."

"You thought you'd heard Joanne say that before?" He was at her side now.

"Yes, but I was wrong. It wasn't Joanne's voice I remembered this afternoon. It was Abby's!"

"Abby's?"

"Yes. When I was a little girl, she was about the same age that Joanne is now. That's why everything sounded so familiar. But it wasn't Joanne's voice that I remembered, it was Abby's. Joanne would have said, 'I'll see you tomorrow, Christina!'"

"Oh, God, you're right," he said, as disappointed as she was. "I'm sorry, Suzy." He put a consoling arm around her. "And here I thought you'd finally latched on to something."

"So did I." Suzy's shoulders slumped dejectedly.

But Rich wasn't as easily daunted. Tightening his arm around her, he held her close. "Don't give up the game until the final whistle is blown," he whispered, his breath gentle and warm in her hair.

"Even if you know you're going to lose?" she murmured.

"You never know that...."

She knew she'd lost one battle, however, and that was with her resolves. They fell like autumn leaves in a windstorm when Rich escorted her up the stairs with a possessive arm around her shoulders. Without so much as a second thought, Suzy cast all her hesitancies aside and welcomed him into her room and into her arms.

Before the door had even closed behind them, they came together in a kiss that not only signaled their trembling desire, but promised release from the feeling of arousal that was growing so swiftly in both of them. With a soft, contented sigh, Suzy tightened her arms around Rich's neck. She was vaguely conscious of the moonlight streaming through the windows, the quiet ticking of a distant clock, the faint smell of roses, all of which came together in a harmonious mingling of sensations...as did the feeling of oneness with the man whose body was pressed so intimately against hers.

Taking Rich's head between her hands, Suzy's lips moved languorously across his face, running moist kisses over his skin. Murmuring quiet nothings, she explored every mound and crevice and ended her luxurious roaming by capturing his lips between hers. As Rich sucked in his breath, she could feel a delicious shudder of desire race through him.

"Let's get out of these clothes," he whispered against her lips.

"Right now," she whispered back.

Suzy was appalled at her own lack of restraint. Without a second thought, she let her skirt and slip drop to the floor and began peeling off her panty hose. In the meantime, Rich divested himself of his clothing with a speed she'd never known existed and stood before her, his naked body glowing and warm in the dimly lighted room.

"Let me do that." Stepping so close to her that the lower regions of their bodies brushed against each other, he began to unbutton her blouse with deliberate slowness. He was in no hurry, and neither was Suzy. Putting her hands at his waist, she pressed her fingers into his muscled body, gently massaging, edging downward.

His fingers moved faster. "You know how to put the speed on, I'll say that."

"You want me to help?"

Rich's body squirmed deliciously beneath her hands. "I like things the way they are," he murmured as he finally conquered the last button and started skimming the blouse off her shoulders. Reluctantly, Suzy released her seductive hold on him to let the blouse slip to the floor. In moments, he had her bra off and was pressing her breasts against his muscled chest.

"Oh, God," he said longingly. "You feel great."

All Suzy could manage was a soft "Mmmm" as his arms closed around her and their bodies melded together in a mutual shudder of desire. Deliberately they moved against each other, teasing the flame, heightening the senses. Suddenly Rich's hungry lips sought her mouth. Sensuously he twined his tongue around hers in an intimate exploration that was so intoxicating Suzy felt herself tremble as though the earth were falling away from beneath her.

They swayed together for a moment, then, lifting her up in his arms, Rich carried her to the bed. He laid her gently on the quilted spread, then stretched out beside her, his lean, sinewy body a stark contrast to Suzy's satin-textured skin. As her head fell back, Rich kissed the vulnerable spot at the base of her throat before trailing his lips downward until they circled a rosy nipple, closed over it, teased it, savored it, before moving to the other breast.

With a soft moan of pleasure, Suzy moved even closer and began to freely explore Rich's damp, muscled back with slow, deliberate strokes. She massaged his back, his waist, his hips and thighs, loving his nakedness as well as the tormenting response of his muscles. Wanting to give as much pleasure as she received, Suzy gradually increased the pressure of her roving hands until she felt his body suddenly tighten with a desire that matched her own.

"Ahh, yes," Rich moaned with delighted satisfaction.

Then, with a sudden surging movement, Rich took control.

Easing Suzy onto her back, he moved over her, instantly taking possession of the valley between her thighs. Suzy felt shock waves of pleasure race through her as Rich's hands stroked down her hips, slowly exploring her needs and responses. Her breath came in short gasps as she repeated his name and clutched his shoulders. Then, instinctively, she wrapped her legs around him, opening herself to him, urging him to join their bodies.

He entered her with slow, steady thrusts that drew a gasp of ecstasy from Suzy's lips. Positioning himself until her hips fit perfectly with his, he slowly began to move their bodies together, pacing himself until their rhythm was even. Then, with deepening urgency, he buried himself in her liquid heat until their bodies flamed into a white-hot fire that swept away everything but the ecstasy of the moment. Their tempo increased, spiraling upward, reaching for the ultimate goal. Suzy was conscious only of Rich's hardness and the answering rhythm of nature pounding through her bloodstream.

"Oh, my God," she cried out as he tightened his grip, gathering momentum. Then suddenly, in a burst of fierce power, he took them soaring out of their orb of naked desire and into the kingdom of total fulfillment.

Suzy sank back into the world of voluptuous rapture, a world she had never dreamed existed before. For a long time, Rich held her in his arms until her throbbing pulse began to subside and the world around her came into focus again. Gently stroking her hair, he nestled her into his arms, cradled her against his chest and nuzzled his face in her hair.

"How do you feel?" he whispered.

"Wonderful. How about you?"

Rich exhaled a long sigh. "Supremely satisfied. We did pretty well for the first time together. We seem to fit like..." He paused, searching for a comparison.

"Like springtime and rain?" she offered.

Rich's mouth curved in a warming smile. "Yes, something like that." Lifting his head a little, he looked into her face, serene and beautiful in the flickering shadows. "Are you ever lonely, Suzy?"

Her eyelids fluttered downward. "Sometimes," she murmured.

"Do you miss the farm life?"

She shook her head. "No. I might if Abby were still alive, but without her, I'd never want to go back to all those hardships." Suddenly she raised her gaze to his. "What about you? Do you miss the excitement of being in school again and planning daring escapades with your friends?''

''Naw. I'm too old for that.''

''Are you ever lonely?'' she asked quietly.

Wrapping his arms around her, Rich held her closer. ''Sometimes,'' he murmured.

Rich was still asleep when Suzy opened her eyes to a shaft of sunlight creating patterns on their tumbled bed. At first she didn't dare move for fear the marvelous moments of their night's lovemaking would disappear, but as she adjusted her eyes to the brightening room, she realized her fears were childish. Nothing could take away what they had shared.

Soundlessly, Suzy slipped out of bed and moved quietly into the bathroom. Closing the door, she inspected her face in the mirror. It was the same Suzy who was there yesterday, no question about that, but there were new lights in her eyes and a seemingly permanent smile at the edges of her mouth. She looked rested, alert and glowing with inner excitement. As Abby would have said, she had apples in her cheeks and sunshine in her eyes. And why wouldn't she have? Hadn't she just spent the night in the arms of the most wonderful man she'd ever known?

Tiptoeing out of the room, she closed the door softly behind her and, tying the sash of her robe, made her way downstairs. Suzy had never been one to stay in bed in the morning, and though she had nothing in particular to do until Rich woke up, she thought that maybe she could explore the house a little and... Ah! Her nostrils picked up the delectable aroma of fresh-brewed coffee. Pushing her way through the door into the kitchen, she found Mrs. Slingluff sitting at the kitchen table. She was wearing a neat blue-and-white print dress with a matching linen jacket and large silver earrings.

"Well, you look ready for church," Suzy said as she breezed into the room.

"Yes, I am, but I have time to—"

"No, no, no." Suzy stayed her with a raised hand. "You stay right where you are. I can get my own coffee. What's that? The Sunday paper?"

"Yes," Mrs. Slingluff bubbled, "and Rich's picture's in it!"

Mrs. Slingluff smoothed her hand across the section that was of such vital interest. It happened to be the society page. "Right there," she announced proudly, pointing to a blurred picture of several people at a party. "That's Marcia Tolbert on the left, over there, and her father on the other side. Good picture of Rich, don't you think?"

Suzy thought it was fuzzy and grayish, but the man in the center of the picture was definitely Rich, and the woman at his side was definitely young and beautiful and smiling up at him as if he were the center of the universe. The man on the other side was handsome, with shocking white hair, a full mustache and a well-cared-for athletic physique. Despite the poor quality of the picture, it was evident that the three of them were strictly class A.

Swallowing a stubborn rising lump in her throat, Suzy took another sip of her coffee and leaned back in her chair, as if by pretending disinterest, the article would fade from view.

But Mrs. Slingluff was not one to let it die. "That was the benefit dinner for the opening night of the art center. Marcia's father is one of the major donors."

"Oh, how lovely," Suzy murmured, trying hard to pump some enthusiasm into her voice and not succeeding.

Lifting her chin, Mrs. Slingluff scanned the page again, making sure she hadn't overlooked something. "Yes," she went on, "Alvin Tolbert is one of the wealthiest men in this area. He's a commodore, you know. Has a beautiful new sailing vessel named *The Symphony Spirit*. I understand he's going to enter it in the America's Cup races next summer."

"Oh, how exciting." Suzy wondered if Rich would be on the crew...as a permanent member. "Do they sail it around here much?"

"They keep it in Newport. That's where all the action is, so Rich tells me. I wouldn't know. I seldom go there—not my kind of country, if you know what I mean."

Suzy nodded wordlessly. She knew exactly what she meant. In fact, she was beginning to feel a little like that herself. "Does Rich sail with them often?" she asked.

"No, not in the past year or so. He seems to have lost interest in ships. There was a time when you couldn't keep him away from them, though. He and Marcia spent many a summer together at the Newport docks, let me tell you, but, of course, they were just kids then."

"How nice," Suzy murmured. What else could she say? It was great that they were still friends? Wonderful that they had remained buddy-buddies all these years? Splendid that their comrade-in-arms status still prevailed? Horse hair! If Suzy had her way, she'd tow Marcia Tolbert out to the briny deep and leave her there. But that was a ridiculous thought, Suzy scolded herself. She'd never even seen the woman. Deliberately she changed the focus to the third person in the tableau, Commodore Alvin C. Tolbert III, according to the blurb under the picture.

"Mr. Tolbert looks like a very handsome man."

"Oh, he is." Mrs. Slingluff nodded enthusiastically. "And very influential, too. He and Rich's father were good friends, you know."

"No, I didn't realize that."

"He's trying to get Rich to run for state representative. With Tolbert's backing, it would be almost impossible for Rich to lose. Every businessman in the area owes old A. C. a favor, and you can be sure he'd remind them of that when it came to supporting his favorite candidate."

"I can see where he'd be very influential." Suzy's spirits began to sink a little. She'd unconsciously placed Rich in a group of hardworking people who struggled with the ins and outs of daily problems the same as everyone else. She'd never thought of him as a political figure with tons of money behind him. He seemed so...so normal.

Getting up, Suzy poured herself another cup of coffee. Unconsciously she rubbed the back of her hand across her eyes, wishing she could drop the subject then and there, but she couldn't resist hearing it all.

"And is Rich thinking of running?" she asked, hoping she'd laced her voice with just the right amount of casualness...politely interested but not unduly concerned.

Folding the paper, Mrs. Slingluff rose and went to the sink to rinse out her cup. "Oh, I don't know." She sighed heavily. "Rich says he's not interested, but I don't see why not. We could use a good representative, and heaven knows he's more than qualified. Besides, with a house this size, he could hold political rallies every week if he wanted to."

The sound of feet scraping on the outside mat brought the subject to a close. Albert opened the door and called in, "You ready, Hermione?"

"Just as soon as I wash my hands." She turned to Suzy. "There's plenty of eggs and some fresh raisin bread and—"

"Now don't worry about us," Suzy assured her. "We can manage a little breakfast. You just enjoy yourself."

"Oh, thanks, I will. I always do." With a final touch to her hair in the small mirror near the door, Mrs. Slingluff picked up her handbag and followed Albert out the door. She took a deep breath and called back in, "The weather is simply gorgeous. Maybe you could get Rich outside to..." But her words faded into the distance as Albert hurried her to the waiting car.

Chapter Seven

As if forced to undertake an unpleasant task, Suzy went back to the newspaper and read the whole article about the new art center. Rich was only mentioned once, as Miss Tolbert's escort, but the picture said it all. Quietly Suzy put the paper down, and propping her elbows on the table, she rested her chin in her hands and stared out of the curtained window at the wide lawn beyond. She sighed heavily.

Despite their lovemaking the night before, Suzy wondered if there could ever be a place for her in Rich's life. They were from entirely different worlds. She was a small town, hardworking woman who had never known the luxuries of a monied life. Rich, on the other hand, knew nothing else. And, though she doubted if he realized this, his whole future was structured around this wealth. He was ideal political material. He not only had looks and personality, but he was one of the old families and would have the support of wealthy influential friends like the Tolberts. Even if he loved her, and Suzy wasn't sure that he did, would they ever marry? Though he didn't seem to be politically oriented today, the time might come when he'd change his mind. In that case, Marcia Tolbert would be a perfect wife for him, whereas Suzy, who knew nothing about the political scene, could only offer him her love and devotion. Was that enough?

Suddenly the door from the dining room swung open and a yawning Rich dragged himself into the kitchen. Mumbling a good morning, he walked up behind Suzy's chair and, wrapping his arms around her, buried a moist kiss in the hollow below her ear.

"I don't usually stir until noon, but when I found myself sleeping in an empty bed, my ego got all bent out of shape. Why didn't you wake me up?"

"Because you looked like a sleeping lamb. Besides," she confessed, raising her arms so that her hands held his head, "I like to have a little time to myself in the morning. It gives me a chance to get my day organized."

"Mmm," he mused, "I don't get mine organized until after I reach the office." Giving her a gentle buss on the cheek, he walked over to the sink and went through the difficult process of pouring himself a cup of coffee, which he started drinking before he even got to the table.

Suzy pointed to the society section. "Mrs. Slingluff found your picture in the Sunday paper."

Rich barely glanced at it. "That Tolbert family is constantly involved in some sort of benefit or other, and they always manage to drag me into it."

"Maybe they think that with your good looks and charm on their side, people will donate more money."

"Yep. You're probably right." He gave her a wink. "Jealous?"

"Yes, as a matter of fact, I am," she admitted. "This Marcia Tolbert is looking at you with adoring eyes."

"Really? Let's see." Leaning over the paper, Rich squinted at the picture. "You're right. She thinks I'm a Greek god or something, but," he said, expanding his chest with true macho élan, "there's nothing I can do about that. If I'm a god, I'm a god." Reaching over, he patted the back of Suzy's hand. "Now what about my breakfast?"

"What about it?"

"What do you mean what about it? Here I sit in regal aplomb and you dare to even suggest that my first meal of the day is not prepared and ready to set before me—"

The phone rang, interrupting his soliloquy, and Suzy laughed. "You'd better answer that, Your Highness. It might be the king of Neja asking to borrow a dozen eggs."

"Oh, all right," he said, getting up. "No wonder royalty vanished. There's no respect for the true—" He picked up the phone. "Hello."

He listened for several minutes. Then, "Well, what makes you think that?" A pause. "And whose decision is this?" Another pause, a short one. "I see. Well, frankly, Mae, I'll have to talk it over with Suzy before I make a decision." They exchanged a few brief parting words before hanging up.

Turning from the phone, Rich sighed disgustedly. "Needless to say, that was Mae Voght. It seems Joanne has a headache this morning and can't see you."

"Oh, no," Suzy said, exasperated. "Now just what in hell does that mean?"

Rich tweaked her cheek. "I think it means that Mae is assuming you're going home today, but little does she know that evil forces are at work here. Why don't you call your boss and tell her you're taking the next week off?"

The suggestion was almost more than Suzy could resist, but she knew better than to spend a whole week with Rich. Then she'd never want to go. "I'll call her in an hour or so and see what she says."

"Good. And I'm going to call Paul Hilton. Not that I want you to spend all day with Joanne, but it galls the hell out of me to have Mae pulling all the strings."

"I know. I feel the same way."

Pulling Suzy to her feet, Rich planted a firm kiss on her mouth and then, not so tactfully, led her to the refrigerator. "Why don't you start cooking breakfast while I try to get hold of Hilton?"

"Oh, all right." Suzy appeared to concede with reluctance, but inside she was delighted to be sharing the kitchen with Rich—sharing anything with Rich.

By the time Suzy had searched the refrigerator and gotten the bacon started, Rich had finished his call. Dr. Hilton couldn't be reached at the moment, but Rich left word for him to call back. Then, sitting down again and relaxing back in his chair, he awaited his breakfast.

"Now wait a minute," Suzy protested. "I'm not the cook here, you are."

"Nonsense, I cooked last night."

Suzy went over and ruffled her hands through his hair. "And you did such a superb job of it that it would be a waste of talent to let you sit idle while I struggled."

Grabbing her hands, he pulled them down around his neck. "Okay, I'll tell you what I'm going to do. I'll conjure up one of my surprise omelets if you'll do everything else, including making a fresh pot of coffee."

"It's a deal." Teasingly she patted his cheek and went back to her bacon, which was already a little overcooked.

When the phone rang again Rich was in the midst of assembling some sort of Chinese concoction. "That's probably Dr. Hilton. Can you get it, Suzy?"

"Sure," she said, and drying her hands, she answered the phone.

"Is that you, Suzy?" It was Dr. Hilton's voice.

"Yes, how are you?"

"Great, but what's going on over there? Is Rich sick?"

"No," Suzy assured him. "Mae called earlier and said that Joanne was sick with a headache and couldn't see me today and Rich is feeling all bashed in about it."

"Oh, ah, well, ah..." He paused uncertainly. Was something wrong? Suzy wondered. But almost immediately Dr. Hilton got his thoughts together and continued. "I talked to Joanne earlier and she really does have a headache. Nothing serious, though. She just had a restless night. She'll probably be fine this afternoon. Have you and Rich planned on doing anything today?"

Suzy glanced at Rich, whose back was to her. "Well, as a matter of fact, we thought we might drive to Newport...."

"Then go right ahead," Hilton said quickly. "You're going to stay over a few days, aren't you?"

"Yes, I think so."

"Good, then you can have Joanne all to yourself for a while, and if Mae gives you any trouble, I'll take you over there myself."

Suzy laughed, her voice soft and lilting. "I hope you mean that. I just might need you."

"Don't worry about Mae. Her bark is worse than her bite. You two take the day off and have a good time."

"Thanks, we will," Suzy replied, wondering if her voice hinted at the closeness that was growing between Rich and herself.

"And Suzy," Dr. Hilton added, "I think I have the answer to one of our mysteries."

"Really? What?"

"On the telephone, you sound exactly like Joanne used to not so many years ago."

"No! Really?"

"You sure do. No wonder David Hepburn was so anxious to meet you."

"Oh, my gosh," Suzy gasped, hardly believing it.

"What, what, what..." Rich called from the stove, but Suzy said good-bye and hung up before she let him in on Dr. Hilton's new discovery.

Rich absolutely beamed. "Whew! We're getting somewhere, Suzy Yoder. I told you to hang in there."

Suzy was just as elated as he was, but still, she had her doubts. "It really isn't conclusive. A lot of people sound alike over the phone. Besides, Dr. Hilton said this was the way Joanne sounded years ago. How can he remember?"

"Believe me," Rich assured her as he flipped his gourmet omelet onto their plates and they both sat down, "his memory goes back to forever. He still knows what my temperature was when I had chicken pox at the age of seven. He has a mind like a computer and..." He stopped in midsentence. "What's the matter? Don't you like the omelet? Too many tomatoes?"

"No," she answered dryly, "too many sardines."

Suzy was still in her robe looking through her suitcase for her bottle of scented bath crystals when Rich came bounding into her bedroom wearing only a towel.

"I'll show you how to work the shower," he announced, his intentions obvious.

"No, you won't. I can manage very well by myself. Besides, I'm not taking a shower, I'm taking a bath. Besides, it's time we got on our way...."

"Speaking of besides," he said, glancing meaningfully at the unmade bed, "why don't we take a few minutes and discuss this more intimately?" Already his hands were on her robe, easing it off her shoulders.

Suzy started to protest, but as soon as her robe fell away from her and her breasts were pressed against Rich's naked chest, she was lost. Skimming her hands down his back, she clasped her palms around his buttocks and squeezed gently. In answer, Rich pulled her into his hardness and within minutes they were in bed again. Once more Suzy felt the power of his hands moving over her soft, rounded curves seeking every nook and crevice, caressing, savoring. She tasted his body with feverish kisses until they were caught up in a bubble of passion that grew and grew until suddenly something snapped in both of them, bringing the inevitable release that their throbbing bodies so desperately sought.

Rich trailed a finger across Suzy's brow, down her cheek and into her hair. "Why don't we stay here all day? To hell with Newport."

She stirred lazily. "Too much of a good thing...."

"I know, I know, but who's to say what a good thing is?"

Opening both eyes, she looked into his still damp face. His eyes were crystal-clear circles of shiny blue glass and his mouth was quirked up just a little on one side, giving him a devilishly handsome look that made her heart turn over. Was he hers only for the moment? she wondered, then quickly dismissed the thought, determined not to let any shadows ruin their cherished hours together.

She gave Rich a hearty slap on the behind and sat up. "Come on, you lazy lug, you promised to show me Newport and I want to see it in the daylight."

"Does that mean you want to be back here by dark, then?" He patted her place beside him.

"No, it means we have to hurry and that I don't have time for a bath and have to take a shower instead."

Instantly Rich was on his feet, his arm around her. "Come on, I'll show you how it works."

The only suitable thing Suzy had to wear was a pair of beige slacks, a white terry V-necked top and loafers. She didn't look or feel very nautical, but then she hadn't expected to be shown the sights of Newport Bay. Rich, on the other hand, looked as if he'd just stepped off a yacht with his white jeans and navy pullover and that rakish pirate's grin of his.

"How much more time do you feel you're going to need before you feel ready to present yourself to Newport society?" Rich asked as he leaned against the doorjamb of her bedroom with a stopwatch in his hand.

Suzy was not to be hurried. "I'm almost ready, but I have to finish drying my hair. So why don't you go downstairs and pack the car or something?"

"What am I supposed to put in it? Blankets?" he suggested hopefully.

"Forget I said that. You don't need any reminders."

"I have one right before me."

Marching over to the doorway, Suzy put both hands on Rich's chest and firmly pushed him into the hall. "Do something while I finish dressing, will you?"

"Okay," he conceded reluctantly. "I'll get the car out. But hurry it up, right?"

"Right."

As he disappeared down the hall, Suzy finished styling her hair and gave her makeup one last inspection. Then, shouldering her handbag, she started out of the room but paused when she spied the phone on the night table. She'd better call Terri and tell her of the change of plans. After all, Terri was expecting her in the office the following morning.

The phone rang five times before Terri picked it up with an impatient "Hello."

"Stop being so grumpy. It's Sunday," Suzy teased.

"Oh, hi, Suzy," came a more relaxed voice. "I was just outside trying to decide what I'm going to plant this year. How goes it with you?"

"Wonderful." Suzy tried to tone down the enthusiasm in her voice. "Rich Link met me at the airport as planned, and I've already met Joanne and the rest of the household."

"And they were delighted to see you?"

"Not exactly."

"Then what's so wonderful? The sheer thrill of being in Bark Cove, Massachusetts," Terri joshed, "or is it just possible that the young man who invited you to visit is young and handsome and single?"

"As a matter of fact he is," Suzy confessed. "In fact, since there aren't any motels around here, I'm staying at his home."

"Oh, how convenient."

"Well, it is," Suzy contended, "but I'll explain all that later. What I'm calling about is that I think I'll stay over a few days, if it's all right with you."

"Of course it's all right," Terri assured her. "I never did think two days was going to be enough time for you to make a decision as big as this."

"I'd just planned on meeting the family and then going back to Windland to mull it over."

"I know, but nothing is as simple as it seems. And now, with that handsome knight on the scene..." Terri's voice trailed off thoughtfully. "Maybe you'd better take two weeks."

Suzy laughed. Though Terri was ten years older than she was, they were as close as sisters and could almost read each other's thoughts. Sometimes this could be provoking, but usually, as now, it was nice to have someone to confide in. Suzy described her meeting at Thrushmore in considerable detail, putting the emphasis on the Hepburn household and not on Rich Link. Terri listened pensively, interrupting occasionally with a question or two. Suzy ended the tale when she and Rich left Thrushmore the previous afternoon. If Terri was aware of the time gap between then and now, she was tactful enough not to mention it.

"Well," Terri expounded. "It looks like you're in it up to your neck, Suzy."

"What do you mean? I'm just staying over a few days to get to know Joanne better, and that's it."

"With that amount of money involved, nothing is going to be that simple," Terri warned. "But at least you have a lawyer at your side, and something tells me you're going to need one. I just hope he's good."

"He's the best, but unfortunately, he's not on my side. He has to remain neutral since he's the executor of the estate."

"But you like him, don't you?"

"Of course." Did she ever!

"Then he's good." Suzy could almost see Terri nodding her head. "What you lack in experience, Suzy, you make up for with your fantastic ability to judge character. If you think he's a winner, I'm placing my bet on him right now."

"You're crazy." Suzy laughed, delighted that Terri approved of Rich. It wasn't that she needed a second opinion, but it was nice to know that someone thought her good sense was still intact. They talked a few more minutes, then hung up. Suzy was just picking up her handbag again when she heard the thud of Rich's impatient footsteps pounding down the hallway.

"What the hell—" he started, but Suzy interrupted him.

"Ready," she said, and before Rich could utter a word, Suzy breezed past him, sped down the hall and descended the stairs. Rich was momentarily stunned, but within seconds he was right behind her, and at the bottom of the stairs he caught her by the elbow. Suzy glanced up at him. "Don't even ask," she said, and marched out of the house and got into the waiting car.

As Rich got in beside her and started the engine, he slid her an oblique glance, which Suzy chose to ignore. For a man who had dawdled away half the day in bed, how could he even think of the word "hurry"?

Rich gave her arm a joshing nudge with his elbow, then started down the drive to the main road and then west to Rhode Island. At first the scenery was more or less typical of northeastern United States, but as they headed south and neared Newport, everything changed. Whereas in Pennsylvania the colors seemed to be green and gold, here they were all blues and whites. There was also an electricity in the air that caught Suzy up in the whirl of activity that abounded everywhere. She could hardly wait to get out of the car, walk on the wharf, see the boats, feel the ocean breezes and close her eyes and let the soft winds—

"There isn't a damn space left!" Rich complained, jolting Suzy out of her reverie. "I can't believe there are this many people out at this time of year. What are they going to do in summer when the crowds really pour in?"

"Right there!" Suzy shouted, pointing to the only empty parking space in sight. When Rich angled the car into it and shut off the engine, he turned to Suzy with a wide, satisfied smile. She shook her head. "You know something? You're spoiled rotten."

"No, I'm not. I'm just anxious. I haven't been here since last summer and I just want to take a nice leisurely stroll on the docks." He clamped his large hand over her knee. "Ready? Let's go."

Getting out of the car, Suzy took a moment to stretch her arms over her head, inhale deeply, hold it, let it out slowly....

"This way." Guiding her by the arm, Rich started hustling Suzy down a narrow street. So much for a nice peaceful day at the water's edge, Suzy thought, but almost immediately, everything changed. They turned a corner.

Before her was a narrow cobblestone street leading to the wharf. It was lined on both sides with quaint shops, old-fashioned pubs, antique signboards and rustic storefronts. Everywhere men and women of all ages, dressed in navies and khakis and sneakers and captain's hats, bustled about with purposeful steps. At the end of the street, stretching far above the crowd, huge masts, packed together like matchsticks, stood tall against the skyline.

Suzy stood perfectly still, taking in everything. Finally she exhaled a long breath and, turning to Rich, gave him a lovely wide warming smile. "I like it," she said simply.

Rich absolutely beamed. "I knew you would." His grip tightened. "Come on, I'll show you the docks." He started walking, but this time he was in no hurry. He was proud of this special place. He wanted to show it off, and Suzy didn't blame him. It was not only a spectacular sight, but it vibrated with a new and exciting beat that followed them through the shopping area and right out to the wharf, where busy mariners readied their ships for a day at sea. These people were also bustling and happy and enthusiastic. They called to each other across the piers, waved to friends on other boats and bantered among themselves before they finally pushed away from the docks and headed out into the open water.

Rich seemed to know everyone there and stopped constantly to chat, introduce Suzy and explain why he hadn't been around lately. Several of his friends wanted to take them on a quick sail around Block Island, but Rich declined their offers, saying they were only staying a few hours and hadn't had lunch yet. Then, taking Suzy's hand, he walked to the end of one of the docks and sat down, pulling her beside him.

He gave her a broad smile. "Well, what do you think?" he asked.

"It's magnificent," Suzy answered excitedly as her gaze swept across the bay. "I've never seen anything like it in my life. But it's so crowded. Don't the boats ever bump into each other?"

Rich laughed. "Don't let anyone hear you say boats. They're ships, and most of them have crossed the Atlantic several times." He pointed toward a jumble of ships near the wharf. "See that cutter over there?" Suzy squinted, trying to discern just which one he was referring to. "The cutter," he whispered, leaning closer, "is the one with the man in the red overalls standing on the deck."

"Oh, I see...."

"That one has just recently been—" He stopped short as someone's hands covered his eyes. Glancing up, Suzy saw a young and beautiful blond woman standing behind him.

Laughing lightly, she lifted her hands. "Now don't try to tell me you didn't know what that was." She gave Suzy a big wink. "You're just trying to make me feel insignificant."

"Believe me, Marcia, no one could do that." Despite Rich's wry sarcasm, however, he seemed delighted to see her and moved over a little so that she could sit between Suzy and him. "I want you to meet Suzy Yoder. This is Marcia Tolbert, Suzy, the worst sailor on the East Coast."

Marcia took the gibe good-naturedly and sat down beside them. "The worst *racing* sailor on the East Coast," she corrected. "I wasn't made for speed." She held her hand out to Suzy. "It's nice to meet you, Suzy. Do you sail, too?"

"Oh, no, not at all. I'm just visiting for a few days."

"Wonderful," was Marcia's surprisingly friendly response. "This is quite a spot if you've never seen it before, and the restaurants are heavenly."

"We haven't gotten that far yet," Rich said, "but my stomach tells me it's about that time. Care to join us?"

"Thanks, but not today. I still have some phoning to do for the political dinner Dad's organizing. In fact, I think your name is on my list, Rich."

"Do me a favor and draw a line through it, will you?"

"Not on your life. You're Dad's pick of the crop, you know that." She turned to Suzy. "Don't you think Rich would make a spectacular state representative?"

"I'll go along with that."

"See? It's unanimous."

"Too bad you don't have the candidate's approval," Rich said dryly. He shook his head. "Honest to God, Marcia, I don't know what it takes to get it through your father's head that I'm not interested in running. If he has to waste his time with all these rallies, he'd better start looking for another candidate."

"Yes, I know," Marcia agreed as she wrapped her arms around her legs and pulled her knees up to her chest. "But you know Dad. This was something your father would have wanted, and he feels it's his duty and so on...." She waved the sentence away.

"That's some reason," Rich scoffed. "Never mind that I'd be sacrificing myself to the masses. I don't have the temperament for that."

"I think you do," Marcia stated firmly. "Don't you, Suzy?"

Suzy bit her lip pensively. "I don't know," she answered honestly, "but then I'm no judge. I'm not up on the qualifications for a state rep."

"Well, I am," Rich replied hastily. "Not only is the campaign a long and boring endurance contest, but if you win, you have citizens calling you twenty-four hours a day, complaining about one thing or another."

As Rich and Marcia went on arguing the evils versus the virtues of public life, Suzy listened, her gaze shifting from one to the other. Marcia wasn't pushy or insistent, but she was obviously familiar with the life of a public official and for every argument Rich presented, she countered with one of her own. It was an interesting discussion, and though Suzy didn't feel left out of it, she refrained from getting into a dispute about which she knew nothing.

After a half hour or so, Marcia stood up. "I hate to break this up, but I have work to do." Once again she turned to Suzy and extended her hand. "It was nice meeting you, Suzy. If you're still here next weekend, maybe we can all get together for lunch."

Suzy also stood up and took Marcia's hand in a firm shake. "I'd like that." She didn't add that she wouldn't be here next weekend, or any weekend.

Rich sat sprawled on the dock. "Bye, Marcia," he mumbled, not even bothering to look up.

Marcia exhaled a "Harummp" and put both hands on her hips. "You know something, Rich? You're a big lunk."

He slid her a wry glance. "Marcia, you've been telling me that ever since I was ten years old."

She turned to Suzy. "Horrid man, isn't he?"

Suzy grinned. "And what's worse, he enjoys it."

Marcia shook her hand. "Maybe he wouldn't make a very good rep after all." Giving Rich's head a gentle push with the heel of her hand, she started off, waving as she went. "See you around," she called to both of them, and strode down the dock.

Suzy dropped down beside Rich again. "I like your friend. She's very down-to-earth."

"Oh, she is that," Rich agreed. "She can also be very outspoken, but that's probably because she knows me so well."

Suzy dangled her legs over the end of the dock; then, holding her wind-tossed hair away from her face, she looked up at Rich. "How well do you know Marcia?"

"Our families have been friends for generations."

"That's not what I meant," Suzy said, trying to make this sound like an offhand remark. "Have you and Marcia ever considered getting married?"

He blinked, surprised. "Hell, no. She's more like a sister to me."

"She doesn't look like a sister," Suzy commented dryly.

Rich spread his hand over her thigh. "Look, Suzy, if there had ever been anything between Marcia and me, we'd have married a long time ago." His fingers tightened teasingly. "I assure you I'm a free man in body and spirit, but," he added, dropping his voice to a seductive murmur, "that doesn't mean I always want to be."

His words, like a flame, spread through her in a hot path, and Suzy knew the bond between them was tightening. It was a delicious sensation, one she'd never experienced before.

Rich persisted. "And now, Miss Curious, is there anything else you want to know?"

"Yes." Suzy grinned. "When are we going to eat?"

"Now!" Suddenly Rich jumped to his feet and pulled her up beside him. Then, cupping her face between his hands, he brushed a quick kiss across her lips. They were both fully aware of the curious glances around them. "See?" Rich said, cocking his brow. "If I were a public official, I couldn't do this."

"I've got news for you," she said under her breath. "You can't anyway."

"Prude."

"Right."

"Let's eat."

Wrapping their arms around each other's waists, they started down the dock. As Suzy felt Rich deliberately bump her hip with his, she wondered if Marcia could be watching them. Maybe Rich considered Marcia just a childhood chum, but Suzy was sure Marcia didn't feel the same way toward him. She'd probably been in love with him her whole life, and no wonder. He'd undoubtedly been irresistible from birth.

Suzy was aware of an insidious feeling of jealousy rising up within her, and she felt guilty. If only Marcia had been the typical cold and heartless "other woman," Suzy would feel justified in competing against her. But Marcia had bent over backward to make her feel welcome and gone out of her way to include her in the conversation, never once monopolizing Rich or flirting with him or referring to previous dates they might have had. Darn, Suzy thought. Why couldn't Marcia have been a real stinker?

Chapter Eight

Though Mrs. Slingluff had a light supper prepared for them, neither Rich nor Suzy could eat another mouthful. They'd not only had a large and late lunch, but several of Rich's friends had joined them for a round or two of beer and story swapping and, not incidentally, an introduction to Suzy. They'd greeted her warmly and seemed genuinely glad to see her, but Suzy had sensed the curiosity that lingered behind their eyes. She knew they were wondering where she'd come from and if there was anything serious between Rich and her...the same two questions Suzy kept asking herself.

"Your room or mine?" Rich asked as they climbed the stairs together that night.

Suzy hesitated, not wanting to be indiscreet while the Slingluffs were in the house.

"Mine," Rich decided, and clamping her head in the crook of his arm, he walked her down the hall and through the door and into his arms.

With an uninhibited sigh of longing, Suzy reached up and laced her fingers around his neck, loving the feel of their bodies pressed close together. As Rich's lips moved down her cheeks and throat and torrents of hot, pulsing longing swept through her, Suzy closed her eyes. She knew her body's responses were beyond the point of logic or reason, but she didn't care and willingly let the heat of passion grow and expand and finally lift her into the world of voluptuous fulfillment she had come to crave.

It wasn't until later, when she lay in the protective warmth of Rich's arm, that she allowed herself to face the question that always lingered at the edge of her mind. Did Rich love her as much as she loved him, or were they just trading pieces of each other's worlds for a little while?

Monday dawned with clear blue skies and a brisk wind that carried with it the faint smell of cherry blossoms. As Rich stopped the car in front of Thrushmore, Suzy looked up at the tall cut-stone structure before her. Thrushmore was a magnificent English Tudor home, but despite its beauty, it lacked something. Activity, perhaps? Warmth? Life? That was it, Suzy decided. It was inert, like a sick animal hiding in the woods waiting for its wounds to heal.

She started to get out of the car, but Rich held her back for a moment. "As long as you're going to be here most of the day, I'm going to go into the office and catch up on a few things. How about if I pick you up at four? Is that enough time?"

"Yes, plenty."

"But remember," he said, gently tapping her chest with his forefinger, "if for any reason at all you want to leave earlier, you call me at the office, and I'll come right out."

"I will," she promised, "but I don't think six hours with Joanne will be too much."

"No, but six hours of Wayne and Mae could get a little hairy."

"I'm planning to keep away from them."

"That might not be so easy."

"You know something? You worry too much."

Rich smiled and, turning her face to his, kissed her on the lips. "I just want to make sure you're not a frazzled heap of shot nerves by the time I get back."

"I won't be." Suzy loved his thoughtfulness. Even though Rich tried to cast his remarks off as good-natured banter, Suzy knew he was honestly concerned.

Rich walked her up the steps and waited until Frank opened the door, then he walked back to the car without kissing her good-bye. Suzy wondered if he'd seen Mae standing at the upstairs window, but she refused to glance up. To hell with Mae; Suzy was here to see Joanne.

After assuring Frank that she could find her way, Suzy went upstairs. Joanne answered her knock with a cheery "Come on in, Suzy," and getting up from her chair, she met her with outstretched hands. Suzy took the thin fingers between hers in a firm clasp, pleased that Joanne was so glad to see her.

"Well," Suzy exclaimed. "You look like you're ready to conquer the world."

"That's the way I feel, too," Joanne exclaimed. "Come on and sit down. Have you had breakfast yet?"

"Oh, yes. Mrs. Slingluff doesn't believe in starting the day on an empty stomach." As Suzy started to take the chair opposite Joanne's, she noticed a movement near the long closet that covered almost one whole wall. Mae was there, flipping through the clothes on the rack, keeping her back to Suzy. Finally she selected a pale blue robe with a white monogrammed pocket. "Would you like to wear this one today?" she asked, holding it up.

Joanne looked at it for only a moment before shaking her head. "No, Mae, I'm going to get dressed. I don't want Suzy to think I'm an invalid."

Mae's eyes became flat, opaque. Her expression was unreadable as she woodenly turned back to the closet and hung up the robe.

Joanne eyed Suzy's dark, tapered slacks, her beige V-necked top and strands of gold chains. "I think I'll wear slacks, too," she announced.

Mae's neck and back stiffened, her chin went up and with a terse sniff, she began looking through the closet again, emerging almost immediately with a pair of brown checked slacks that had been in style about ten years before, Suzy guessed. She threw them across the bed.

"Thank you," Joanne said pleasantly, and crossing to the bed, she looked at the slacks. "I think we can manage by ourselves, now, Mae. Why don't you go downstairs and have your breakfast?"

Joanne's firmness surprised Suzy, but evidently Mae was accustomed to it. With a perfunctory nod, she turned on her heel and left the room, closing the door behind her with a firm smack.

"Don't let Mae's little bursts of temper worry you. That's just her way. I'm immune to them by now," Joanne explained as she picked up the slacks. "Now all I have to do is find a sweater to go with these."

As Suzy watched, Joanne started rooting through drawer after drawer, pulling things out, stuffing some of them back, tossing others on the chair. The more she hunted, the more bewildered she became. Her hands started to shake.

"Here, let me look," Suzy offered, jumping to her feet. "It seems to me that between the two of us we should be able to come up with an outfit for you to wear."

Joanne relinquished the task gratefully. "Mae always takes care of my clothes. I don't know where anything is."

"We'll find out," Suzy assured her, and within a matter of minutes she handed Joanne a blouse and sweater before going into the chest to look for shoes. On the inside of the closet door was a full-length mirror, which reflected the room behind her. Suzy realized what a lovely room it was, with a flavor of distinction and a sense of refinement that was missing from what she'd seen of the rest of the house. If this was an indication of Joanne's taste, it had been confined to this one room. Strange, Suzy thought, how one could have so much and yet have so little.

With Suzy's help, Joanne got her brown, gray-streaked hair up in a soft bun and even applied a little makeup before turning to Suzy for approval. "You look great," Suzy assured her.

Joanne beamed. "I feel great, too. I haven't felt so up-to-date in years." Putting her hands on Suzy's shoulders, she looked into her gray-green eyes. "Thank you, Suzy."

Suzy smiled. There was a warmth about Joanne that came from deep inside, as if it had been hidden away. "You're very welcome, you know that."

"Of course I do." Joanne dropped her hands to her side, but the smile still lingered. "Now what do you say we go for a walk?"

"Sounds great. You can show me the grounds."

"There really isn't much," Joanne said as she took Suzy's arm for support. "Just a tool shed and a fish pond and some hard stone benches...." Her voice trailed off as they descended the stairs to the lower hall, where Frank met them. He was obviously as surprised as he was pleased and hurried to bring Joanne's jacket from the hall closet. She slipped into it, then with a brief "Thank you" she took Suzy's arm again and they stepped out into the brisk but sunny day.

Suzy inhaled deeply. "Ah, I smell freshly tilled soil. Is someone planting a garden?"

"Oh, yes, we have several of them. I guess the gardener is putting in the annuals." She looked up at Suzy. "I understand you know a little about planting yourself."

"Yes, I was raised on a farm, but Abby leased most of the land out. Neither one of us was into tilling the soil."

"How did she make her living, then?"

"Her main source of income was from her flea market sales. That's where she found me, you know, in a flea market."

"Yes, I know." She directed their steps down a cement walkway. "Paul Hilton stopped by yesterday and filled me in on a lot of your background. Abby must have been a very special person to have taken a strange child into her home like that. It isn't easy to raise a child to be a responsible adult, even when it's your own."

"She was a wonderful person. I realize it now more than I did when I was younger." Shoving her hands in her pockets, Suzy thought back. "I can remember going to the flea market with her every Monday. She had a little chair for me, and I'd sit behind her booth and pretend I was the owner of the store."

"But didn't people wonder where you came from?"

Suzy shook her head. "They had no reason not to believe Abby. If she said I was a distant relative, then I was. No problem."

Joanne shook her head. It was hard for her to believe this could happen...it was hard for anyone to believe it, but those were the facts and Suzy couldn't change them.

"Do you think Abby ever felt guilty?" Joanne pressed.

"No," Suzy said, shaking her head. "I think Abby convinced herself that someone had left me with her because they couldn't keep me for one reason or another and thought she would give me a good home."

"But didn't you have trouble getting into school without a birth certificate?"

"None at all. The Amish school I went to didn't require them, and when I transferred to high school, all they asked for were my grades."

"Oh, I see," was the quiet response.

They'd approached a concrete bench and Joanne sat down, motioning Suzy to sit beside her. Against the massive stone seat, Joanne looked very fragile. She was smaller than Suzy and much thinner, but her features were perfectly sculpted and her hair, like Suzy's, curled slightly in the damp air. She wasn't as distressed as she'd been the last time Suzy saw her, but she was restless, as though she were struggling with a difficult decision, something Suzy well understood. Suzy was doing the same thing.

"Don't you remember anything at all prior to the day Abby found you?"

Again Suzy shook her head. "Nothing."

"Paul says you could have had amnesia brought on by the shock of the kidnapping and the sudden environmental displacement. It's very common, especially in small children. They're so impressionable. Besides, if children have no one to remind them of various incidents in their lives, they are more apt to forget them."

"I suppose so," Suzy murmured.

"Tell me," Joanne urged. "What was it like growing up on a farm?"

Suzy thought for a moment. "Well, I guess I could sum it up as a lot of freedom and a lot of hard work. The winters were bad because we were constantly worrying about the livestock. Abby didn't have much, just a few pigs, a dozen sheep and chickens, but they all had to be fed and watered and bedded and cared for even in subzero weather. Every morning Abby would go out to the barn, and I'd go with her. When I was very small, she used to put my boots on, then wrap my feet with strips of woolen cloth." Suzy laughed. "I looked like a mummy and walked like a robot, but at least I never had frostbite."

"It sounds as if Abby was a very good mother."

Suzy nodded. "She was the greatest. We didn't have much. In fact, as I look back, we didn't have anything, but never once did I feel deprived. As I got older and went to school, I couldn't go to the market with Abby on Mondays, but she made it a special day just the same. Every week she brought me home a soft drink, and I mean *a* soft drink," Suzy repeated. "A six-pack on our budget was unheard-of. Each week it would be a different brand, a Coke or a Seven-Up or a Pepsi or whatever, and I can remember sitting in school all day Monday wondering what I was going to get, but never did I have to worry if I was going to get it. Abby was very dependable."

"She sounds like the Rock of Gibraltar," Joanne agreed. "But what did you do for entertainment?"

That was easy to answer. "Nothing. We didn't have TV or radio, so when we finished our chores, we went to bed. As soon as I learned to read, though, I spent many an hour buried in a book."

Joanne's face lit up. "I like to read, too. So did my mother. I think it must run in the family."

"I guess that's possible," Suzy murmured, realizing that Joanne was unconsciously trying to fit her into the vacancy left by Christina. She didn't want to hurt Joanne by telling her there was no chance of that at all, because that wouldn't be true. On the other hand, she couldn't encourage her, because this whole episode could end up in another broken dream for Joanne.

They sat in silence for several long minutes. Then Joanne reached over and gave Suzy's hand an affectionate pat. "I'm sorry I didn't get to see you yesterday, but maybe it was just as well. I made a big decision." Leaning back slightly, she crossed her legs. "When I woke up, I had a slight headache, nothing serious, and a few hours later Mae told me she'd called you and told you not to come. Not long after that, Paul stopped by and said he'd told you to wait until today to come. So instead of seeing you, I sat and listened to Paul tell me about you." She looked at Suzy. "Does that make sense to you? Of course not," she answered herself. "Why did I have to hear everything secondhand? Because I was letting these people live my live for me, that's why. And then I remembered what you'd said: 'Joanne can't spend the rest of her life in her room.' So I decided that starting today, I was going to get out of my room and stay out."

"All day?" was Suzy's surprised response.

"All day," was the firm answer. "I'm not so ill that I have to sit in a lounge chair with my feet up. In fact, I've decided that now that David's gone, I'm going to handle all the household matters. There's no reason why Wayne has to do that."

"Oh, Wayne," Suzy murmured, suddenly remembering the unpleasantness of the situation.

Joanne smiled. "Don't let Wayne get under your skin. He's just a very dull person and his wife is even duller, but he's a good accountant and David trusted him completely."

Maybe that was because David was able to check up on him, Suzy thought, but what chance did Joanne have against a clever businessman? She held her tongue, however. The Hepburn family arrangements were none of her business.

Joanne looked around her. It was still windy, but it was a beautiful spring day. Inhaling deeply, she turned to Suzy with an expectant look. "Well, Suzy, we have the whole day together. What would you like to do? Look at the rest of the gardens?"

Suzy stood up. "That sounds fine to me, but don't overdo on my account."

"Don't worry about that," Joanne said. "I think a little 'overdo' is just what I need." She took Suzy's arm again and they started walking down the path. "I'm afraid there isn't much for a young girl like you to do here."

Suzy knew that Joanne was worrying about keeping her entertained, but this was an additional stress that Joanne didn't need. "Maybe I can think of something," Suzy suggested lamely.

Joanne exhaled an elaborate sigh. "I hope so. Even I'm bored with Thrushmore today."

Suzy's steps slowed, then stopped as an idea began to take form. She turned to Joanne, who stood beside her, waiting expectantly. "Do you really mean that?" Suzy asked.

"Yes, indeed I do."

As Suzy and Joanne sped down the highway in David's Mercedes, they exchanged a look of shared delight. Behind them were a stunned Frank and a furious Wayne, who had pulled into the drive just as they were leaving. Suzy didn't even pause to explain and Joanne didn't ask her to. The two women merely waved a cheery good-bye to them all and turned into the road leading to Bark Cove.

Joanne looked around her like a child in dreamland. "Heavens, it's been years since I've been out for a drive. David always hated drives in the country."

"It sounds as if he was a very stern person."

"In a way, he was," Joanne agreed, "but I could understand this. David was very efficient and exacting, with guidelines for everything in life. In fact, that was one of the things I admired in him the most when I first met him. I was a little like that myself at the time. But after the kidnapping, it was me, not David, who changed." With a long sigh she glanced out of her window. "When I came back from the hospital and found that everything in Christina's room had been thrown out and hauled away, my entire world collapsed. There wasn't a single thing left that I could hold and cherish. The shock was almost as bad as the kidnapping itself."

"Rich told me David had been acting under your psychiatrist's orders. Some psychiatrist!" Suzy scoffed.

Joanne nodded. "He did more harm than good. Even David was sorry later that he hadn't kept something of Christina's for himself. He knew he'd made a terrible mistake and tried all of his life to make it up to me. He shielded me from financial problems, he kept Mae on, he ran errands for me, he bought my clothes, he kept me stocked with records and books and always there were fresh flowers in my room...." Her voice trailed off on a sigh.

"Didn't he realize he was severing you from the rest of the world?"

"No, he never did, and I never let either David or Paul Hilton think that. Actually, I didn't realize it myself until several years later, and by that time my life had fallen into a pattern that was very unexciting, but very hard to break, too." She opened her hands and shrugged her shoulders. "My attitude was, why bother? It was easy for me just to drift along, and easy for David, too. He had his life's project—taking care of me—and thought that by doing this, it would somehow atone for the hurt he'd caused me."

"Oh, God," Suzy murmured. "What a sad existence."

"Oh, it wasn't that bad." Joanne turned to her with a small smile. "Don't believe everything you hear, Suzy."

"I won't." The only gossip she'd heard had been started by Wayne, who insisted that Joanne wasn't rational enough to make a decision. Why would he start a rumor like that? Suzy wondered. Joanne was as mentally sound as anyone she'd ever met.

Smoothly Suzy slid the Mercedes into a parking space just off Bark Cove's main street. Joanne watched as she took the keys out of the ignition. "Well, I'll say one thing, you sure are a good driver."

"I should be. I've driven everything from kiddie cars to tractors in my day." *Of course,* she thought, *nothing as elegant as a Mercedes....* "Now what do you say we take in the sights of Bark Cove, all three blocks of it?"

"Sounds good to me."

Joanne seemed genuinely excited about her rare venture into the world of consumerism, but when they started to walk down the street, Suzy noted that she was leaning heavily on her arm as though fatigued already. Looking around her, Suzy spied the little ice-cream shop she and Rich had visited several days ago. She glanced at her watch. "Twelve-thirty!" she exclaimed, as though surprised as the lateness of the hour. "Time for lunch."

Joanne looked dismayed. "I keep forgetting the appetites of you young people, but now that you've mentioned it, I could go for a little something myself, perhaps a cup of tea...."

"How about a hot-fudge sundae with pecans?"

Joanne didn't even pause. "Wonderful!"

Evidently the shop's supply of hot fudge had been replenished, and they were served two tall sundaes smothered with nuts. "I'm going to have to tell Rich about this," Suzy commented as she dipped her spoon into the ice cream. "We were here on Saturday, and they were all out of fudge. I thought he was going to have a heart attack."

"Men take their food very seriously. They're worse than children sometimes." Joanne scooped up a pecan and popped it into her mouth, then slid her eyes to Suzy. "What do you think of Rich Link? I've known him, or rather of him, since he was a child, but I seldom saw him. He seems to be a very pleasant young man."

"Oh, he is," Suzy agreed, trying to keep her voice casual.

"David said he was every bit as good a lawyer as his dad."

"I don't doubt that," Suzy said warmly. "He has all the attributes of a successful attorney. He speaks well, he's mannerly, handsome and intelligent. He's just, too," she added almost as an afterthought.

Joanne's eyebrows lifted slightly. "You think he's also impartial? Unprejudiced?" she asked meaningfully.

"Oh, of course," she answered quickly.

"Hmmm," Joanne mused. "I suppose that's very exemplary, but when you like someone it's hard to accept him if he's not on your side one hundred percent, don't you think?"

Suzy was a little surprised at Joanne's intuitiveness, but her gentle prying didn't offend her. In fact, it was good to have someone to confide in. "He's been wonderful to me, and frankly, I think he's terrific," Suzy confessed. "From the very moment we met, he accepted me for what I claimed to be. He wasn't suspicious, he didn't cross-examine me, he never even hinted that I could be a fraud. And I appreciate that. I'd hate to think he'd ever question my integrity."

"Oh, he'd never do that," Joanne assured her. "You're as open and honest as anyone I've ever met, and I'm sure Rich feels the same way. Trust between two people is very important, and he'd never risk losing that, any more than you would."

"I guess so." Suzy sighed and pushed the empty sundae dish away from her. "Unfortunately, our relationship doesn't seem to have any place to go, anyway. We're from two different worlds."

"That doesn't make any difference," Joanne assured her. "Cupid's arrows have been known to spin very strange paths."

Suzy laughed. She liked Joanne. She was easy to talk to, to confide in, and if she'd expressed her feelings more than she'd intended to, she knew Joanne would never repeat their conversation. Instinctively, Suzy knew an allegiance had formed between them.

Once outside again, Joanne seemed to feel a little stronger, and though she still held Suzy's arm, she wanted to pause in front of every shop window. She stayed longest at a display of women's casual clothes.

"Do you want to go in?" Suzy asked.

"Oh, I don't need anything...."

Suzy tugged on her arm. "Come on, let's go in and see what they've got anyway. I could use a pair of shorts and some sneakers if they have them."

"I'll just sit in that chair by the window and wait for you."

"Look and see what they have," Suzy urged. "Maybe you could find a pair of slacks or something."

Joanne slid Suzy a sly look, then glanced down at her brown checked slacks. "Are you trying to tell me something?"

Suzy threw her hands up. "What can I say?" She grinned mischievously.

Joanne, good sport that she was, smiled, too. "Where do they keep their slacks?"

"Right over here, ma'am," came the voice of a saleslady. "We've just gotten in our summer whites."

Fifteen minutes later, Suzy rubbed her chin thoughtfully as she tried to determine if the cotton twills Joanne had tried on were a good fit. "I think they're a little too baggy in the butt," she finally decided. "Here, try these Calvin Kleins."

"I can't believe I'm doing this," Joanne kept murmuring under her breath, amazed at her own daring yet obviously thrilled to be out, to be shopping, to be a part of the world again. Suzy felt so happy for her that she actually felt tears stinging her eyes.

When they emerged from the shop an hour later, they were carrying several packages. Pausing, Joanne looked up and down the short shopping section of Bark Cove.

Suzy read her thoughts. "I'm afraid this is the only women's store in town, but if you feel up to it tomorrow or the next day, we can tackle something a little larger. I'm sure Rich can tell me where the nearest mall is."

"It's a date," Joanne said, and taking Suzy's arm, she started for the car. Normally, Suzy would have driven to the nearest shopping center right then and there, but she realized that Joanne, despite her enthusiasm, was beginning to tire. Her footsteps were definitely slower than when they'd started out.

"What do you say we call it a day?" Suzy suggested. "You don't want to overdo and land in bed for the rest of the week."

"Oh, don't worry about that, but I admit I'm a little tired." She turned to Suzy with a wide, sunny smile. "But I've enjoyed every minute of it, Suzy. You're just the medicine I need."

"You just need to get away from Thrushmore," Suzy assured her, but she was flattered that Joanne had enjoyed their short outing so much. She'd enjoyed it, too, but as they got into the car, she crossed her fingers that Joanne hadn't gotten too tired. A confrontation with a sour-faced Mae wasn't Suzy's idea of how to end a nice day.

They took a different road back to Thrushmore, and about halfway there, Joanne spied a roadside stand. "Oh, Suzy, could you pull over?" she asked excitedly. "I just love little stands like this, don't you?"

As Suzy dutifully pulled off the road, she smiled. She was accustomed to seeing stands like this all around Windland, but never had she seen a Mercedes like this parked in front of one of them. It made her realize that she was on a seesaw, and this worried her. She couldn't jump off anytime she wanted to without hurting the person on the other end.

Joanned passed by the fruit and produce that was offered and headed straight for the rows and rows of potted plants and flowers. She loved everything she saw, and within an hour the entire backseat of the car was loaded with pots of daisies, begonias, geraniums and mums, all commonplace plants but all bursting with color and freshness and the reminder of springtime. Though Suzy realized that Joanne was trying to bring some of the outdoors inside, she couldn't imagine Thrushmore bedecked with flowers. Nonblooming houseplants, maybe, but never flowers.

As soon as the car pulled into the drive, Mae burst out of the front door. She eyed the flowers with total distaste, but to Suzy's surprise, she didn't voice her feelings. Her main concern was Joanne, who, though still bubbling with excitement, was definitely showing signs of fatigue.

"You go inside and tell us where you want these," Suzy told her, "and Frank and I will do the toting."

Joanne didn't argue, but she didn't give in to Mae's fawning, either, and helped place the plants all over the first floor. By the time all of the flowers were inside, Thrushmore had taken on a new look. Once, Wayne came out of the office to see what changes had been made, but when he saw Suzy he gave a disgusted grunt and went back to the study, closing the door behind him.

It was a small thing, but it bothered Suzy. She'd never known disrespect before, let alone open hostility, and wasn't sure how to deal with it. Unconsciously, she glanced at her watch. It was only three, another hour before Rich would be here. She realized suddenly how much she missed him. They'd been so inseparable for the past few days that he'd almost become a part of her. She refused to give in to her impulses, however, and call him up and tell him to come early. He'd spoiled her enough already. Besides, they'd have the whole rest of the day together and all night long....

Joanne's voice interrupted her thoughts. "What do you say to coffee and sandwiches in the sunroom?"

Suzy grinned at Joanne's growing independence. "I'd love it, but we'll have to make it fast. You look like you're ready to fall asleep standing up. What do you say we give it thirty minutes?"

"That sounds fine to me."

Within the allotted time Suzy and Joanne had finished off almost everything on the tea tray and were still chatting when Suzy saw a movement in the hall. It was Mae, pacing up and down. Odd that she hadn't come into the room, Suzy thought, but she was glad that she hadn't. Her possessiveness made Suzy nervous. Still, Suzy glanced meaningfully at her watch. "Time's up," she declared; then, with a lift of her eyebrows, "Will I see you tomorrow?"

"I'd love it, Suzy, you know that."

"Good. It's a date, then."

Mae, who'd obviously been listening at the door, strode into the room to claim her patient. "Ready?"

"Yes, Mae." With a tired sigh, Joanne stood up. She glanced at Suzy. "Until tomorrow...."

"I'll be here early," Suzy promised.

As they moved off down the hall, Suzy exhaled a long sigh; then, picking up an outdated magazine, she sat down again. As she started thumbing through it she saw another movement in the hall. Glancing up, she was surprised to see it was Wayne. What did he want? she wondered.

"Is Rich picking you up?"

"Yes, at four o'clock."

"You're welcome to take the Mercedes home if you want to."

Suzy blinked. This? From Wayne? Had she heard right? And then she remembered that the Mercedes had been David's car and wasn't under Wayne's jurisdiction anyway. But she managed a polite smile. Why stir up trouble? "Thank you, Wayne. Perhaps some other time."

Then, standing in front of her chair, he typically got right to the point. "Did you know Rich was running for state representative next term?"

"I've heard a lot of rumors, but Rich said he wasn't interested."

"Maybe that's his tune today, but a month ago it was different. Of course, he had Commodore Tolbert in his camp then, but now..." The sentence trailed off portentously.

"Now what?" Suzy demanded. She hated these innuendos.

Wayne leaned forward. "Yesterday Rich went to Newport with you on his arm. Needless to say, Tolbert would have preferred to have seen his daughter there instead."

"That's understandable, but Tolbert will have to learn the facts of life."

"You're missing my point." His voice was cold and steady. "Rich can't win an election unless he has a lot of money behind him. Therefore it stands to reason that if he's willing to forgo the Tolbert support, he must have other plans. Perhaps the Hepburn fortune?"

Suzy looked up sharply. The urge to jump to her feet and shake Wayne's head loose was almost overpowering, but she knew he was just trying to stir up trouble, and she wasn't going to allow him to do that. Still, one quick shove was very tempting.

She settled for a stony glare. "For your information, Mr. Hepburn, Rich Link does not have to resort to subversive tactics to get where he wants to go. If and when he chooses to run for public office, he'll manage quite well on his own."

"Perhaps," Wayne smirked, "but it would be much easier to marry into wealth. I'm sure you realize that." His eyes narrowed. "Just as I realize that you and Rich are working together to bilk the Hepburn estate."

For a moment Suzy was so stunned she couldn't speak. Then suddenly it all came together. "What did you say?" she demanded, jumping to her feet.

"You heard me," Wayne sneered, his words loud and menacing. "Don't you think I know why Link contacted you after David's death? Because he wants to be fair and square? Who are we kidding? You two had this whole thing planned before you ever got here. With Rich's knowledge of the Hepburn family, it'd be easy enough to pull off."

Suzy was so furious that she was shaking. Never had it occurred to her that Wayne, or anyone else, would accuse her of fraud. But then, she wasn't accustomed to the hazards one encountered when large sums of money were involved. Also, she'd never known anyone as miserable as Wayne.

"If there's any double-dealing around here," she retorted icily, "you're the one who's doing it."

"Me!" Wayne tapped his chest with his finger. "I'm the victim!"

"I don't know how you could call yourself a victim when you're going to inherit a minimum of fifty million dollars," Suzy snapped, her eyes blazing. "In my opinion you're nothing but a mercenary old fool who—"

"Hold it!" Rich's voice came from the doorway. "What's going on?" he asked as he strode into the room and glanced from Wayne to Suzy.

"I'll tell you what's going on," Wayne snarled. "If you two think you're going to pull one over on me, you're crazy. I'm on to you now, and by God, nothing's going to stop me."

"What are you talking about?" Rich demanded.

"You and her, that's who." Backing up a step, Wayne tugged down the sleeves of his shirt and straightened importantly. "I hope you don't think that

I'm so naive that I don't know you two are trying to milk the Hepburn estate. Well, let me tell you something." His voice was shaking with anger. "I'm getting a lawyer and a detective, and I intend to expose you for the frauds you are."

"Frauds!" Suzy repeated in a loud, astonished voice. Instinctively, her hand rose as if she were going to strike him, but Rich reached out and grabbed her wrist in a viselike grip, holding it to his side.

He was the epitome of self-control, so much so that Suzy even found him irritating. "If you feel that way about it, Wayne, you have every right to take whatever steps are necessary to prove your allegations. Now," he said, glancing down at the table, "if you two have finished with your tea, we'll be going. Ready, Suzy?"

"Ready!" she fumed. "I'm not leaving here until—"

"Yes, you are." Clasping her shoulder in a grip of steel, he nodded a polite good day to Wayne and together he and Suzy marched out of the room.

Chapter Nine

As Rich helped Suzy into the car, he gave her arm an extra squeeze. "And here I always thought that adage about redheads having a quick temper was just an old wives' tale, but I can see—"

"He's the most obnoxious man I've ever known," Suzy cut in, still furious. "Accusing me of fraud!"

"I heard most of the discussion. Frank opened the door just as you got into the wild part. And I have to admit that, had my adrenaline been up as yours was, I would have probably taken a swing at him."

"I wish you had."

"I'm glad I didn't. He's looking for trouble."

"Well, he's not going to find it."

"He doesn't intend to find it, Suzy. He intends to invent it."

Suzy glanced up quickly. "What do you mean?"

"I don't think we've been taking Wayne seriously enough, but we'd better start. To begin with, he's going to try to prove Joanne is incompetent."

"Oh, baloney," Suzy scoffed as the car rolled out of the drive. "She's saner than I am."

"If you say so, I believe it, but I've only met Joanne about a dozen times in my life."

"She's very pleasant, intelligent and perceptive, and I think she's great."

Suzy's voice was firm and decided and left no room for argument. Rich glanced at her. Though she was sitting quietly and appeared to be idly watching the scenery, he knew that she was struggling to get her emotions under control. He admired her for that. Even though she'd lost her temper with Wayne, she was still a person with marvelous self-control and firm convictions and staunch loyalty. Odd, he mused, how very much like David Hepburn she was.

When they returned to Link Hall, they decided to change into walking clothes and go for a hike in the woods, something they both needed.

"Darn," Suzy grumbled, "I left my new sneakers over at Thrushmore."

"You went shopping?" Rich asked, surprised.

Suzy laughed. "We certainly did. You should have seen Wayne's face when he drove off in the Mercedes."

"Oh, my God." Rich clapped a hand to the side of his face. "No wonder he was so hysterical."

"Serves him right," Suzy muttered, but her anger had diffused some time before and she had even reached the point where she was able to laugh at herself. Taking Rich's hand, she let him lead her through an abandoned cherry orchard toward the hills behind the house. As Suzy chatted happily about her day with Joanne, Rich realized what delightful company she was, so different from any woman he'd ever known. The thought of her leaving soon was unbearable.

When Rich woke up in the middle of the night, it was just past three o'clock. Suzy's body was curved into his, her arm stretched across his chest, her head pressed against his shoulder. Even in sleep her young slender body had a raw sensuality about it that made him ache to wrap her in his arms again and feel the intoxicating heat of her flesh tremble under his touch, awakening flames that leaped from her body to his until the heat of passion burned in both of them. Suzy was an ecstatic lover, returning the pleasure she received with deep sensual strokes that not only encouraged but dared him to travel higher and farther in the journey of completeness.

As Rich smoothed a strand of hair away from Suzy's face, he realized that he felt very protective toward her. She was here at his invitation; she'd met Joanne at his insistence; she'd exposed herself to Wayne's humiliating accusations because he, Rich Link, had instigated it. Though he didn't want to alarm her, he knew that this was just the beginning. Wayne's threats were not the meaningless rantings of an angry man. He was too avaricious for that. Rich knew that Wayne fully intended to hire a detective to investigate Suzy's background, and in a little town the size of Windland, Pennsylvania, that would probably cause quite a stir. Did she need that? he asked himself.

Rich was up before Suzy and by eight o'clock he'd already contacted an old college friend of his, Matt Drechsler, who now operated his own private detective agency in downtown Boston. They made arrangements to meet at Matt's office at eleven o'clock. Though Rich wanted to fill him in briefly on the purpose of the visit, he didn't want to chance Suzy's overhearing him. There was no point in alarming her until he'd gotten some facts straight.

On the ride over to Thrushmore, Suzy was her usual ebullient self and full of plans for her and Joanne. "I think we'll spend the day going through her closet and throwing out old clothes," she decided.

"Isn't that a little premature? I mean, the poor woman has to have something to wear to the store to buy some clothes, doesn't she?"

Suzy eyed him askance. "You know something, Richard? You don't know anything about women."

"I've never professed to, but it seems logical to me that if a woman is going to spend all of her time shopping, she'll have to have a shopping wardrobe."

"We're not spending all of our time shopping." She grinned up at him. "We like to eat, too."

"Well," he said, nudging her with his elbow, "at least your interests are diversified. Frankly, though, I'm a little surprised that Joanne is so well rounded. I'd always thought of her as a recluse."

"She might have been, but I think David's death has brought her out of her cocoon. She's really a fun person to be with once you get to know her."

Rich glanced at Suzy, his face serious. "Do you like her? I mean a lot?"

Slowly Suzy nodded her head. "Yes, I do," she murmured, "and to be perfectly honest with you, I have the feeling that there's an invisible thread that wants to tie us together, but it's so frustrating." She sighed. "I just can't put my finger on it. It's an elusive thing...."

Rich gave her arm a reassuring pat. "Don't push it, Suzy. These things take time. Just be grateful that you and Joanne get along so well."

"And we do," Suzy assured him, "but that doesn't necessarily mean we're related. Many mothers and daughters get along very well, but others can't stand each other."

Rich stopped the Trans Am in front of Thrushmore again. Reaching over, he held Suzy's head between his hands and gave her a resounding kiss. Then, reluctantly, he released her. "You and Joanne just enjoy each other and don't worry about trying to prove something. Even if you're not related, I think you need each other."

"What do you mean?"

"I think you miss Abby very much, Suzy, and it's possible that you're trying to put Joanne into the role."

Suzy frowned, perplexed. "Are you saying that I want to be Christina Hepburn because I want a mother like Joanne?"

Rich shook his head firmly. "No. Just the opposite. You want to be Suzy Yoder with a mother like Abby."

Suzy looked at him for a long moment, then quirked a mischievous eyebrow upward. "Rich, be forever grateful that you pursued law as a career and not psy-

chology. You'd never have made it." With a final reassuring pat on his cheek, she got out of the car. "See
you at four?" she asked.

Rich grinned broadly. "You betcha."

When Rich walked into the offices of Drechsler Investigative Enterprises, Inc., his friend Matt was
waiting for him. Though they rarely did business together, they often saw each other in the courthouse
and managed to meet for lunch about twice a year.

Matt was a big beefy man with a seemingly nonchalant air about him, but Rich knew that behind his
buffoon pose was the keen, calculating mind of a man
who knew his business well. Sitting opposite Matt in
a black leather chair, Rich eased back into its depths
and proceeded to tell all he knew about Suzy Yoder.
Matt taped the conversation, but he also took notes,
interrupting frequently with questions to make sure his
facts were straight. He was very thorough, and very
attentive. Nothing escaped him.

"Do you know the name of the detective Wayne's
going to hire?"

"No, no idea."

Tossing his pen on the desk, Matt leaned back in his
chair. "You know, a clever interrogator is like a clever
lawyer. He can ask questions in such a way as to plant
the answer in the mind of the testifier."

"I realize that."

"It's illegal, but it's done every day. Now, if someone, anyone, were to go to this little town of Windland and ask some of the old-timers if they remember
how Abby Yoder got this child she raised, they'd
probably say they weren't sure. Abby said she was a

distant relative and they never questioned her, something like that. But if a clever detective went there, he'd ask, 'Do you remember Abby Yoder's Uncle Amos?' Of course they'd all say no, and then the interrogator would add, 'He's the one who had the little redheaded girl that Abby raised.' 'Ahh, yes,' they'd say. 'Suzy. Lovely child. Her uncle's daughter, did you say? I've always wondered.'"

Matt leaned forward on his elbows and wagged a finger at Rich. "And let me tell you something. Once that idea gets planted in their minds, nothing will change it. And there goes Suzy's story about being found in a flea market. Everyone in town is going to swear she was the daughter of Uncle Amos even if they never heard of the man until last week. It's human nature for people to want to tie up the loose ends, and in your case, it can be devastating."

Rich nodded, concurring. "Don't I know it. So what do we do?"

"We have several options. Number one—we can get there first and lay our own groundwork; and two—we can check the statistics Suzy gave you, her age, schools attended, jobs held and so on. While we're at it"—his eyes narrowed—"we'll also make sure that Abby Yoder really did exist."

Rich's head snapped up. "What are you talking about?"

Matt slapped his hand on the desk. "Look, pal, we've been friends for years, okay? And I want to do a job for you, but you've gotta face facts, man. How do we know this Suzy is everything she says she is? She could be the cleverest con artist in the country. She could even be working for a syndicate for all we know."

"No, never...."

"Yes, often...."

"You don't know Suzy."

"But I know my job, and I'd hate to tell you how many guys have fallen for a good-looking babe who claimed she was just a small town girl, only to find out later that she's the superstar of a well-planned con game. It happens all the time."

"But this is different," Rich insisted. "Suzy doesn't have a dishonest bone in her body."

Matt leaned forward on his elbows. "Hey, pal, didn't you say that once before when you and Morgan Arnold got involved with a woman named, ah..." He snapped his fingers, trying to remember.

"Ratonia Zinsky," Rich furnished wryly. Would he ever live that one down?

"Yeah, that's the one. She came on as Miss Rural Poland or something, and you walked right into a bear trap. Now, do me a favor, will ya, pal? Let me handle this. I promise to be discreet, but"—he wagged his finger again—"you can bet I'll be thorough."

"You sound good, Matt, but tell me, what are you going to look for?"

"First of all, we'll establish Suzy's growing-up years. Then we'll move on to her friends and business associates and see if we can find a tie-in, someone who could be a coconspirator." He shrugged. "Hell, for all we know, it could be Joanne."

"Joanne! Oh, God, this is going too far."

"Why not?" Matt persisted. "You say she's not as mentally irresponsible as everyone has been led to believe. Her husband cut her out of his will."

"But she has a fortune of her own."

"Do you know this? Are you her lawyer? Her accountant?"

"Well, no. I just represent David."

"For all we know, she could be dead broke, right? Who's to say she and this woman Mae didn't hire someone to play the part of the daughter Christina?"

"But Mae doesn't agree—"

"Of course not," Matt interrupted. "Not now, that is. But she will. Then the three of them will get the fifty million, split it up and live on easy street the rest of their lives."

"Oh, cripes, Matt, you're on another planet. This just isn't possible." Shaking his head, Rich ran his fingers through his hair, a habit he had when he was in doubt. After an hour with Matt, all sorts of things were swirling around in his head. There was the slim, very remote possibility that Matt could be right. Though Rich knew better than to take everything he said at face value, it was hard for him to forget his experience with Ratonia. He'd really fallen into the trap then, one hundred percent, but that was ten years ago. He was fresh out of school and lacked the maturity he had now.

Still...

He stood up and started pacing the room. "God, Matt, I don't know what to say."

Matt swiveled his chair around to face him. "I could be wrong as hell, you know," he admitted, easing off a little, "but why don't I check out the statistics anyway? I'll keep it low key, no one will know. She hasn't been in contact with anyone from Windland since she's been here, has she?''

"No, I don't think so."

"Well, that's encouraging."

Suddenly, Rich snapped his fingers. "Oh, now, wait a minute," he said. "She talked to her boss, a woman named...oh, God, I don't remember."

Leaning back in his chair, Matt folded his hands over his stomach. All he said was, "Oh?"

The realization that a clever con game might be in progress hit Rich like a tidal wave. It wasn't that he didn't believe these things existed, they happened every day, but to think Suzy could possibly be involved made him sick with despair. Was there any truth in Matt's suspicions? Was it possible that his feelings toward Suzy had blinded him to reality? Was a woman he loved going to make a fool of him again?

He turned to Matt. "Okay, I've got the message, but let me think about it for a while. I have to get my thoughts in order."

"Take all the time you want. You know how to get hold of me." They parted with a handshake, and Rich drove back to his office, left orders with his secretary not to be disturbed and sat down with his head in his hands and tried to get his facts together. He realized now how important Suzy was to him, how much he loved her. Never had a woman pleased him so much, given so willingly. Nevertheless, the thin thread of uncertainty persisted. It was this, plus a natural curiosity about Suzy's background, that brought him to a decision.

He called Matt. "You go ahead and check out the schools, jobs and so on, but don't send a man to Windland to interview Suzy's friends. I'm going to do that myself."

"You're going to Windland?" came the surprised response.

"Yes, I am. I decided that if anyone is going to do some questioning and plant some answers in people's minds, it's going to be me."

"Well, God knows you're qualified," Matt assured him. "Good luck. Keep it low key and call me when you get back."

Rich left the office early. He couldn't concentrate on the brief before him or put any enthusiasm into the phone calls he returned. Though he'd made the decision to go to Windland, he hadn't brought himself to actually making a plane reservation to Harrisburg. Not yet.

When he arrived at Thrushmore, he noticed that Wayne's car wasn't parked in its usual place. Odd, he thought. Wayne never deviated from his set daily routine. Was he contacting his lawyers? he wondered. A detective agency? Frowning, Rich got out of the car and had just reached the steps when the door was flung open and an exhilarated Suzy flew down the stairs and into his arms.

"Oh, is it good to see you," she exclaimed excitedly. Locking her arms around his body, she squeezed hard; then, tipping her head back, she looked up into his face. Her eyes sparkled with flecks of green, and her smile, beautiful and bright, was unlike anything he'd ever seen before. It reached clear to his heart.

Suddenly, all his doubts disintegrated. Folding his arms around her, he held her close for a moment. "I missed you," he murmured huskily.

She laughed, lightly, easily. "I'm glad. I'd hate to think you'd forgotten me. Come on," she said, pulling him by the hand. "Joanne and I are in the sun-room. I want you to see how beautifully she's doing."

Before he could protest, Rich found himself being tugged up the stairs and into the house by an eager Suzy. Joanne sat on a couch in the sunroom surrounded by fashion magazines. She had a pair of scissors in her hand and beside her was a pile of clippings.

When she saw Rich, she smiled up at him. "I'd get up, but I don't think I can. Come on, sit down." She gestured toward a gaily colored chair. "Suzy and I have spent the whole day planning my new wardrobe," she began, and went on to explain how they had gone through her closets and drawers and weeded out almost everything. Suzy added comments here and there and began gathering together a few clippings of her own.

As the two women chatted companionably, Rich injected a few appropriate remarks occasionally, but he was barely aware of the essence of the conversation. He was struck first by Joanne's apparent normalcy. Though he'd never known her well, he'd always thought of her as a shy shadow of a woman who rarely spoke. But as he watched now, he could see what his father meant when he'd said Joanne had been one of the most beautiful women he'd ever met. She was still attractive, and though she wasn't as ebullient as Suzy, she certainly had a degree of enthusiasm.

The room itself was an unexpected surprise, too, he noted. He'd been to Thrushmore many times to see David, but always their business was confined to the office. Though Rich knew the sunroom existed, its windows faced the front of the house, he never dreamed it was so bright and cheerful. Had it been closed off all these years? he wondered. What a pity. What a waste.

In less than fifteen minutes, Suzy was ready to go, promising Joanne she'd be back bright and early in the morning. As Rich took her arm and they started down the hall, Suzy let her glance rove over him, teasingly seductive.

"Too bad you're not wearing shorts. It's so early we could have gone to the beach."

"I can change in five minutes."

"So can I."

The water was still too cold for swimming, but Rich managed to get Suzy out over her knees, a major achievement for a stubborn farmer, as she liked to call herself. It wasn't long, however, before they both retreated to the warmth of the sand, and lying on their backs, they stretched out on the blanket, side by side, and stared up into the clouds above them.

Suzy emitted a long, satisfied sigh. "Oh, this is heavenly. What is there about the ocean that makes you forget everything else?"

"Maybe it's because it's so massive that, by comparison, your own problems seem insignificant."

"Hmm, sounds logical," Suzy murmured lazily. "I should bring Joanne out here."

"From what I saw, she doesn't look like she needs it. She's as alert as anyone I know."

"That's what I've been telling you all along. But she's not physically strong. For instance, she could never make it down this path"—Suzy indicated the narrow rocky trail behind her—"but I think a lot of her fatigue is just due to lack of exercise. If she keeps on the way she's been going, she should be up to par in a couple of weeks."

Propping himself up on one elbow, Rich looked at Suzy. She was lying on her back with her eyes closed, her long thick lashes looking like fuzzy shadows on her cheeks. Taking a strand of russet hair that had fallen across her forehead, Rich held it between his fingers, fascinated by the burnished streaks of gold that danced in the late afternoon light.

"Suzy," he said quietly, "do you have any special feelings toward Joanne? I mean, do you think you remember her at all?"

Suzy opened her eyes, then immediately shaded them with her hand. She looked up at him. "Nothing that I can be positive about. I like her and we get along very well, but I don't remember her voice or her face at all." She paused for a long moment before continuing. "Something did come up this afternoon, though. We were cleaning out Joanne's drawers, and she was getting rid of a lot of old costume jewelry. One of the pieces was a heart-shaped pendant with a pearl in the center. It wasn't valuable and I was surprised Joanne even owned anything like that, let alone that she'd kept it so long." Suzy's eyes met Rich's. "I remember that necklace very well," she said quietly.

"Are you sure?"

"Positive. I even remember holding it in my hand and looking at the pearl and turning it over to see if there was one on the other side."

"Did you say anything to Joanne?"

"No." Suzy sat up and, hugging her knees, stared out at the ocean. "If you remember, Abby used to sell a lot of junk jewelry. I could have seen it then. In fact, she might have even given it to me to play with." She sighed heavily. "Darn."

Rich knew Suzy was frustrated and wished there was something he could do, but he was powerless. He hated being so helpless. Sitting up, he put an arm around her shoulders. "Why don't you plan to stay over another week, Suzy? In that time a lot of these little pieces will have fallen into place."

Suzy shook her head. "Stop dreaming. This thing will never come together. It's too late, too many years have passed. Maybe a few instances will pop up here and there, but I doubt if there'll ever be anything substantive."

Rich could sympathize. He was beginning to think the same thoughts himself, but at the moment he was more concerned with keeping Suzy at Link Hall for another week than he was in finding Christina Hepburn. Just the thought of her leaving made him feel empty. "How about it?" he pressed. "Can you stay another week?" His eyes roved longingly down her slim but shapely figure. He made no attempt to disguise the intense feeling of longing that surged through him.

She turned to him with a wide smile. "I'll think about it," she teased.

Laughing, he tumbled her back onto the blanket and rolled her beside him. "Well, you'd better think in a hurry. I'm an impatient man." To prove it, he splayed one large hand across Suzy's soft bottom and pressed her to him. Then, tipping his head back a little, he looked into her face. Her eyes were like emerald seas, beckoning, coaxing...

A lazy smile touched the corners of her mouth. "You don't seem to be in a hurry now," she observed wryly.

"This is different," he murmured, and curving one arm around her shoulders, he held her close to him, delighting in the moist warmth of her breath against his neck and the feel of her fingers as they traced a path up the side of his face and burrowed into his hair.

Subtly, Suzy shifted her body, fitting it into his, and for many moments they lay enfolded in the silent comfort of closeness. But soon the glowing warmth of their bodies began to fan into an aching need for more, arousing the familiar passion they had come to crave. Pressing against her, Rich began to seek her mouth with his, but Suzy met him with parted lips, encouraging his tongue to enter her mouth and entwine with hers in a sensuous and mutual exploration. Drinking deeply of her sweetness, he was as amazed at the depth of his arousal as he was at the swiftness of Suzy's response. It triggered an instant and consuming desire for more. As a sublime dizziness washed over him like a giant wave, his body cried out for her.

Surrendering to his desperate hunger, Rich began to explore, to enjoy her, to return the passion she gave him. Starting with her moist lips, his mouth journeyed downward, his slow, teasing kisses intensifying the heat between them. Then, sliding his hand under her shirt, he pushed her bra aside and captured one breast in his hand. As he moved his thumb across the nipple with slow, sensuous strokes, he delighted in the feel of it hardening under his touch. Lowering his head still further, he captured the rosy mound between his lips and drew it into his mouth, savoring the satin sweetness with his tongue, reveling in the rapturous heat of her exposed skin and the feel of her hands circling the back of his head and pressing him even closer into the soft fullness of her breasts.

Suzy's hands slid downward to caress his back in seductive, mesmerizing patterns until their bodies began to rock together slowly. Rich could feel the beginning of a tormenting tremble. It started in a searing path down the length of his body and settled in his loins with a hard, demanding insistence.

As his blood heated in the consuming desire for more, however, a voice of caution overruled his throbbing hardness. Vaguely the realization that they were not in a private spot caused his body to still.

Reluctantly he pulled away a few inches. "God, let's go home where we can express ourselves more freely."

"Oh, I don't know," she answered drolly. "It seems to me if you start something, you should finish it."

"Okay, if you say so!" He started reaching under her skirt again.

Laughing, Suzy pushed against him. "I was only kidding."

"But I wasn't," he rallied. "You seem to forget I'm a very serious person."

"You're a very sensuous one, too," she reminded him as she began pulling down her shirt. Her eyes sought his. "Did they teach you that in law school?"

"No." Clasping her hand in his, he brought her fingers to his lips. They were trembling slightly, and he knew she was fighting the same battle of restraint he was. It was a small but revealing response and brought with it a strange and new kind of joy. "I'm only sensuous when I'm with you, Suzy. You're so different from any woman I've ever known." Releasing her fingers, he gently framed her face with his hands. "I love you, Suzy."

For a moment she looked startled, then doubtful, and then suddenly a well of tears sprang into her eyes. "You mean me? Just plain old Suzy Yoder from Windland, Pennsylvania? No frills? No outstanding achievements? No heritage?"

"That's the one...."

"Oh, gosh, I wish I could think of some flowery way to say I love you, too."

Grinning broadly, he hugged her to him. "You mean me? Somber lawyer Rich Link from Boston, Mass.?"

"Yes," she whispered. "That's the one."

Chapter Ten

The following days passed so swiftly that Rich could hardly believe it. He'd practically moved into Suzy's bedroom and spent every moment possible with her. If the Slingluffs were shocked by his behavior, as he realized they'd have to be, they were also discreet. In fact, Rich was quite sure that Mrs. Slingluff, who was very fond of Suzy, was probably knitting a baby blanket behind the closed doors of her apartment.

Suzy spent all of her days with Joanne, and though Rich was quite sure she'd given up trying to prove she was Christina, she rationalized extending her stay in Massachusetts by claiming she was on a two-week vacation with the two people she loved most in all this world, and what was wrong with that? Nothing, he thought, absolutely nothing.

The harshness of reality, however, returned in the form of a phone call from Matt Drechsler. "How'd it go?" Rich asked breezily.

"So-so," was the dour response. Rich could hear papers rustling. "There's no record of Suzy Yoder's grammar school years."

"The Amish school she attended was probably lax in their record keeping," Rich reasoned.

"But there was a student by the name of Suzy Yoder enrolled in high school there as well as the local college. Of course, even an amateur con man could pick the name of some student and use it. We'd have to check that out by comparing a recent picture of her with her college ID. Have you any photos around?"

No, he hadn't, and Rich wasn't sure this was necessary. Suzy was everything she claimed to be, and he actually felt guilty about contacting Matt in the first place. What had he been thinking of?

"Wayne's on the move," Matt went on. "He's hired Burrows and Pierce to do an in-depth investigation."

"Well, let them," Rich replied confidently. "They're not going to find out anything we don't already know."

"Maybe, maybe not. They're a slick outfit, and if Wayne offered enough up-front money, they could do a lot of damage."

"Like what?"

"Like bribing someone in that little burg of Windland to swear that they knew some imaginary distant relative of Abby's and could even remember when Suzy was born."

"They'd have to prove it."

"Right, but fake IDs are easily come by and to disprove them in court takes two years," he reminded Rich. "If you want, I can send a man out there. We could lay a little groundwork."

Rich told him no. He realized now that Wayne was gearing up for a lawsuit, and though Rich was confident that Suzy's story of being a foundling was true, he knew this would not be an easy case to win. It wouldn't be an easy one for Wayne to win, either, because he had no evidence unless, as Matt suggested, he could bribe some witnesses. In which case, Rich told himself, he'd better start doing his homework.

Tomorrow he'd go to Windland.

Rich didn't want Suzy to worry, so he decided not to tell her where he was going, not just yet, anyway. He simply said he'd be out of town on business and made arrangements for Albert to drive her to Thrushmore. She didn't doubt or interrogate him, just told him to hurry back; she missed him already.

Taking an early morning plane for Harrisburg, Rich arrived around ten o'clock. After purchasing a map at the newsstand, he rented a car and headed south to Windland. It was a beautiful spring day, sunny and warm and full of buttercups and early violets and, as he got farther south, the earthy smell of winter wheat. It was the sort of day that made one feel exultant, and he breathed deeply of the fresh air blowing in the window. But, strangely, Rich felt irritable and unsettled. At first he tried to blame it on the time of day and the inconvenience of the trip, but in his heart, he knew that his grumpiness was caused by a dull, nagging feeling of guilt.

He realized there was really no reason for him to come to Windland at all. The supposition that Wayne might bribe a witness was more fantasy than fact. Trying to brainwash Suzy's friends was a project suitable for a sociological experiment, certainly not a legal responsibility. Then why was he here? he dared to ask himself. The answer was slow in coming, but eventually he admitted that Matt had planted the tiniest seed of suspicion and Rich wanted to stamp it out before it grew.

He had no trouble finding the farmers' market that sprawled at the edge of an open field. This wasn't market day, however, and the place was deserted. Parking the car, Rich got out and went into the long narrow building that Suzy had described so well. It was a shaky wooden shack with stalls on both sides and an aisle in the middle. Though it was illuminated only by shafts of sunlight streaming through the cracks between the planked siding, it was easy for Rich to picture the market as it would be when it bustled with activity.

Slowly he walked down the aisle, looking right to left, wondering which stand had been Abby's. He could almost picture an old woman with a dark shawl around her shoulders, sitting in a chair behind her stall and waiting for customers, smiling and nodding to friends and talking in low tones to the little red-haired girl beside her. The child was sitting in a small-sized chair, her head was bent over a book. Behind her, the wide stall door was open and an old beat-up truck, its springs sagging with wear, waited in the hot sun.

Suddenly, Rich shook himself. God, if he wasn't careful, he'd hypnotize himself into a trance, he thought as he left the building. As long as he was there, however, he decided he'd walk around before he returned to the car. Everything was exactly as he'd pictured it from Suzy's description, and he could see how easy it would be for someone to dispose of an unwanted child here on a busy market day.

Just as he was rounding the corner at the far end of the building, an ancient station wagon turned into the lot and stopped. A young woman with an Amish cap on her head and an old man with a long gray beard got out and walked toward the stalls. They seemed to be looking for something and paid no attention at all to Rich. But he wasn't one to be easily brushed off. Lengthening his strides, he caught up with them and gave them his most winning smile. The woman smiled back, but the old man eyed Rich with disapproval.

"Good morning," Rich greeted them. "I wonder if you could tell me how I can find Abby Yoder. I understand she used to have a stall here."

Sullenly the man shook his head, but the girl was quick to answer. "I'm afraid she died several years ago."

"I'm sorry to hear that," Rich said, "but actually, I didn't come here to see Abby Yoder. I understand her daughter, Suzy, has some property for sale."

The old man shook his head. "Suzy weren't her daughter. I think she were her cousin's niece," he grumped.

"I see." Rich smiled again. "Well, perhaps you could tell me where Suzy's farm is."

"She sold that several years ago," the girl answered. "She lives in an apartment now."

"Oh, do you know her?" Rich asked. The old man was scowling.

"Yes, we went to school together, right from the first grade. We just lived a mile apart." She looked up at Rich expectantly. "Are you a friend of hers?"

He wished now he'd taken another approach, but it was too late to change. "Well, I've met her several times, and she spoke so highly of this property that I thought since I was in the area, I'd take a look at it...if I can find it, that is."

The old man stared straight at him, and without lifting his hand at all, he said, "Dern this road to the feed store and turn your left."

"I see." Rich nodded politely. "And I thank you." He glanced at the girl again. She'd been studying him very closely, but when he caught her gaze, she lowered her eyes. Then the old man gave her arm a tug and they disappeared into the market building.

Rich got back into the car. He'd already removed his suit coat, but now he took off his tie, opened his shirt collar and rolled up his sleeves. He looked down at his neat shoes and pressed pants and knew he still looked like an alien, but it was the best he could do. He followed the old man's direction and drove to the feed store. After parking the car, he walked inside. An older woman in an ankle-length lavender dress eyed him suspiciously from behind the counter. He decided to come right to the point. This time he didn't smile. Forget that.

"I'm looking for the farm that used to belong to Abby Yoder. Can you tell me how to get there?"

With a slight tip of her head, she indicated the road that ran behind the store. "West three mile on your right."

"Thank you," he said, nodded politely and left. He didn't smile until he got back into the car. Visions of a smart Boston detective trying to get information out of the residents of this close-mouthed Amish community made him laugh. "Lots of luck, Wayne," he said out loud, and pulling out of the lot, he headed west.

At first three miles seemed like very vague directions, but after a mile, when the asphalt ended and the gravel began, Rich realized the farms were so far apart out here that "three miles on your right" was as accurate as any map.

He drove slowly, enjoying his surroundings. On both sides of the road, acres and acres of newly planted fields stretched in neat rows as far as the eye could see. Dotted here and there were clusters of farm buildings and even an occasional windmill could be seen against the horizon. As Rich drove, he became more and more aware of the vast greatness of the countryside that opened out before him with an awesome serenity. It was unlike anything he'd ever experienced before, and several times he was struck by the sudden beauty of clumps of wildflowers at the side of the road or a copse of weeping willows or the sight of a horse and plow in the distance.

He didn't realize how far he'd gone until, suddenly, he crested a hill and there it was. Below him on the right was a small farmhouse hugging the side of the road. Several outbuildings and an old barn were clustered around it, and a woman in a pink dress was in the yard hanging clothes on the line. Near her were two small children playing with a wagon. He could almost hear their laughter and see their shining faces.

Rich knew instinctively that this was Suzy's farm. How like her it was, he thought, with its clean white buildings, its neat rows of trees, the wild hyacinths and daffodils at the side of the lane. Though there were traces of wilderness and languor, there was also a strict sense of order and privacy.

Rich feasted his eyes on the little farm for many long minutes, and then he turned the car around and headed east. He realized how out of place he was both in thought and presence. He could never intrude upon these people with his phony questions and clever explanations. Like Suzy, they were as quiet and honest and uncluttered as the peaceful fields around them.

Rich felt like an absolute jerk. At first he tried to make excuses for himself by rationalizing that his experience with Ratonia had left him skeptical, which was a lot of garbage, and he knew it. Here he was, checking up on the woman he loved more than anyone else in the world as if she were a common criminal, when in truth she had more honesty in her little finger than he had in his whole body. *Go home, Rich Link*, he scolded himself. *You don't belong here.*

Albert drove Suzy over to Thrushmore earlier than usual, but she'd gotten up to see Rich off and was dressed and ready to go. Since she was sure Joanne wouldn't be up yet, Suzy decided she'd take a walk under the pretext of seeing how the newly planted gardens were doing. Actually, she just needed some time alone. A nagging sense of disappointment had dampened her spirits, and she realized she'd have to come to terms with it. This was Thursday, the end of her second week, and on Sunday she'd be leaving. Rich was as aware of this as she was, but he hadn't insisted she stay over as he had before. Though he'd said he loved her, he hadn't even hinted that he wanted to marry her and keep her there forever.

Fortunately, Suzy was basically an optimist. She tried to rationalize Rich's behavior by telling herself that he was a cautious person and simply wasn't ready to commit himself to any one person yet. He needed more time and, she thought ruefully, perhaps more distance. Though the thought of leaving him made her feel sick, Suzy managed to bolster her spirits by telling herself that Rich was going to miss her as much as she would miss him and that within two weeks' time, he'd come for her, and she'd go with him...anywhere.

A voice jarred her back to the present. "Suzy, good morning," Joanne called from the patio.

Suzy waved and started toward her. To her surprise, Joanne wasn't only up and dressed, she was even having her coffee on the patio. "Good heavens," Suzy exclaimed as she looked at the dainty breakfast china, "this place is beginning to look like *House Beautiful*."

"Thank you, Suzy. I'm glad you appreciate my efforts." As she poured Suzy's coffee, she chatted excitedly. "I've decided I'm going to do some redecorating around here. I think I'll start with that dismal library and get rid of those awful drapes."

"Wow! You really meant it when you said you were going to open Thrushmore up again. Once you've finished with the library, that about does it, doesn't it?"

"Well, there's still the upstairs."

Suzy glanced up quickly. "Christina's room?"

"Yes. I've decided I'm going to throw out every stick of furniture in that room and have it completely redecorated in a bright airy country look. I'm going to open the doors and the windows and let the sunshine in." She turned to Suzy with a big smile. "What do you think?"

"I think it's great," Suzy approved wholeheartedly. "I looked in that room one day thinking maybe I'd recognize something, the windows or the ceiling or whatever, but nothing was familiar. In fact, I got out of there as soon as I could. The room is like a tomb."

"I know," Joanne said, sighing. "David put that old furniture in there and shut the door. We've never used it, not even for guests."

Suzy leaned toward Joanne a little. They'd come to know each other so well that she felt free to discuss almost anything with her. "Joanne," she said quietly, "are you trying to make that room into something that would be suitable for me?"

Leaning back in her chair, Joanne folded her hands in her lap. "Yes," she admitted.

"But I'm leaving Sunday," Suzy reminded her. "I have a job to go back to. I just can't extend my stay here any longer."

Suzy knew Joanne held out an almost childish hope that she was Christina, and though Suzy hated to dash her dreams, she realized they had reached an impasse. There was no positive proof that she was Christina Hepburn, and she was sure there never would be. As much as she hated to admit it, it was time for her to go home.

Joanne sat back and looked at Suzy with long, loving eyes. "Can I be perfectly frank with you?"

"Sure."

"I understand how you feel, but in my opinion, Suzy, you are Christina. I have a feeling about you that's different from anything I feel toward other people. And though of course I don't recognize you physically, there's a certain chemistry about you that's identical to Christina's. I know I can't be mistaken. Now," she said, clasping her hands together, "I realize that this is just my opinion and it's not based on facts. I also know that you, like David, will not be content until you have proof positive." She glanced up at Suzy. "Am I right?"

Suzy grinned. "Am I really as stubborn as all that?"

"Not stubborn, dear, factual. You're looking for proof, and I admire you for that, but don't blame me if I don't show too much enthusiasm. As far as I'm concerned, the search is over, and I'm not going to waste any more of my life looking."

"I wish I felt that sure," Suzy murmured.

"Keep digging until you're satisfied, dear, and don't hesitate to ask me anything you want to know. In the meantime... Uh-oh, who's that?" Getting up, she walked to the edge of the patio and looked toward the drive. "It's Paul Hilton." She waved to him and watched him approach. "What are you doing here?" she called. "I've never felt better in my life."

"I just stopped in for a second to see what a well person looked like," he joshed, "and oh, my God, what's this, a tea party?"

"We're having breakfast on the patio," Joanne explained.

Suzy grinned. "It's done in all the magazines."

"Oh, well, I'll have to get my nose out of the medical journals, I can see that." He lowered himself into one of the bright yellow lounge chairs and looked from Suzy to Joanne, where his gaze lingered for a long moment. "Well, I must say, I've never seen you looking so good."

"I've never felt so good, either, but Suzy tells me she's still planning on going back to Pennsylvania this Sunday. I was hoping she'd stay...forever," she added quietly.

"I see." Dr. Hilton nodded sagely. He turned his gaze to Suzy. "Why are you leaving?"

"What a question," she answered. "You know very well why."

"Because you can't prove you're Christina?" It seemed incredible to him.

"Of course."

Hilton threw up his hands. "But that's the most ridiculous thing I've ever heard. What the hell difference does it make? You don't have a mother, Joanne doesn't have a daughter. You get along great. Who's to keep you two from just deciding you belong to each other?"

"But legally there's—"

"Oh, to hell with legally." Dr. Hilton wasn't a man to let minor details stand in his way. "You are two adult women. You don't have to answer to anyone. All you have to do is decide you're mother and daughter and that's it."

Suzy smiled. She loved the way he pushed aside stumbling blocks. "And what about Wayne?" she asked.

"All Wayne wants is money," Hilton explained. "That's all he's ever wanted. And though half of David's inheritance would net him fifty million dollars, that isn't enough for Wayne. He wants it all."

"Well, let him have it," Joanne interjected. "I have more money than Suzy and I together could spend in a lifetime. Why should we waste any more years trying to prove a point?"

"My sentiments exactly," Dr. Hilton agreed. "How about it, Suzy? What do you say?"

She realized she was on the spot, and though she hated to disappoint the two of them, she knew she could never live under Joanne's roof pretending that she was Christina.

Joanne knew this, too, and reluctantly came to the rescue. "Stop trying to force Suzy into a decision she's not ready to make yet. Besides," she said gamely, "we have three more days, and I don't intend to waste them arguing about who's who." She turned to Dr. Hilton. "We were just discussing new drapes for the library when you arrived."

"Oh, my God," he said, getting up, "I hope you're not going to ask my opinion."

"That was the last thing on my mind."

Dr. Hilton smiled. "You know, Joanne, you're beginning to get your sense of humor back."

"You can thank Suzy for that."

"I know, and I do." He gave Suzy an affectionate pat on the shoulder. "I sure hope you can see your way clear to staying. In the meantime, I'll try to come up with some kind of a solution. There has to be one somewhere."

"I hope so," Joanne answered.

As Suzy watched Dr. Hilton drive out of sight, she found herself trying to hold back a tear. Quickly she wiped it away and began bustling about being as noisy as possible. Joanne, however, still had her back to Suzy and was obviously struggling with the same problem.

Suzy went over to her and put her hand on her shoulder. "You know, just because we're not related doesn't mean we can't be friends. We can phone and write and visit back and forth...."

Joanne nodded; then, taking a breath, she turned around. "Of course we can. Besides, even if you were my daughter, that's the way things would be, isn't it? You'd have a job someplace and we'd see each other occasionally." She put a loving hand on Suzy's cheek. "It's good having you so close that we can visit." She smiled, a small smile but a firm one. "Now, how about it? Are we going to Plymouth today? We could look for drapery material for the library."

"If I'm going to be coming back to visit, why don't we start by looking for wallpaper for that back bedroom?"

Joanne absolutely beamed. "Oh, that's wonderful, Suzy." She swallowed heavily. "How about a small print in a contemporary country design?"

"Sounds good to me. Why don't you go get your purse and I'll back the car out and meet you in front?"

"I won't be a minute."

As Suzy watched Joanne's departing figure, she sniffed a final sniff, picked up her handbag, slung the strap over her shoulder and was just starting toward the walk that led to the garage when Mae appeared on the patio.

She held out a bottle of pills. "If you aren't going to be here for lunch, Mrs. Hepburn should take one of these after each meal."

Suzy tried not to appear too stunned. "Why, thank you, Mae."

The old woman's answer was a brief nod. Then, turning on her heel, she marched back into the house.

Well! Suzy thought. *What a surprise. Mae must be thawing a little.* She'd actually gone out of her way to speak to her, and that was the only reason for the contact. Not only did Joanne not need the pills, but she was quite capable of carrying them herself.

While Suzy and Joanne were in one of the large shopping malls, the weather turned cool. The skies darkened in the early afternoon, and by the time they were ready to leave, it had started to rain. Suzy was a little apprehensive. She remembered Rich telling her that Joanne was afraid of storms, but when she looked at Joanne, she seemed to be more concerned about protecting her armload of home decorating magazines than she was with getting wet herself.

When they got into the car and slammed the doors, Joanne turned to Suzy with a broad smile. "Do you realize this is the first time I've been out on a rainy day in twenty-two years?"

Suzy nodded. "I heard that it stormed the night Christina was kidnapped. Rich told me."

Joanne's only answer was a nod in agreement. She busied herself then by settling into her seat and watching the road ahead as Suzy drove out of the parking lot and onto the main thoroughfare. Then she turned to Suzy with a raised eyebrow. "We're a little late. I hope we don't keep Rich waiting."

"Oh, that's all right. He had some business out of town today and said he might be a little late himself."

Satisfied that they weren't holding anyone up, Joanne opened one of her magazines and began folding back pages she wanted to refer to later. She left the driving to Suzy, whose thoughts drifted to Rich and the hope that he'd be waiting for them when they returned. She missed him. One day and she missed him. What was she going to do next week? she asked herself, and then shook the answer off with a shrug. She'd decided long ago that a lot of hurt later was worth even a small amount of pleasure now. Actually she was getting a bonus, because being with Rich was not a small amount of pleasure but a lot of it...and worth every tear.

To Suzy's delight, Rich's car was in the drive when they pulled in, and Rich himself opened the door for them. He looked devastatingly handsome with his broad shoulders, taut beneath the confines of his shirt, his tousled hair, his captivating smile and, most of all, his outstretched arms. Suzy didn't care who was looking. She ran right into them and hugged him to her. God, it was good to be home again, she thought.

Frank hurried out with an umbrella for Joanne, who was obviously pleased to see Rich there. She offered him a drink, but he declined, saying that Mrs. Slingluff was probably pacing the floor. Joanne understood and didn't press it. But she did wave them off, like a mother seeing her daughter depart for the senior prom.

In the car, Rich gave Suzy a long, deep kiss that reached all the way to her toes. "God, I missed you," he whispered. "You've been in my thoughts all day long."

Suzy circled his lips with the tip of her finger. "Didn't that interfere with your work?"

"I'll tell you about that later. Right now I just want to get you home and to myself before this weather kicks up into a real storm." Releasing her, he put the car in gear and sped down the drive.

Vaguely Suzy wondered what he wanted to tell her, but since it was obviously job related, it could wait, she decided. Right now all she wanted was what he wanted...to be alone together.

Chapter Eleven

Just how, Rich asked himself, did a man go about telling the woman he loved that he'd had doubts about her and had taken the precaution of verifying the facts she'd given him? That was commensurate to announcing one's lack of trust, not the sort of thing a man did if he had plans of marrying the woman...and this was Rich's goal. He couldn't even conceive of life without Suzy. She was everything to him, his days and nights and tomorrows and forevers.

Though Rich had no intention of taking any risks that might result in his losing her, he did feel that he should tell her he'd been to Windland. Admittedly, part of the reason he'd gone was because of the doubts that Matt Drechsler had planted in his mind, but Rich realized now that his curiosity was equally to blame. He'd wanted to see where Suzy had grown and flowered, so that he could put the last dab of paint on the picture.

He decided to wait until after dinner to tell Suzy, but by that time the rain was coming down hard and he and Albert had gone through the whole house making sure all the windows were closed. Then Suzy took a bath and got into her robe, and then the phone rang three times, and then he needed a snack, and then... Oh, hell, he'd tell her later.

They were in the library and Suzy was inspecting the French doors, which opened onto a sheltered porch. "Why don't we open these?" she suggested. "It's still warm out, and I love listening to the rain, don't you?"

"Of course." Though Rich had never considered this as a pleasurable experience, somehow it went with the spring night and the low lights and the dreaminess they both felt.

After opening the doors wide, he stretched out on the couch and pulled Suzy beside him, cradling her in his arms. Her hair, still damp from her shower, smelled faintly of lilacs and her face in the dim light was beautifully serene. Suzy's eyes were partly closed, and Rich watched, fascinated, as the dark shadows of her lashes made patterns on her cheeks. Then his gaze moved downward to her mouth. The corners were tipped slightly upward in a half smile, so typical of her whole personality, he thought.

Suzy stirred slightly. "Did I tell you I saw Dr. Hilton today?" she murmured sleepily. "He and Joanne have very strange philosophies."

"Like mine?"

She twisted her head until her round green eyes were gazing into his oval blue ones. "I hate to tell you this,

Rich, but you are very predictable, at least to me you are. I can tell what you're thinking without you even saying it."

"But if I never say it, how do you know you're right?"

"It's called magic."

"Oh, I see." Gently he pressed his fingers into her waist. "And what about what I'm feeling? Can you figure that out, too?"

"Of course." Her eyes glowed mischievously.

"Then how about telling me out loud?"

Idly, Suzy fingered a button on his shirt. "Well, let's see. First you're glad I'm not wearing a blouse with buttons on it like this." Slowly she undid two of his shirt buttons. "And then you're glad I don't have it tucked into my waistband like this." She pulled a part of his shirt out of his pants. "And then you're grateful I don't have a stubborn buckle like this one."

"You should talk." Reaching out, he skimmed his hand under the V of her robe, and sliding it around to her back, he fumbled with the fastener of her bra without success. "See what I mean?"

"Stop complaining. Think of me. I have a zipper to conquer."

"All right," he conceded, and quickly proposed a solution, one that would expedite operations. "Let's trade jobs. We'll both undress ourselves." He nudged her chin with his knuckle. "I'll give you sixty seconds to get out of that underwear."

"Please, lingerie."

He gave the cord of her robe a tug. "Whatever it is, it has to go," he teased.

Unbuttoning his shirt, he tossed it aside, then swiftly disposed of the rest of his clothes. Suzy, however, was moving with tranquil ease and had only managed to get her bra unfastened.

Pulling her to her feet, Rich eased the robe off her shoulders and let it fall to the floor at their feet. Within moments, her panties lay on top of the robe and Suzy was standing before him, unashamed of her nudity. And well she should be, he thought. She had a perfectly proportioned body and skin that was so satin soft it was absolutely irresistible.

Putting his hands on her waist, Rich let his eyes feast on Suzy's gentle curves. She wasn't a highly experienced lover, but she was the most sensual one he'd ever known. There was a certain undefined wildness about Suzy that made Rich's body react with a strange sort of primitive excitement. It was more powerful than anything he'd ever experienced and immediately sent his arousal level soaring.

With a mesmerized "Mmm," he wrapped his arms around her and pressed her to him. She felt warm and soft and intimate, as if her body were aching to fuse with his, exactly what he wanted, too. Splaying his broad hand over her buttocks, he pressed her even closer and was immediately rewarded with a burst of heat and desire that shot through both of them.

"Oh, God," he murmured pleasurably. "It seems like we've been apart for ages."

"Too long," she whispered huskily, the breath of her passion as hot as his. Then, circling her arms around his shoulders, she pressed her hands into the back of his head and daringly moved her tongue back and forth across his lower lip before tasting the inner moistness of his mouth. As Rich tightened his grip, he felt his body tense with an ache for completion.

Despite the raw hunger he felt, Rich was in no hurry. He wanted to savor the feel of Suzy's hardened nipples against his chest, the painful teasing of her hands as they explored his muscled torso, searching for pleasure points...and finding them. But all too soon, his body grew rigid and expanded powerfully as the heat of passion settled in his groin.

"Time's running out," he gasped, his voice breathless with urgency.

"Then take me," Suzy pleaded raggedly.

Hugging her to him, Rich eased Suzy to the floor. Then, rolling her onto her back, he straddled her with demanding possessiveness and began to stroke her body. Starting with her hips, he massaged a path up to her waist and then to her high, taut breasts. Bending over, he caught a rosy-pink nipple between his lips and stroked it hungrily with his tongue while his thumb teased the other nipple until it, too, became firm with the ache of desire.

Suzy expelled a gasp of wondrous satisfaction. Tauntingly, her hips began to move beneath him and soon their bodies were moving together as if they were one. But within minutes, Rich felt Suzy's body heave with an uncontrollable shudder and he knew that her need for sexual fulfillment matched his own.

"Now," she coaxed.

"Now," was his ragged response.

Parting Suzy's legs, Rich bore down on her, giving her his full weight. Then, with strong, steady thrusts, he joined their bodies in a swift union of heated passion. To his delight, he could feel Suzy's body writhing beneath him, merging with his in the precious dance of sweet agony that began to build and grow and strengthen and expand until...suddenly, with an explosive cry of ecstasy, their bodies convulsed together in a climax of such torrid radiance that both of them went soaring into a world of golden rapture and voluptuous fulfillment, a world that only lovers had ever found.

As they lay cradled in each other's arms, they floated down a gentle stream of pleasure into the soothing waters of serenity. Their bodies were still damp as they snuggled together. Sighing contentedly, Suzy caressed Rich's neck and shoulders. He lifted her slightly and eased his arm beneath her before fitting the length of his body along hers. As his mind began to slip into a dreamy state, a small frown furrowed his brow. Where had he ever gotten the idea that Suzy could be anything but what she was—sincere, unequivocal, warm-hearted and totally trusting?

Lifting her head slightly, Suzy looked up at him. "You get an 'A' for accomplishment," she murmured sleepily.

"It takes two," he assured her, tightening his arm. "Are you cold?"

"A little. How about you?"

He could have stayed there forever, but he didn't want Suzy to be uncomfortable, especially tonight.

Getting up, he pulled her with him; then, easing her down on the couch, he left to close the doors. When he returned, he pulled her robe over both of them and they snuggled together under its warmth.

"I love you, Suzy," Rich said quietly. "I don't ever want to be away from you for so long again. This has been the longest day of my life."

She didn't answer; she just lay quietly in his arms.

Putting his hand under her chin, he tipped her face up to his. "Suzy," he whispered, "will you marry me?"

At first her expression was amazement and then slow, dawning realization and then, to his surprise, he saw tears trembling on her lower lashes.

"Oh, Rich," she cried in a choked voice, her cheeks glistening with teardrops of happiness. "I thought you'd never ask." Throwing her arm around his neck, she pressed her cheek against his.

His hands tightened around her. "You didn't think I'd let you go, did you?"

"I wasn't sure. I thought perhaps you were still making up your mind."

Rich thought of Windland and the little white farmhouse and the rows of newly planted fields. "I was," he admitted, "but today I realized you were everything I wanted and that if I didn't get my act together, I might lose you. I'd never get over that."

"Oh, Rich, you say the nicest things," she said, sniffing. "It's too bad Abby isn't here to meet you. She'd love you as much as I do."

"I'm sure I'd love her, too," Rich said with sincerity. "I almost feel as if I knew her."

Suzy snuggled comfortably into the curve of his arm and sighed, a long and peaceful sigh. "Well, Abby may not be here to congratulate us, but I'll bet Joanne will. She's very fond of you. Besides, there's nothing in the world she'd rather have than for me to get married and stay here.''

''She's a smart woman.''

They talked for a while, but all too soon they both got so sleepy that they couldn't even finish a sentence. Finally, gathering up their clothes, they straggled up the stairs to Suzy's room and fell into bed, their arms and legs so entwined they were almost as one. As Rich felt Suzy's body relax into sleep, he held her even tighter. How lucky he was, he thought, and how glad he was he hadn't told Suzy about going to Windland. Why spoil such a beautiful night by reminding himself of his own absurdities?

Despite Suzy's fatigue, she woke up before the sun rose. The rain had stopped and the birds were busy with their early morning feeding. As she listened to their chatter and watched the sky lighten into another sunny day, her thoughts skipped happily ahead to the day when she and Rich could marry and start the rest of their lives together. It seemed like heaven waiting....

Yet for some reason, Suzy felt a heaviness of mind. Idly she looked around the daintily furnished guest room with its antique furniture, its thick carpeting and ruffled curtains. She found herself wishing she, too, had something to bring to their marriage, and for the first time since that auspicious trip to the dentist so many months before, Suzy wished that she were Christina Hepburn. With a name like that and the money that went with it, doors would open like magic for Rich.

Suddenly she stopped and blinked her eyes. What was the matter with her, anyway? If Rich had wanted to marry into a dynasty, he could have had Marcia Tolbert years ago. And as for the money, wasn't Suzy the one who had told Wayne just last week that Rich didn't need money? He could get anywhere he wanted to go without outside help. Besides, she thought dreamily, from now on there'd be two of them and that was stronger than anything material.

Feeling chagrined over her brief but mercenary thoughts, Suzy decided she'd better get up and get her head cleared. She knew Rich wasn't planning on going into the office today. He'd told her he was going to sleep until noon, at which time she could serve him his breakfast in bed and then, after a leisurely nap, they could spend the rest of the day in Newport. It sounded wonderful to Suzy, but she wanted to see Joanne. She couldn't wait to tell her that she and Rich were getting married. In fact, she thought, if she didn't tell someone, and soon, she was going to burst.

Dressing hurriedly and silently, Suzy went downstairs, where Mrs. Slingluff was in the kitchen making home-baked breakfast rolls.

Closing her eyes, Suzy sniffed appreciatively. "Mmm, they smell heavenly. How long do I have to wait?"

Mrs. Slingluff smiled. "Just fifteen minutes. How about a cup of coffee? And the orange juice is freshly squeezed...."

Her words were interrupted by the ringing of the phone. Mrs. Slingluff practically flew across the room to answer it on the first ring so it wouldn't awaken Rich. No wonder he was so spoiled, Suzy thought.

"It's for you, Suzy," Mrs. Slingluff said. "Do you want to take it in the hall?"

"Oh, no, this is fine." Suzy couldn't imagine any reason to be secretive. She was a little puzzled, though, when she heard Terri's voice. "What's going on?" she teased. "Can't you get along without me?"

"Oh, we're hanging in there," Terri assured her, "but that's not why I'm calling. I saw Mary Hofstater at the garden store this morning, and she told me someone was at the market yesterday inquiring about buying Abby's old farm. Is it up for sale or something? Do you have it listed?"

"Why, no," Suzy frowned, perplexed. "How could I get a listing if I haven't been there for two weeks?"

"Well, that's what I thought, but Mary said the man asked specifically about how to get there."

"What man?" Suzy asked.

"I don't know. She didn't get his name. Said he was very handsome, tall with dark, kind of curly hair, blue eyes, young..."

Suzy felt a hard, uncomfortable lump start to form in her throat. "Did she say what he was wearing?" she asked, keeping her voice low so Mrs. Slingluff couldn't hear it over the sound of her mixer.

"No. She said he was dressed like he was from the city, though. Do you know who it could be?"

"No. No, I don't," Suzy murmured, but the icy knot that twisted in her stomach told another story. She did know; it was Rich. His out-of-town trip yesterday had been to Windland. But why would he go there? she asked herself. And worse, why didn't he tell her?

The rest of the conversation was a blur of mundane words and phrases that Suzy wasn't even aware of uttering. By the time she hung up, she was almost numb.

Leaving the kitchen, she wandered into the library, but when she saw the couch and the French doors, she turned and went out a side door to the yard. Tears of shock and dismay stung her eyes, but her primary emotion was confusion. She simply didn't understand. Why was Rich hiding this from her? What was he doing there? Checking up on her? she wondered. Didn't he believe her? Had he been sleeping in her bed all this while and wondering if she was a hypocrite? But if that was true, she argued, why did he ask her to marry him?

The sound of a door opening startled her. It was Albert. "Your breakfast is ready," he announced with a pleasant smile.

Suzy's shoulders slumped dejectedly. "Gosh, I'm sorry, Albert, but I don't think I'll have breakfast this morning." As he nodded and started to turn, however, she added hastily, "Do you think you could drive me over to Thrushmore?"

"Of course I could. Anytime at all."

"Could we go right now?"

"I'll have the car up to the front in five minutes."

When Albert pulled up in front of Thrushmore, Joanne called to her from a side garden. Mae was with her, and they seemed to be in the middle of planting something. Suzy waved and walked over to them. They'd been trying to decide how close to plant flowers in what looked like a newly turned bed. When Mae saw Suzy, she put the trowel down and brushed off her hands. She looked almost pleasant.

"Go ahead with what you're doing," Suzy said quickly. "I didn't mean to interrupt."

"Oh, that's all right," Joanne assured her. "We were just measuring, anyway. We don't have the petunias yet."

"If you want, we could go and get some."

"Maybe we will, but later." Joanne took Suzy's arm and patted her hand affectionately. "Right now you look like you could use a cup of good strong Irish coffee."

"You're more right than you know," Suzy lamented.

"Oh? Did you and Rich have an argument? I noticed that Albert brought you over."

"No, no argument." Suzy sighed heavily. "Maybe that's the trouble. We don't seem to be communicating. I found out this morning that his out-of-town trip yesterday was to Windland."

"Oh?" Joanne was neither surprised not alarmed, and this puzzled Suzy. She'd expected a ready ally.

"I don't know why he didn't tell me," Suzy went on as they left the walkway and started across the lawn. "Am I that hard to talk to? Or doesn't he trust me?"

"No to both questions," Joanne stated firmly. "And frankly, I'm not at all surprised that he went there. Rich is a very thorough person. As a lawyer, he has to be. He's learned to leave nothing to chance, even if it's something he wants so badly that he's afraid to substantiate the facts."

The hurt in Suzy's eyes was obvious. She looked at Joanne. "Then he did go there to check up on me," she complained petulantly. "He says one thing and means another."

"Don't be so hard on him, Suzy," Joanne coaxed. "I hate to think of all the times David went out look-

ing for Christina and never told me. He assumed I'd
never find out, but of course I did. At first, like you,
I felt hurt and left out, but as time went on, I realized
that part of his search for Christina was just an ego
booster. He loved imagining himself in the role of a
clever detective and delighted in finding the one little
clue that proved that someone or other was ineligible.
Sometimes I used to think he was more interested in
not finding Christina than he was in finding her, but
of course that was ridiculous. It was just the little boy
in him crying out, 'Look, Ma, no hands!'"

A little smile touched the corners of Suzy's mouth,
but it quickly faded away. "But all this while I thought
Rich was on my side one hundred percent."

They'd reached the stone benches, and sitting down,
Joanne motioned for Suzy to sit beside her. "I don't
think that's the only reason he went there. I think he
was curious to see where your roots were."

"But he already knew that. I'd told him enough
times."

"That's just it. Supposing you'd met Rich on a trip
someplace and he'd talked about Link Hall. Wouldn't
you have wanted to see it?"

"Of course, but we could have gone together. Why
didn't he wait?"

Joanne shook her head. "I don't know, Suzy, but
I'll bet at this very minute Rich is wondering the same
thing. I wouldn't be surprised if he's trying to rationalize his actions as much as you are. Something probably triggered his imagination, and he just acted
impulsively. Believe me, Suzy, he didn't act
maliciously."

"I suppose not," Suzy conceded. Joanne was right Rich would never hurt her deliberately. He didn't have a mean bone in his body.

Joanne gave Suzy's hand a reassuring pat. "If you'll just be patient, dear, I guarantee you Rich will explain this whole trip to you someday. In the mean time, you'll just have to have faith in him."

"Oh, I do," Suzy murmured. "I know it doesn't sound like it, but I'd trust him to the end of the world."

"Do you love him?" Joanne said quietly.

"Oh, yes." As a sudden wash of relief flooded through her, Suzy's face broke into a wide smile. "I'd better. We're getting married."

"Married!" Suzy could hear Joanne's quick intake of breath. "Married? Suzy, are you and Rich getting married?"

Suzy absolutely beamed. "That's right."

"Oh, my God, Suzy, I've never heard such good news in my life." Tears of joy sprang to her eyes. "I can't believe it. For once in my life all of my dreams have come true. Oh, Suzy, how wonderful." Putting her arm around Suzy's shoulders, Joanne hugged her tight. "And to think you'll be living right next door to me."

Suzy grinned. "Well, at least for now. But of course, that might change in the future."

Joanne wasn't ready to listen to unpleasant speculations. "Oh, well, I'm not going to worry about what's down the road. I believe in taking life one day at a time, and right now, this is my day of glory." She squeezed Suzy again, then released her and clasped her hands together. "To think after all these years..."

She didn't finish the sentence, but she didn't have to. Suzy knew what she meant. It was as if Christina had finally come home for good, and Suzy realized that, to Joanne, she had. Though Suzy knew this was just a fantasy on Joanne's part, she didn't have the heart to remind her that she wasn't really Christina. Besides, what difference did it make now? They'd always be close friends; perhaps even as close as mother and daughter, and that's all Joanne really wanted.

As they sat in the sunlight and chatted excitedly about all the joys the future held, Suzy realized how lucky she was to have found Joanne, how lucky they were to have found each other. As she listened to Joanne's bubbling enthusiasm about the coming wedding and her sometimes outrageous suggestions about where it would be held and how lavish it would be, Suzy was reminded of Dr. Hilton's remark several days ago. Joanne was indeed a changed person from the physically weak and pale woman she'd met two weeks ago. She'd become a very beautiful and vibrant person and, though she still had a long way to go, she was becoming more and more independent every day.

But best of all, she'd come out of her inner shell and had given freely of her depth and perception. Strange, Suzy thought, how the role of "the guiding light" was now shared by both of them. She smiled inwardly. Joanne was an extraordinary friend, indeed.

Chapter Twelve

When Albert told Rich he'd driven Suzy over to Thrushmore several hours before, Rich was surprised and slightly disturbed. But when Mrs. Slingluff told him Suzy had gotten an upsetting phone call, he was downright worried. He surmised it was from her boss, Terri, and that it concerned his trip to Windland. He didn't completely understand why he'd gone there himself. Was it because Matt Drechsler had urged him to go or because he'd just been idly curious? In any case, he realized it would naturally be upsetting to Suzy that he hadn't told her, but the opportunity just hadn't come up. Besides, how was he to know those close-mouthed Amish would spread the news so quickly?

Despite this faux pas on his part, however, Rich was full of happiness. He'd found the girl who was more than anything he'd dared to dream of in a woman, and she'd agreed to marry him. God, how lucky can you get? he thought as he stepped into the warm shower. Then he paused a moment. Of course, he'd be even luckier if Suzy were with him right now.

Rich was shaving and looking at himself in the mirror when it suddenly occurred to him that he'd reached another decision. In the two weeks that Suzy had been here, he realized that there would never be any positive proof that she, or anyone else for that matter, was Christina Hepburn. The absence of such proof, as well as Suzy's reluctance to fight for the Hepburn estate, simplified Rich's job as executor. At the end of the year when the estate was settled, Rich would simply agree that Wayne should inherit the Hepburn fortune.

There was nothing Rich wanted more.

He loved Suzy for what she was—straight-thinking and big-hearted with indisputable integrity and loyalty. Yet as much as he loved her, he knew that if Suzy had turned out to be Christina Hepburn, he'd have hesitated a long while before proposing to her. He knew that Suzy would never think that he'd wanted her for her name and money, but other people would, and this could cast a pall over their marriage that they'd never be able to shake. It wouldn't be fair of him to do this to Suzy. But hell, he thought, what was he worrying about? This wasn't his problem. Trying to come up with a reason for going to Windland was his problem, but he'd think of something by the time he got to Thrushmore.

As soon as he got out of the car, he could hear Suzy's and Joanne's voices coming from the garden. When he called out, Suzy hailed him from behind a clump of shrubs.

"Over here," she shouted. Then, laughing, she started toward him on the run. Her legs were long and straight and her hair, the color of cinnamon in the bright sunlight, tumbled loosely over her forehead. She looked absolutely radiant.

Rich held out his arms. As Suzy ran into them, he took her full weight and, lifting her off her feet, swung her around in a circle. Then, tightening his grip, he gave her a big bear hug before releasing her.

"Well," he exclaimed in a teasing voice, "it looks like you're in good spirits today." His glance took in her shorts and tennis shoes and sea-green pullover. "It also looks as though you're ready for the beach."

Suzy laughed. "You do, too," she said, toying with the sunglasses in his pocket. "But before we go, I want you to hear all the crazy plans Joanne and I have been hashing out." Taking his hand, Suzy led Rich back toward the garden, but Joanne met them halfway.

She took both of Rich's hands in hers and, leaning back a little, eyed him discerningly. "I hope you know what a lucky man you are."

"I do," he assured her. "Believe me, I do, but you're pretty lucky yourself. It seems to me you've suddenly inherited a daughter."

Joanne smiled. "I feel the same way, but then, I've thought of Suzy as my daughter ever since the first day I saw her." She glanced at Suzy and started to say something but evidently changed her mind. She shook her head. "Anyway, we've decided we're not going to let a lot of legal hang-ups spoil our fun."

"What do you think of the idea of getting married right here in the garden?" Suzy asked breathlessly.

"Sounds good to me," Rich agreed. "I'm not up on weddings, but as long as I get the bride, I'll go along with anything."

"Now there's a good sport if I ever heard one." Smiling, Joanne looked from one to the other; then, as if suddenly remembering something, she straightened and turned to Suzy. "While you're filling Rich's head with all the ideas we've been dreaming up, I think I'd better get back to Mae. I don't want her to think I've abandoned my flower bed project." Without waiting for Suzy's protest, she gave them a saluting wave and started toward the house.

Circling their arms around each other's waists, Rich and Suzy strolled leisurely toward the stone benches. To Rich's surprise, Suzy seemed rather quiet. He'd expected to be inundated with excited wedding plans, but Suzy seemed content to just walk beside him. Her thoughts were probably filled with dreams of their life together, knowing, as he did, that it was going to be long and full of love and passion and...

His brow furrowed into a frown as a nagging sense of guilt crept back into his consciousness. Marriage was supposed to be based on faith and trust in each other, wasn't it? In that case, he certainly wasn't starting out very well. If he didn't want any shadows between them, he'd better explain his trip to Windland to Suzy. Though he wasn't quite sure himself why he went, he was determined to make a stab at it. Now.

"Suzy," he said quietly, "there's something I want to explain to you. I guess you already know I went to Windland yesterday."

"Yes. Terri called me this morning and told me."

"I'm sorry I didn't tell you. I meant to, but, well, there just wasn't an opportunity."

"Why did you go?" she asked.

Rich exhaled a long breath. "I'm not even sure myself. I think I was—"

"Boosting your ego?"

"Huh?"

"Sometimes men like to think of themselves as detectives, and they act out all sorts of charades trying to find some little clue or other which will prove that they're smarter than they've given themselves credit for. This is a very normal chauvinist action."

"Now, wait a minute," he protested. "I wasn't playing detective. I was—"

"Just filled with curiosity," Suzy finished for him. "You wanted to see where I'd spent my childhood, and I don't blame you one bit. If we'd met on a trip someplace and you'd told me all about Link Hall, I'd have been dying to see the place. It's only natural for people to be interested in the roots of the ones they love."

"Well, yes, sure." This was going better than he'd thought it would.

"Of course, I would have liked to have taken you there myself, but you know, Rich? You have a little impulsive streak in you."

"I have?"

"Definitely. Someone probably triggered your imagination and you just went into action, without thinking. I'll bet you never realized how curious you are."

"No, I suppose not...." His voice trailed off uncertainly. Rich tried to rationalize the twist the conversation had taken but found himself hopelessly lost. He shrugged. What difference did it make? At least he wasn't hiding anything from Suzy now, and that's what mattered.

Rich was aware she was watching him with a decidedly devilish glint in her eyes. Mischievously she pressed her fingers into his waist. "What do you say we get organized and go to the beach?"

But Rich had better plans. "How would you like to spend the whole weekend in Newport? I'd like to look around for a wedding gift for ourselves."

"Oh? What kind of a gift?" There was something in the tone of her voice that told him she already knew.

"Well, something small at first. That hundred twenty horsepower Grand Banks cruiser with the autopilot has been highly recommended. Of course the fifty-three-foot Hatteras is a hot selling item, too, though many people will argue that the Burger cruiser has better stability. But personally, I don't think that's—"

"Rich...hey, Rich! Whoa!" Suzy passed a hand before his face and grinned. "I think your idea of buying us a wedding gift is terrific. Give me a moment to say good-bye to Joanne and I'll be right with you."

"Do you want me to go back to the house and throw a few things in a bag for you?"

"No, absolutely not."

Framing her face with his hands, he kissed her before he reluctantly let her go. "Okay, I'll wait for you on the patio. But hurry," he warned.

"I will."

Giving Rich an affectionate pat on the flank, Suzy started off to look for Joanne. Since she wasn't in the garden, Suzy surmised she'd gone upstairs. Hurrying into the house, she took the steps two at a time but paused at the top of the stairs when she heard Joanne talking to Mae. Their voices were low, but their tones were pleasant and they reminded Suzy of two sisters who were in the habit of sharing their thoughts with each other. Suzy shrugged. Maybe Mae wasn't so grumpy after all, she thought as Joanne's words drifted out into the hall.

"Surely I must have some old garden shoes in here, Mae."

"No, nothing," was the firm reply. "Why would you? You haven't been in the garden for twenty-two years."

"Well, I'm going to be in it today. I want to get those petunia beds started so that they'll look like a blaze of color within a month."

"Is that when the wedding is? A month?" Mae asked.

"No date has been set, but if I know Rich and Suzy, they're not going to wait long. That suits me. I'm anxious myself. It's about time Thrushmore got jolted out of its placidity."

Suzy felt like an eavesdropper standing out in the hall listening, so with a light knock, she pushed the door open and walked inside. Mae and Joanne were both in the closet on their hands and knees. All around them were shoes of every size, shape and color in the world.

Joanne smiled when she saw Suzy. "I was wondering where you were."

"I was looking for you. Rich and I are going to Newport for the weekend."

"Oh, how nice. The weather's supposed to be perfect. We're going to work outside. Mae, here, is an excellent gardener."

Mae shook her head. "I used to be," she corrected brusquely, "but now all I do is tend the houseplants."

Joanne wagged a finger at her. "Well, all that's going to change. You and I are going to get out of our cocoons and start doing some of the things we used to enjoy. Now that I'm well, I have all sorts of plans."

Joanne was busy looking down at the array of shoes and only Suzy saw the swift look of concern that flashed across the older woman's face. Then, as if she were ashamed of her own emotions, Mae lowered her head and took a calming breath.

"And you are well, too," Mae agreed, her voice low and quiet. "More than I ever thought possible." She blinked several times, then, swallowing tightly, she forced herself to go on. "In fact, that's something I wanted to talk to you about."

Joanne looked up quickly. "What is it, Mae? Is something wrong?"

"No, no, of course not. In fact, just the opposite." Bravely Mae lifted her chin. "Since you're doing so well now, I realize you won't be needing a n—" She started to say "nurse" but faltered on the word. Suzy felt so sorry for her she thought she was going to burst into tears.

Not so Joanne. Instantly she was on her feet. "Mae!" she exclaimed, incredulous. "Are you saying what I think you are? Do you honestly believe that now that I'm well there's no place for you here?" She stepped back. "Why, I'm ashamed of you."

Slowly Mae stood up and busied herself by smoothing down her skirt. She wouldn't look at Joanne, whose eyes, like Suzy's, were bright with tears. Gently Joanne put her hands on Mae's broad shoulders and sighed heavily. "Oh, Mae, do you think I could ever forget all the years you've given me? All the days you made me go for walks and eat and take my medicine so that someday I'd be well again? Or the hundreds of times we talked and shared our hopes and frustrations and read to each other while we both bravely tried not to think of Christina? Do you think my getting well could ever erase the caring and the closeness we've shared for twenty-five years?''

"No, of course not." Slowly Mae lifted her head. Tears were in her eyes, but she blinked them back. "You're very loyal. More than I am."

"That's ridiculous."

"And forthright and honest, too," Mae added dryly.

Instantly Joanne sensed something was wrong. She certainly knew Mae well, Suzy thought as she watched Joanne's eyes, keen with interest. "Mae? What's wrong?"

"I'm afraid I haven't been as honest with you as I should have been." Reaching for a tissue, she dabbed at her eyes while Suzy and Joanne watched in silence. "All these years when you were so anxious to get Christina back, I sympathized with you and agreed with you and consoled you when one clue after another led to a blank wall. But all the while, in my heart, I was afraid."

"But why?"

"Because I knew as the years went on that Christina would be growing up, and even if she did come back, she could never be the same little girl who left here. And that's what you were looking for."

"Yes," Joanne murmured, "I suppose I was."

Mae nodded. "And I know that young girls of today aren't raised like they used to be. A lot of them are cold and heartless and even cruel. Who's to say how Christina would turn out if she was raised by strangers? Why, she could walk in here, nice as you please, take Mr. Hepburn's money and turn on her heel and march right out again.'' She looked at Joanne, her eyes soft with compassion. ''If that had ever happened, it would have destroyed you.''

Joanne paused for a moment, then nodded thoughtfully. ''Yes, I suppose you're right.''

''Mr. Hepburn thought so, too. That's why he was so careful to screen everybody. But,'' she said with a weary sigh, ''I can see now that we were wrong. Our Christina could never be anything but the kind and bright-eyed little girl who left here.'' Lifting her head, she looked straight at Suzy. ''She's turned out to be a very lovely person, inside and out.''

They all stood still, motionless in suspended silence. The only movement was the blink of Suzy's eyelashes.

Joanne was the first to rally. ''Oh, my God, Mae,'' she gasped as she put her arm around the older woman's shoulders. ''Do you really think Suzy is Christina?''

Mae nodded firmly. ''I've thought that ever since the day she arrived.''

Joanne's face broke into a big, beaming smile. ''And so did I, Mae.'' Laughing, she turned to Suzy. ''Didn't I tell you you had the same chemistry as Christina? I sensed it right away, didn't you, Mae?''

To Suzy's surprise, Mae shook her head. ''I don't know anything about chemistries,'' she stated firmly. ''I'm basing my decision on facts. The first day Suzy came here, she said that Abby had given her a soft rag doll, and she had named this doll Lucky.'' She turned to Joanne. "Don't you remember? The day before Christina was kidnapped, you and Mr. Hepburn took her to a fair, and you bought her a little stuffed horse and she named it Lucky."

"I remember the fair, of course," Joanne murmured, "but I don't remember the horse."

"It's a wonder you even remember the fair after what you went through, but I remember the horse very well." Mae was on firmer ground, now, and back to her habit of not mincing words. "If you can remember back, you and Mr. Hepburn went out to dinner that night and Christina and her horse, Lucky, and I had supper right here." She pointed to the floor, indicating the dining room below. Again she looked at Suzy. "I'll never forget it," she added quietly.

Mae was very sure of her facts, and since she was such a practical and exacting person, it was almost impossible not to agree with her. Still, though Suzy's hopes had risen considerably, a dull, nagging doubt still prevailed.

"But Lucky is a pretty common name for a child's toy, isn't it?" she asked.

"You have to take into consideration that it was the last toy given to you," Mae persisted. "It was the last toy you held in your hands. Of course you'd remember its name." Mae's mouth closed firmly, but her expression was one of concern. She glanced from Suzy to Joanne. "I still have it," she said quietly.

"What?" Joanne leaned forward. "You what?"

"I still have it," Mae repeated, slightly chagrined. "I stole it. When Mr. Hepburn said he was going to throw out everything that Christina owned, he forbade the staff, and especially me, to keep anything that would remind you of her. He was afraid that you might find them someday. Of course at that time, no one knew—"

"Yes, Mae, I understand, but go on," Joanne urged.

"I couldn't let everything go," she confessed. "I loved Christina as much as you did, and I had to have something to cling to. So I took the little horse and hid it in my old cedar chest."

"Oh, my God," Joanne gasped. "Is it still there?"

"Yes, just like the day you bought it. Do you want to see it?"

"Do I!" Joanne turned to Suzy, her eyes sparkling with joy. "Can you believe this? I'll bet anything that this is going to be that one little link to your past that you've been searching for, Suzy. Oh, won't it be wonderful to get all of these doubts swept aside?" Taking Suzy's arm, she squeezed it affectionately. "Come on, Mae, lead the way. And hurry up."

Joanne's spirits were so effervescent that Suzy couldn't help but be caught up in her bubbling excitement. For the first time in weeks, Suzy tossed her prudent cautions aside and let her dreams soar beyond the limits of practicality into that mesmerizing state of euphoria. If she really was Christina... But her mind boggled at the thought. All she could see was the thrill of wondrous excitement in Rich's eyes when she told him.

Eagerly Joanne and Suzy followed Mae down the hall to her room. It was a large room with wide windows and many plants. At the end of the meticulously made bed was an old cedar chest with a portable TV and a neat stack of books on top. Removing them, Mae opened the lid. In unison, Joanne and Suzy leaned forward to stare into the chest. Suzy was scarcely breathing. After moving a few things to one sie, Mae reached down and brought forth a little gray stuffed horse with a white mane and tail and an ornately decorated pink felt saddle. She handed it to Joanne.

As Joanne reached out to take it, tears spilled down her cheeks. "Of course I remember this," she cried, and cuddling the little horse in her hands, she gazed at it lovingly. "They had a whole table of them at the fair, and Christina chose this one because the saddle was so beautiful." She shook her head. "Children of three always love glitter, don't they?" Turning, she held it out to Suzy. "Do you remember this?"

Numbly, Suzy took the little horse and tried to imagine how big it would feel to a small child. She studied the saddle carefully and the long mane and the black button eyes. She turned it over and over in her hands, and finally she handed it back to Joanne. And slowly shook her head. "I don't remember it at all."

Both Joanne and Mae stared at her with disbelief. "No? Don't you even remember the saddle?" Joanne pressed.

Again Suzy shook her head, but Joanne wasn't to be discouraged. "Well, that just goes to prove that what Paul Hilton said was right. You probably had amnesia from the trauma of the kidnapping. Isn't that right, Mae?''

"It certainly is possible."

As Mae and Joanne rationalized Suzy's inability to recognize the little horse, Suzy felt a heavy letdown. She was sorry now she'd even seen the horse. It was just another bitter disappointment to add to the frustration of searching for her identity. Would it ever end? she asked herself. Or would she always be—

Suddenly Suzy's eye caught a bright speck of color in the bottom of the chest. It wasn't typical of something Mae would own. "What's that?" she asked, pointing. Both Mae and Joanne peered into the chest, but their expressions were emotionless. "There," she said. Bending over, Suzy lifted out a pile of blankets. On the very bottom of the chest was a large piece of manila paper with smears of bright color all over it. It was a child's finger painting.

Mae and Joanne lifted it up together. "Oh, for heaven's sake," Mae said, clapping her hand to the side of her face. "I forgot all about this. It was taped to the back of Christina's closet door, and I found it after her room had been emptied out. I knew Mr. Hepburn would burn it if I gave it to him, so I hid it." She shook her head. "Lord, it's been here so long I forgot about it myself."

"How Christina loved to finger-paint." Joanne smiled as she let her eyes feast on the painting. She held it out so Suzy could see it.

This time Suzy only gave it a casual glance. She could easily say she recognized it, because in a sense, she did. As a child, Abby had let her finger-paint all the time, and in the course of her growing-up years, she'd probably turned out thousands of pictures exactly like this one. There was nothing distinctive about Christina's finger painting. It was just the daubing attempts of a three-year-old and nothing more.

Again she shook her head. "I'm afraid not."

Seeing the disappointment in Suzy's face, Joanne put a reassuring arm around her. "I just wish you could be more accepting like me and not as factual as David, but we love you just the same." She looked at the picture. "Frankly, I don't recognize this painting, either, but that's not going to stop me from having it framed and hanging it in my bedroom." Picking up the picture, Joanne and Mae tried to discern what the daubs meant. They lifted it a little to see better and moved it slightly into the light. All of a sudden Suzy let out a yell.

"Oh, my God! Look!" she shouted. Reaching out, she took the finger painting and turned it over. Dotted all over the back of the paper were a child's fingerprints. Some of them were smeared, some were barely visible, but many of them were clear and distinct.

Chapter Thirteen

For many moments, even the air seemed to hold its breath. Finally Joanne expelled a long held sigh. "Christina's fingerprints," she murmured, her voice faint with astonishment. As reality dawned, she lifted her eyes to Suzy, who was still so stunned she felt as if she were frozen in place. "Do you know what this means, Suzy? This is your proof. This is what you've been searching for." Holding out the painting, Joanne gazed at it lovingly. "Here in all these glowing colors is your answer."

"And this is rock-solid proof, too," Mae put in. "No one had better dare suggest this isn't Christina's finger painting."

Dropping the picture on the bed, Joanne put her arms around Suzy and hugged her. Suzy hugged her back. Her whole body began to throb with excitement and happiness as the clouds of nagging doubts dissipated and the sun shined in. For the first time Suzy was as exhilarated as Joanne. The proof she'd been searching for had unfolded before her like a gift. It was almost as if the little three-year-old who had left here so many years ago was saying, "I'm back! I'm no longer just a memory in your heart. I'm real. I'm alive. I'm home."

Carefully Suzy took the picture. Her eyes were glistening with tears, as were Joanne's, as were Mae's. They looked at each other and then they blinked and then all at once they started to laugh. The sudden release from uncertainty and hesitation was like an absolution for all of them, especially Suzy. It made her realize how adrift she'd felt. But no more. At last she was on a steady course and would never again have to wonder. She'd know now for sure and could stand strong against anyone.

"I can't wait to tell Rich," Suzy exclaimed excitedly. She looked at the painting. "Can I take this down and show it to him?"

Joanne smiled. "You can do anything you want to with that picture, dear. It's all yours. Now hurry along."

Suzy practically flew down the stairs. "Rich, Rich," she called as she ran through the house. "I've found it. I've found proof. Rich?"

"Out here on the patio."

She burst through the door with a gush of excitement. "Look," she gasped breathlessly. "This is a

finger painting Christina did when she was three years
old. Mae's kept it all these years."

Rich looked at the painting with a critical eye. "Are
you trying to tell me this shows a lot of talent?"

Positioning herself behind his chair, Suzy leaned
over him and, folding her arms around his neck,
planted a warm, moist kiss against his temple. "Ready
for a surprise?" she teased.

"Right here? On the patio?"

"There you go with your wishful thinking again."
She tightened her grip. "Come on, look at the back."

Rich flipped the painting over and, like Suzy, stared
with disbelief at the fingerprints. His initial shock was
as great as hers had been, as she'd expected, but his
response was totally different. Instead of jumping with
joy and bursting out in laughter and tears, he seemed
to stiffen. It was almost as if he were still skeptical,
and perhaps he was. Rich was a very thorough person, and there was still the possibility that her fingerprints didn't match Christina's. From what Joanne
and Mae both felt, however, that seemed rather remote, but Suzy realized that Rich had a legal responsibility here. He wasn't in a position to express his
opinion until he'd actually seen a report of the fingerprint analysis.

"You won't have any trouble settling the estate
now," Suzy said encouragingly. "Either I'm Christina or I'm not. There won't be any fuzzy in between
this time."

Covering her hands with his, Rich lowered his head
and pressed his lips against her fingers. His breath was

warm and deep, as if he'd been holding it a long while. He remained motionless for several minutes.

Gently, Suzy laid her cheek against his. "Is something wrong?" she asked quietly.

Rich cleared his throat. "No, I was just thinking. You're right. This is going to make my job a lot easier for me. Too bad David didn't have this painting years ago. It would have saved him a lot of work and a lot of disappointments."

Suzy was not sympathetic. "Well, it's his own fault. He told Mae he didn't want her to keep one single thing of Christina's. So what was she supposed to do? Trot it out three years later?"

"I can understand her predicament, but I can understand David's, too." He held up the picture. "Wow! This painting's going to be a windfall."

Suddenly the door banged open and Wayne strode out onto the patio. He looked smaller than the last time Suzy had seen him, but his eyes were just as dark and glaring, and as usual, he was steaming with anger. Obviously he'd been eavesdropping.

"What painting are you talking about?" he demanded. His voice was not only threatening, but loud. Suzy knew everyone in the house could hear.

Rich showed him the paper. The daubs of color seemed even brighter out here. "Suzy tells me that this is a picture that Christina made and that Mae kept all these years. On the back"—he turned it over—"are some of her fingerprints."

Wayne barely glanced at it. Instead he turned his wrath on Suzy. "What kind of a hoax is this?" he roared. "You could have painted this yesterday for all we know."

"But if Suzy's fingerprints match the ones on this paper," Rich reasoned, "how do you explain the difference in the size of the fingers? Obviously the prints on the back of this picture are those of a child."

"You can do all kinds of tricks with finger paints," he scoffed.

"You can't make them smaller, Wayne."

He wasn't to be discouraged and pointed accusingly at Suzy. "You could have painted this when you were a child and saved it all these years. Who's to say you didn't bring it with you and plant it—"

"I say so!" Mae shouted as she barged through the door, her face red with fury. Joanne was right behind her, but she made no effort to soothe the old nurse's temper. Mae, her face dark and scornful, put her hands on her hips and marched right up to Wayne and looked him straight in the eye. "Don't you dare try to tell me this isn't Christina's finger painting. I put it in my cedar chest myself and it's been there all these years. And I'd just like to see you or anyone else try to prove otherwise."

"Well! Get a good look, Mae, because that's exactly what I'm going to do." Stepping back, he looked down his nose at her. "Just how much is Suzy paying you to aid and abet—"

Mae slapped him right across the mouth. Suzy was so stunned she was paralyzed, but Rich was on his feet in an instant, and none too soon, because Mae seemed to be readying for another swipe. All Suzy could think of was, *Thank God she's on my side.*

"That's enough," Rich said. "This isn't getting us anywhere." Mae backed off to stand beside Joanne, but Suzy could see she was still shaking with fury. "You should be grateful we found these prints, Wayne," Rich went on. "It'll save years of red tape in the probate courts."

"Not if it's challenged." He sneered.

Rich took a calming breath. "That's strictly between you and your attorney."

"But you must admit that this does look like solid proof," Joanne interjected.

"What do you mean—proof?" he scoffed. "I don't see any fingerprint expert standing around here."

"No problem," Rich assured him. "I'll take this painting into Boston tomorrow...no, tomorrow's Saturday. I'll take it in Monday morning first thing. Suzy can come with me, and we'll get this thing settled within an hour." He looked from one to the other. "Is that agreeable with everyone?"

"I want my lawyer there," Wayne growled.

"By all means, bring him."

"Well," Joanne exclaimed, "as long as everyone is going..." She turned to Mae. "What about it?"

Mae blinked with astonishment. "You're going to Boston?"

"Certainly. Do you want to come or not?"

"I wouldn't miss it for anything in the world."

It was Rich who finally got tempers calmed down, for the moment, at least. Then he and Wayne went into the office and talked at length while Suzy supervised Joanne and Mae's gardening, which was subordinate to their lively chatter about Wayne and the painting and Monday morning and the wedding. Finally, they heard Wayne's car leave, and right after that, Rich appeared to say he was ready to go, too. Once again Suzy said her good-byes, and this time she actually got into the car. It seemed to her she'd been trying to leave ever since she had arrived.

Rich got in beside her and they rolled out of the drive and headed in the direction of Link Hall. "That Wayne is the stubbornest man I've ever known," Rich grumped. "This estate could be tied up for ten years if he carries through with all his threats."

"Do you think he will?"

"I don't know." Rich shrugged the question off as if the whole thing were out of his hands. Suzy was a little surprised at his lack of spirit. She thought he'd be as anxious as she was to get this settled and, if she was Christina, to share the rewards. Maybe he was having trouble comprehending the enormity of the situation as well as its resolution, she rationalized. It did sound like something from a fairy tale.

Suzy exhaled a long sigh. "Boy, if I really am Christina, just think of what it would mean to us."

"Frankly, all I can think of is trouble, trouble and more trouble."

"For heaven's sake, why?"

"Well, to begin with, the moment we walk into the police lab with this painting, you can expect the news media to start crawling all over us."

"You can't blame them for that," she said as she placed the painting onto the backseat. "It is an unusual situation."

"It's more than that, Suzy. It's international news. When Christina was kidnapped it was in every headline in the country."

"But that was twenty-two years ago."

"Even more reason for the media to make a big event out of it. The great follow-up story! Pictures of you, then and now. And pictures of Windland, too. This is where she lived, this is her school, her classmate, the grocery store she went to..."

"Oh, stop it," Suzy scoffed. "You're exaggerating. Besides, even if they do take a lot of pictures, it'll just be for the first week or so, and then it'll be back page news."

"Maybe," he groused, "if you're lucky."

Suzy lapsed into silence. She knew Rich was just being grumpy, which wasn't like him at all, but then everyone had a bad day once in a while. Besides, she thought, he could be feeling a little jealous about all the upcoming publicity. A man liked to think of himself as the dominant partner who had complete control of every situation. But this didn't worry Suzy. She knew Rich was basically good-natured. He'd get over this in a few days. Besides, as he said, it could be in probate for years, so why should she worry about it today of all days?

As the car stopped in front of Link Hall, Suzy turned to Rich with a broad smile. "What do you say? Are we still going to Newport?"

"Sure, if you want to."

"Of course I want to. We're buying ourselves a wedding present today, don't you remember?"

Reaching up, she pinched his cheek. Rich grinned and caught her hand. "You can get in trouble doing that," he warned.

"I'm willing to chance it."

"Then what do you say we get on the move?"

"That's what I'm trying to tell you." As Suzy got out of the car, she took the painting in with her. "I don't want to lose this," she said as she sailed past him into the house.

While Rich went looking for Mrs. Slingluff to tell her they would be going away for the weekend, Suzy went upstairs to pack her bag. Since they'd probably be shopping for a boat every minute they were there, she decided to take slacks, shorts and sneakers. If Rich wanted to go someplace fancy for dinner, he'd have to wait until their next trip. She finished in record time and was starting down the stairs just as Rich was starting up.

"Hurry," she urged. "I'm all ready."

"Won't be a minute."

After putting her bag near the front door, Suzy wandered into the library looking for a newspaper to read while she waited. The French doors were open and a slight breeze was blowing, ruffling the papers on the desk. Suzy went over to anchor them with a paperweight and had just gotten them in order when she saw a rubber stamp resting on the metal lid of a stamp pad.

She stared at it for a long while. Would it be possible for her to take her own fingerprints? she wondered. Was this inked pad so different from what they used at the police department? Without waiting for her own answer, Suzy picked up a clean piece of paper and laid it flat on the desk. Then, opening the lid of the stamp pad, she pressed the forefinger of her right hand onto the pad and then onto the paper. She lifted her finger quickly so as not to smudge it and, sure enough, there on the white paper was a perfect fingerprint. Eagerly, Suzy set to work and did each finger until she had ten distinct prints on the paper. Then, wiping her hands on a tissue, she picked up the paper, waved it in the air a minute to dry it, then ran upstairs to her room.

Putting the paper on the table near the window, she went to get Christina's drawing to set alongside it. She wished she had a magnifying glass. Maybe Rich had one somewhere, she thought, but then, why bother? Her decision wouldn't be valid anyway. Scooting the two papers side by side, she leaned over eagerly and studied first one and then the other and back again and again many times. The silence in the room grew longer. Finally Suzy straightened and stared unseeing out the window. Though she'd never analyzed fingerprints before and didn't know a loop from a whorl, she was sure of one thing.

Her fingerprints did not match those of Christina.

Rich tossed a few things into his canvas zippered bag. The enthusiasm he'd felt earlier over the excitement of looking for a boat had dimmed considerably, and he hated himself for it. It was as if his mind were saying "I will love Suzy as long as she never changes," and only a fool would think that. Everybody changed, as did circumstances. Just because she could prove to the world now that she was Christina Hepburn, the kidnapped child, heir to the Hepburn millions, was no cause for him to think she'd feel any differently toward him. That simply wasn't Suzy's style.

Grow up, Link, he reprimanded himself, and picking up his bag, he started down the hall. As he passed Suzy's door, he was surprised to see her in her room. Her back was to him, but she didn't turn around. Puzzled, Rich dropped his bag on the floor and, standing behind her, put his hands on her shoulders.

"What's wrong?" he asked.

With a weary sigh, Suzy leaned back against him and closed her eyes. "My fingerprints don't match Christina's," she said tonelessly.

"What?" Glancing down, Rich saw the two papers side by side on the table. Curving one arm around Suzy to bring her closer to his body, he reached out with the other hand and picked up the paper with the black prints on it. "Did you make these yourself?" he asked, and when she nodded, he added jokingly, "What do you know about fingerprint analysis?"

"I don't have to know anything. Look for yourself." She held up Christina's drawing so Rich could compare the two.

His first glance told him they didn't match but still he studied them carefully for several minutes. He wanted to be sure. Suddenly he flung the paper across the room and let out a whoop of delight. "They don't match! They don't match, Suzy!" Turning her around, he folded her in his arms and squeezed her tight againt him. "Oh, God, that's the best news I've ever heard in my life. Think of it, you're not Christina. You're not Christina!" he repeated, still not quite believing it himself.

Suzy's face stirred softly against his shoulder as her hands locked behind his back. He knew she was trying hard not to cry. "How can you be so happy when I've just lost everything I've ever wanted?" she grumped.

"Suzy, that's not true and you know it. When you first came here, all you wanted was to meet Joanne. You didn't care about the money or the Hepburn name. And you can't tell me you've done an about-face since then."

"Well, I have. I want to be from a socially prominent family like Marcia Tolbert. With name and money and influence like that, you could have become a congressman in a couple of years."

Leaning back a little, Rich eyed her critically. "To begin with, all congressmen do not come from wealthy families, and secondly, what makes you think that's what I want?"

"From the way Marcia talked, it sounded like it."

Putting his hand under her chin, Rich tipped Suzy's face up to his. "That's what Marcia Tolbert

wants, but what I want is my beautiful, unspoiled Suzy
Yoder from Windland, Pennsylvania.''

She looked up at him and he could see a smile
starting at the corners of her mouth. It reminded Rich
of a sunrise. She leaned back against his arms. ''No
wonder I love you so much.''

''And I love you so much that I'd already decided
to marry you...even if you were Christina.''

''Now what is that supposed to mean?''

''Suzy, you've no idea of the publicity you'd have
gotten if you'd turned out to be Christina Hepburn,
and it would follow you all of your life. If I married
you, I'd always feel like I was walking in your
shadow.''

She gave him an oblique glance. ''I can't imagine
you walking in anyone's shadow, Rich.''

''Well, it's happened to a lot of my friends,'' he
finished lamely.

Suzy's reply was to pull his face down to hers until
their lips met in a warm, moist kiss that was so gentle
and loving and so full of anticipation and promise that
Rich's pulse beat immediately went into high gear.
Closing his arms around her slim body, he covered her
soft, rounded bottom with his hand and pressed her
against him. A moan of pleasure trembled against his
lips, and Suzy's response was a low echoing
''Mmmm.''

She parted from the kiss and leaned back a little, her
gray-green eyes studying the passion she couldn't help
but see in his gaze.

The phone rang several times, but Rich didn't answer it. Finally someone downstairs picked it up. Someone, he smiled to himself, who was probably wondering what was going on up here and hoping it was exactly what it was—two people in love and not caring who knew it.

Suzy exhaled a long sigh. "I guess I'd better call Joanne," she murmured. "She's going to be sick with disappointment."

Rich shook his head. "I doubt that. She'll always think of you as her daughter. Mere proof will never change Joanne's mind. If you're worried about it, though, why don't I call her while you get your things together?"

"My things have been together for half an hour, but I could stand a little freshening up."

"You look just great the way you are, but if you insist..."

"And I do..."

"You have five minutes."

Grabbing his bag, Rich went downstairs and put their things in the car before calling Joanne. When he explained what had happened, she took it exactly as he thought she would. She was surprised but not devastated.

"Who cares about legalities, anyway?" she said. "But if this thing is going to upset Suzy, tell her I'll adopt her. But we'll talk about that later. She's still planning on having the wedding here, isn't she?"

"I suppose so, but I'll check with her to be sure."

When Suzy went downstairs, he hustled her into the car. "We've got to hurry," he said, but still he stopped to repeat the conversation with Joanne.

Suzy frowned worriedly. "It's going to be such a small wedding, it doesn't seem worth all the effort Joanne's going to put into it."

"Why don't we just get married in the courthouse?" Rich suggested.

"Or in an open country church in Windland."

"Or on the deck of a fifty-six-foot Broward motor yacht."

Suzy smiled up at him. "You're crazy, Rich, but I love you anyway. Now hurry up, or we'll waste the whole day."

"We're off."

Putting the car in gear, Rich swung around the drive and down the hill. As he stopped at the road, his eye caught the old sign at the side of the drive that read "Link Hall." He smiled. It looked as though the old place was going to undergo a renovation...and about time, too.

Epilogue

"Oh. Oh, thanks, Mae," Suzy said into the phone. "I'll call back tomorrow." Replacing the receiver, she cocked one hand on her hip and frowned. "I don't know what's going on over there at Thrushmore lately."

"What's the matter?" Rich teased. "Joanne and Mae making plans without consulting you first?"

"Mae says she's definitely decided she's going to England next month to visit her sister for the summer, but that doesn't surprise me. But guess what? Joanne has gone out to dinner with Dr. Hilton."

"So? What's wrong with that? He's always loved her."

But Suzy wasn't listening. "If that old codger thinks he's going to take advantage of an innocent woman, he has another guess coming."

"Suzy, Joanne is a big girl now."

"I don't care. She isn't experienced. She's lived a sheltered life."

"Let's face it. The real problem is she didn't ask for your approval first."

Straightening, Suzy stepped out of the phone booth. "She probably didn't have a chance to. The minute I turned my back, he swooped in like a fox and whisked her off to Boston."

Rich grabbed Suzy's arm. "I like the way that guy operates," he declared as he whisked her down the dock to their fifty-six-foot wedding gift. Jumping aboard, he turned and, catching Suzy with both hands at the waist, swung her into the boat beside him. Then, brushing his face against her ear, he whispered, "Why don't we go below where we can discuss this more privately?"

If you're ready for a more sensual, more provocative reading experience...

We'll send you 4 Silhouette Desire novels

FREE...

and without obligation

Then, we'll send you six more Silhouette Desire® novels to preview every month for 15 days with absolutely no obligation!

When you decide to keep them, you pay just $1.95 each ($2.25, in Canada), *with no shipping, handling, or additional charges of any kind!*

Silhouette Desire novels are not for everyone. They are written especially for the woman who wants a more satisfying, more deeply involving reading experience.

Silhouette Desire novels take you *beyond* the others and offer real-life drama and romance of successful women in charge of their lives. You'll share precious, private moments and secret dreams... experience every whispered word of love, every ardent touch, every passionate heartbeat.

As a home subscriber, you will also receive FREE, a subscription to the Silhouette Books Newsletter as long as you remain a member. Each issue is filled with news on upcoming titles, interviews with your favorite authors, even their favorite recipes.

And, the first 4 Silhouette Books are absolutely FREE and without obligation, yours to keep! What could be easier...and where else could you find such a satisfying reading experience?

To get your free books, fill out and return the coupon today!

Silhouette Desire®

Silhouette Books, 120 Brighton Rd., P.O. Box 5084, Clifton, NJ 07015-5084

Silhouette Special Edition

COMING NEXT MONTH

SUMMER DESSERTS—Nora Roberts
Blake Cocharan wanted the best, and Summer Lyndon was a dessert chef *extraordinaire*. She had all of the ingredients he was looking for, and a few he didn't expect.

HIGH RISK—Caitlin Cross
Paige Bannister had lived life from a safe distance until she met rodeo rider Casey Cavanaugh and found herself taking risks she had never thought she would dare.

THIS BUSINESS OF LOVE—Alida Walsh
Working alongside executive producer Steve Bronsky was a challenge that Cathy Arenson was willing to meet, but resisting his magnetic charm was more than a challenge—it was an impossibility.

A CLASS ACT—Kathleen Eagle
Rafe had always thought that Carly outclassed him, but when she was caught in a blizzard nothing mattered other than warming her by his fire...and in his arms.

A TIME AND A SEASON—Curtiss Ann Matlock
Two lovers were thrown together on a remote Oklahoma highway. Katie found Reno easy to love, but could she embrace life on his ranch as easily as she embraced him?

KISSES DON'T COUNT—Linda Shaw
Reuben North hadn't planned on becoming involved, but when Candice's old boyfriend threatened to take her child away, Reuben found himself comfortably donning his shining armor.

AVAILABLE NOW:

THE HEART'S YEARNING
Ginna Gray

STAR-CROSSED
Ruth Langan

A PERFECT VISION
Monica Barrie

MEMORIES OF THE HEART
Jean Kent

AUTUMN RECKONING
Maggi Charles

ODDS AGAINST TOMORROW
Patti Beckman